The Gambling Master
of Shanghai

and other tales of suspense

The Gambling Master
of Shanghai

and other tales of suspense

Joan Richter

PCW

A PEACE CORPS WRITERS BOOK

A Peace Corps Writers Book
An imprint of Peace Corps Worldwide

FIRST PEACE CORPS WRITERS EDITION, April 2011

This collection of short stories is a work of fiction. All of the characters, places, and incidents
are the product of the author's imagination or used fictitiously.

The Gambling Master of Shanghai and Other Tales of Suspense
Copyright © 2011 by Joan Richter

Library of Congress Control Number: 2011921224

Designer: Maria Miller Design
Cover photograph: Bruce Dale/National Geographic Stock

ISBN 978-1-935925-02-6

For Dave, Rob, India and Kai

ACKNOWLEDGMENTS

———◆———

I am indebted to the Peace Corps for challenging me to wander the world with a purpose, and to those fellow adventurers, near and far, whose lives significantly intersected with mine, thank you for a life-time of enduring memories.

My gratitude to Frederic Dannay, founding editor of Ellery Queen Mystery Magazine for publishing my first two stories, and to Janet Hutchings, the magazine's current editor, who has followed in his footsteps. Special thanks to my friend, Maria Miller, for encouraging me to work on this book and for designing it.

It is my good fortune to have two loving sons, Dave and Rob, whose creative and productive lives continue to enrich my life, as do the remarkable pursuits of my endearing grandchildren, India and Kai. My husband, Dick, has been a constant source of love and inspiration in the amazing journey we have shared.

ABOUT THE AUTHOR

———◆———

Joan Richter is an award-winning short story writer, whose fiction has appeared in *Ellery Queen Mystery Magazine* and anthologies. Raised and educated in New York City, she has a BA from Hunter College, and went on to study at Sarah Lawrence College and Georgetown University. She lived in East Africa for two years, when her husband was deputy director of the Peace Corps program in Kenya. Along with their two small sons, they visited volunteers in remote villages, and traveled extensively in Kenya, Uganda and Tanzania. She consulted for Peace Corps Washington on the role of staff wives overseas.

On returning home, Richter worked as a freelance writer and editor. She was a stringer for *The New York Times* metropolitan section and contributing editor to *Westchester Magazine*. She became travel editor of *The Trib* and then joined American Express, publishers of *Travel & Leisure,* as director of public affairs. She was the company's representative to the United Nations World Tourism Organization. In her career she traveled to more than sixty countries.

Most recently from Washington DC, she and her husband, Dick Richter, now live in Issaquah, a suburb of Seattle.

TABLE OF CONTENTS

———◆———

ASIA AND EUROPE

The Gambling Master of Shanghai ◆ 12

The Dance of the Apsara ◆ 28

Assignment in Prague ◆ 52

———◆———

AFRICA

The Ones Left Behind ◆ 72

Love and Death in Africa ◆ 82

The River's Child ◆ 98

Bitter Justice ◆ 108

Only So Much to Reveal ◆ 116

Intruder in the Maize ◆ 128

The Prisoner of Zemu Island ◆ 138

———◆———

THE UNITED STATES

Recipe Secrets ◆ 156

A Legacy of Questions ◆ 172

Last Harvest ◆ 186

The Oak's Long Shadow ◆ 194

The Waste Pile at Apple Bow ◆ 210

A Matter of Trust ◆ 226

The Last Rendezvous ◆ 232

———◆———

Publication Sources and Dates ◆ 254

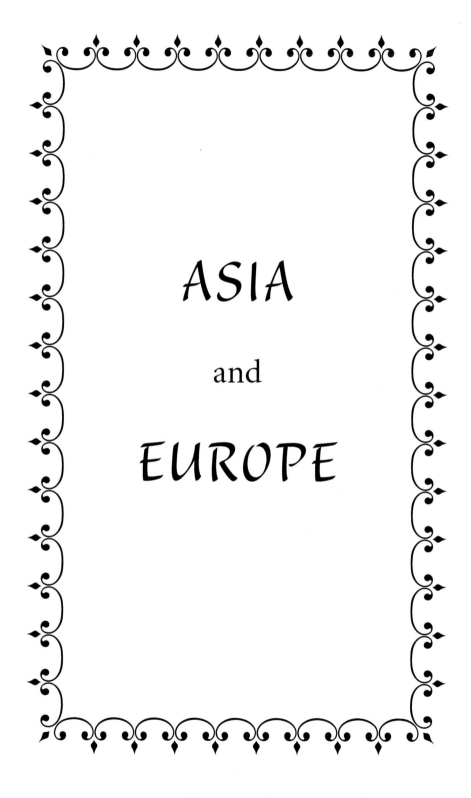

ASIA

and

EUROPE

The Gambling Master

of Shanghai

The three of us were hanging out in the kitchen that Saturday afternoon, when we heard the mail truck pull up at the end of our driveway. I'd come back from basketball practice a half-hour ago and was having a coke. My mother was at the counter slicing vegetables for a stir-fry for supper that night. Dad was at the table with the newspaper spread out in front of him. "I'll go," he said.

He was gone a while. Mom and I figured he'd probably run into the man next door, who liked to talk baseball, but as soon as Dad came back inside, I could tell something was up. His face had that tight look it gets when things aren't quite right.

My mother heard him come in and stopped her chopping and turned around.

"It's a letter from Shanghai," he said, nodding at the light blue envelope in his hand. We could see he had opened it.

Mom stared at him. "From Shanghai? We don't know anyone there."

Both my parents had been born in China, but came to the states when they were little kids. They met one another in their last year at Northwestern and were married a couple of years after that. I was born in Chicago.

"It's from Uncle Ho," my father said.

My mother put down her knife and wiped her hands on a kitchen towel. "I thought Uncle Ho died in the Cultural Revolution."

My father nodded. "That's what I thought. That's what everyone thought."

By everyone, my father meant our relatives, who were scattered all over the U. S. In typical Chinese fashion we got together every few years for big reunions. The elders liked to exchange memories and tell Uncle Ho stories, which always led to talk of gambling. It seems, at a very early age, Uncle Ho had been a Gambling Master, which in Chinese lingo makes Michael Jordan a Basketball Master.

Everyone liked telling Uncle Ho stories. The relatives tried topping one another with a new piece to an old story, or an entirely new one. And since they all thought Uncle Ho was dead, it didn't matter if the truth got bent a bit.

"Uncle Ho is coming here," my father said.

My mother frowned. "What do you mean he's coming here?"

"I mean here. Las Vegas."

My mother had the next toss, but her sudden stony silence said she was deferring to my father.

The way he cleared his throat told me she wasn't going to like what he had to say.

"He's coming to Vegas on one of those casino-sponsored deals there's been so much talk about."

"You mean Uncle Ho is one of those "whales?""

My mother sent me a look that would freeze Salt Lake.

I should have known better, but it just popped out. I dipped my head in apology and tried to look contrite. I did a retake on the "whales" story.

It hit the news a couple of months ago. American casino interests had decided to take advantage of the big economic boom in China and the Chinese centuries-old love of gambling. They were sending agents over there to scout for rich guys who liked high stakes games. They called them "whales." Once a "whale" was sighted the only thing he had to do was offer some proof of his wealth, then the agents took care of the rest. They helped with visas, air travel, and hotels. It was only at the gaming tables in Vegas that the high rollers were on their own. And guess what? The casinos were counting on them losing big.

The media loved the story and ran all over the place with it. Reporters speculated about where the "whales" money came from, with edgy suggestions that it was hot, embezzled or siphoned off from companies and corrupt government agencies. Another flyer was that the money came from smuggling—drugs, arms, trafficking in women.

A few reporters got to the practical question of how these rich guys managed to get their money out of China, since the country had rigid restrictions on currency going offshore. The conclusion was that a lot of people were getting paid to look the other way.

"The whole thing is going to start all over again," my mother said.

She was a little off the point, but I knew what she meant. So did my father. He nodded.

Three years ago the relatives had come to Vegas. It was the off season, rates were good and we took over one of the small hotels on the outskirts of town. There was a swimming pool for the kids and a room large enough to have a real Chinese banquet on our first and final nights. The Strip offered plenty of entertainment of all kinds. The relatives weren't opposed to gambling, in fact they loved it.

My parents never went near the casinos. They skirted the slots, which were everywhere, as if they sprayed the plague. The relatives didn't quite believe it. Some came close enough to suggesting my parents were secret gamblers. It was in our blood, after all. It could be traced to Uncle Ho, which is what my mother meant when she said it was going to start all over again.

In all fairness, when someone moves here it's sort of taken for granted that gambling is a big draw. I was only five when my parents made the move, so I don't remember a lot, but I've heard their story enough times so it feels like it's my own. We had been living in Chicago, where my father had a good job as an accountant, when out of the blue, through one of his clients, he was offered a partnership in a big firm in downtown Las Vegas. Mom freaked out. Sin City!

The two words became a drumbeat in her head, until she was driving home from work one day and heard a long-range weather forecast for the Midwest. The coming winter was supposed to be the coldest in fifty years. Record snowfalls, ice storms and power outages. She started thinking about the bitter winds off Lake Michigan and soon she was on the phone checking out housing, schools for me and job opportunities for herself. She was a physical therapist. When she discovered she could line up a job before we even left Illinois, the deal was done. Vegas it was.

According to my mother, when the relatives got wind of our Nevada move the phone lines crackled with so much gossip they could have caused a power failure all their own. It went on, not just for months, but years. It's sort of quieted down, but it's not a dead issue. And now Uncle Ho was coming to *our* town.

The relatives would have to be told. First, of course, that he was alive and then that he was coming here to gamble, at the invitation of the casinos. It was easy to see why Mom was upset.

She looked at my father and reached for the letter. He handed it to her and pulled a chair away from the table and sat down.

"It's in English," she said.

Dad laughed. "Did you think I'd suddenly learned to read Chinese?"

Neither of them had ever learned to read the language.

"How is it that *your* Uncle Ho knows English?"

I was careful not to laugh. Actually, Uncle Ho *was* my father's relative. It's a bit complicated. He was the youngest son of my father's grandfather's youngest uncle. It's easier to say in Chinese.

My father shook his head. "I don't know any more about Uncle Ho than you do. I never met him. All I know are the stories. You've heard the same ones I have."

"Maybe he had someone write the letter for him," I said.

This time my mother eyed me with approval. "That's a possibility. You were right about something else, James. It looks as though *your* Uncle Ho *is* one of those 'whales.' He's going to be put up at one of those fantasyland hotels on The Strip."

Now he was *my* uncle.

She looked at my father. "At least that means he doesn't expect to stay with us."

This didn't sound like my mother at all. It seemed a little inhospitable for the legendary Uncle Ho to come all the way from Shanghai and not stay with us, if only for an overnight. We had a guest room with its own bath, so it isn't as though we didn't have the space. But I kept my mouth shut.

My mother handed the letter back to my father. "He's arriving tomorrow. You didn't tell me that."

The level of electricity between them had just shot up. I decided to make myself scarce. I put my coke can in the recycling bin, mumbled that I'd be back later and went out the side door, grabbing my basketball out of habit. It was hot, but I was used to it. The court was about three blocks away. Some of the guys were bound to be there. A few shots and another pickup game wouldn't be bad. Then I'd run home and get cleaned up again in the outside shower. I didn't remember much about Chicago, but in terms of climate the change had been a great trade.

At supper that night we sat down to the stir-fry and steamed rice and Dad gave me the news. "We've decided to meet Uncle Ho's plane. His flight from Los Angeles gets in at four tomorrow afternoon. We'll let him decide if he wants to spend time with us."

Somehow I didn't think Uncle Ho would be satisfied with a quick hello at the airport, otherwise he wouldn't have sent us the letter. But my parents were feeling their way, and there was no point in my adding to their confusion.

"How will we recognize him?"

"Your mother thought of that. We'll take along a sign with his name on it, put it on a stick and hold it up. That way *he* will be able to find *us*. Maybe you could take care of the sign, James."

"Sure. What should it say? Uncle Ho?"

My mother was quick to answer. "No. Mr. Ho."

"Got it."

The other thing they decided was not to call the relatives just yet. "It's better if we wait until Uncle Ho gets here. There will be more to tell them after that."

———◆———

It's hard to remember exactly what happened that next day, except that there were more surprises. We left for the airport with lots of time to spare. My parents were nervous. I was curious. When we got there, parked the car and started for the terminal, I was carrying the sign. There weren't a lot of people around. Sunday can be a sleepy day. A lot of people go to church, although it was a little late in the day for that.

I was the first to see him, seated on a bench off to the side of the terminal entrance, in the shade of some eucalyptus trees. He was holding a sign with his name on it. He saw mine. We waved our signs at each other. His baggage was alongside him, not very much—a small suitcase and two square boxes, tied with heavy cord. A bamboo pole was threaded through a loop at the top of each box. They were identical, cube-shaped, the size that could hold a basketball.

My father apologized for being late, even though we were early. He explained we thought the plane wasn't due for another half-hour.

It turned out Uncle Ho hadn't come by plane. Someone had driven him from Los Angeles.

"Where are all the others?" my mother asked.

Uncle Ho looked puzzled. "Others?" he repeated.

"Your traveling companions. Your letter said you were coming with a group."

He nodded. "They will come later. They are taking a trip to the Grand Canyon."

Through the years, without really knowing it, I'd formed my own image of Uncle Ho—someone sort of ancient, drawn in charcoal, stepping out of the pages of an old storybook. Since yesterday, I had been trying to recast him as a high roller, wooed to Las Vegas by big gambling interests. I couldn't get it to work. And now, here he was, in the flesh. What I saw didn't match anything I had imagined.

It was hard for me to get a fix on his age. His hair was thick like mine, but streaked with a lot of silver. He wasn't real old, but he sure wasn't young. He would have been ordinary looking if it weren't for the scar that ran from the center of his forehead down to his left eyebrow. I couldn't help but wonder how he'd got that. It must have been some gash. Blood must have poured into his eyes.

The pajama-like pants and gray quilted jacket he was wearing sure made him look more like a peasant than a millionaire. But a lot of Chinese dress that way. Besides, during the Cultural Revolution, Uncle Ho *had* been a peasant. He'd been sent to the countryside to work in the rice fields. According to all the stories I'd heard, he had died there, drowned in a ditch. It wasn't an accident.

I was a bit surprised by what my father said then, but Mom wasn't having any trouble with it, so I guessed they must have worked it out.

"Uncle Ho, we would be glad to take you to your hotel, but if you would like to come to our house, you are welcome."

Uncle Ho stared ahead for a minute and then responded with a nod. "I would be glad to go to your house."

My father nodded to me and motioned to Uncle Ho's suitcase. I picked it up. Uncle Ho reached for the bamboo pole and centered it on his right shoulder, balancing one box in front of him and the other behind. Another charcoal drawing slid across my mind.

My parents led the way. Uncle Ho followed and I took up the rear. We were an odd little procession.

At the car my mother suggested Uncle Ho sit up front with my father. I helped him with the seat belt. We didn't usually drive along The Strip, unless we had to, but Dad thought it was a good idea to show Uncle Ho where he would be spending his time when he hooked up with the rest of his group.

As we approached the skyline of hotels, archways and towers, brightly lit even in broad daylight, Uncle Ho leaned forward. He nodded. "I have seen many pictures in travel brochures. But it is different, when you see it with your own eyes. It reminds me of when I went to Beijing for the first time and saw the Forbidden City. It can be described, but it cannot be imagined."

———◆———

Our house was in one of those residential communities that have a tidy look about them, uniformly landscaped plots, planted with cactus and shrubs indigenous to the desert, and ground cover that doesn't need much water. Ours was a two-story with a two-car garage. On the first floor there was a large family room, kitchen and dining area, and my parent's bedroom. The second floor had three bedrooms.

My parents left it to me to take Uncle Ho upstairs. I carried his suitcase up first and then came down to help him with the two boxes. He took one and I reached for the other. I'd been expecting it to have some weight, but it was so light, it almost flew out of my hand.

Uncle Ho chuckled. "It flies like a bird, even when the bird is not there."

I'd already spoken more Chinese that day than I had in a year, but even so I thought I'd misunderstood him. I replayed what I thought he'd said, and it came out the same way. I didn't get it.

I led the way into the guest room and showed him where the light switch was and how to work the blinds. I opened the empty bureau drawers, the closet and the door to the bathroom. I demonstrated how the shower worked and decided I didn't need to show him how to flush the toilet. If he had traveled this far, he knew what that was all about.

"I don't know your name," he said to me.

"It's James.

"That is short, like my name. Ho."

There were a lot of questions I would have liked to ask him, but it didn't feel right just yet. I said he probably wanted to unpack and take a rest. He should come down when he felt like it, or I would knock on his door when my mother had supper ready.

Back downstairs I saw that my parents' bedroom door was closed. I could imagine the questions they were asking each other.

———◆———

When we were seated at the dinner table that night my father explained to Uncle Ho that he and my mother had to leave for work early the next morning. "James is on vacation from school this week, so he will be here to take care of you."

Uncle Ho nodded. "My needs are simple. I will try not to be too much trouble."

An awkward silence began. It didn't look like Uncle Ho was about to initiate anything and my parents had the idea that it was impolite to ask questions. We'd heard so many stories *about* Uncle Ho, I thought it would be great to hear his side of things.

I began slowly, wary of my parents' reaction and a little uncertain of my language skills. I apologized in advance for mistakes I would make.

"You are doing very well," Uncle Ho said. "You have a question to ask me, I will try to answer it."

That put me on the spot. If I clammed up now, it would be a great loss of face. The relatives talked a lot about that.

What I really wanted to know was how he had gotten to be a Gambling Master, but I sure couldn't start off with that.

"I was wondering where you lived when you were my age. What sort of things did you do?"

"And you are how old?"

"I'm sixteen."

Uncle Ho nodded. "We lived in Shanghai then. I also went to school. I was studying mathematics, but my family was poor and I needed to earn money. I raised crickets, Fighting Crickets. I learned how to be a cricket handler and then to manage cricket fights. Many people came. They paid admission and they placed bets. The profits were good." He stopped there, and I could see he was waiting for my next question.

I wasn't sure just what to ask. I sure didn't know anything about crickets, so I went with the obvious. "How did you get interested in crickets?"

He chuckled. "Many children in China have crickets as pets. They are good companions. You can keep them close to you at night and listen to them sing. They are small and fit in a box you can put in your pocket. There are many different kinds of cricket boxes. Some are made from dried gourds, others from bamboo, clay and fine woods. It is said that the last emperor kept his cricket in a box inlaid with ivory and gold. Antique cricket boxes are collectors' items now."

We heard a lot more about crickets that night, with Uncle Ho describing a cricket fight. "Fighting Crickets are very aggressive," he said. "When two rivals enter an arena, they will jump at each other's heads, biting sharply, until one is vanquished."

———◆———

I heard my parents leave for work the next morning and rolled over, looking forward to sleeping in. It was spring break. Then I remembered Uncle Ho. I set my alarm to sleep another hour.

When I got up I saw that my mother had slipped a note under my door. "Try to find out when the rest of Uncle Ho's group is supposed to arrive, and what hotel he will be staying at. I'll try to get home early, but it won't be before five. Dad and I are driving in together, so you can use my car. You might want to take Uncle Ho on a little sight-seeing tour."

Uncle Ho's door was closed when I headed downstairs, but he heard me and opened the door.

"Hi, Uncle Ho. How about some breakfast?"

"I would like to show you something first." He motioned me into the room.

He had slept in the twin bed close to the window. The quilt was neatly folded back. But it was the other bed that got my attention. Two birdcages sat on top of the bedspread.

I *had* understood him. "It flies like a bird even when the bird is not there."

"I will need your help," he said. "I must find a shop that sells birds."

Okay. What's a birdcage without a bird?

"The name of the shop is Fragrant Hills," Uncle Ho said.

I just so happened I knew the shop. It was in a strip mall next to a computer store where I'd had a summer job last year. A Chinese woman owned it.

"Fragrant Hills. I know where it is. But you just got here. How come you know about it?"

He smiled. "I will tell you when we get there."

Okay. He wanted to be mysterious.

———◆———

My mother had set two places at the breakfast table and left English muffins out on the counter, along with a bowl of fruit and a canister of tea. I turned on the kettle and reached into the fridge for milk and a carton of eggs. I thought I'd scramble some and toast the muffins. I told Uncle Ho what I had in mind.

"I will have whatever you have, but only a small portion," he said.

He walked to the window then and looked outside, squinting. "The sun is very bright. It makes the sky look very big."

I hadn't thought of it that way, but he was right. Nevada has big skies.

Over breakfast I tried the same thing I did the night before, only this time I asked him about birds, not crickets.

"When I was a small boy in Shanghai, I liked to go the bird market with my grandfather. He kept his birds in the bamboo houses you saw upstairs. He was very old and I often went with him when he took them for a walk."

"What do you mean, *took them for a walk?*"

Uncle Ho chuckled. "I will show you when we go outside."

Breakfast didn't take long and we left the house by the side door. Uncle Ho had a birdcage in each hand, held by the rings at the top of their domes. He grinned at me and set out past the garage door for a stroll down the driveway and back, swinging the cages at his sides. "Birds like the air. It makes them think they are free."

We got into the Toyota then and I set out for the store named Fragrant Hills. I'd looked it up in the yellow pages to be sure it was still there. Small businesses in Vegas come and go.

There were no customers in the shop when we arrived, but with all the twitters and birdcalls it was a lively place. All kinds of birds were flitting about in large and small cages, and in mini aviaries suspended from the ceiling. Along one side there were shelves stacked with boxes of birdseed and whatever else people might want to buy for their birds.

At the far end of the shop a woman was seated behind a counter. She reminded me of one of my older aunts, who had been a dancer, and wore her hair the same way, pulled back from her face into a knot high on the top of her head.

The woman was bent over a ledger, a pen in her hand, but looked up when we entered. She stared at Uncle Ho uncertainly and then a look of disbelief moved like a wave across her face. Her hand flew to her mouth, suppressing a cry.

Uncle Ho placed the birdcages on the counter and leaned toward her. She was transfixed as he began to speak. His voice was soft and tentative at first and then gathered speed in a waterfall of words. Her hands rose to her throat and a whisper of wonder passed her lips. "Ho," I heard her say, again and again throughout their exchange, but I understood nothing else of what they said to each other. They spoke in a dialect that was strange to me.

Uncle Ho moved one of the birdcages close to her and she reached for it, clasping it with both hands. Beginning at its dome, she ran her fingers over its intricate webbing, feeling her way, until she reached the base. There she paused and began to explore in detail. She seemed to find what she was looking for, and I saw her ease one small finger between two narrow bamboo struts. She looked up at Uncle Ho. He nodded. She pressed down hard. A drawer sprang open.

A shallow cry escaped her and she bent her head to stare at the contents of the drawer. When she looked up, there was a mixture of wonder and fear in her eyes. Frantically, she pressed her finger down again. The drawer closed, hiding what was there. What I had seen looked like a collection of dried up brown peas.

I stepped aside to let her by as she ran from behind the counter, headed for the front door. She bolted it and pulled down the shade.

I looked questioningly at Uncle Ho. A smile was playing at the corners of his eyes. "Madam Jia has put up a sign saying the shop is closed. Her home is behind that curtain. She has invited us to go there."

I followed them down a short corridor, lined with more shelves of bird supplies, to a door the woman unlocked with a key hidden in a jar. It opened onto a sitting room, bright with the light from a window that looked out onto a small garden. She motioned for us to sit down, and then looked toward Uncle Ho.

"I have told Madam Jia that you are a member of my family and that I stayed at your home last night. Jia and I are friends from a long time ago. Our grandfathers knew each other. As children we played in the alleys of the bird market in Shanghai. We made plans to have a bird stall of our own some day. Although they did not have names then, Jia said we would call ours Fragrant Hills."

He smiled at the woman. "Our lives have taken different paths. I am glad you chose that name for your shop here in the United States, or I might not have found you."

Their glances held for a moment and then Madam Jia turned to me. "Forgive us for having spoken in the language of our childhood. We will not do that from now on. Ho has many things he wants us both to know."

"Actually there are not so many, it is just that they are complicated. You already know how I gained entry into the United States. I was invited by one of the big casinos. I am sure you are both wondering how that came about." He smiled at each of us in turn.

"Even after so many years there are those who still speak of my days as a Gambling Master. Time and repetition of the story have magnified the truth, but that is what is believed. When the casino agent approached me, he referred to that reputation and assumed I was a wealthy man. At first I thought I should tell him that had been a long time ago, but as I listened to him I realized that what he was offering me was the answer to a long-held dream. My old standing would enable me to get to this country, to find Jia. And, so I let him speak, and said nothing to contradict him."

"So it is true that you have come here to gamble?" Madam Jia leaned forward, her sharp eyes, staring intently at Uncle Ho.

"Life is a gamble," Uncle Ho said with a soft laugh, and then nodded. "It is true, now that I am here, I am expected to gamble. I know very little about the kind of gambling that goes on inside the glittering palaces on the wide boulevard you call The Strip. The only gambling I know is the betting that takes place in cricket fights. I will not find a cricket fight here, I am sure. Casinos do not like winners, so they are hoping I will lose. That might not be very difficult."

I thought of the "whales" story again, and the big bucks the casinos expected their high rollers to play. It didn't sound like Uncle Ho had that kind of money. It was scary to think what might happen if he reneged on his part of the bargain. The days of back street murders were gone, but there was still a lot of talk about those times, when a cheat could be found in an alley with his throat cut.

Something else was bothering me. It was those brown peas. I've seen enough old movies set in Macao and Hong Kong and Shanghai, to know something about opium dens. If those little brown pellets had anything to do with the poppy, I was in big trouble.

I set the opium thought aside for a minute and went back to my other worry. "Uncle Ho, do you have any money to gamble with?"

"If by money, you mean American currency, I do not have that. All my wealth is there." He nodded toward the birdcages.

Madam Jia's impatient voice startled me. "Ho! I cannot wait any longer. How did you manage to hide them all these years? You were in prison for so long, and then you were sent to the countryside. I thought you had died there." Tears sprang into her eyes.

"You must not be sad," Uncle Ho said. "Those times are in the past. I am here. Did you ever think that would happen?"

"Years ago I used to dream …. But enough of that. I am not the little girl you chased in the market alleyways. I have lived many years. You must tell me, now. Where did you hide them?"

"I am surprised that you have not guessed." Mischief sparkled in his eyes. It was clear Uncle Ho wasn't about to be hurried. "Do you remember the caves?"

"Of course, I remember the caves! How could I forget?"

Uncle Ho turned to me. "In Shanghai there was a small mountain range near where I lived as a boy. I climbed there often with my friends. The paths were steep, with giant boulders and tall pine trees that gave off a fine fragrance when the wind blew. We were always looking for treasure. We found pinecones. It was a child's game.

"We wouldn't let Jia come with us. She was too small, and she was a girl. But she was curious."

Madame Jia leaned back into her chair, a quiet smile lighting her face.

"I should have known when I told Jia that we had found some caves, she would not be content to be left behind. Without our knowing, she trailed after us one day, but once she entered the caves she lost her way."

"Jia did not come home to her family that night. No one knew where she was. The next morning her grandfather came to my house and spoke to my grandfather."

"Ho found me," Madam Jia said, her eyes sparkling with the delight of memory. "He guessed what I had done and he came for me. I was in a cave that had many niches carved into its sides. Before the light was gone, I counted them, from right to left and back again until I reached the top. There was one large niche all by itself. It seemed it was as high as the sky. I called it the moon niche. When Ho found me I told him that if we ever had any treasure to hide, that would be a good place."

Uncle Ho nodded, and their glances held for a moment, sharing an old memory. "It was many years later, when the country was under Mao's grip that I thought of those caves. The government had been watching me and I knew one day they would come to my door and I would be thrown in prison. It had happened to many of my friends.

"I might die or I might live, but if I were to live I was determined to save my treasure for that day. I chose a dark night and made my way back to the hillside of my childhood and hid my winnings in the niche Jia had given the name of the moon.

"It would be a long time before I would return to that place and to Shanghai. When I did, I hardly recognized the city of those early years. Towering buildings were everywhere, old ones had been torn down, streets and alleyways I had known were gone. At the foot of the hillside that led to the caves, bulldozers and cranes were in place, waiting to level the land and collapse the caves. I had come just in time.

"I dressed as a peasant, with a bamboo pole across my shoulder and my two bird cages. I set out to climb the steep hill for the last time. I found the cave I was looking for and came out on the other side, so that if someone were watching they would simply see an old man taking his birds for a walk, and not guess what treasure he had."

Madam Jia brought her hands together and, pressed them to her lips. "Ho," was all she said, until she rose from her chair. "The time has come for us to see your treasure. I will bring the water and the bowls you asked for." She nodded toward a long table in front of the window. Sunlight splashed on its light blue cloth cover. "We will do our work there."

She asked me to come with her into the kitchen. She put a large basin in the sink and began filling it with hot water and gave me a stack of dishtowels and some soup bowls to take to the table. When the basin was full I carried it there. She followed with a large sieve.

I thought about asking a few questions then, but it looked as though I'd have some answers soon. And besides, it was their story to play out.

I stood to the side as Uncle Ho sprang open the drawers in each of the birdcages. In small handfuls he dropped the brown pellets into the sieve which Madam Jia lowered into the water. It gradually turned muddy.

"They must soak for a while," she said.

We changed the water several times, until it finally became clear and the pellets were no longer brown. Uncle Ho counted and separated them, and Madam Jia carefully spread them on the dishtowels to dry in the sun streaming in through the window.

There were twenty-nine star sapphires, thirty-six rubies and forty-seven emeralds, sparkling in the sun's bright light.

Uncle Ho was a rich man.

"There were many men who did not have the money to pay their gambling debts," Uncle Ho explained. "They paid me in gems. That gave me the idea to convert some of my other earnings into what you see here. I wrapped them in bird droppings so no one would know what they were."

He turned to Madam Jia then. "I think it is best to wrap them now, in soft cloth, and put them back in the birdcages. It has been a safe place for many years. I will take them with me to James's house and think about what I should do next. But I must decide before tomorrow afternoon."

"Why tomorrow afternoon?" I asked.

"I must be at the airport then to rejoin the group."

"Were you supposed to go with them to the Grand Canyon?"

"Yes, but after we arrived in Los Angeles and passed through immigration, I slipped away. Since there were only six of us, it is certain that I was missed. When I join them, I will just say that I lost my way in the airport in Los Angeles. It is a confusing place."

Maybe they'd believe him, and maybe they wouldn't, but what I wanted to know was what happened after that. "And just like that, you found someone to drive you here? How did you manage that?"

Uncle Ho smiled. "I will tell you the details at another time, but we must be going now."

I got up and said goodbye to Madam Jia and told Uncle Ho I'd wait in the car for him. Madam Jia let me out through the garden.

It wasn't long before the front door of the shop opened and Uncle Ho appeared with a birdcage in each hand. Madam Jia held the door for him. To anyone who might be watching she was just saying goodbye to a customer, not someone she had known a lifetime ago.

———◆———

It was well past lunchtime when we got home. Uncle Ho said he wasn't hungry and wanted to rest for a while and think about what he should do next. I helped him upstairs with the birdcages, aware of how much wealth I held in one hand.

I made myself a sandwich and thought about all that had happened since my parents had left for work that morning. I grabbed a coke from the fridge and went into the family room and turned on the TV. It was set to the local news channel. A bulletin came on, obviously a follow-up to a story they'd been monitoring all morning. One of the local anchors was reading an announcement.

Two helicopters collided and crashed in the Grand Canyon shortly after dawn this morning in a surprise lightning storm. There are no survivors. The bodies of both pilots have been identified. The passengers were Chinese tourists, traveling in a group. Their final destination in the U. S. was Las Vegas. There is some question as to whether there were five or six passengers on board the flights. Only five bodies have been found.

I sat there, staring at the screen, thinking I should probably call my parents, but I couldn't imagine telling them all of this over the phone. I thought of Uncle Ho. I wasn't ready for that either.

Another bulletin came on.

The families of the pilots have been notified of their deaths. Authorities have released the names of the six Chinese tourists who were scheduled to be aboard the two helicopters. As a special service to our viewers in the Chinese community, their names can be found on our website.

I went up to my room and sat down at my computer. The website listed the names in Chinese with English transliterations beside them.

There were six names. Ho was one of them. I went back downstairs and flipped on the TV.

I must have fallen asleep, because the next thing I knew my mother's hand was on my shoulder, shaking me awake. Dad was standing beside her. The TV was still on. I sat up and stared at them. For a minute I thought the whole thing had been a dream.

"We heard the news as we were driving home," my mother said. "It's dreadful. I wonder if it's the group Uncle Ho was traveling with."

"Where's Uncle Ho?" My father asked.

"We got home a short time ago. He went to his room to take a rest. I'll go get him."

I started up the stairs. All sorts of questions were chasing around in my head. One thing was sure. The next time the relatives got together, I'd have an Uncle Ho story to top them all.

The
Dance
of
the
Apsara

Pochetong Airport in Phnom Penh can be hairy for someone arriving in Cambodia for the first time, so that was the excuse Mike Swann had ready for meeting her plane. She was coming in on Thai Air's morning flight from Bangkok, en route from New York.

He stood outside of customs and spotted her right away, white T-shirt, jeans and blazer, fair-skinned in a sea of Asian faces. As he got close he saw she had Jingo's eyes. That was a bit of a jolt. Lady-killer eyes, the guys used to say. Nothing else of her father had been passed along that he could see. She was beautiful. Slim as a reed. Her brown hair gleamed.

He walked toward her. "Jill Winfield?"

She looked up in surprise, and he got the full blast of those hazel gold eyes.

"Mike Swann," he said, introducing himself, and then played with the truth. "I've been asked by the folks at *The Cambodia Monitor* to welcome you to Phnom Penh and be your local guide for the next few days."

"Oh, really?" She eyed him quizzically. "We haven't met before, have we?"

"I don't think so," he said shaking his head.

She continued to stare at him, and then in a slow wave of recollection, it came to her. "You wouldn't happen to be Michael J. Swann, foreign correspondent, Pulitzer winner, National Book Award?"

He hadn't expected that, and felt himself blush. "I have to plead guilty," he said, not missing the irony in his words.

"I read your novel last year. I've read books that gave me sweeter dreams, but I liked it a lot."

The photograph on the book jacket hadn't romanticized him, she decided. No question he was a good-looking guy, lean body, lean face, dark brows arched over serious gray eyes. His brown hair had a few wisps of gray.

He could tell she wasn't quite satisfied. He waited.

"Tell me, what have I done to rate you? You must owe someone at *The Cambodia Monitor* a big favor."

He laughed. "The truth is I'm between assignments. I planned to use the time to take another look at this town." His response wasn't a lie, but it left out a lot. How the hell did I get into this? It would be just fine, if he could just play it straight. Leave it to his old buddy Jingo to complicate things.

That seemed to satisfy her, so he motioned for a porter to pick up her bags, and then led the way through the confusion of arriving and departing passengers to where his Toyota was parked. The air was hot and steamy.

She had a reservation at the Lucky Siam, not a bad little hotel on a quiet side street, run by a Thai he knew. She said she'd picked it out of a guidebook.

"Good choice." He was glad she hadn't chosen the sprawling Cambodiana, a draw for many Americans. It catered to high-end tour groups which gave Phnom Penh an overnight and then headed for the temples at Angkor.

"You've had yourself a bit of journey. How's the jet lag? Are you up for some sightseeing this afternoon?

"I'm a bit groggy now, but a quick nap and a shower should take care of that. I'd love it, if you have time."

"I do. And I'm looking forward to it," he said as he turned onto Phnom Penh's only wide boulevard. He eased in behind a pedicab, and felt her stiffen when he crossed two lanes of oncoming traffic to make a left turn on to a narrow side street.

"Sorry. I should have warned you. The Cambodians haven't gotten around to traffic lights. The rule of the road is that anything goes. People are pretty polite and most small cars can stop on a dime."

In wasn't long before he pulled up in front of the Lucky Siam. Tall palms framed the wide white steps. Mike accompanied her to the reception desk, and waited to make sure there were no glitches.

"Is there anything special on your list of things to see?"

"I'd be happy to leave that to you today. At some point I want to go to The Killing Fields."

Mike nodded. "I thought you would. But it takes some emotional stamina. We should leave that for tomorrow, and start out easy today. How is three o'clock? I'll give you a call first."

"Sounds great. I'll be ready," she said, smiling at him. "I hope you won't mind. I ask lots of questions."

He grinned. "That's okay. So do I."

———◆———

The publisher of *The Cambodia Monitor* and Mike had been in the Special Forces together. It wasn't something they broadcast then, or now. After their tours were over Larry had settled in Hong Kong and turned into a businessman, with a wide range of investments in Southeast Asia, including an English language newpaper in Phnom Penh. As expats in the same neighborhood, they kept in touch, exchanging a high-five now and then. An E-mail from Larry was no surprise, but his most recent one, with the subject "JINGO" was something else. Mike read it and thought of hitting delete and leaving town.

A young woman, named Jill Winfield, is headed your way. She's the daughter of our old buddy Jingo. You're not to let on you know that. She's divorced, and is using her married name. I'm not sure what the story is, but she wants a newspaper job out here. It's arranged. I've talked to the editor at The Monitor. Jingo asked that you take her under your wing for a few days. She's never been to Asia, no less Cambodia, so you've got your work cut out. For some reason he wants her to have a look at The Apsara Project. It's part of a community development program up north. Cambodian named Ving is in charge.

That's it for now. The Senator says thanks.

Mike stared at the computer screen and wondered who else knew the Senator as Jingo. If rumors of a run for the oval office had any substance, "his old buddy" might like to keep that under wraps.

The three of them had saved each other's ass more than a few times. Jingo had been extra trouble, always into high risk games. He must have turned the corner and channeled all those juices into political ambition. His picture was in *Time* and *Newsweek* off and on. He'd put on some weight and had a bit of jowl. Well, a lot of years had rolled by. The Senator was twelve years older than Swann.

Mike guessed Jill was somewhere around twenty-five, almost young enough to be his daughter, if he had started early, but then he hadn't started at all. He'd known Jingo had a family back home, but he hadn't talked much about that. Jingo was into the thrill of the moment, and if things got dull, he'd find some way of stirring them up. Jesus! It's a wonder we got out alive.

What the hell was his daughter doing out here? A job with *The Monitor* made no sense, not for her and not for the Senator, for sure. The English-language paper did pretty well covering the current mess of Cambodia, a desperately poor country, struggling to dig out of its beleaguered past. It had been ruled by the French, occupied by the Japanese, bombed by Uncle Sam and invaded by Vietnam. Add to that Pol Pot and the Khmer Rouge, and all the unexploded mines that were still around.

The Monitor staff was the usual foreign outpost mix. There were a few lonely planet types, some serious students of Asia, a handful of green journalism grads, and a couple of guys who had no other place to go. It was sure off the beaten track, unless you had a special reason for being out here. How did Jill Winfield fit into that?

———◆———

He phoned her at three, as promised. As soon as her voice came on the end of the line, he saw her smile and those eyes. It was no lie; he was looking forward to showing her around. She was out in front waiting for him, standing in the shade of one of the palms, in a sleeveless yellow dress, a straw bag slung over her shoulder.

"It's hot, so we won't walk far," he said. "I should have told you to bring a hat. The sun is fierce."

"I have one in my bag. It's one of those roll-up straws. Not the Madison Avenue look but it's okay." She put it on and peered up at him from under the brim.

She looked great.

He hailed a pedicab at the next corner. "This may feel a little unprotected, at first, but you'll get used to it. On a hot day like this, it's the best way to see the town." They settled into the wicker seat, with the driver peddling behind them.

It was a kick watching her take in the scene, and getting caught up in a detail he no longer noticed, like the towers of mangos and pomelos, piled on fruit-sellers trays, defying gravity.

"Why is there so much rubble?" she asked after awhile. "Half the buildings look as though they're falling down."

"Some are. Some just look that way. Most of it's neglect, but some is left over from the war. Foreign aid is finally beginning to pour in, and agencies are scrambling for office space and housing. Reconstruction makes for more mess."

They came to the Royal Palace and the Silver Pagoda, ornate structures with golden spires blinding in the reflected light of the sun.

Jill shook her head in wonder. "Just think of all that wealth behind those walls. According to my guidebook, there's a life-size Buddha inside, encrusted with 9584 diamonds. Our pedicab driver has all of his wealth in his leg muscles."

"I was counting on your fresh eye."

She laughed. "Where's home to you, when you're not here?"

"I grew up outside of Los Angeles. My parents are still there, in the same house. When I was a kid we were surrounded by acres of orchards— nectarines, plums, oranges. Now it's track housing. I try to get back once a year, but I don't always make it. My mother writes, at least once a month. I try to match her, if it's only a post card. If we kept score, she'd win." He waited a moment before he followed up. He wondered how she would answer him. "And you?"

"Boston most recently. It was a natural transition. I'd gone to boarding school in New England and then Connecticut College. It had a good performing arts program, still does. I thought I wanted to be an actress. It turned into just fun. I decided on journalism instead. I worked on *The New London Day* for a while and then went on to freelancing for *The Boston Globe*."

No mention of her family. It wasn't the time to ask.

Along about five he had the driver let them out at the Foreign Correspondents' Club. They were a little early. No one was at the bar. He chose a table in the corner.

"The FCC is a mecca for journalists passing through, and a hangout for those who live here. There's a small auditorium behind those double doors where they have cultural events and panel discussions every couple of weeks. Visiting dignitaries and politicos give speeches. Sometimes you can get a story out of it. The expat community loves it. It gives them a handle on the outside world."

Their beers came, and they touched glasses.

He took a deep swallow, and decided to plunge in. "So what brings you out here? *The Monitor* is a good paper for what it sets out to do. But it's a little far from New England."

Jill sent him a level gaze. She liked him, but she knew he wasn't playing straight with her. It was time to call him on it. "Mike, *The Monitor* isn't expecting me for another ten days. I came out early to have a look around on my own. If I hadn't read your book and looked at that jacket photo often enough, I wouldn't have had a clue who you were, at the airport, except some guy trying to pick me up. That didn't seem to fit then, and it still doesn't. So what's going on?"

He smiled sheepishly, at the same time filled with relief. Jingo, it looks as thought your cat is about to pop out of the bag.

"I know the publisher of *The Monitor*. Larry lives in Hong Kong, but we often exchange e-mails. He passed along a message from your father."

"My father!" The words burst from her mouth. "What do you mean you got a message from my father!"

"The Senator and I knew each other a long time ago."

Her bewilderment had turned to anger. He saw it in her eyes. He didn't think all of it was directed at him, but he wanted to make sure it stayed that way.

He leaned toward her. "Here's the story."

"I can't wait to hear this." Her voice was as sharp as a knife.

He chose his words carefully. "Your father and Larry and I were in a special unit here in the seventies, just before Pol Pot took over. That's twenty-two years ago. The three of us were in some tough situations together. With effort we were a good team. But when our tour was over, we went our separate ways. Your father and I didn't stay in touch. We were too different." He decided to leave it at that. "I followed your father's political career. It wasn't hard to do. And I guess he's kept track of what I've been up to. Anyhow, that's what I deduced from Larry's e-mail. The word was that you were coming out here to work for *The Monitor* and your father wanted me to take you under my wing for a few days." He shrugged. "I have to admit it came as a surprise. But I didn't have a problem with it, except that there was a catch. I wasn't to let on I knew whose daughter you were." He sat back and opened his hands. "That's it."

She glared at him, her eyes blazing now. "Oh, come off it! You smelled a story. Get at the Senator through the daughter. You've heard the rumors—my father's talking of running for president."

He shook his head. "I don't blame you for thinking that. I'll admit I'm curious about what your father is going to do, but I'm not after a story. I've hung up my reporting hat for a while. I have another book contract. I'm taking a year off. I leave here in two weeks. That's what I meant when I said I was between assignments."

He had her attention, but she was still trying to figure out if she could trust him. Dammit, Jingo! Your side of this thing smells.

"Just to make sure everything is out on the table, your father had another request. He wants me to take you to see the *The Apsara Project*."

She didn't hide her surprise, but she said nothing.

"I'm familiar with the project, but I have no idea what interest it holds for your father. I went up country to check it out about five months ago. I filed a story. The *apsara* is an icon in Cambodia. *Apsara* dancers performed in the courts of kings, way back in the days of the early Khmer Empire. There are stone carvings on the temples in Angkor depicting them in all their traditional dance positions."

"I'm familiar with the *apsara*," she said with a nod. "My father had a bronze replica of an *apsara* in his study at home, and several books about the temples at Angkor. I didn't see much of him when I was little, but certain things stand out. We'd sit together on the sofa in his study and he'd turn the pages of books that were too heavy for me to hold." Tears sprang to her eyes, but she blinked them away.

Out of the corner of his eye Mike saw two guys walk in and sidle up to the bar. Happily it wasn't anyone he knew. He didn't want any interruptions now.

"Tell me about the *Apsara Project*," she said.

"It's part of a larger mental health program in this country, which uses art as therapy. It teaches the dance of the *apsara* to young girls who have suffered some form of trauma. I don't have to tell you the depth of the brutality that once gripped Cambodia. The project was having some trouble getting off the ground due to lack of funding, but I heard recently that a benefactor has appeared on the horizon, so it looks hopeful."

She looked at him, and wondered just how much she should tell him. She was almost convinced he was telling her the truth, but how could she be sure? She had to risk it, because she needed him. There was no one else she could turn to.

"I heard about the *Apsara Project* from my mother. She told me it was her private deal. She said my father knew nothing about it. Even though it made no sense, I believed her. She has no connection to this part of the world. My father has. That was years ago. He has other interests now."

She frowned. "The mental health side of it fit. That's been my mother's area of interest. A political wife needs to have a cause." Jill sighed, and her voice trailed off. The light in her eyes was fading. She looked totally fagged.

Mike leaned toward her. "I think we should call it a day. We can chew on this some more tomorrow. I think it's time for me to get you back to the Lucky Siam."

With his arm lightly on her elbow, he led her to the exit. Darkness had fallen, and the winding stairway to the street was in shadow. A hissing whisper startled her. "Missy, Missy," were the words she heard. Mike held on to her arm and guided her past the huddled figure at the foot of the stairs.

"He's here most evenings," Mike explained, and drew her toward a line of pedicabs. "Someone drops him off. He works at a bike repair shop off and on. He's one of Cambodia's landmine victims. You probably couldn't see it, but he was sitting in a shallow basket on wheels."

"There is so much sadness in this country."

Mike spoke to the pedicab driver and then turned to Jill. "If you can keep your eyes open a few more minutes, we'll have a quick look at the river. The Mekong and the Tonle Sap meet just over there. The fishermen are out in their boats now, and the lights from their lanterns cast wonderful reflections on the water. It's a beautiful sight. It will give you sweeter dreams."

When they reached her hotel, he walked up the steps with her. She looked up at him with a weary smile. "Thanks for meeting my plane ... and for the lights on the Mekong. I'll let you know about those dreams tomorrow."

He lay awake for a long time, thinking. He watched the shadows, cast by the palms outside his window, sway back and forth across the ceiling. He wished he knew what Jingo was up to.

They did the markets the next morning. "Central first," he said. "You need to see it. It's a storehouse of goodies for the expat community here: refrigerators, croissants, smoked salmon, antibiotics, TVs … you name it, and they've got it."

"I thought Phnom Penh was a hardship post."

"Only for Cambodians."

The Russian Market was a labyrinth of local goods—fabrics, clothes, hand crafts. He showed her where the silver was—intricately patterned bracelets, necklaces and serving spoons. "Cambodian silver isn't the silver we know. It's a mixed metal of sorts. It blackens quickly and needs polishing. But the pieces can be beautiful. I sent my mother some. She said she loved them, but I'm not so sure. Polishing silver isn't her thing."

She patted his arm. "It's the thought, Michael. She loved you for that."

They had lunch at a small restaurant with outside tables shaded by pink umbrellas. The menu was in French. "I keep seeing such contrasts. Is it like this all over the country?"

"Not really. In the countryside everyone is poor. There are so many landmines around, farmers can't get back to planting rice."

"What makes you stay?"

"It's hard to say. This is where I got started. I've bopped around most of Southeast Asia, in and out of Cambodia a lot. It's what I know. If my first job had been in Latin America, would I be there now? Who knows? Sometimes the roll of the dice determines your life." He nodded, putting a period to his thought, and went on studying Jingo's daughter. He had decided to leave it to her to return to their conversation of the previous evening. She did then.

"When I woke this morning I was afraid you might have decided you'd had enough of the Senator and his daughter. As much as I hate to admit it, I don't think I can figure this out by myself." She smiled, a look of quiet mischief in her eyes. "I need you, Michael J. Swann. And since you promised yourself to me for a few days, I'm going to hold you to it."

He laughed. "You don't see me running, do you?"

She stared at him for a long moment and thought, I like this guy.

"Okay," she said. "Here goes. Do you know a man named Ving?"

Mike had expected the question.

"He's head of a community development center about three hours north of here. The mental health program and *The Apsara Project* were his idea. When I dropped in on him about five months ago, I found him working out of a couple of thatched roof lean-tos. He was trying hard to get things going.

"I met Ving for the first time in the spring of 1995. That was the year many Cambodians were returning home. It was an anniversary of sorts. Twenty years before, Pol Pot had marched into Phnom Penh and the killing began. Those who managed to escape found exile in a variety of places around the world. Ving was a doctor, then, working at the hospital in Phnom Penh. If the Khmer Rouge had known that, his life would have ended right there. He pretended to be a cobbler, and joined the thousands who were force-marched into the countryside. Eventually he escaped through the jungle into Thailand and then found exile in the United States.

"I hadn't seen him again until five months ago. Although he remained optimistic about making a go of it, I knew he needed funding. I was afraid he was in for a long wait. But as I told you, I heard he'd gotten some funds, from an anonymous donor. I hope it's true. I've wanted to pay him another visit. Now I have a double reason, yours and mine." He looked at her questioningly. "If you like, we can drive up there tomorrow."

She nodded, but turned away, and looked off in the distance. It was hard to guess what she was thinking, except that she wondered if she could trust him.

"I don't know what this is all about and I don't know where it's going," she said slowly. "There are things I shouldn't tell you, but I'm about to. But I want your word that anything I say is off the record."

He reached into pocket and took out a card. He wrote a few words on the back and signed his name. He handed it to her. "You've got it."

She looked surprised. "You didn't have to do that."

"Yes, I did. We didn't get off to a good start. You have every reason to wonder if you can trust me. I want you to know you can."

"Okay," she said and took a deep breath. "You said Ving got the funding he was waiting for, from an anonymous donor. It was my mother."

That was a curve.

"I told you her cause is mental health. About two years ago she chaired a major fundraiser in the U. S. in support of research in the mental health field. She got a tremendous amount of national publicity. After that tons of requests came pouring. One came from a Cambodian woman, named Mei. The proposal included a description of Ving's plans for a program that would use art as therapy. She called it *The Apsara Project*. My mother met with Mei. And Mei won her over."

"So, your mother organized a fundraiser for *The Apsara Project?*"

Jill shook her head. "No. That wouldn't have made sense. My mother has always done things to bolster my father's political ambitions. Putting her efforts behind a project that would benefit people in a foreign country wouldn't have satisfied that. The mental health aspect of it was right, but Cambodia? Most people don't even know where that is."

Mike nodded.

A puzzled look came into her eyes, and when she spoke it was clear she was searching for an answer. "There was something about *The Apsara Project* that captured my mother's interest. I'm not sure just what it was. Maybe it was the Cambodian woman herself. My mother hired an attorney to arrange for the anonymous donation. She told me it was her secret. No one was to know about it, not even my father."

"But your father does know," he said gently.

She nodded. "So it appears. I can't argue with that. You wouldn't be here, if my father didn't know." She shook her head. "You can see why I'm having so much trouble making sense of it all."

She fell silent then. Mike waited, not wanting to intrude too quickly into her thoughts, but her plea for help was unmistakable.

"What was it that prompted your mother to tell you now?

Jill took a long breath. "She wanted me to come out here and take a look at the project."

"To check up on Ving?"

"Sort of. But she also thought I should get away for a while. I had just been through a divorce, and although I'm okay with it, my mother doesn't think so." Jill smiled. "She thought I needed a change of scene. Cambodia sure fits that. But there was also some urgency on my mother's part about my getting out here. Since I was at a bit of a crossroads, I decided just to do it. The idea of a job with *The Cambodia Monitor* was my idea. I needed my own purpose for coming out here. It seemed to make sense then, but it doesn't now."

———◆———

He picked her up later that afternoon and they set out for the twelve-mile drive to The Killing Fields.

"It's something I have to do," she said. "It would be disrespectful not to. It would be like going to Normandy for the wine and not visiting the battlefields."

"I'm with you on that. But no matter how much you've read and how many pictures you've seen, this is going to be rough. The Cambodians haven't softened a thing. They want everyone who comes here to know what happened."

He walked through the entry gates with her and then let her set her own pace. He didn't want to crowd her, or encroach on the emotions that were sure to rise.

Her first view of the pagoda was as it was for everyone, a simple and sedate memorial against a clear blue sky. A closer look was when shock set in. Behind its glass windows were the skulls of Pol Pot's victims. Stacked layer on layer, they stared out in silent accusation across a landscape of communal graves, turned into shallow craters by the sun and rain of passing years. Bones lay scattered like shells on a beach.

———◆———

He took her to The No Problem that night. It was Rick's Café Asian style, straight out of *Casablanca*. Patrons settled into high-backed wicker chairs, sipped Singapore Slings, or whatever else they fancied, while ceiling fans stirred the hot moist air. Pierre had his own repertoire, but was always happy to oblige with *As Time Goes By*.

You could count on a collection of regulars at the bar, and if you came in alone, they would lay it on about how they'd finally gotten to understand the country. Swann never entered that cloud of hot air. No one understood Cambodia. Not even the Cambodians.

He'd known their appearance would get a rise. Her dress was a sleeveless white linen, hugging the curve of her high breasts and showing off her slim, suntanned legs. The mirror behind the bar signaled their arrival. All heads turned. He made the introductions. Guys, who could be hard and crass, were transformed into charmers. He gave them some room, but not for long. It was a sweet trip having her on his arm.

Yellow orchids floated in the bowl in the center of their table. The lights were low and the fans' soft whir blurred nearby conversations. "Here we go with contrasts again," she said. "Just think of where we were this afternoon. Now, this. It's so lovely. I can't imagine wanting to be any place but here, right now."

In the soft light her eyes were the color of amber. Steady, Swann. Off limits.

He took a deep breath and reached for his wine. "It's a nice spot," he said casually. "I had a feeling you'd like it. As for contrasts, there will be a few more tomorrow. The road is bad—trucks, cars, oxcarts, all trying to navigate around ruts, potholes and assorted debris. No one drives it after dark. There's an okay hotel run by a Frenchman, not far from Ving's. I called ahead."

Their waiter came with the first course, shrimp remoulade, over slices of avocado.

"I've guessed your secret, Michael Swann. You stay because of the food."

He laughed. "That's one good thing the French left behind. Actually, as colonizers go, they get some good marks."

"We've talked about Ving, but tell me what you know about Mei," she said.

"I can't help you there. I never heard of Mei, until you mentioned her."

"According to my mother, she's out here now, working with Ving."

"We'll soon find out. I called Ving early this morning to let him know we were coming. I said I was bringing along another journalist, but I didn't mention your name. I wasn't sure how you wanted to play that."

"Winfield isn't my family name, as you know. And since my mother's donation is anonymous, my family name wouldn't mean anything to Ving, anyway."

"But it would to Mei. She's met your mother, which means she knows who your father is."

"You're right. That's another thing that makes no sense. For some odd reason my mother trusts Mei. The more I think about it, the stranger it gets."

That's for sure, Mike thought. Why would the Senator's wife support a project with none of the usual benefits? And why the need for secrecy?

Pierre was back at the piano and the strains of *La Vie en Rose* reached them. Jill reached across the table and brushed the back of his hand with the tips of her fingers. "Mike, let's forget about my parents for a while. I don't want to spoil all this."

He lifted his glass, "Just one last question. How serious is your father about pursuing the nomination?"

"Major serious. He's had his eye on that prize for a long time. My mother, too. For years she's talked about their walking down Pennsylvania Avenue together. She teases him about wearing a top hat."

JINGO FOR PRESIDENT. Wouldn't that be a slogan!

She started to smile, but her lips never got to it. He waited, wondering where her thoughts were taking her. He thought he knew, but she wasn't there just yet.

"That's what this has to be all about—my father running for president ...." Her voice trailed off in disbelief.

"He would never discuss what he did out here. It was so off limits I didn't dare ask, even later on. The only thing he talked about was Angkor Wat and seeing the ancient temples. I loved the story, the jungle swallowing up an entire civilization and keeping it hidden for centuries. Then a French explorer just happened along and found one of the temples. For a while I had it confused with *Sleeping Beauty*. But I got it straight after a while. The pictures were amazing, gigantic heads on top of towers, a snake that went on for miles and a huge parade of elephants carved in stone. There was a double spread of dancers in the most intricate positions. That's when I first heard the word *apsara*."

She shook her head. "But that was all a long time ago. What does it have to do with now?" She leaned toward him. "Something has my parents worried. Something must have happened out here that could be damaging to my father's candidacy. That could explain how Mei got to my mother."

Mike had arrived at the same thought. It came from instinct and knowing Jingo, but he was glad she had gotten to it on her own. He thought of all the times he had been close to decking his old buddy. His hand was itching now. Senator, what the hell are you doing to your daughter?

"Mike, don't look at me that way. He was never a great father, but he's the only one I have. I don't want your pity. I want your help. I need you to tell me what happened out here. What was my father into that would make him a target for blackmail? Was it drugs? Was he dealing in arms? Was he involved in a black market of some kind? Help me, I don't even know the right questions to ask."

He waited, thinking hard. Okay, Swann. Let's see how objective you can be.

"Your father didn't talk to you about his work, because those were the rules. They still are. What we did was covert. I'm sure that doesn't surprise you. But that's all I can say about it. I wasn't his keeper, but I'm sure he wasn't into smuggling drugs or arms. He took unnecessary risks, just for the hell of it. Your father was a handsome guy and he had a way with women."

"What do you mean he had a way with women? Are you talking sex, or something else?"

"Sex. He could never get enough of it. He loved the game."

She rolled her eyes. "Are you telling me I had a horny father, or is there a whole orphanage out here with kids that have eyes like mine?"

"Jill, there's no point in getting mad at me. I've I told you as much as I know."

"God, there are times when my father can be such a jerk."

The waiter came along then with another bottle of wine. It was Jill who changed the subject after he had gone. She asked Mike about his novel. "How long were you working on it?"

"It was in my head for a few years, but when I actually sat down it took me about ten months. I'm not as far along on this next one. A few years ago I bought a cabin in the hills in southern California. That's where I'm headed after here. I'm hoping to work things out."

When they left The No Problem, Pierre had just finished playing *Moon River.*

Jill slipped her hand through his arm. "Let's go look at the lights on the Mekong."

The dreaminess in her voice told him it was the wine talking. There was nothing that he would have liked more than to take her anywhere she asked. But there were enough people taking advantage of her. He wasn't adding his name to the list. "Jill, it's late. We've got a lot ahead of us tomorrow. It's going to be a long day."

On the way out of town the next morning they drove past a small farming village. The roofs on the houses were sagging, but there were vegetable patches and a few banana trees in each of the yards. It would have passed as a quiet picturesque scene, except that at the doorway to each house a dark effigy-like figure stood guard.

"What are those all about?" she asked. "They're the most frightening scarecrows I've ever seen. They must have more on their minds than a flock of crows."

"The enemy has many faces in this country.

"I'm beginning to understand that."

The road had gotten worse since the last time he drove it. The ruts had multiplied and the potholes were deeper. Dust devils swirled in the dry fields and then danced across the road. The sun played its own tricks, creating mirages that dissolved and reappeared. Mike kept his eyes straight ahead, and his hands steady on the wheel.

"Is that for real?" she asked. Signs posted along the shoulder warned of land mines in the fields beyond.

"I don't suggest we check it out. Land mines are all over this country. Most places aren't marked, particularly along streams and old rice paddies. Foreign aid is out here digging them up, but it will be years, maybe never, before the land is clear. The enemy didn't leave any maps. Some of the mines they dig up don't get detonated. Now there's a market in live mines."

"Who buys them?"

"Cambodians. They put them around their houses to keep the enemy out. It's another kind of scarecrow. Then they forget where they've buried them. Someone in the family trips one and another amputee is added to the list."

"The stories don't get any better, do they?" she said.

"There are a lot of bad things still happening out here. Good things, too. They're harder to find. Ving's project is an example. But to complete the land mine lecture, don't go wandering off on your own. Keep to defined roads and paths. The hell with modesty. The woods are off limits."

"I hear you." She looked out the window at the yellowed fields with their tufts of high grass, dense enough to provide modest cover, and suppressed a shudder.

———◆———

Mike expected that Ving's new building would be one of the prefabs cropping up all over the developing world, with a corrugated tin roof, so he was startled to see the structure that had replaced the rickety lean-tos. Made of bamboo and woven palm, it had a sloping roof of thick thatch, which sheltered verandas with half walls and inner rooms. It was a replica of the houses built before the Khmer Rouge.

"It's beautiful!" Jill exclaimed. "Did you expect this?"

"I sure didn't. I knew it was what Ving wanted, but the chances of finding some one to put it together were pretty slim. Those were the kinds of skills Pol Pot did a good job of snuffing out."

When Mike had called, Ving asked that they come early. "I have many things I would like to show you and much to talk about. The young *apsaras* will give their first performance in the afternoon."

That explained the small crowd that had already gathered. Women and children sat on the ground in a wide semi circle that followed the perimeter of the yard, hugging the shade of the giant fig trees that edged the surrounding forest.

"There's Ving now," Mike said and returned the wave of the man who had come out onto the veranda of the new building. He was dressed in a loose-fitting light blue shirt and trousers. There was an air of tranquility about him.

When he reached them he brought his hands together in the traditional greeting. "Welcome. I am honored that you have both made the journey today."

"Ving, it's good to see you," Mike said. "I'd like you to meet Jill Winfield. She arrived in Phnom Penh just a few days ago to work on *The Cambodia Monitor*."

"You are both most welcome. You have chosen a special day. Our new building is finished and, as I told Michael, the young *apsaras* will give a performance this afternoon." He motioned then to a young woman standing off to the side, and spoke in Khmer. "Lok speaks only a little English," he said to Jill, "but she will take you to refresh yourself."

Lok led her to a screened-off area, shaded by trees. The facilities were primitive but clean, and in a few minutes Jill rejoined the men on a side veranda where a breeze stirred the hot, moist air. Ving poured tea, and Lok reappeared with a bowl of seasoned rice and vegetables and small individual bowls. Ving explained they were the polished halves of coconut shells.

"You would be amazed at how much can be derived from a coconut palm. We use all our natural resources wherever possible. If we can pluck something free from the forest, we do. This building, as you can see, is made of our natural materials. It is very cost effective. Finding someone who knew the old skills was the challenge."

"I'd sure like to know how you managed that," Mike said.

Ving smiled, obviously pleased by the question.

"I sent word to the local villages. An old man came to see me. He said he had some memory of the way our houses were built and thought he could work out the puzzle, but he was not strong enough to do the hard labor. I knew some farmers whose land had been taken from them by mines. They were poor and depressed by their idleness. It did not take much to persuade them to let the old man be their teacher."

A mischievous gleam came into Ving's dark eyes. "I'll admit, it was a bit of a gamble, as you would say in your country, but their endeavors proved more than satisfactory and beneficial to everyone. They have become a team now and have gone on to do similar work, smaller houses than this. You will see one shortly."

"It's certainly a beautiful building, Ving, but beyond that, it represents is a major achievement. You should be very pleased."

"I will not deny that I am," Ving replied and then glanced at Jill. "Much of what we are doing, now, were only ideas when Michael was last here. The entire time I lived in your country I hoped to return to Cambodia and work with the mentally wounded. There are so many who suffer the post stress of the Khmer Rouge. Art as therapy is common in the United States, but it is unknown here. It intrigued me. As you know, Pol Pot targeted the educated, so there are few left with the memory of our traditional arts and crafts. The program I proposed had two goals: retrieve our lost skills and heal the mentally ill. *The Apsara Project* is the cornerstone of that effort.

"There is someone I should like you to meet. She knows you are here, and she is waiting for us. Mei is responsible for the progress of our young *apsaras*. Like myself, she found exile in the United States. Toward the end of her stay she took it upon herself to seek funds for our efforts here. I know nothing of the magic she worked, except that she found a benefactor."

Magic. Jill heard the word, and thought it an interesting choice. Without a doubt there was an unusual aspect to Mei's influence over her mother.

"There are some things you should know about Mei before I take you to see her. What I say may sound disloyal to someone on whom I have learned to rely. But it would not be fair to you to keep silent." A ripple of emotion passed over his face.

"By now the entire world knows of the atrocities Pol Pot committed here. Some Cambodians still have the need to repeat their tragic stories. I do not fault them, but it is not my way. When Michael and I first met, I had already made the decision to no longer speak of how my wife died. The details are too strong. When spoken, they render people impotent.

They cannot endure the thought, so the man Ving disappears; only pity for him remains." He paused for a moment.

"Mei is different. She is compelled to speak of her tragic story. My wife and Mei were sisters. The three of us were together when my wife died. There is no forgetting. There is only the hope of healing.

"I thought that our work and the passage of time would help to heal Mei's wounds. It seemed so when she was in the United States, but it is different now. She has returned to longing for things that cannot be. There are times when she thinks with great clarity and then others when she slips into fantasy. It is difficult to predict what she will say, or do." Ving rose, the look on his face wistful.

"Come, I shall take you to her house. She is looking forward to meeting you." Hesitating, he added, "I hope it will not be a troubling visit."

As Jill and Michael followed Ving out into the sun-drenched yard, they exchanged glances, guessing they were sharing the same thoughts.

At edge of the forest, Ving paused. "It is not far, but be sure to follow in my footsteps and do not stray off the path."

Mike's earlier warning reverberated in Jill's ears.

They came to a clearing and a small building, built in the same style as the one they had just left. Off to the side was a circular enclosure, with a raised thatched roof. The sound of singing drifted toward them.

A soft smile played across Ving's face. "What you hear are the voices of the young *apsaras*. They sing now to give strength to their voices. When they came to us, some could not speak at all. Others spoke no higher than a whisper and their words were few. Mei's approach was not to bring attention to their disability, but to distract them from it. She began by telling stories. Using a lantern, she cast shadows with her hands, creating animal images that entertained them and made them laugh. Laughter was a new experience for them. One day one of the girls put her hand alongside Mei's and began imitating the motions of her hands and fingers. From there, Mei went on to introduce them to the dance of the *apsara*.

"The enclosure is their school room and dance studio. The small house is where Mei lives. They were both built by the new building team."

Ving raised his voice then and called out, a few words in Khmer.

From behind the half wall of the veranda of the small house the figure of a woman moved toward them along the passageway. When she stepped into the sunlight, it was with the composure of someone accustomed to the stage. She was not young, but she had the aura of studied beauty. Her jet hair was wound into a coil, resting on the top of her head like a crown. The skirt of her dark green dress skimmed the ground. She walked slowly, leaning on a cane.

Mei acknowledged Ving's introductions, inclining her head in a graceful bow, and then motioned toward the veranda. "Please," she said, "It is much cooler out of the sun." She led them under the overhang of thatch to where four chairs were arranged around a low table. The air was humid and still, but the direct rays of the sun were gone.

"I should like to add my welcome to Ving's," Mei said when they were seated. "The young *apsaras* have been the focus of my attention, but Ving has other programs in place that follow the same model, art as therapy in combination with the revival of our old traditions.

"The making of baskets and weaving is art. As is fishing, planting, and the keeping of bees. So, too, is building a house such as this." With a graceful movement of her hands, she embraced the space in which they were seated.

"It is amazing what you have accomplished in so short a time," Michael said, directing his words first to Ving, but carefully including Mei.

"Ving has spoken of your visit here some time ago. I am sure it would give him great pleasure to show you a few of the other projects." She turned then and smiled at Jill. "You have come a long distance. I would like us to have some time together."

Although Jill was surprised by the suggestion, she felt no ill ease at the idea of being left alone with Mei. For that matter, she was rather intrigued.

"You will be going to the hives, I am sure," Mei said as the men rose. "Ving, I would be pleased if you brought me some honey."

"Ah yes, you asked me yesterday, and I did not remember. Today I will not forget."

Mei turned to follow their departure, giving Jill a chance to study her profile. Her mother had never mentioned how beautiful the Cambodian woman was. Mei's gaze lingered in the direction the men had gone, long after they were out of sight. Jill began to wonder if Mei had forgotten that she was there. When she finally turned, Jill was struck by the change in her expression. A distant look had replaced the cool directness that had been present before. Her eyes seemed unfocused and when she spoke it was with a lilting cadence.

"I have dreamt that you would come. I saw you when you arrived. When Lok took you to refresh yourself, I was nearby. I have seen you before. Many times. Yours is a face that comes to me in my dreams. I knew a man with eyes like yours .... "

Jill held back a gasp, stunned by the words she had just heard. "I knew a man with eyes like yours." They seemed to hang in the hot, still air.

"You are wondering about me .... I was an *apsara* when the Khmer Rouge came. My life was to dance. Pol Pot took my legs from me, but he did not take my memories or the dance my hands can still do."

In a studied motion, her hands rose from her lap. One gesture flowed into another, detailing sequences of the *apsara's* secret story.

"My sister was an *apsara,* too," she said and brought her hands to rest in her lap.

"Kaa was Ving's wife. They marched us from Phnom Penh into the forest, with no shoes on our feet and only grass to eat. They tied us in a circle of trees, so we could know each other's pain as well as our own. They tortured us until we begged for death. It was Kaa and her child who died. They slashed open her belly and ran off with her child."

Jill recoiled from the horrific image, feeling as though her own blood had drained away. She thought of Ving's warning. "The words are too strong. They render people impotent."

"The man I loved had eyes like yours. I have dreamt that you would come .... I have longed to see the child I might have had ...."

Mei was staring at her, but she wasn't seeing her at all.

Jill took a deep breath, and began in a gentle voice, as one might to a sleepwalker, who should not be startled awake. "Mei, this man you knew who had eyes like mine, can you tell me his name?"

"I did not know his full name then. I learned it later. But it is not the name I knew him by, so it is gone from me now. I know him only by the name of my memories, the name I whisper in my dreams—Jingo." She brought her palms together then, and slowly bowed her head. After a long moment, she looked up, her face washed of its daze. When she spoke her voice was firm and composed.

"The men will be back soon. We must hurry." She rose, leaning on her cane. "I told Ving I would introduce you to the young *apsaras.* There is not much time. They are expecting us."

In the circled enclosure, which Ving had pointed out to them, eight young girls, dressed like dolls for the grandest of parties, welcomed Jill with the deepest of bows.

She returned their greeting with a smile and then turned to Mei. "The girls are beautiful. Their costumes are lovely. I am eager to see them dance. Will you tell them that for me?"

Mei spoke in Khmer and the girls bowed once again. Then at Mei's prompt one of the girls stepped forward, her small hand extended to meet Mei's outstretched palm.

"Kaa was the first to put her hand alongside mine. I saw it as my sister's hand and so I gave her my sister's name."

Ving's voice reached them then. Mei spoke hurriedly to the dancers and turned to Jill. "They have come for you. You must join them. It is almost time for the *apsaras* to perform. I will see you there."

A wave of relief swept over her as Jill walked to where Mike and Ving stood waiting for her. She caught the look of concern in Mike's eyes, but she turned to Ving, who was about to speak.

"So you have seen our young *apsaras?*"

"Yes. I have. They are lovely. Mei has taught them well." There was a tremor in her voice, she knew both men heard.

Ving smiled sadly. "I had hoped that your time with Mei would not bring you pain, but I fear that is not the case. I can see it in your eyes. I assume she told you her tragic story."

Jill nodded. "Yes, she told me."

"I had hoped to spare you, but there are times when hope is a feeble defense.

"The tale Mei tells is not as it happened. I am not sure why she had reconstructed it as she has. It is no less harsh or more so than what happened. It is true that my wife died a cruel death, but there was no child in her body. It was Mei who lost a child.

"Everyone was malnourished. Starving is a truer word. The child just slipped from Mei's body, without life. She still mourns that loss. I never knew the man she loved. People came in and out of our lives we never saw again." He turned slowly, away from Jill, and looked at Michael.

"So, my friend, now you have heard more about me than I ever wished to say. But I am not afraid to have you know, not now. You have seen my fishponds and our beehives, and much of what is happening here. Soon you will see the *apsaras* dance. I have no fear that you will not continue to see Ving, the man." He pressed his palms together, and bowed. He turned and started back along the path.

Jill looked after the pale blue figure receding into the forest shadows. The tears she hadn't shed at The Killing Fields flowed from her, gathering together all the sorrows and betrayals that had touched her young life. Mike drew her into his arms and held her, absorbing the rise and fall of her sobbing breasts. He stroked her hair, waiting until she was ready to continue on.

———◆———

A red carpet was spread on the ground in front of Ving's new building. Lok led them to a place in the shade where two chairs had been set aside. Mei and Ving soon appeared and took their seats off to the side, positioned close enough so Mei could give the dancers their cues.

A hush fell over the crowd, when the young *apsaras* appeared. Their costumes were complete with small pointed crowns. They greeted the audience with graceful bows and then with the slowest of movements began the dance. With the positioning first of a hand and then a foot, a ribbon of motion flowed through their young bodies. Their gestures followed the ancient choreography of the Khmer Empire, designed to appease the gods. They gave life to the stone figures carved on the temples in Angkor.

As Jill watched the young *apsaras*, she saw the book of her childhood open on her father's lap. A tremor flowed through her and she felt the sting of tears burning at the back of her eyes.

———◆———

At the end of the day, they sat in the flickering light of a kerosene lamp in the hotel's small courtyard. Dinner had been an omelet, fresh vegetables, bread, cheese, and wine. A bottle of water and a flask of brandy were on the table now, compliments of the proprietor. They were the hotel's only guests. Night had fallen a long time ago.

"I feel like I've been talking forever," Jill said, reaching across the table to touch Mike's hand. "You must be tired of it by now."

He shook his head and smiled at her. "I signed on for this, remember? My time hasn't run out yet."

She had thought it would be easy, that the words would just pour from her, in a torrent, but they stayed locked inside her. She didn't want to repeat the words Mei had said, or interpret what they meant, not to herself, not to anyone. She wanted to pretend it hadn't happened.

But eventually the words began to form, in jagged, halting phrases that needed re-explaining, but gradually smoothed into an unselfconscious flow that went on for a long time. She decided she had said it all, except for one significant detail. She wasn't quite ready.

She leaned into the pool of flickering light and looked across at Mike. "Before we went to The Killing Fields you warned me that no matter how much I'd read or how many pictures I'd seen, it was going to be rough. You were right, of course. There are some things you can't prepare for.

"My experience with Mei falls into that category. I knew so little about her when I arrived in Cambodia, only her name. Then Ving described her wonderful work with the young *apsaras*, and then cautioned us about her fragile mental state.

"She had such a take-charge attitude when we arrived, that I forgot Ving's warnings. They didn't seem to pertain to the woman he introduced us to. But as soon as you and Ving left, a change came over her. She went into a sort of trance. It was all there, full blown, just as Ving described."

She shook her head. "Even if I had held on to Ving's warning, I wouldn't have been prepared for the things she said."

Mike waited for her to go on, not sure she was finished. Mei's graphic story would give her nightmares for a long time. But he had a feeling there was something more she wanted to say.

"I keep thinking back to why I came out here. I thought seeing Mei would give me some answers. It hasn't, not yet. But it's taken care of one thing. Mei is too unstable to be a threat, if she ever was one. I can take that home with me." In the flickering light sadness filled her eyes. "But there is little pleasure in that."

———◆———

They were surprised to find Ving waiting for them in the courtyard the next morning, where they had gone to have breakfast.

"I have come to wish you a good journey. But there is something else I have to tell you. It is about Mei.

"If you remember, she asked me for honey, and I brought it to her, wrapped in a palm leaf. When you cut honey, sometimes there is a bee still inside. I made sure there was none, because for Mei the sting of a bee is fatal. She knew that.

"It was her custom at the end of the day to sit on the veranda until sleep seemed not far off. She did this last evening. She took the packet of honey with her and opened the palm leaf wrapping, knowing the bees would come. Lok and I found her there early this morning."

His eyes sought Jill's. "You are new to Cambodia. Our history is strewn with many sorrows. Some are greater than others. Life had become a torment for Mei. Her passing should not make you sad for too long. She would not want it to."

———◆———

Mike picked Jill up at the Lucky Siam the next morning and drove her to Pochetong airport for her flight home. "Are you sure I can't persuade you to go with me to Angkor? You've come this far. It's a shame to miss the temples first hand."

She flashed him a wistful smile. "I won't say I'm not tempted, but there are so many things I have to settle back home, and then get on with my own life. Maybe I'll come back here another time, without the family baggage. There are stories out here that need to be told—remember you said I had a fresh eye? I want to think about that."

"Okay, but come visit me in California. I'll be doing some thinking, too." He reached into his shirt pocket and took out an envelope. "Here are the particulars, even a map. I won't be hard to find."

She reached out and touched his arm. "You're a nice guy, Michael J. Swann. I'm not all that anxious to say goodbye to you. I may not know my way around Cambodia, but California shouldn't be that hard for me to navigate." She lowered her eyes, and then looked up at him. "I wanted to ask you this last night, but somehow I just couldn't get the words out. Why don't you think of it as my last question."

Mike laughed. "I won't hold you to that. It's hard for me to believe that you'll ever have a <u>last</u> question."

"Well, at least for now it is."

"In that case, go ahead, whenever you're ready. I hope it's not too hard."

"You spent a lot of my time with my father. Did he have a code name?"

This was the loaded question he'd been expecting. He'd thought it would come sooner, and wondered what prompted it now. He was sure it had something to do with Mei.

"You've read enough spy novels to know the answer to that."

"Will you tell me what it was?"

He shook his head. "Jill, I can't do that, not even now."

"Let me guess, then. Was it Jingo?"

He looked at her for a long moment, trying to come up with an answer that wasn't an outright lie. "It's not that I never called him that. Jingo was a name we had for guys who needed to prove they were hot stuff. There were plenty of them around."

He drew her toward him then and tipped her face up to his. "Now get going. I know that's what you want to do. Come to California and we can start all over again."

Assignment
in
Prague

She looked up from her desk and glanced out her office window. On clear days she could see for miles, across the sweep of lower Manhattan, into New Jersey, but today swirls of gray fog drifted by. Even the close silhouettes of the Twin Towers were obscured from view.

This was definitely not one of her sunny days, on any count. Monday was always a downer after the week end. She loved Sunday, with time to curl up on the sofa of her Westside apartment with *The New York Times.* Yesterday a look at the society pages had upended that. There was Michael, smiling at his bride, in a froth of white.

Gail winced at the returning image, grateful for the task before her, the final preparations for an international conference on the environment. She had been working steadily for more than an hour, when her secretary poked her head through the doorway, waving a white envelope.

"You were waiting for this. It's a plain envelope, marked URGENT & CONFIDENTIAL."

"That's right, I was. Thanks."

It was an odd assignment. Her boss had admitted as much when he presented her with the idea. "If you say no, I won't hold it against you, but I'd be less than candid if I didn't say I'd consider it a favor."

Ron Samuels was chairman of The Foundation for a Safe Environment where Gail had worked for six years. They'd met in Washington at a series of hearings on the environment, where she had interviewed him, and then written a story about his organization. She was a reporter then, working for a wire service, the environment was one of her beats.

When the hearings were over Samuels invited her to lunch, and broached the idea of her joining his organization. Over the next few months they met and worked out the details.

"I'd like you to come on as my special assistant. That will give you an overview of what we do. After that, you can choose your area." That was five years ago. She was now the foundation's Vice President of International Affairs.

Last week they had been in the small, unpretentious conference room across the hall from Samuels' office. The walls were painted a light gray, decorated with pleasing water colors of seascapes and beach scenes.

They had just gone over a variety of items, when Samuels leaned toward her and broached the subject.

"There isn't much I can tell you about this assignment." Samuels said. "Except that the request comes from a reputable, high-powered search firm. They don't want to be identified, so I can't tell you that. They're interested in a man who will attend the conference in Prague. I have no idea who he is or what they're looking for."

She listened and waited for Samuels to tell her more.

"You've attended a dozen of these overseas conferences. You know the scene, and the players. You're a keen observer and you've got good judgment." He smiled at her almost shyly. "I'm sure you'll be able to give them what they want."

She asked a few questions, but it was clear Samuels had told her all he knew, except for the name of the search firm. He wouldn't budge on that. She would prefer knowing which one of the agencies it was, but decided it wasn't all that important. She knew the man she worked for was a man of integrity, and she trusted him. On that basis she accepted the assignment.

He smiled his appreciation. "Good. You'll hear from them directly. The envelope will be marked CONFIDENTIAL & URGENT."

With the envelope now in her hand, she had been going over their conversation. The conference was just a week away. It was the fifth in a series, held in a different city each year. Last year it had been New Delhi, before that Rome. This year it was Prague, where she was one of the vice chairs.

The extra work had helped keep her sane after Michael had walked out. They had been together more than a year and had talked about a wedding date. They wanted a small wedding. Her sister Janice was to be her maid-of-honor and Michael's older brother his best man. Then, out of the blue, Michael told her he had met someone else. The next day he was gone. That was four months ago.

She stared at the envelope, oddly reluctant to open it, yet curious to know what she had gotten herself into. There was only one way to find out.

Her disappointment was immediate. All she found was a single sheet of paper, without letterhead, salutation or signature. Two paragraphs floated on the page.

SUBJECT: *Elgar Krinn, 43-year old male, Austrian passport, first-time delegate to environment conference.*

ASSIGNMENT: Observe social demeanor, professional competence and idiosyncrasies. Make no effort to instigate or promote relationship with subject. Evaluate in context. File report within ten days. Mail to post office box indicated.

She tossed the sheet aside.

The material was skeletal and the rules struck her as ridiculous. There were hardly enough lines to read between. She looked at it again, reading each word, searching for a missing piece, but there was nothing else there. She methodically lined up what she knew.

An unidentified agency is interested in a man named Elgar Krinn. She said the name out loud and decided it had a pleasant, somewhat elegant sound. The first name was unusual, not one she'd be likely to forget if she'd heard it before. Why, then, did it sound so familiar? She thought a while. When nothing came to her, she went on.

Austria might be Elgar Krinn's birthplace, or it might not. Was it important? She had no way of knowing. Given the rules, unless Elgar Krinn was a talker, there was a lot she wasn't going to find out.

He was five years older than she was, the same age as Michael, forty-three. She shook off the comparison. It was time to stop using Michael as her yardstick.

She let herself imagine what kind of man Elgar Krinn might be, and gave herself free rein, reminiscent of a game she and her sister had played on summer nights at the family cabin on Crystal Lake. Gail had found it useful since. It broke up mental log jams.

They had no TV at the lake, only a small radio which they pulled under the covers with them when they went to bed, making a kind of tent. They kept the volume low, so their parents wouldn't know they were still awake. There was only one station, a late night disk jockey who invited friends to drop by. They listened to the twangy voices and silly stories, smothering their giggles. It was Janice who began conjuring up images and giving personalities to the voices they heard. They loved topping each other with extremes.

Gail tried it with Elgar Krinn. She decided he wore well-tailored gray suits, crisp white shirts and elegant silk ties. He was tall and debonair. Gold cufflinks flashed at his wrists. His fingers were long. He played the piano.

With a twitch of annoyance, she pushed back her chair. You're losing it! Elgar Krinn is probably bald and fat! Why the piano?

———◆———

Her flight from JFK to Prague the following Monday was overnight via Frankfurt. She had a window seat, and an empty seat beside her, so she was able to sleep during the flight across the Atlantic. She felt rested when she arrived in the Czech capital at noon.

She checked into the hotel where the conference was to be held, one of a number where blocks of rooms had been booked for delegates. She was eager to see something of Prague before the opening reception that evening, so quickly took care of a few chores. She hung up the evening suit Janice had given her. It was a beautiful moss-green. Her sister was taking a sabbatical from a law career and was at home with a four-year-old and a newborn. "By the time I get around to wearing this again, it'll be out of style. Besides, it's your color."

Gail smiled. It was as much Janice's color as hers. They were eighteen months apart, and shared their mother's honey-blond hair and gray-green eyes. Their brother Jimmy was the image of their father, with brown eyes and dark curly hair.

———◆———

Wenceslas Square was a short walk from her hotel. In the warm spring sunshine she joined the flow of locals and tourists strolling along the wide boulevard, pausing to browse at shop windows. She marveled at the vibrant mood of the city, in stunning contrast to the gloom when the Russians had been in power.

The scent of coffee reached her as she passed one of the many sidewalk cafes lining the street, with displays of delicious-looking pastries in their windows. She was tempted, but decided to save the treat for later.

There were a number of shops showcasing the intricately cut glass for which the country was known, beckoning to passersby with the sparkle of elaborate candelabra, wine goblets, and vases of all shapes and sizes. Some of it was too ornate for her lifestyle, but she wanted to find something for her sister, and perhaps herself. It seemed odd that the shops all had the same name—SKLO. It was on banners strung over doorways and printed on store windows.

Her purchases needed some thought, so at the next café she found an empty table with a view of the busy boulevard. She ordered coffee and apple strudel, which came sprinkled with powdered sugar. It was as delicious as it looked. She settled back to enjoy the passing crowd, then glanced at her watch and headed for the last SKLO shop she'd passed. A vase in the simple shape of a sphere appealed to her. She could see it on the corner table in her living room, filled with the yellow roses Michael often brought home. The lapse was brief. If Michael were still buying yellow roses, they were no longer for her.

She chose a different shape for her sister. While the vases were being wrapped, she spotted a miniature punch bowl with tiny cups, perfect for her four-year-old niece.

———◆———

The packet of conference material was waiting for her at the hotel when she picked up her key. In her room, she glanced at it briefly, familiar with its contents, extracting her delegate's badge to wear that evening.

The weightiest item on tomorrow's agenda was the planned protest against China's decision to build a dam in the Yangtze River. No one expected that the Chinese would be moved by the arguments opposing their plans, but environmentalists wanted their views on record. The dam would displace millions of people and create unaccountable ecological changes for generations to come.

There were other issues to be addressed, too many perhaps. It would be a challenge to keep things moving along. Part of her role was to see to that, and at the same time make sure delegates had an opportunity to air their views.

And then there was the matter of Elgar Krinn. She wondered how they would meet. With three hundred delegates expected, it was possible their paths might not cross at all. If she followed her instructions to the letter, she could do nothing to engineer an encounter.

The odd notion that Elgar Krinn played the piano had stayed with her. On the flight over, she had thought of it, and in a semi state of dozing, saw his hands moving authoritatively over a polished keyboard. She heard the music, the pronounced beat of a march. It returned to her again, now in the hotel room, as she dressed for the evening. Her foot began to keep time, and with that the source of her fantasy revealed itself. She almost laughed out loud. It was her brother's hands she saw, his dark curly head bent over the keyboard, fingers flying, practicing for his high school orchestra audition. "Pomp and Circumstance," was the selection. Elgar was the composer. She saw the name in dark gothic letters on Jimmy's sheet music. Sir Edward Elgar.

The tricks the mind will play, she thought, and smiled at her reflection, as she added the final touch to her make up. "Elgar Krinn," she said out loud.

She left the room and turned down the long empty corridor toward the elevator. It has been a good day. Her flight had arrived on time and she'd had a successful afternoon shopping spree. She was pleased with how she looked in Janice's green silk suit. As she drew close to the elevator a man approached from the other hallway. He was tall and had the long easy stride of a runner. The distance between them shortened, and she spotted a delegate's badge, swinging from a chain between the lapels of his dark blue suit. He was not someone she had met before.

"I see that we are colleagues," he said with a formal smile, as they stood waiting for the elevator. "I should not be surprised. There are many delegates in the hotel."

Gail returned his smile. He had blond hair and his eyes were intensely blue. His badge was flipped over, hiding his name. "Yes, you're quite right there are many delegates in this hotel." She introduced herself. "Gail Jennings."

"Ah yes. I have seen your name on the correspondence this year. You are one of the vice chairs. You have come from New York, a much longer journey than mine." He bowed. "My name is Krinn. Elgar Krinn. I had only a short distance to travel, from Vienna."

"I envy you your short trip," she said hiding her astonishment. So much for wondering if, or how they would meet. "Did you come by train? I understand it's a short ride from Vienna to Prague."

Before he had a chance to answer, the elevator sprang open and Gail was drawn into a flurry of greetings from delegates she knew from previous years. The ride down was noisy, hardly conducive to continuing her conversation with Elgar Krinn. She lost sight of him which they reached the main floor.

Delegates were filing into the reception, where drinks were already being served. Gail moved from one conversation to another. She caught sight of Krinn from time to time. His height and fair hair made him easy to spot, but it was always from a distance. She was surprised and a little irritated that he made no effort to seek her out. At dinner she was at the head table with the other officers, ending the possibility of any further mingling.

She was exhausted when she returned to her room, but as she got ready for bed, she thought more about Krinn. Perhaps her position as a vice chair was a barrier. Europeans had a sense of class distinction Americans did not. He might have thought it was her place to make the overture. It was easier on her pride, to seize that as his excuse, than to think she had stirred no interest in him at all.

It took a long time for her to fall asleep. Jet lag, a full day, the anticipation of tomorrow, all lined up behind her frustrating questions concerning Elgar Krinn. She lay trapped in that place where conscious thought crosses into dream, and wanders down strange paths, creating realities that in the light of day are quickly unmasked. She was dreaming of Michael, but his familiar face dissolved into that of Elgar Krinn. He was walking toward her across a stretch of green lawn, a bouquet of white flowers in his hand. When he gave them to her, he drew her hand into the loop of his arm and led her down a long carpeted corridor to a pair of wide double doors. They opened onto the convention hall. An orchestra began to play. The delegates rose and turned to watch them march down the aisle. She was wearing a white satin wedding gown with a long train. The music was "Pomp and Circumstance."

When she woke the next morning it was with the sense of having had a bad dream, which she couldn't remember. She gave it no further thought and dressed for breakfast downstairs. She was on the dais before nine-thirty, in time to see Elgar Krinn enter the room. Her elevated position made it easy to observe him, without seeming to. Late in the morning when he requested the floor to propose an addition to the agenda, she was attentive to his slightly accented English and admired his poise. She made notes in the margin of her pad, decipherable only to her. His proposal was an interesting one, that countries be required to alert tourists to areas within their borders of questionable environmental safety.

As she studied him, the recollection of the dream returned. Her fingers clenched round her pen. For an instant she thought everyone in the hall had been witness to her dream. She took a long, slow breath and refocused her attention as Krinn finished speaking and the next agenda item was called.

The afternoon session moved according to plan, with the Chinese Yangtze dam the last item of the day. The Chinese offered no counter arguments, choosing silence instead, so it took less time than had been allotted.

Delegates had been asked to gather outside the hotel at seven that evening for transport by bus to the National Museum for a reception. Gail arrived a few minutes early, thinking it would give her an opportunity to see Krinn, but there was no sign of him. She boarded the bus, delighted to see the bright smile of Antoine Lyon, who was seated on the aisle. He waved to her. "I have been saving this place for you, *Mademoiselle*." He rose to let hers slide into the seat by the window.

"How kind of you, *Monsieur*," she said, mocking his formality, and sparking to his flirtatious smile. They had been at a number of conferences together and enjoyed each other's company.

"I looked for you at lunch today, but you were already taken. I apologize for arriving a day late. As usual my minister had a crisis." He shrugged. "I am used to it, but it is still a pain."

In recent years Antoine had talked about leaving the government for the private sector. She asked him about that.

"I have waited this long. I want to get through next's year's conference. It is in Paris, as you know," he said with ironic emphasis.

She smiled.

"Why do you have to live so far away? I will need your help. I have begun to realize it is big job to run this conference."

"Whatever gave you that idea?" They laughed.

Lights illuminating Prague's night skyline had just come on, and they turned to look out the window.

"It is a beautiful city," he said over her shoulder. "Some say it is even more beautiful than Paris. What do you think?"

"I think that's a trick question."

"You are quite right. If you said Prague, my ego would be ruined. If you answered Paris, I would be delighted, but then I would ask why you do not come to my city more often."

She smiled at him. "How are things with you and Yvette?"

He grimaced. "She has left Paris for a job in Bangkok with the embassy. It is her way of saying it is over between us." He shrugged. "*C'est la vie.* Should I ask you about Michael?"

"Not necessarily, but since you have ... we are not together anymore either. But it is more final than a geographical separation." She turned away toward the window to avoid saying any more and was surprised to see Elgar Krinn standing on the corner waiting to cross. The bus had stopped for the same light. Their glances met. Krinn raised his hand in a formal wave. The light changed and he walked on.

"Who is that?" Antoine asked over her shoulder.

"His name is Elgar Krinn. It's his first time at the conference."

"I knew I had not seen him before. I would have remembered. He is a handsome man. What do you know of him?"

"Not much. We haven't really spoken, only to say hello. I met him at the elevator."

"He has the right idea—to walk. It is a beautiful night. The museum is not so far from here."

After a brief tour of the museum's private galleries delegates were then ushered into a chandeliered salon for a cocktail buffet.

"It's a good thing the conference is only three days," Antoine said, helping himself to a slice of liver pate. "All this rich food will make us fat. You choose well," he said with a glance at her plate. "Salmon, cucumbers and tomatoes. Now I know your secret to staying slim. Did I tell you, you look marvelous this evening?"

She smiled. "No, but now you have."

Throughout the evening Gail caught glimpses of Elgar Krinn but again only at a distance. She thought of suggesting to Antoine that they welcome the new delegate, but then decided it might give Antoine the wrong idea.

She had reason to add a few more notes to the margin of her pad the next day when Krinn rose to speak on his agenda item. During the discussion that followed, his delivery remained controlled, but a surprising darkness slide into his eyes when his challengers grew in number. The blue turned almost black. She found his expression ominously threatening. She sketched a dark eye on her pad.

On the last day of the conference some recommendations were finalized, others were left in drafts to be pursued at regional meetings during the year. Krinn's proposal was in the latter category. Adjournment came and delegates gathered for a brief farewell. No one lingered long. There were late planes to catch and early flights the next morning. Antoine took Gail's hand and kissed her on both cheeks. "Are you flying home tonight or tomorrow?"

She shook her head. "Neither. I'm staying on for a day."

"You must give Paris more time than that next year. But why wait so long?. What can I do to persuade you to come to see my city of lights … and me?"

She laughed. "I'm sure you will think of something."

In her room that night she took a mini bottle of Scotch from the bar and poured it over ice. The conference had gone well, but her contact with Elgar Krinn had been non-existent. Her report was going to be very brief.

She dressed for sightseeing the next morning in slacks and a light blazer over a white T-shirt. The conference and Krinn were behind her. A guide to Prague was in her hand when she paused at the entrance to the dining room, waiting to be seated. With most of the delegates gone, the room was almost empty, so she was quick to see Elgar Krinn at a table by the window. He rose as soon as she appeared, which made her think he had been waiting for her. That was confirmed by the maitre d' who led her to his table.

"I hope you will not think me too forward," Krinn said, and remained standing until she was seated. "I was hoping I would see you this morning. I heard you say last night that you would be staying on in Prague."

Gail hesitated, thrown off balance by his sudden interest in her. It seemed less awkward to simply sit down.

A waiter brought them coffee and waited to take their order. Gail ordered scrambled eggs and toast. Krinn said he would have the same.

"Do you know Prague well?" he asked, nodding at the travel guide she placed on the table.

"No, not really. I was here once before—a long time ago. The weather was awful and the Communists were in power." She paused. "What about you? With Vienna so close, you must know Prague well."

"I was here, also many years ago. The times were different then. It is a happy city now. I like to see it that way. Unless you have other plans, I would like to suggest that we see Prague together."

Gail was mystified. He had no trouble approaching her today. Why not before?

He didn't wait for her answer. "There is only one thing I would like to do. There used to be a small shop on the hill near the castle. I should like to try to find it. It is a lovely walk in that direction, across the Charles Bridge over the Vlatava River. One is always looking up at the castle on the hill.

"If I can persuade you to join me, we should make a list of what you would like to see. A day is not much time. I have only to look for my shop, but you must tell me what interests you."

She glanced at the guide book lying alongside her coffee cup. "You interest me," she played with saying. But was that still true? The conference was over. Her report was essentially written. He'd had his chance.

It was curiosity that determined her answer. "I hadn't decided on a route, except to begin with The Old Town Square and go on from here, to the castle, of course. My idea was just to walk and look."

"Then that's what we shall do—walk and look. Perhaps you will bring me luck and I will find the shop."

They started out in the direction of the old square. "It is the heart of Prague," he said. "It is where everyone goes in good times and bad."

She remembered it from her previous visit, all the glorious old buildings, crowned with steeples and spires. "Look, isn't that the clock tower over there?" She pointed to where a crowd was gathering.

He nodded and glanced at his watch. "It is almost time for the hour to strike."

They joined the crowd and as they waited Gail noticed a young couple in front of her, their arms about each other's waists. She envied them.

The hour struck and all eyes lifted to where a trio of tiny figures appeared and performed their mechanical ballet. Children giggled and clapped their hands. There was a flutter of applause when the performance was over and the crowd began to disperse.

Krinn nodded in the direction of a passageway marked by a stone arch. "We can go that way to get to the Jewish Cemetery. It is not far from here."

She had not been there before, but she had read about it, and seen photographs, so she was somewhat prepared for the stark emotion of the scene. There was no grass, no flowers, only weathered tombstones, fallen and collapsed against each other, skeletal symbols of the tragic lives they commemorated. An overwhelming dryness burned in her throat. Tears stung her eyes. Neither one of them spoke.

At the next street, lined with serene and lovely old buildings, the change in mood was a welcome relief.

"The University is very close," Krinn said, motioning at the next corner, at which point the school's doors burst open, flooding the cobblestone passageways with boisterous students eager to be on their way.

Krinn took her elbow and raised his voice above the noisy crowd. "They are all going to the Charles Bridge. When the light changes, they will cross. We will wait for the next light. By then most of them will be gone."

It turned out to be a good suggestion. They crossed the street and approached the entrance to the bridge. Krinn led her to the chest-high wall from which there was a view of the river traffic—tankers, tugs, barges, pleasure craft and sightseeing boats moved in a defined channel toward the spans of other bridges beyond. Sun glimmered on the surface where the water rippled. Along the nearby bank a forest of willow trees trailed their thin branches into the water.

Krinn pointed in that direction." If you look closely, you will see the swans." She tried to see through the camouflage of silver leaves and detected only shifting shadows. She watched as the leafy curtain parted and a pair of swans appeared, gliding on the open water, staying close to shore. With their snow-white plumage puffed and full, they were proudly on parade.

She turned to Krinn. "I've seen *Swan Lake,* but I've never seen real swans before."

He nodded. "The swans were always here."

"When was that?" she wanted to ask.

The pedestrian bridge was a busy thoroughfare, even with the students gone. She guessed it was mostly tourists who stopped at souvenir stands and in front of impromptu art galleries, where open portfolios and paintings were propped against the stone walls. A mime and a juggler vied for an audience. Gail and Krinn watched them for awhile and then moved on to where an old man with a beard was playing a violin. Krinn tossed a coin into his open violin case. The melody had a mournful sound.

"What is he playing, do you know?" Gail asked.

"Smetana, a Czech composer. It is a piece from his big work, *Ma Vlast—My Country.*"

"Are you a musician?"

He shook his head and laughed. "No. I am only a listener."

So, I was wrong. You don't play the piano.

She suddenly had a longing for home, not her Westside apartment, but the home of her childhood, the house where she had grown up. She thought of the living room and her father's big chair, with its worn foot rest. She saw Jimmy at the piano, his eyes intent on the sheet music where notes leapt like flags across and between the thin black lines, the bold dark print of a composer's name—a different Elgar.

She wondered what this Elgar would say if she told him the story of Jimmy and Sir Edward Elgar's "Pomp and Circumstance." Would he laugh? Would he find her imaginings endearing, as Michael might have, not all that long ago?

The haunting strains of the violin's melody faded as they continued on, but there was more music up ahead, of a different kind. "Hey Jude," was the tune, strummed by a new generation hippie with DAKOTA stamped on his T-shirt.

She shook her head in amazement. "It's like a carnival."

"Life has come back, but it is too much. It is without discrimination. That will change, perhaps. But I don't think it will ever be as it was years ago, before our time, before the war, before the Russians—a city full of music and intellectual subtleties."

Intellectual subtleties, an interesting phrase. "Tell me more," she wanted to say.

When they reached the end of the bridge they stood with their hands shielding their eyes against the sun, their gaze directed to where the castle stood, a shimmering gold fortress on the hill.

"It's right out of a fairy tale," she said.

"It is a favorite of artists to paint the castle on the hill, the *Hradcany*. The word is hard for non-Czechs. *Hradcany*. The H and the r run together liked a soft growl. The c is pronounced like ch."

"We must go toward the *Hradcany*, to look for my shop, but first we should stop for something to drink. I'm sure you are thirsty. It is very warm."

A strong sun had turned the spring day to summer. The sky was clear and without clouds. They crossed to a small cafe perched on a stone balcony overlooking the river, its tables shaded by yellow umbrellas. Gail asked for lemonade. Krinn ordered a beer.

"You present very well," he said.

"What do you mean?" It was her first direct question.

"You could use your looks as a tool, but I saw none of that at the conference. You relied on your expertise and your diplomatic skills to make your points, to move the agenda along. I admire that, a woman who does not play the games society still forces on your sex." He paused, his eyes holding hers. "You have a lovely smile."

Why had he waited until now?

She thought he was about to say more, but when the silence went on for too long, she asked him about the shop he wanted to find. "Does it have a name?"

"There are many with that same name now. You will laugh when I tell you."

"What is it?" He's playing with me. Why?

"*SKLO*." He spelled the word, but he needn't have.

She shook her head, but she didn't laugh. If she had, it would have been only to please him. She told him of her afternoon on Wenceslaus Square, the vases she had bought for her sister and herself, and the tiny punch bowl for her niece. "For a while I couldn't understand why all the glass shops had the same name. I decided to ask when I was inside the shop. I was told it meant glass." After that she laughed, but it was at herself. "*SKLO* is the only Czech word I know."

She glanced away, to keep from babbling on, and to be released from the steady gaze of his blue eyes.

She looked back to the part of the city where they had just been, across the long arch of the bridge, marked with its medieval statues, to a complex of chimneys and domes and towers, darkly outlined against the sky.

How old were you when you lived here? When did you leave? Why? These and other questions were crowding behind the barrier of rules she had been given. She could argue that the assignment had ended on the final day of the conference. The regulations no longer applied. She could ask Elgar Krinn anything at all and pursue the relationship as she chose. Is that what she wanted? Where would it lead?

"Tell me about your glass shop. How will you recognize it?"

He looked off in the distance, his brows drawing together in a way that suggested he was entering a passage of a private memory. He began slowly, his voice melancholy in tone. "The shop was on the ground floor of an ancient building made from stone the color of red wine. There was a lantern over the front door. When it was lit it was quite beautiful. It was made of triangles of clear glass and blue glass."

She sat watching him. It was a performance, a seduction of sorts, she told herself. "Fuel wasn't wasted on lanterns in those days. The family who lived behind the shop was poor. Everyone was then. Johan's mother rendered scraps of fat and sometimes soaked a piece of cloth to use as a wick. When it was lit, it smelled like pork roasting. We could smell it in the tower room where we used to hide when I came. It made our stomachs growl."

She tried to see past the words, to understand the story he was telling. *We smelled it in the tower room ... where we used to hide .... It made our stomachs growl.*

She thought of the folder back at the hotel, the draft of her report, spare, tidy and complete. What am I going to do with this?

They left the crowds behind them when they started up the steep incline, a winding walk over uneven cobblestones, leading in the direction of the castle. A family, on their way down, passed them. The parents were steadying each other over the uneven ground, while their two young boys ran ahead, laughing, and racing one another downhill. They were alone after that.

Narrow streets and alleys were lined with buildings made from huge blocks of stone. Some had intricately carved arches and facades, evidence of the skilled labor of an earlier time. They were empty and abandoned now, with broken windows and massive doors sagging on heavy hinges. How long would it take for a generation of renovators to appear and send the price of real estate skyrocketing?

Krinn's stride suddenly lengthened and she watched him move out ahead of her, struck by the steady rhythm of his walk. Again, she wondered if he was a runner.

At the next turn he stood, waiting for her and she hurried to close the gap, but he continued on before she caught up. She paused to catch her breath. The day had grown warmer still. She found him in front of a massive stone building, the color of dark red wine. The ground floor windows were boarded over and the heavy door was fastened with a rope of twisted wire. The bent frame of a lantern was over the doorway. Its glass was gone, except for one small fragment that had a hint of blue.

She stayed to the side, sensitive about crossing into his emotional space, yet close enough to follow his gaze as it traveled up the side of the building, past the first floor up to the second and on to the tower.

"That's where we were," he said, turning to her. "There was a way to climb up the side then. Johan's family lived on the first floor, behind the SKLO shop. There was no glass to sell then. His father worked in a boot factory. His mother did laundry."

He walked up to the front door and pressed the weight of his body against it, pushing hard. A few strands of the rusted wire frayed, but it took several more attempts before they all gave way. His hands gripping the edge he tugged, and with a rough scraping sound, he pulled the door open.

She followed him into a large room where cobwebs trailed from high beams and filled the shadowed corners. Empty shelves lined one wall. It was damp and cool. Shafts of sunlight spilled down from the upper floors, revealing a wide stone staircase.

He mounted the first step, and then stopped, offering her his hand. She moved toward him, but he didn't wait. At the first landing he hesitated and glanced over his shoulder, waited, but moved on and disappeared around a turn. She continued upward, passed the second floor and followed the echo of his footsteps. She heard the sound of another door forced open. A billow of light bloomed above.

When she reached the tower she saw Krinn through the arch of the open doorway. She shielded her eyes, adjusting to the brightness after the semi dark, and then stepped over the doorway's high sill. Only when she was outside did she see that the outer curve of the stone balustrade was gone. She hugged the inside tower wall, staring at the blue haze that rose over the city, far below.

"On summer nights we came out here. We liked to lie on our backs and look up at the stars. We asked each other if there really was a God."

She heard his words and tried to imagine the boy he must have been, the child he was remembering, but her thoughts hit a wall. She was trapped into absorbing his silhouette, stark and unreal, with nothing behind him but sky. A terrifying chill came over her. Where had her judgment gone? What am I doing here?

His movement was so slow it took her by surprise. He drew her toward him as if in a dance and spun her in the narrow curve of the tower floor, releasing her to stand with her back to where the city lay. He stood with his back to the tower wall.

Terror pumped her heart.

"Johan's mother was lame and needed a stick to walk. She never came up here. His father worked hard and went to bed early. We didn't hear him coming up the stairs that night."

She was watching his eyes.

"His father found us, boys doing things together that boys are not supposed to do. He hit me first, with the back of his hand, but when he turned on Johan his fists were tight and hard. He was a big man. The blows were very hard."

His glance slid to where a rubble of stones lay loose near the tower door. "There weren't so many stones then, but one was enough. I hit his father, hard."

The heat of the sun pounded down on her head, but ice was in her veins.

"We ran away that night and hid by the river among the willows. The swans were there. Johan couldn't stop crying. He knew his father was dead. He held on to me until he fell asleep, but the next morning when I woke, he was gone. I never saw him again, but I knew he had come back here."

A light breeze swirled a pile of dry leaves near the doorway, sounding as though someone was there. Krinn turned to look. It gave her courage.

"Why are you telling me this?"

The expression on his face was calm and appraising. "When I saw you that first evening by the elevator, I thought, here is a woman I would like to know. Throughout the conference I watched you, and I was almost sure."

She shook her head. "You never spoke to me."

The change was sudden, the blue of his eyes gone black. She thought of the eye she had drawn on her pad. The blackness she saw there now was her warning of the movement to come before it began. With her arms stretched out like a swimmer, she dove to the side of him and slid on her knees across the rough stone floor. She grabbed for the sill of the tower door. His movement was a blur, too propelled to be reversed, sweeping past the space where she had stood and beyond to where the city lay. She thought she saw the fleeting shadow of his fall play out across the tower wall.

———◆———

Her report was less than a page and followed the expected form. It covered the time of the conference and nothing more.

She was afraid for a while. But if anyone knew they had been together that day, no one came forward.

That didn't end it, of course.

Elgar Krinn appears in her dreams now and again, and some days when she approaches a corner she imagines she sees him waiting for her. But she doesn't rush after him anymore. She knows he will be gone.

She left the foundation, but consults for them from time to time. She accepts no assignments from high-powered search firms. She lives in Paris with Antoine. They are married and expecting their first child.

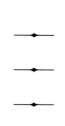

AFRICA

The Ones Left Behind

He stared out of the window and watched the dust settle in the long driveway. That was all that was left of the Europeans—the red dust from their car. The house was empty. Beds, books, clothes, dishes—everything was gone. The house was ready for the next family to move in. And like the others before them, the new family would stay a few years and then be gone, returning to America, to England, or wherever they had come from. Some families he remembered happily. Others he tried to forget. That had been before Independence, when a white man could do anything he pleased with an African.

In one of the empty rooms, a closet door opened and closed. He turned, hopeful for a moment, thinking that it was the Memsab, that she had not gone, but he knew it was his mind playing tricks. It was Kama he heard, sweeping out the closets, the last of the chores to be done.

It was important that the house be clean, so that the new people would see that he and Kama knew how to keep a fine house, and that they had worked for Europeans before. Yesterday the windows had been washed and the floors scrubbed, and this morning he had polished the dark wood once more, using the sheep skins that fitted over his sneakers. The little boy, whose hair was the color of ripe maize, had liked to skate alongside him, helping.

Tetu looked out the window, past the line of pepper trees to the lawn where the boy had often played. In the sun, his hair had gleamed with the brightness of a polished brass bowl. Tetu wondered if the new family would have any children. His own children lived in his village, a day-long journey by bus. He saw them only once each year, on his annual leave.

He reached into the pocket of his trousers to feel the thick wad of twenty-shilling notes that rested against his thigh, a month's salary and two months' farewell bonus. That was something to be happy about—the extra money. It would take care of the school fees for his two oldest children.

And tonight, or tomorrow, he would go to the cinema in Nairobi. He did not always understand what he saw—his English was not good enough, but he watched the colored pictures that moved so fast he was afraid to close his eyes and miss something. They told stories of strange people in places different from anything he had ever seen.

Kama came up behind him, his footstep silent, but Tetu knew he was there. The oil Kama brushed into his hair and rubbed on his arms had the sweet smell of a ripe mango. Tetu knew when he was coming, or if he had just passed from a room.

He was seventeen, younger than Tetu by ten years. He spoke with gruff impatience. "Why do you stand at the window, looking after them?"

Tetu ignored his question. He did not want to talk about the family who had just gone. "Have you swept all the closets?"

"All. Now I am ready to go to town." Kama leaned his broom against the wall and reached into the pocket of his shirt and fanned the twenty-shilling notes.

"That is a lot of money," Tetu said, knowing it was more money than Kama had ever seen before. Tetu had worked in the city a long time, but this was Kama's first year. There was no work for them to do in their village.

Kama put the money back in his pocket. "Let us go into town."

"I will take lunch first and then have a small sleep. I will wait until tomorrow to go into town."

"How can you sleep when there is money to spend?"

"It would be better if you went to the post office first and started a savings account. Then go to town."

"You talk like the Memsab."

It was an insult to be compared with a woman, but Tetu decided to let it pass. They were of the same clan and therefore brothers. Kama was young and he did not mean the words the way they sounded.

"I will worry about a wife and children when the time comes," Kama went on. "Tonight I will go to the cinema and after that I will go to Mary's."

He thought Kama went to Mary's too much, but he said nothing. He went there himself sometimes, but not often. The women were not like the women of his tribe. Their heads were not shaved clean and their painted mouths smelled of too much *pombe*. Even good sweet African beer turned sour when someone drank too much. He looked out the window again.

"Why do you look after them?"

He was surprised sometimes by how much Kama did not understand. "Who knows what the next ones will be like? These were good people. I told you about the first white people I worked for—the day I drank water from a glass that belonged to them and the woman threw it away. Then she took the price of it from my wages."

"Yes, you told me that. Why do you tell me again?"

"So you will know the difference. So you won't be fooled and think that they are all alike—good, like the Memsab who has just gone."

"Why was she so good? We worked. Did we not? I do not understand you, Tetu. You think only of small things that do not matter—drinking from glasses. Have you forgotten about your wife?"

Kama voice sounded loud in the empty room. His words echoed in Tetu's ears. "My wife?" he said slowly, "Why do you speak of my wife?"

"Because you have been talking of the *good* Memsab. You seem to have forgotten that it is this *good* Memsab who is to blame for what happened."

Tetu frowned, aware that a strange heat had risen inside of him. It made his head feel swollen and his mouth dry. "I do not understand you. For what is the Memsab to blame?"

Kama looked down at his feet and reached for the broom. "If you do not know I cannot tell you. There are some things a brother knows about a brother that he cannot say. I am going to town."

Tetu stayed by the window and listened for the kitchen door to open and close, and then watched Kama walk along the path that led to the servants' quarters behind the high hedge of bougainvillea. He waited at the window until Kama appeared, dressed in the clothes that he wore when he went to Mary's, dark trousers and white shirt. For just a moment Tetu wished he was going with him.

In the cookhouse he shared with Kama, Tetu heated his tea, but he did not take time to warm the *posho*. Instead he rolled the cold corn meal into balls and ate them quickly. But there was no reason to hurry today. The Europeans were gone. Today, he could take his sleep and not set the small clock the Memsab had given him, so he would be awake before she returned. He would not have to listen for her car or carry her baskets into the kitchen, full of the fruits and vegetables and meat she had bought at the market. She would not be here to tell him what to fix for the evening meal, or stay to show him how to make something he had not cooked before.

He remembered the time she wanted to make a special cake the Bwana liked. It needed many egg whites. Tetu had never separated a white from a yolk then and his hands were clumsy and there were many mistakes. He thought she would be angry, but she laughed and said it did not matter. "We'll have those messed-up eggs for breakfast tomorrow."

Tetu remembered this as he stretched out on his bed and pulled the thin blanket over his shoulders. There was no evening meal for him to prepare. It would not matter how long he slept.

With the door closed it was dark inside his room, and sleep usually came easily, but it was far off today. His mind had started on a long journey, with many stops along the way, times and places not forgotten, but set aside.

It had been Easter time. He and the Memsab and the little boy were in the kitchen making cookies, shaped like rabbits. The little boy was giving them raisin eyes.

"Has your wife ever been to Nairobi?" the Memsab asked him.

"No, Madam. My village is very far from here. The journey by bus is very long, and it costs many shillings."

"Would you like her to come here for a visit? If you would, the Bwana and I will give you the money for her bus fare."

He had never thought that his wife might come to Nairobi, that he could show her the city's busy streets, and the big house where he worked, that she would stay with him in the small room where he always slept alone.

He had to swallow before he spoke. "Oh, yes, Madam, I would like that very much."

It took many weeks for the arrangements to be made, but the day his wife was to arrive he woke at dawn and went to the bus station to wait. The buses were never on time, but he wanted to be sure to be there.

It was late afternoon when the bus finally came, its roof piled with baskets and boxes and bundles tied in big squares of cloth. Tetu watched one person after another step down from the bus, and he began to worry that something had happened and she had not come. When it seemed that everyone had gotten off, she appeared in the doorway. She had on a blue dress and a blue headcloth to match. She was wearing shoes. He smiled. In his village none of the women wore shoes. He pushed through the crowd, calling her name, "Ruth!"

Her head turned, and the shadow of fear he had seen in her face disappeared and her eyes brightened like stars coming out from behind a cloud.

"Ruth is not a name that belongs to our people," his father had said. It is a name that comes from the white man's God book. It would be better if you chose another wife. Besides, she is small. She will not bear you many sons."

Times were already different then and a man could choose his own wife, even against his father's wishes. His father's prophesy had been wrong. In the first year Ruth bore him a son. And each year thereafter, ten moons after his annual leave, another child was born.

When he finally reached her, she looked up at him with shy, uncertain eyes, and only then did he see the child at her breast.

"This is your new son. I could not leave him—he is just new-born."

Tetu stared down at this newest child, and realized that he had never seen one so small. He had never seen any of his other children when they were so new-born.

———◆———

How big a man he felt before his wife that week. In the cinema Ruth held tightly to his arm and sat as still as the child that suckled at her breast. But it was the quickening of her breath and the tilt of her head that told him how full of wonder she was. The week went by too fast and he asked the Memsab if she could stay one week more.

"All right. Tetu. But your wife needs to go home to be with your other children, so only one more week." She looked at him steadily, in that way she had that told him she was thinking of something that was difficult for her to say.

"How many children do you have, Tetu?"

"Six, Madam. My father had two wives and he had many, many children. I have only one wife, but already I have many children." He shook his head. "Times are different. They must go to school. School fees are very high. It is not good to have too many children."

She nodded, and spoke slowly. "Your wife is very young and so are you. You could have many more children. There is a clinic at the hospital in Nairobi, where a doctor can tell you about how you can stop having children. I will take you and your wife there, if you want me to."

He had heard talk of such things, but they were mysterious to him and made him think of a boy in his village who had gone to a clinic with only a sore on his leg and had come back with his leg cut off.

"The doctor will talk to you and your wife, in a way that I cannot. I don't know the right words or how to say them properly. Tell your wife about the clinic. I will drive you into town so you can go together and listen to what they have to say."

That night in his room he told Ruth what the Memsab had said. He thought she would be surprised, but she told him that the women at the coffee co-op spoke of such clinics. There was none near their village. Her head was turned so that the light from the flickering candle on the table beside his bed shone on her cheek. She looked at him shyly. "I would like to go with you to the clinic."

———◆———

He became an important man in his village. Not only had his wife been to the city, she had been to a clinic where something special had been done so she would have no more children. With no new child growing, she could work longer hours in the coffee fields, which meant there was money for food and clothes and for school fees. Someday maybe there would be money for land and then Tetu would not have to go to the city to work.

He told Kama about the clinic and said he should go there so he would know, before he took a wife, how to keep his family small.

"When I marry, my wife will have many children. I do not want to waste my seed."

He was impatient with Kama's foolish words. "It is a waste to plant more maize than the ground can grow!"

"You are a fool, Tetu. You have begun to think like a European!"

"It is you who are the fool, Kama. Listen to me. What was good for our fathers is not good enough for our children. I do not want a son of mine to be a houseboy, like me. And you—what are you? A houseboy's helper! Is this what you want for your sons?"

The look that had come to Kama's face told Tetu that his insult had been felt, and he was glad, but soon the softness in his heart made him wish he had not made his words so harsh. But when Kama spoke again his regret was less.

"We are not talking of the same things, Tetu. You talk of school fees. I am talking of your wife and what you had done to her. And what has happened to you because of it."

"What has happened to me?"

"You are no longer a man."

Tetu shook his head and smiled. "Those are old thoughts. These are new times. I am a bigger man now because I am thinking ahead."

"You are a bigger fool. Now your wife can lie with any man and you will never know."

Tetu had turned away, telling himself Kama was young and knew only the ways of the women at Mary's. Some day when he had a wife he would know the difference.

Kama's words had made him angry and Tetu was glad that a few days later the younger man left for their village on his annual leave. But his words came back to Tetu and grew in his mind. He thought of Ruth and the brightness that came into her eyes when they were together. He could hear her small laugh and see her fine bare legs, strong from working in the coffee fields. He remembered how it felt to have them entwined with his. It was five months since he had been with her and his longing was great.

The hunger began to burn in him and he began to think of going to Mary's, but then the Memsab told him that the family was leaving on a month's holiday and he could go home to be with his family until they came back. He had never been so happy.

Tetu had made the journey home many times, but never had it seemed so long, or did he want to get there more quickly. The bus was like an old woman carrying too heavy a burden up a steep hill. He looked out the window and saw villages not so different from his own. The houses were made of mud and wattle and the roofs were thatched with palm leaves. Goats and chickens wandered in the yards. On the hillsides women planted their crops of beans and potatoes and manioc.

When they reached the highlands, where the coffee grew, it began to rain. If only the big rains would not come until after the bus had passed the low stretch near the river, but even before they got there, the dirt road had turned to mud and they could not go on.

By road, it was still a long way to his village, but he remembered there was a shorter way across the valley, a path he had taken when he was a boy and had gone to the mission school. With his head bent against the slanting rain, he set out. Gusts of winds swirled and clattered the leaves of the banana trees. Thunder rolled from low clouds across the valley and added an earlier darkness to the coming night. A streak of lightning crossed the sky, and in its eerie light he found the path. The storm moved off, but the rain continued to fall, as icy as the waters of Mount Kenya's rushing streams. When he reached the cluster of thatched houses that was his village, his bones were chilled and his teeth would not stay quiet in his head. Night had fallen a long time ago and the village was asleep. At the doorway to his house, he pushed aside the heavy curtain made from a cow's hide and stepped into the room where his children slept. It was warm from their breath, fragrant with the smell of *posho* left in the cooking pot. He took off his wet clothes and felt the familiar comfort of the room flow over him. The dry earth floor was warm under his feet.

He moved quietly past the half wall to where his wife slept. Even in darkness he knew the place. A stool was in the corner and to the side there was the large wooden box with nails on its lid, a storage place for grain. A few steps away was the reed mat on which she lay. He knelt beside her and spoke softly, so not to frighten her. He whispered words she would recognize as only his, and leaned close to touch the smooth curve of her cheek. His hand drew back, startled at the touch of hair that was coarse and crisp.

He reached behind him to feel for the box that should be there. Was he not in his own house? His hand passed over its lid, and he felt the familiar pattern of nail heads rise under his fingertips. Not a breath in him moved.

In the darkness he heard the frightened whispered voice of his wife. "There is a noise. Go! Go quickly!" A rustle of cloth gave way to a movement of limbs, and though he could see nothing, Tetu knew a man had risen from the mat, and with the swiftness of a mamba was gone.

Tetu felt the cold heat of his body explode into a flame. It licked at all his parts. It consumed his heart and set fire to his brain. He fell upon his wife and found the small pulse in her throat. It was warm and soft and fluttered like the heart of a tiny bird. It grew strong and fought him, but only for awhile. And then it stopped, and there was nothing, only the sound of the wind and the rain outside, and the roar in his head that went on and on.

Without conscious thought he drew on his clothes and walked out into the night where the blackness swirled and the rain still fell. He followed the path along which he had just come until he reached the bus.

———◆———

It was a whole day before the rains stopped, another day before the road was dry enough for the bus to move on. By then the roaring in his head was a fever and his tongue was as dry as charcoal in his mouth.

Someone brought him water—a woman with wrinkled cheeks and sunken eyes. She lifted his head and helped him drink. He thought she was his mother, and tried to call her name, but he knew his mother had been dead many years. In his sleep her skin turned smooth and above the gentle curves of her cheeks her eyes shone like stars. She was his wife and he dreamed that she had come to lie down beside him and keep him warm.

He woke, but for awhile his kept his eyes closed. He knew Kama was there. He smelled the sickening sweetness of his oil. It made his stomach roll. He was in Kama's house and the old woman who was his nurse was Kama's mother.

"You have been sick a long time," Kama said when he opened his eyes, and told him that it was two weeks since the bus had brought him to the village. "Two men carried you here."

Tetu's tongue moved slowly around the words he tried to say and when he spoke he did not recognize his voice. "Why did they not take me to my own house? Where is my wife?"

The look in Kama's eyes made Tetu try to sit up, but he could not even raise his head.

"You do not remember?" He heard Kama say, but he was already asleep.

The next time he woke, Kama's mother was holding a bowl of warm broth to his mouth. He tried to speak, but she pressed the bowl against his lips. "Drink first, my son."

When he was done, he could not remember what he had wanted to say. He took her hand. "*Asante sana, Bebe.* Thank you for all you have done." She nodded and looked at him sadly. Then he remembered what he wanted to ask her. "Where is my wife? Why is she not here?"

Her wrinkled eyes squinted at him, and filled with tears. "Two days before the men carried you to this bed there was a big storm, with much rain. The sky was filled with noise and the wind blew. That night your wife went to sleep, but when morning came she did not wake."

The fever returned and so did the roar in his ears. Days passed and he remembered nothing except the sorrow that filled his heart. Then one day the fever was gone and he was able to sit up and slowly he began to walk. Soon he was well enough to go back to the city, to the house of his employer, where Kama had already returned.

The little boy saw him coming up the driveway and he ran down to meet him and took his hand. The door of the house opened and the Memsab came outside. She was smiling, sadly, and clasped his hand. "We missed you. I'm glad you are well again."

———◆———

Tetu sat up and pushed the blanket away. He lit a candle and looked at the small clock that stood on the table beside his bed. He had rested a long time. It was night now and Kama was at the cinema and would soon be on his way to Mary's. He wished he had not let Kama's words anger him. They were of the same tribe. They were brothers.

He looked around the small room, at the wall where the light from the candle made shadows that shifted and swayed. He went to the door and opened it. The night air was cool. There was a large moon, so bright it made the stars seem dim. There was no rain. It was not like the dark night he had been hurrying home to be with his wife, when the road had turned to mud and the rain kept falling. He had been numb with cold when he pushed aside the curtain to his house that day, and stepped into its comforting warmth. He smelled the breath of his sleeping children, the *posho* in the cooking pot. He felt the warmth of the earth floor under his feet. But there was also something else. He remembered it now—the sweet scent of oil, that had clung to Ruth's body, and to his, for a long time afterward.

Love and Death
in Africa

The Thorn Tree was the kind of place where a cold bottle of Tusker or a cup of Kenya's fine brew bought you time to sit back and watch the passing scene. It had been a favorite of mine when my family and I had lived in Nairobi, so that's where I headed my first morning back after five years. I was staying at The New Stanley and the café was right out in front.

I chose a table that faced Kimathi Street, with Kenyatta Avenue off to the left. I could see the purple haze of the jacaranda trees that lined the wide boulevard, named after the country's first president, Jomo Kenyatta, an anthropologist, educated in Britain. He had been a great leader when he first appeared on the scene. He believed in the land and he fought for his people's right to it. A flamboyant figure, he was often seen in public gatherings wearing a leopard skin across his chest and used a fly whisk as his scepter. Flies are major pests throughout Africa. Corruption is another scourge. It would tarnish Kenyatta's legacy.

The cars and trucks moving along the street were not too different from what I remembered—all makes, shapes, sizes and vintages. Some showed wear, others the shine of freshly applied polish by the owner's house servant. The dusty, mud-caked Land Rovers and carryalls established where I was, in a city surrounded by the bush with its vast stretches of beautiful, untamed land.

A waiter came to my table. His proud bearing was enough to identify him as Masai. His earlobes confirmed his tribal origins, long open loops that swung as he walked. In the grasslands where the Masai tended their cattle it was common to see the stretched skin plugged with a piece of wood, sometimes a flashlight battery. I wondered how he had made his journey from cattle herder to waiter in one of Nairobi's major tourist hotels.

"Good morning, Sir."

I returned his greeting with a smile, gave him my order and watched him move off. He hadn't lost his graceful stride.

As I settled into the shade of the giant thorn tree that gave the café its name, I thought of how in earlier times someone I knew would happen by. I couldn't expect that now. Everyone I'd known had left. Sadly, even Lisette.

The shops across the street began to open and I saw that Woolworth's was no longer there. My wife wouldn't consider it a great loss. Ann had preferred the *dukas* on Bazaar Street, a string of shops and stalls connected to each other by back doors and blood relationships. They were owned by the descendents of immigrants from India and Pakistan, the Asians of East Africa. They had come in the early 1900's to work on the East African Railway, and stayed on.

You could find almost anything on Bazaar Street—cooking pots and spices, hardware, school uniforms, shoes, cottons, fine silks, a good tailor, just for a start. The scent of curry was always in the air. But the *dukas* were gone now, as were their owners. Their absence from the city was stark to see. They were missing among the people passing by.

The departure of the British had been underway in my time. It was the beginning of a major land resettlement program, and had been a somewhat orderly process. It was prompted by Independence with its promise of returning the land to Kenyans, land the colonizing British had taken as theirs and farmed for decades. But the expulsion of Asians had been a different matter. It was sudden and swift. I had already returned to the States when they were forced out, but I'd followed the story in the international press. Headlines told of displaced Asians seeking asylum in England and other parts of the British Commonwealth, but finding themselves unwelcome.

My breakfast arrived. The aroma of the cheese omelet and sausage told me how hungry I was. I ate with relish and watched the city come to life.

There were many changes that jarred my nostalgic eye. Although westernization was a sign of progress, I was dismayed to see that Kenyan women had adopted western dress. Gone were the colorful *kikoys* and *kangas* they wore with such grace, bright lengths of cloth fashioned into sarongs and slings for *totos* who rode at their mothers' breasts or on their backs. In the face of seeming economic progress, it was troubling to see the number of bedraggled people in tattered clothes, walking aimlessly along.

I thought of my son, and the challenge it would be to tell him about the changes I would find. Though he was only eight when we left Kenya, his recollections are vivid, re-enforced by our colored slides. Plugging in the projector was always a family treat and a prompt for retelling old stories. Danny's favorite was when we took Musembe to the game park for the first time.

An amazing bond developed between our little boy and our Kenyan house servant. They were an unlikely pair, the lean black man and our fair-haired child, running a soccer ball on the back lawn, Danny challenging his sturdy plump legs to imitate Musembe's smooth, elegant moves.

Before I left on my trip Danny extracted a promise from me. "You'll try to find Musembe, won't you?" I wasn't surprised by his request, but I had little confidence in being able to fulfill it. When our family had prepared to leave Kenya, Musembe made plans to leave Nairobi and return to his village to farm, which was many miles north. I reminded Danny of that.

"I know. That's what he said, but he might have changed his mind," my son insisted. "He might have come back to Nairobi. He could be working in our house, for the people who live there now. Dad, you could go there and have a look, couldn't you?"

I ruffled my son's blond hair. "I'll do that, for sure."

"If you find him, give him this. There's a picture inside of me in my soccer uniform, and some Kenya shillings notes Mom had." The small white envelope, with Musembe's name on it was in my pocket now.

Prompted by that recollection, my glance toward the newspaper kiosk on the corner of Kenyatta Avenue took in a young Kenyan I'd noticed earlier. He resembled Musembe. He was about the same height and wore a short-sleeved white shirt and black trousers. Shedding his workday suntans, this is how Musembe dressed when he went into town, on his day off. On Sundays we saw him come through the gate of the high bougainvillea hedge that separated the servants' quarters from the main house. His head held high, as he set off across the lawn to the path that led to the lower road, to catch a ride into town. Danny would wave to him, shouting the Swahili goodbye, "Kwaheri."

Musembe always raised his arm and returned his call.

I continued to study the man on the corner. He turned so that I should have had a clearer view of his face, but sunlight flashed off his dark features and transformed them into a shining blur. The sudden brightness made his full silhouette clear, and with that, my fantasy collapsed. The sag of the man's shoulders dissolved whatever resemblance might have been there. This was not the posture of the proud man we had known.

I sat there absorbing the disappointment, when something else captured my attention. In times of stress, Musembe often lifted his hand to his forehead and then slowly passed it over his head and down to his neck. I saw that happening now.

I was almost certain he was not the man I wanted him to be, but I couldn't walk away without making sure. The distance between us was short. As I approached he eyed me warily.

Up close, all my doubt was gone. It had been five years. Would he remember me? "*Jambo*, Musembe."

He stared at me, startled. A seeming stranger, I had called him by name. Slowly the look of recognition filled his eyes.

"*Bwana!*" he exclaimed. "*Bwana* Williams, is that you?"

Words failed me for a moment, but a grin gradually spread across my face. "*Jambo sana*, Musembe. It is good to see you again." I reached to shake his hand, continuing the Swahili greeting. "*Habari gani?*" How are things?

"*Nzuri, Bwana.*"

The answer was always the same at first. Good. The details would come later. We stood for a moment, looking at each other in mutual amazement.

I explained that I had been seated in the The Thorn Tree, having breakfast when I saw him. I knew he had walked by the café dozens of times, but he would have never been inside. I asked him to join me. I had seen that sausage rolls were on the menu, and I remembered how much he and Danny liked them.

Ann had often bought the tasty savories at a bakery in Westlands, on the way from picking up our son at school. As soon as he had changed out of his school uniform Danny ran to the servant's quarters, clutching the small bakery bag, eager to share his snack with Musembe.

Musembe smiled. "I have not had sausage rolls in a long time. I like them very much. Danny liked them, too. He must be a big boy now." A shy look came into his eyes. "Does the *Bwana Kidogo* remember me?" Little Bwana, that had been Musembe's special name for Danny.

I swallowed hard. "Oh, yes, he remembers you, very well. He tells lots of stories about his Kenyan friend, who taught him how to play soccer."

"You have not come back to Nairobi to stay," Musembe said quietly, cutting to what was important to him. There was a question in his voice, but I suspected he knew the answer.

"No. I've come to attend a conference at the University. It begins later this morning. I will be here only two weeks."

Disappointment shadowed his eyes, but only briefly. It was a matter of pride.

I leaned toward him. "When I told Danny I was coming to Nairobi, he asked me to try to find you. I didn't think you would be in Nairobi." I shook my head and looked toward the kiosk. "But there you were."

I reached into my pocket. "This is from Danny."

Musembe studied his name on the envelope and opened it slowly. He acknowledged the folded shillings with a serious nod and bent his head to study the photograph. He read the message Danny had printed on the other side.

"These are very good presents, *Bwana*. I am happy to know Danny remembers me. Please tell him, *asante sana*." His eyes were glistening.

The waiter brought a plate of sausage rolls and more coffee for me and tea for Musembe. I asked him if he had gone back to his village as he had planned.

"Yes, *Bwana*. My brother and I planted maize with the bonus money you gave me. Our first crop was good. But there was trouble for me. No one in my village has ever been to Nairobi. They did not like that I had lived in the city. They said it made me act like a big man."

Ann and I had speculated about Musembe's adjustment to a life without electricity and running water, to a house made of mud and thatch, after having worked in European households for so long. It hadn't occurred to us that his village might not welcome him.

"If I had stayed, there would have been more trouble, so I came back to Nairobi to find work." His voice trailed off and his shoulders drooped. He was thin. He had lost weight.

"I am An Applicant now."

I frowned, uncertain of the word. "An Applicant?"

He nodded. "That is what we are called. There are many men like me looking for work. There is not enough to go around. Every day I go to the employment office. This morning I was waiting for it to open."

The extremity of his situation stunned me. Like Danny, I had kept him in a memory box, and had not considered how he might be affected by the swirl of Kenya's economic strife.

We talked a while longer and I asked him a few more questions, all the while wondering what I could do to help him. The last thing I wanted was to raise his hopes, and then not be able to deliver, so I decided not to say anything until I had a chance to explore the possibilities.

"I would like us to meet again, Musembe, so we can talk more. Can you meet me here, the day after tomorrow, Wednesday, at nine o'clock?"

"Yes, *Bwana*. I will be here. I will be very happy to see you again."

"I'm staying here at The New Stanley. Here's my name and my hotel room number." I wrote it on my business card. "If you need to leave me a message, just go to the man at the desk inside and tell him."

Musembe nodded, but I saw the uncertainty in his eyes.

"Let me show you," I said, and led the way into the lobby, and took him to the desk where he could leave me a message. We shook hands then, and parted ways until Wednesday.

I had often walked from The Thorn Tree to the University, so I set out on the same route, curious to see what changes I would find along the way. They were not quite what I expected. The well-kept buildings I remembered had sagging roofs, collapsed walls and were surrounded by broken concrete. Empty lots were strewn with litter and shattered glass. Even more unsettling were the clusters of listless young men sitting on the ground and idling in doorways. They eyed me sullenly as I passed. I became uneasy when I realized there were no other pedestrians around, and it had been a while since a vehicle had passed. The temptation was to quicken my step, but I decided I would attract less attention if I held to my stride. If I were lucky the neighborhood would soon change.

The next empty lot offered some promise. It had been cleaned up a bit and there were no idlers hanging around, or so I thought, until three men stepped out from behind a rusted Coca-Cola sign. They started toward me, with nasty expressions in their hooded eyes. I kept walking, measuring the distance between us. I shifted my briefcase from my left hand to my right, thinking I could use it as a shield.

I'd just about decided running might not be a bad idea, when a loud explosion close behind me rocked the air. Smaller explosions quickly followed, and I recognized the sound of backfires. A quick glance over my shoulder revealed the source, a battered truck trailing puffs of black exhaust. It had startled my stalkers as it had me. They stood in their tracks, as if in a trance. Eager to take the advantage, I hurried on, and when the truck drew abreast of me I moved to hug its flank, seeing it a haven of sorts. At the next corner it turned and I followed.

As I had hoped it brought a new change of scene. Tidy plantings hugged a long white-washed wall. Flags framed a gated driveway where two men in uniform stood guard, rifles at rest. Beyond the gates, I caught the glimpse of red tile roofs, manicured lawns, flowering shrubs and tall trees. The scent of oleander that drifted toward me reminded me of Lisette and her painting of oleander blossoms.

Coffee was being served when I arrived at the University, but I'd had my fill for the morning. I shook hands with the committee chairman and made my rounds of the other delegates. We represented different disciplines and came from different countries, but we all had a common goal, to review Kenya's development needs.

During the morning session I was seated next to a Kenyan journalist who had an enlightened take on his country's problems and was remarkably open with his opinions. I was glad to spend more time with him over lunch. His name was Stephen Githau and he worked for *The Nation.* I told him about Musembe, certain he would be able to shed some light on local employment problems.

"No question, there are no jobs for men like your former house servant," Githau said. "He speaks some English, can read and write a little, and do some sums. That makes him too big a man for his village, but in the city he is not big enough. There are hundreds like him in Nairobi, looking for work that does not exist. This is true of many cities in Africa."

"But what does a man do without an income?"

"In our culture, it used to be that no door was closed to a relative or a friend. There was always a place to sleep. Food was shared, even when there was very little. But times are harder now for many people. A man cannot live off others. There is a lot of crime in Nairobi these days. When you lived here before, there was petty thievery, but it is much more serious now. I should warn you, it is not safe to be on the streets after dark. Even during the day people are killed for just a few shillings."

I thought of my own close call, but didn't mention it. I was more interested in hearing what else Githau had to say.

"Our biggest problem is corruption. Politicians and government officials are stealing right and left. All our systems have broken down. The push to Africanize was too strong, and too fast." He paused and looked at me. "You are surprised to hear an African speak this way."

"I suppose I am."

"So much has gone wrong, that sometime I must speak my mind. I am careful of my audience. A big mistake was to expel the Asians. They were the *fundis,* the fixers. They were retailers, plumbers, carpenters, office managers, and accountants. Some were doctors and lawyers. They knew how to do everything. We forced them out. It was stupid. No one was left with the skills do their jobs."

Githau had my full attention, and he knew it.

"Don't misunderstand. Throwing out the Asians did not happen without cause. They had treated us as the British had treated them, like lesser beings. So when we had the chance, we sent them packing. I will admit, there was some pleasure in seeing them scramble to find asylum and be left dangling."

He leaned back in his chair. "You are still wondering why I am speaking so openly." He laughed. "It is good therapy, and you are a good listener. I will be honest. I am taking advantage of you. You will go home, and tell others. Eventually the world will know. I do not write such things. I take chances, but I do not go too far. It is said that the pen is mightier than the sword. I believe that. But you have to stay alive to be able to choose your weapon."

I looked at him and hoped he knew who his enemies were.

He had read my mind.

"I think it is safe for me to speak out in this forum. But one can never be certain. The government has its spies."

I was back at The New Stanley by mid-afternoon, my mind a swirl of all I had seen and heard on my first day back. I kept replaying my chance meeting with Musembe and my conversation with Stephen Githau. Although worlds apart intellectually, frustration dominated each of their lives. Musembe wanted to work and couldn't find a job. Githau wanted to write the truth, but it might cost him his life.

If Ann were with me, I would be talking to her about all of these things, instead of talking to myself. I missed her, and Danny, too. It was too soon to be homesick. But we had been here together as a family. Memories of those times swirled all around me.

I was jet-lagged. A shower would give me a lift, but I wanted a quick look at *The Nation*. Maybe I'd come across Stephen Githau's byline.

I'd gone halfway through the paper, still looking, when a photograph leapt out at me. There was no accompanying story, only a caption. *Artist Lisette Manet Conducts Story Hour at Harambe Orphanage.* Through the blur of newsprint I stared at Lisette's lovely face. A group of small children sat in a circle at her feet.

I sank back into the large arm hair, imagining what it would be like to see her again, to hear that soft French-accented voice for real, not in an idle daydream. Lisette had done some volunteer work at the orphanage when I knew her five years ago. This had to be an old photo, used to fill empty space. It was just too unlikely that she would be in Nairobi now.

We had met at an art benefit, held in the gardens of the American Ambassador's residence. Temporary scaffolding had been hammered into the lawn, as support for the paintings on display. I had been there awhile, enjoying the diversity of the work, when I came to a large canvas filled to its very edge with oleander blossoms. Their white petals were luminous in the reflected light of the sun. I wasn't surprised to see the painting marked SOLD and a gold ribbon pinned to its frame.

My shadow fell across the canvas, startling the young woman who stood alongside it. She looked up quickly and I saw the sparkle of tears in her eyes.

"Forgive me. I am so happy to have my painting sold. The money will go to the orphanage, but I am sad to think I will not see it again. I wish I were a writer or a musician. It is only painters who must say goodbye to their work."

I had never thought about that before.

"You must think me quite vain," she said.

"Not at all. You've educated me. From now on I will look at paintings and their creators in a totally different way."

Lisette Manet was her name. Her hair was chestnut-colored, her eyes a golden brown. She was lovely. Her husband worked for an oil company and traveled all over Africa. They had been in Nairobi a year and a half.

"Sometimes I go with him, but not so often. I love it here in Nairobi. We will be here five months more. It will be good to go home to Paris, but I will miss this Africa."

The day was warm and it turned out that we were both thirsty. I had noticed a bar off in the corner of the garden and we went there for a cold beer. We sat in the shade and talked until she had to leave for a reception. She invited me to visit her studio the next day, a cottage on a coffee estate owned by her uncle. His name was St. Claire.

I saw her that day and the day after that, often, in the four weeks left of my stay. My family had returned to the States early, so Danny could be home for the start of school. Conveniently, Lisette's husband was in West Africa.

After three rings, I heard that unmistakable French 'ello, and then the rising lilt of her voice on the second syllable.

"Lisette?" I said her name as a question, but I had no doubt she had answered the phone.

There was a pause, and then a quick breath, followed by that no-non-sense tone I remembered. "*Oui!* It is Lisette. And you? Who are you?"

"It's Brian. Brian Williams."

"It is not possible. I don't believe it! But I do. Brian, your voice ... I recognized it right away. No one says my name like you. I thought it was a trick my mind was playing. This is my first time back to Nairobi. And I have been thinking of you so much."

"I saw your picture in today's *Nation.* I have it in front of me. I'm look-ing at it now."

"You are here? In Nairobi?"

I laughed. "Where do you think I am?"

"I don't know. Phones can be anywhere."

"I'm at The New Stanley. And you? I know where you are, but what are you doing here?"

"I got lonesome for this part of the world. I've been here almost two months, but I must go back to Paris next week. My husband is there."

I hesitated only an instant. "When can I see you?"

I heard her soft laugh. "Perhaps you could come for tea today."

A grin spread across my face. She had teased me about being invited for tea and staying on for breakfast.

"I'm on my way."

"Drive carefully. And remember to stay on the left side of the road."

As I hung up the phone, I realized it was something Ann might have said. The thought was fleeting. Right then my family seemed far away.

I took Uhuru Highway out of the city, through the roundabout at Westlands, past the shops with the bakery that sold sausage rolls, and then turned on to Loresho Road. With my window rolled down, I breathed in the softly scented air. It was tinged with smoke from the charcoal fires that smoldered in the *shambas* on the hillsides, the unmistakable smell of Africa. There was some urban sprawl on either side of the road, tract housing where farmland had once been, a gas station, a mini mall, but enough thatched houses and vegetable patches dotted the softly rolling hillsides to make me feel that not everything had changed.

I had rented a car on my arrival. It would make it easy to get to the game park and to keep my promise to Danny. I smiled. Looking in on our old house to see if Musembe was working there wasn't necessary now. I had found him.

Up ahead, I saw the beginning of the coffee estates. A dark green swath stretched across the horizon and spread from ridge to ridge, marking the acres of land planted in the lucrative crop. I drove more slowly, looking for the stone pillars that framed the wide driveway of the property that belonged to Lisette's uncle. It was the flash of sunlight glancing off the bronze plaque that caught my attention. I shifted into a lower gear to make the turn and then eased on to the pebbled track that led to the cottage.

I found her in the garden, cutting orange daisies. She looked up at the sound of the tires on the loose stones and stood still, like a child caught in a game of statues. The flowers fell from her hands onto the grass. She came toward me, suntanned, in a pale yellow dress that swirled around her slender legs.

"I can't believe it—that you are here." Her open arms reached out to me. I kissed her forehead and then her hair. "How lucky we are," she said and offered me her mouth.

She led me along the side of the small house to the rear garden, glancing at the flowers lying on the ground. "They are in the shade. The dew will keep them cool. Saba will collect them when he returns from town. I had to do something after you called. I could not sit still, waiting for you. I came outside to cut flowers."

We walked in the small garden, linking arms, holding hands, exclaiming, dropping bits and pieces of our lives into the silence that surrounded us. The sky was wildly streaked with color, a signal that the sun would soon be gone. Darkness comes suddenly on the equator.

She drew me toward the small verandah, and I followed her inside.

Afterwards she lay with her head in the hollow of my shoulder. "How long before you go back to Paris?" I asked.

"Six days." She raised her head and looked down at me, her topaz eyes happy and sad. "Time will go so quickly. Afterwards it will be hard."

"I let myself forget what it's like to be with you." My voice was hoarse.

"I too," she said softly. "I couldn't go on from day to day, wishing I could be with you." She took a quick breath. "Perhaps it's not good to say such things. But I need to say them ... here, when we are together, because when we are not, and I think of you, I am as silent as a stone. I never say your name."

We had dinner at a small table in the living room. Saba had left us chicken, a rice salad, slices of papaya with lime, and a bottle of cold white wine. The orange daisies were in a low brass bowl on a side table.

She told me how much she had missed Kenya. "Others have said it before, so much better than I. It is all there in Karen Blixen's *Out of Africa*. I feel it, too—the skies that go on forever, the wide plains, the sounds that one hears only here. I am working on a book for children, set here. I needed to come back. As sharp as my memories are, I could not get the feel of Africa, walking along the *Rue Madeleine*."

Later we sat on the sofa, facing the small fireplace where soft flames flickered, taking the chill out of the night. I had been telling her about Musembe.

"It was eerie. It was as though I had wished him there—on the corner of Kenyatta Avenue. But I wasn't ready for his sad news. I wish I could find a way to help him."

She turned to me, her eyes shining. "I think there is something you can do. There are trade schools here now. They offer a variety of courses— carpentry, electrical work, hotel training, and other things. If Musembe acquired a special skill, he would be able to find a job. Perhaps you could help him attend such a school. I will get some information for you."

I drew her toward me. "You have an answer for everything."

She shook her head. "No, not everything, my love."

I talked about the conference then. "We're taking a look at Kenya's development programs. The country had so much potential after independence, but it has done poorly in so many areas— in family planning, education, health, agriculture. There is a Kenyan newspaperman in the group, Stephen Githau. He is intensely critical of the current regime."

"I have met him. He is an interesting man, and a good journalist, but he should be more careful. Journalists have disappeared. Others died in accidents that everyone knows were not accidents."

Her eyes had grown troubled and sad. "Because I am here for such a short time, I have tried not to let things touch me, but it is not possible. I ease my conscience by spending some time at the orphanage. Life is hard for so many Kenyans. When you and I lived here before, we used to have *askaris* to guard our houses from petty thieves who poked fish poles through our window grills. They would hook a bracelet or a necklace from a dressing table, and then run off. There is so much poverty here now. Thieves carry guns and knives. They use them. Nairobi is not a safe place now." She pressed my arm. "You must be careful."

"So must you," I said. "Is it safe for you to travel into Nairobi alone?"

"My uncle talked to me about that when I arrived this time. He insisted that I take Saba with me whenever I went in to town. I did that for awhile, but I don't any longer." She saw the concern in my eyes. "Don't worry. I am careful. I am never out after dark."

She smiled then, a little sadly. "Some say it is wrong to live in the past, to long for things that were, but when I go back to Paris next week, I will remember the Africa of my first memory. Like your Danny, I will have my old slides. They will not change."

"We were lucky to be here then. Danny's memories are happy ones. He will have a hundred questions waiting for me when I get home. That worries me. But if I can help Musembe, I will have good things to tell him."

———◆———

On Wednesday morning I arrived at The Thorn Tree a few minutes early, armed with the information Lisette had collected for me on trade schools. I half expected to find Musembe already there. He had always been prompt, so I was certain he would be along soon. I was eager to talk to him about the possibilities of his acquiring a skill that would help him get a job. As I sat there, imagining how much this would please Danny, I thought back on Musembe's first trip to the game park. It was Danny who had initiated the idea.

Danny had been sitting on the front step of our house, waiting for me to come home from work. I had no sooner pulled into the driveway, when he came running toward me. "Dad! You won't believe it!" His blue eyes were wide with indignation. "Musembe has never seen a lion! Or a zebra! Or a giraffe! He hasn't seen any game at all."

"How do you know that?"

"He told me. I was talking about all the animals we saw at the game park on Sunday. He said he's only seen their pictures on postcards."

That was a surprise to me, too. For some reason I'd taken it for granted that all Kenyans had seen some wildlife. I realized how wrong I was.

"How come, Dad? Musembe's lived in Kenya all his life."

I'd time to give the question some thought. "Years ago there was game every where, but now that so much land has been cleared for farming the only way to see game is to go to a game park. You need a car for that, or go on a tour. Musembe doesn't have a car, and tours are very expensive."

We were in our own car the next Sunday, a solid little Cortina. Ann and I were up front, with Danny and Musembe in back. We drove to the game park a few miles outside of Nairobi and followed a dirt track that wound through grassland, dotted with acacia trees. Overhead the sky was a clear crystalline blue, with puffs of high white clouds. We hadn't gone far when Musembe's gasp of wonder filled the car. On a rise, caught in the full light of a brilliant sun, was a herd of zebra. Their stripes were dazzling in the sun's white light.

We saw lots of animals that day. Once Musembe regained his voice, he began providing Danny the words for the animals in Swahili. *Simba* was lion. Musembe admitted he was afraid of the lions. His favorite of all the animals was the zebra herd.

"I will never forget them," he told us that evening. "I did not know that there are so many animals and that they are so beautiful. It makes me proud to know this about my country. It is important for a man to have pride in where he lives and where he knows he will die."

———◆———

I came out of my reverie startled to see that it was close to nine-thirty. Musembe hadn't come. Immediately an uneasiness crept over me. I rose, signaling the waiter that I would return. There was no message at the hotel desk.

Back at my table I glanced at the packet of information I had brought with me. I had felt so close to being able to help Musembe, but if he didn't show up that would be the end of it. I had no way of reaching him.

At ten o'clock I took a taxi to the University, feeling pretty low. It was pointless to try to guess what might have happened. He could have overslept, or pride might have kept him away. He had faced me as An Applicant once. He might not want to do that again.

I would have preferred to talk to Githau later, but he was waiting for me in the courtyard when I arrived at the University. He headed toward me, with great purpose in his step. It seemed he had something important to tell me. A newspaper was folded in his hand.

"I assume you have not seen this story." His voice had a somber tone.

I shook my head and reached for the paper.

He hesitated. "I must warn you. It is not a good story." He handed it to me, then, pointing to a column headed **Street Crimes**.

It is hard to recall what I thought when I read the short item for the first time, except that I didn't believe it. It had to be a mistake.

An unidentified man was found dead in an alley off Compos Road yesterday. He died from a stab wound to the heart. His pockets were empty, but under his body was the photograph of a European boy holding a soccer ball. The writing on the back said: To Musembe, who taught me this game. Asante sana. Danny.

Finally I looked at Githau, who had been silent until then. "I am sorry. This man was important to you and to your son."

I wasn't ready for condolences. "We can't be sure that it's Musembe," I said. "It could be someone else." I shook my head. "We had an appointment to meet this morning, at nine o'clock. He didn't show up. It wasn't like him. He was always punctual. I waited until ten. I knew something had to be wrong, but not this."

Githau drew me to a bench off to the side. "You are right. It is possible that it could be someone else, but since Musembe did not keep his appointment with you, it is not likely. If you want to make certain, I can help you with that."

I nodded. "I need to know. I need to be sure."

"That is what I thought you would say. I have already made inquiries. The body is at the morgue." He paused for moment. "There are some things you should know before you decide to make the identification. The authorities will be glad to have the morgue population reduced, if only by one. They have no resources and therefore no interest in finding out who the dead man is. Musembe was a man without a job, without an address and without a name, except for the one you knew him by. If you identify him as the man you knew, they will expect you to take care of his remains."

I frowned. I hadn't thought that far. I hadn't even accepted that Musembe was dead. I had admired Githau's directness before. It bothered me now, but at the same time I appreciated it. He was providing me with a road map of what I was about to face.

"You will be expected to pay for his burial or his cremation. The latter is a simpler matter, and it is not a big expense. If I am with you, they will not ask you for money under the table."

I almost laughed. It had to be nerves.

It turned out that the morgue was closed until two that afternoon. Githau needed to go back to his office for a while, and we agreed to meet in front of the morgue at two-thirty.

I was grateful to have him with me. He had told me he had been there before. I hadn't asked why. This was a first for me. I anticipated it would be grim, and it was.

There is no privacy in death. Large cabinets held large trays on which the deceased lay sandwiched side by side. It took some time for the attendant to find the right tray. I kept hoping that it would not be the man I had known. It didn't turn out that way.

The procedure that followed was tedious, but eventually all the forms were filled out. I was handed a receipt and told to present it at the crematorium the next day. The ashes would be turned over to me.

———◆———

I waited to tell Lisette when I got to the cottage that evening. As it turned out, she already knew. She had seen the story in the paper that morning and when she hadn't been able to reach me, she had thought to call Stephen Githau. He returned her call after our visit to the morgue.

It made it easier for me. There were some things that no longer had to be said, which made room for others. We sat on the sofa facing the fire. I was trying to work through what I would tell Danny.

Lisette's hand rested lightly on my arm. "It is too soon to know the answer to that," she said softly. "It will come to you."

"Whatever I tell him, it will change everything."

"Not everything. Danny will always remember the Kenyan he knew as a small child, who showed him how to play soccer. When Musembe spoke to you of *Bwana Kidogo*, he was telling you he remembered your little boy. They had their memories of each other. Danny will always have those."

Her words sounded good, but they didn't work for me. "Memories are one thing, but reality is something else. If I hadn't seen Musembe on that street corner ... if I hadn't given him the envelope with the few shillings, and Danny's photograph ... he would still be alive. How will Danny feel when I tell him that?"

"You will have to think hard about what you say when you get home." Her eyes bore hard into mine. "Truth may seem right, but it is not always kind. You have had to make such choices before." In the soft flickering light, I studied the pale oval of her face and knew she was talking about us.

———◆———

The day after Lisette flew home to Paris I drove to the game park on the outskirts of Nairobi and followed the same winding track we had taken that day when Danny and Musembe were seated together in the back of our car. The terrain hadn't changed, sprawling, lush grassland dotted with acacia trees. The sky overhead was that same amazing crystalline blue, dotted with puffs of high white clouds.

It was Danny who had given me my direction. At each recounting of that special day, he repeated the words Musembe had said. "It is important for a man to feel pride in where he lives and where he knows he will die."

The track curved and I rounded the familiar bend, my hand on the container on the seat beside me. There on a grassy rise, dazzling in the bright light of an African sun, was the zebra herd. It was as though they had been waiting.

The River's Child

From the porch of his small house with its overhang of thatch Luka watched the African sun set and looked out over his land. The acres of cultivated ground did not fill his thoughts the way they once had, or take him on the backward journey to the days when he was young and strong and had challenged the bush and planted his first crop of maize. This night his thoughts were of Begay who had been his small wife. The river had brought her to him. The river had her now.

He watched the sun fight its last battle of the day, streaking the sky with all the hidden colors of its fire, but darkness would come soon, suddenly, as it does on the equator, when the sun drops into the next world. It was only when darkness came that Luka said her name out loud. From the shadows of memory he heard her answering voice, and he lifted his hand and stroked the empty air.

"The cora player still sings your story," he called out to the night. "He sings of your life before your river journey, of your second birth and how you became a woman warrior."

If he had not gone to the lagoon that day, the river would have claimed her, sweeping her past the great flat rock that jutted out like a shelf into the cove, to where the rapids swirled and then plunged to a great water fall. On tranquil days, the great flat rock was where the women of his village did their wash and the men sometimes went to fish. But on that day none of the villagers were at the river.

In the east the season of heavy rains had begun and Luka had gone to the lagoon to see how high the water was. The rock where the women spread their clothes to dry was darkly hidden by the rising tide. Only a narrow strip of shore was left where he could stand. Beyond, in the wide channel where the river surged and foamed, tree limbs and matted balls of leaves and straw swept past. The broken roof of a house sailed by. The roar of roiling water filled his ears.

Then, riding the current like a wildebeest galloping across the plain, the carcass of a giant tree appeared. It swerved, and with tremendous force, plowed into the cove. A wave rose, and almost reached his waist. The tree would have knocked him over, had the submerged rock not been there. The tree reared and shuddered from the impact, its tangled branches clawing at the sky. Luka's heart was pounding and a chill swept over him as he stared into the crisscross of twisted limbs. Caught in the tangle was a bloated sheath of straw, the burial shroud of a distant tribe. The great tree rocked from side to side, and the movement spread upward to its limbs, tricking him into thinking something stirred within the shroud.

He closed his eyes and called upon the river to move its cargo quickly on, but when he looked again, the tree was closer than before. The envelope of death was swollen and straining at its seams. A split appeared and through it a small hand reached out. Over the wild, roaring of the river he heard a whimpered cry.

———◆———

Around the cook fires and in the fields word spread of the child the river had brought, who from death had cried out Luka's name.

They called her Begay, The River's Child, and gave her many stories. It was the cora player who sang of the land from which she had come, far to the east where fighting had soaked the ground with blood and the smell of death filled the air. She was the child of a warrior who had been killed in battle.

She was lighter than a stalk of maize that day when Luka carried her to the village, to the compound where his three wives lived. They had already heard the news. Word traveled more quickly than a man could walk. Nyanza, his first wife took her from his arms. "Begay, The River's Child," she exclaimed and thereby gave the child her name.

Luka's two younger wives went to the forest to gather roots and herbs for potions of great power. Nyanza bathed the child and fed her strong tea, chanting a song of welcome. When the other wives returned they put poultices on her wounds. For days the women watched over her, calling her by name. "Begay. Begay. The River's Child." They told her stories about the spirit of the river and of how it had called Luka to its shores. It was from the river that she had been given strength.

The women knew they spoke in a language Begay did not understand, but their words were as much for themselves as for the child. Her ordeal was beyond their imaginings.

At the end of each day, Luka came to sit by her side, and told her of the land to which she had been brought. With wide eyes she listened to all the words and song, but for a long time no voice moved past her lips.

"Her spirit is strong, but her body is weak," Nyanza told him. "It will be longer than a growing season before she will be well." As his first wife spoke, her face grew dark and her eyes filled with a sadness he had not seen before. "She will never be like other women. She will be no man's wife. The place in her body meant to accept a man's seed will never nourish a child. It has been plowed like a furrow and destroyed."

Begay grew stronger and she began to repeat the words she heard, and when the season had passed she started to speak the language of Luka's tribe. It was many more seasons before she was well enough to work beside the women in the fields. She planted beans and potatoes and helped to harvest the maize. She did not have the broad flat palms or the wide foot soles of Luka's people, and she would always be small, but she was no longer a child. Luka built her a house in the compound where his other wives lived. He called her his small wife.

On the days when the women took the children to the river to bathe and wash their clothes, Begay walked to the farthest point of land and knelt down by the river. The women saw her lips move. "She speaks to river spirit," Nyanza said.

In the evenings when Luka was alone, Begay joined him under the overhang of thatch and sat at his side as he looked out over his farm. She liked to hear him talk about the days when he was young and strong and first began to work his land. But often she asked him to tell her about the day he had gone to the river and had seen the giant tree riding the current like a wildebeest, holding in its branches the sheath of death in which she was robed.

"Did I call out your name?"

He smiled. "If you did, I did not know it. A small voice is what I heard. A small hand is what I saw."

There were times when she looked at him with eyes that shone like stars, but then a shadow passed, like when a cloud moves before the moon. He wondered if she had begun to remember more than she would say.

One night the village woke to her screams, so wild and high that the weaver birds left their nests and flew shrieking across the sky.

In the morning she asked him, "Why did the birds cry out last night? By day their song is strong but gentle, like the flutter of their yellow wings."

He did not want to tell her it was her voice that had shattered the stillness of the night, and frightened the weavers from their nests. But she pressed him, and he gave her an answer that was true. "It is an unknown fear that made the birds cry out."

"But of what are they afraid? "

"Something they do not understand."

One day she came to Luka and asked him if he had ever thrown a spear.

"A long time ago my people were a nation of hunters, skilled with the spear and the bow and arrow, but in my grandfather's time the game began to disappear. We had to turn to the earth for food. Maize was the first crop I planted, near where the maize field is now, but it was only a small patch then. I had no hoe or axe, only the *panga*." He looked to where the knife with its wide blade and wooden handle stood beside his doorway. "Every house in the village has a *panga* by its door. It feels right in our hands and it is good for many things." He saw her smile and he laughed, remembering how surprised she had been at all it could do, how strong it was. She had jumped back, afraid, the first time she saw him split a coconut in two.

"It was all forest in those days. There were trees to cut down and roots to pull. I cleared it all, except for the palm trees where the weaver birds still build their nests." He looked off to the corner of his land at the stand of towering palms, the home of the tiny yellow birds. "We are farming people now. We have no need of spears and arrows—only the sling shot, but even that is not meant to kill."

She nodded. "I have watched the lookout. He stays by the maize from dawn until the sun begins to drop, waiting until the last yellow weaver has returned to its nest for the night. He told me he watches for the lead bird. When a leader flies toward the maize, the lookout lets fly a stone. His aim is sharp and true, but your orders are not to maim or kill, only to frighten, so the other birds will not follow and strip the maize field bare."

"When I was young and worked to clear my first piece of ground, it was the birds who woke me in the morning and told me when the day had ended. This land is theirs more than mine. They were here before I came."

She looked at him and frowned. "That is so, but I have heard that men from the capital have been to the farm. They have other ideas. It was Nyanza who told me that they came because your maize seed is strong. She says they told you to get rid of the birds."

Luka nodded. "That is true. But the city men come and then they go. And the land is mine."

"What is it that they would have you do?"

He looked at her and shook his head. "You do not want to know."

"But I do!" She spoke with a defiance he had not heard in her before, and so he answered, not hiding the truth.

"At nightfall they would have me string a net alongside the field, and lay brush alongside. At dawn, without the lookout to scare them off, the birds will fly into the trap."

"And then?"

"They would have me set the brush on fire, and the birds would die."

The next day she came to Luka and told him she had asked the lookout to teach her to use the sling shot.

"What use have you for a sling shot?"

"I don't know. It reminds me of something, a voice and a hand that reached out. The voice said, *Take this, you will need it to save your life.* I don't know whose voice or hand it was, or what it offered."

Luka spoke to Nyanza and told her what Begay had said to him. "Tell me, good woman, what you think of this."

His first wife looked off to where the silhouettes of the palm trees were dark against the sun. "What I think and what I know are different things. Begay was a child when she came to us. She had known great fear and great pain, but she had no memory of the cause. She is a woman now and has more questions than she had before. She has begun to remember, but nothing is clear. Each day there will be more. She will remember many things that will make her afraid. But she will be strong. She has been given the river's strength."

Then one day, without warning, men from the capital came to inspect Luka's farm. They came in a big truck, wearing black uniforms with gold buttons and heavy boots laced to their knees. They marched between the rows of potatoes and beans, as though they were on parade. They pretended indifference to the ripening field of maize, but Luka knew it was the maize they had come to see.

Although he knew they were his enemies, custom made Luka offer them food and drink, beer from a common bowl that was passed from mouth to mouth. One of them drank more than his share and in a loud voice told Luka that until now the land that he had cleared had been his to plant and harvest in his own way. "Things are changing. Prepare yourself for different times."

While the men had been at the farm Begay had hidden in the shadows of the mango trees, watching their every move. That night Luka waited for her to come to him, but it was late before he felt her hand on his arm.

"I have been to the river," she said. "There are things I have remembered. I have seen men like those who came today, before I began my river journey, before I called out your name."

Through the long night she told him about her father and her mother, her brothers and her sisters and a school to which she had gone. She told him of houses set on fire and of days and nights filled with gunfire, the screams of slow death and bewildering pain. "There was so much blood," she said.

He covered her small hand with his large palm.

"My mother told me that to live I would have to pretend to die, and so in the custom of my people she wrapped me in a blanket of woven straw and sewed it closed. Before she made the last stitch, she put a small sharp stone in my hand and told me to hold it tight. When the time was right I would need it to cut myself free."

In the deepening darkness Luka closed his eyes against the visions Begay had drawn. The stone she spoke of had been in her hand the day he carried her to his village and placed her in Nyanza's arms.

Begay stayed with him that night, but at dawn she rose and stood before him, seeming tall. The sun fell in silver stripes on her face, across her breast and to her waist. She had the look of a warrior holding a shield.

"I know it is no longer the custom of your people, but I will learn to use a spear. I will go to where bamboo grows, at the edge of the farm. There I will cut and shape my spears, and practice until my arm is strong and my aim is clear and true."

Luka looked at her. "How is it you know about spears?"

"I was small, when my brothers were full grown. I followed them into the forest when they went to cut the bamboo. They chose it when it was green enough to accept the knife, but not so soft that it would not be hard when it dried. The points they cut were so sharp that not even the skin of an elephant gave them challenge. I pestered them into showing me how to throw. I have not forgotten how."

Luka went to Nyanza, who listened to him in sadness and wonder. "She is a warrior's child, and a child of the river. She will choose her own way."

Another harvest passed and a new season began. With it came distant rumblings, like the coming of locusts, the gathering of storms. Although there was nothing to see, everyone knew it was there. Then as sudden as a thunder clap, it was upon them. The government had been overthrown. Unknown men were in command. Proclamations came each day, announcing new and changing laws. Luka was ordered to go to the capital.

In troubled silence the women watched him leave. They packed him food and water and wished him well. In his absence, they tended to the land as they always did, but they spoke of him more than when he was there. What would he have to tell them when he returned? Would their lives be changed? What if he did not come back?

They had been working in the mango trees and were almost finished for the day, when against the nearby sky they saw a moving line of dust and recognized it as the sign of a vehicle coming toward the farm. Begay signalled them into hiding.

The sun was low in the sky and the shadows were long. The weaver birds were already in their nests when a truck drew up beside the maize field and four men stepped out, large men in black uniforms and high boots.

The lookout walked toward them, his arm raised in cautious greeting. But with his next step a sharp crack sounded, as when a limb is split, followed by another. Hidden in the shadows of the dark-leafed trees the women saw his body jerk and then topple to the ground. In silent terror they watched, as each man took his turn stomping on the fallen man. Then without a backward glance they turned to the task that had brought them to the farm. They dragged a roll of netting across the ground and stretched it along the edge of the maize, heaping brush as they went.

For only a moment Begay closed her eyes against the sight of what the dawn would bring, licking flames and tiny beating wings. She thought of Luka, and what he had said, "The birds were here before I came."

She waited until the men had gone and then raised her voice above the women's quiet sobs. "They will be back at dawn to light the fire. There is much for us to do."

She explained her plan and the women moved with her as one. Throughout the night they worked to fell each tall palm. Nyanza led them in a chant of tribal songs that kept their spirits high and help calm the frightened birds. When the trees were down and the birds dispersed in search of other nesting places, with torches flaming, the women set the abandoned nests on fire. Sparks floated toward the darkened sky.

The same four men returned at dawn and found the trunks of charred and fallen trees. In befuddled rage they raised their guns and fired, looking for an enemy, but it seemed there was no one there. They stomped among the ashes, shouting threats. Their answer was the mocking call of birds from every corner of the land.

Following the example of her brothers, Begay had cut the bamboo and sharpened it according to that memory. She had practiced long and hard. Her arm was strong. Now, with her weapons at her side, she watched and waited. Her intent was not to frighten, or to maim, but to surely kill. The silence of her spears would keep her hiding place secure and give no warning to her foe.

The first spear flew and the first man fell. The other three, bewildered by their ambush, did not know where to look or what to do. In wild confusion, they raised their guns and fired without direction or design. Begay's second spear found its mark, followed by a third. Only one man was left.

The last spear was in her hand and raised, when with the randomness of battle, a stray bullet found her heart.

———◆———

Luka woke at dawn. The night had passed almost without his knowing, so active were his memories that they flowed without interruption into dream. With the dawn the weavers took flight from their scattered nests and filled the morning with their song. No uniformed men had come to his farm since that fateful day. Official word was that they had more important things to do, but everyone knew it was their fear of the river child that kept them away. The legend of Begay had spread far and wide.

"Yes, the cora player sings your story," Luka cried out into the morning. "He tells the story my small wife, the child of the river who became a woman warrior."

Nyanza was beside him and listened to the call with which Luka began each new day. Since his return from the capital she was always at his side, and when dawn arrived they sat together under the overhang of thatch, and she would wait for him to turn to her and ask that she tell him what had happened during the time he had been gone.

She began at the beginning and took the story to its end. "In the custom of her people, I wove her a sheath of straw and sewed it closed, but before the last stitch was done, I put the small stone in her hand. I returned her spirit to the river."

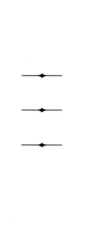

BiTTer JuSTiCe

The African sat behind the big desk and stared through the slanting blinds of the open window. The air was hot and humid, but he didn't notice. In earlier years he had lived inside the stifling uniform of a policeman—the heavy twill tunic, and high shoes with leg bindings that left lines on his flesh at the end of the day, like the markings of a snake on dusty ground.

When he'd become an official of the new government, Kamau left the police force and discarded his uniform. He was comfortable in the loose robe that fell to his ankles. His large feet moved freely in sandals made of antelope skin.

A small breeze stirred and the blinds moved lazily against the window frame. His eyelids lowered and lifted, clearing his vision, enabling him to take in a wider view of the yard surrounding the government building. Two Jeeps were parked beside a Land Rover. On the other side of the red hibiscus he could see the gray Toyota.

Directly opposite the window was a thorn tree strung with the basket nests of weaver birds. Each morning they were out in great numbers, flitting and twittering among the branches, so many that the tree seemed as though it were in flower, each bird a yellow blossom. Many had flown off, but they would be back at nightfall and again tomorrow morning.

Sometimes he wondered what life would be like if he had been born at another time. Not ten years earlier or ten years later; but fifty years. The past was not so easy to recall, but it was far more difficult to imagine the future. It was impossible to know what the next day would bring. Yesterday, for example, he would not have guessed the decisions facing him now.

The approaching sound of a motor reached him and he listened attentively. Kamau recognized the rattle of its worn body and rusted fenders, and knew it had just crossed the wooden bridge by the grove of mango trees. It was the vehicle he had been waiting for, a truck owned at one time by a European chicken farmer who had used it to transport live fowl. This morning it had been sent to round up Asians.

As the truck grew near, he thought about the decision he would have to make. Some men did not stop to think before they took action. Perhaps that was easier. Through the window he could see the sign nailed to the trunk of one of the nearby trees. *Thievery will be punished by public death.*

In recent months robberies and thefts of all kinds had begun to sweep the country like a plague and the government had grown impatient with its inability to cope with them. It had been decided that the severest of punishments must be meted out to set an example. The sign had been posted everywhere, nailed to fences and trees, to the sides of buildings. Executions were to be held daily.

When the truck rattled into the yard he turned from the window. He did not need to watch. He had seen it before. He waited for the squeak of the doors and for the clamor of the Asians seeking air, for dozens of feet padding on dusty ground. In a few moments he heard the front door of the building swing open and the murmur of voices in the outer room. Then the knock came.

"The Asians are here."

Kamau hesitated for a moment, then in a loud voice he called out. "Send in the shopkeeper named Patel."

The door closed and opened again. A guard pushed in a small man with oily hair, wearing a dirty white suit. His beady eyes held the frightened, cunning look of a jackal. The African stared at him and felt the saliva in his mouth turn bitter.

"Let me see your passport."

The Asian's mouth opened, but then quickly closed as he reached into the inside pocket of his jacket and withdrew the document.

"You name is Patel. Is that correct?"

"It is correct," the Asian nodded.

"This says you are a British subject."

"Yes, that is true, I am."

"At Independence you chose to remain a British subject. Why? You have lived here most of your life. You made your money here. Your children were born here."

Kamau stood up, but stayed behind his desk. He was a big man. Before him the Asian was a pudgy, pitiful figure. "Why? I want an answer. I want you to tell me. Speak!" His voice had begun softly, but had risen. His last word was an explosion in the small room.

The Asian trembled, but it gave the African no joy. If they had been equals, perhaps. But they had never been. Once it was he who had trembled before this man. It was the recollection of that time and others like it that brought the bitter taste into his mouth. Their roles were now reversed.

"Tell me why the land that made you a rich, that kept you in women and food and gave you sons, is not the country you choose to give allegiance."

The shopkeeper's lips twisted and his hands fluttered at his sides. The cunning was gone from his eyes.

"You have no answer? Then I will give you one. Fear. But why are you afraid? What have you done that should make you fear an African government?" Kamau came from around his desk, his hands clasped in front of him. The Asian backed away, his hands clenching at his sides.

"What are you afraid of? What can I do to you that you did not at one time do to me? You do not remember me, do you? Shall I pick you up by your coat collar and throw you out the door and call you a thief?"

Terror leaped in the small man's eyes.

"In those days I was not so big as I am now. I was only a child. Your clothes were clean and new and mine were dirty rags from a missionary's barrel. I had one shilling in my pocket and I came to your shop to buy some rice. You called me foul names and said I smelled like an animal. You took the shilling from me but gave me only a half shilling's worth of rice. When I tried to take what was due me, you threw me out onto the street, calling me a thief. I was beaten over the head by your relatives.

Kamau looked away, out the window and across the yard to where the weaver birds nested. His heart was pounding and his head was beginning to ache. Tomorrow morning the birds would wake with the dawn. What else would tomorrow bring? What unknown thing? What regret?

His glance returned to the man cowering in front of him, and wondered why he was hesitating to use the power that was now his. He returned to his desk and sat down. He picked up the Asian's passport, opened it, and then closed it. He folded his hands and looked up. His decision was made.

"Two and a half months ago the government decreed that all Asians who had chosen not to become citizens of this country must leave within three months' time. Why have you not left?"

"There is nowhere to go."

"There is Britain. You are a British subject. This says so." The passport was tight in his hand.

"But there is a waiting list."

"You have no time to wait. The three months are almost up."

"What will happen to me if I don't leave?"

"That has not yet been decided. But whatever, it will not be pleasant. Would you like to stay? Is that your choice?"

A flicker of cunning returned to the Asian's dark eyes. It was what the African had expected.

"Yes, yes, of course," the shopkeeper said.

"Perhaps you can buy your right to stay. I am surprised you did not think of that."

"But I have. And I have paid, but..."

The African looked away from the sorry figure in front of him, to the window again, and his eyes fastened on the sign, *Thievery will be punished by public death.*

"Who did you pay? And what did he promise you?"

"He promised me I would be allowed to stay in my house and keep my shop. That was last week. Then today the truck came and brought me here."

"Perhaps you will have to pay again."

"I already paid. I have no more money. He took my money, but did not keep his promise. He is a thief!"

"Then he must be punished. Tell me his name and we will charge him with thievery and you can witness his execution in the yard." Kamau nodded toward the window. "Come here and look. There is a stone wall against which he will stand, alongside another man who will be executed today for the same crime. It will only take a few minutes. Come, look out the window."

With a faltering step the Asian walked to the window, and looked outside. The African rose and gripped the Asian's shoulder. The small man whimpered.

"I am only returning your passport," he said quietly as he turned the man around, pulled open the jacket's dirty lapels, and slipped the document into the inner pocket.

"Now, then, tell me the name of this man you are calling a thief. Surely you did not give money to someone whose name you do not know. Tell me his name!"

The beady eyes canted. "His name is Saka."

"Saka," the African repeated softly, nodding. "You understand that by telling me his name I have no choice but to put this man to death?"

"He is a thief."

"Someone else has made the same accusation against him, another Asian, like you. We have already apprehended Saka. He is the man scheduled to be executed this morning, against the stone wall outside."

The Asian's eyes shifted and his tongue flicked across his dry lips. "When you seized him, did you find much money?"

"A large sum. I have it in an envelope on my desk. It is a pity that the person to whom it belongs will not claim it. Bribery is not a crime punishable by death, but the prison sentence is very long. I do not think the money is worth it."

The Asian remained silent.

"I will show you, the money, though." The African shifted some papers on his desk from one pile to another. Then slowly he looked up. "But why should it interest you? It is of no importance. And it is getting close to the time for the execution."

He rose and walked to the door that led to the outer office. The man who had brought in the Asian was standing guard outside.

"Take the shopkeeper Patel and the others outside into the yard. Call the villagers. I will be there soon to give the order."

Alone again, Kamau walked to the window. Each office had been given a copy of the government order. *All thieves must die. They must be executed, publicly, as soon as their crime is discovered. There will be no exceptions.*

"Saka," he whispered the name.

It was Saka who had found him that day long ago when the shopkeeper Patel had cheated him out of his fair share of rice and he had been left half dead in the street. It was Saka who had swept up the grains of rice that had spilled from the small paper bag beside him, so they would have something to eat. And it was Saka who had bathed his wounds in the river, and helped him back to their village. And now it was Saka who had been charged with thievery and would have to die.

The villagers were gathered in the yard waiting. The Asians, rounded up in the truck, were huddled together. Saka stood alone, his hands tied in front of him, his back to the stone wall.

Kamau stepped out into the bright sunlight and walked across the yard to where the spectators were assembled. Most would have preferred to stay away, but they were there because the law demanded it. His gaze traveled over the expectant, fearful faces until he found the shopkeeper, huddled with his kind, shivering in the heat.

He turned then toward the stone wall and sought out the eyes of his childhood friend, and addressed the crowd, saying what Saka had been charged with. He finished with the solemn pronouncement, "The government has decreed that to steal from another man is a crime, punishable by death. And so Saka will die."

He turned away from the face that would haunt him from this day on, and sought out the shopkeeper. With great purpose in his stride, he walked toward him, across the dusty yard. When he was but a few feet away, he stopped and spoke again, starting with a quiet voice that grew louder with each word, until it boomed in the quivering sunshine.

"Patel, you have stolen from men and from women and from children. You have thrived on their hunger. You have grown fat on their deprivation. Asian, I charge you with a life of thievery. And for those crimes you will die today."

An ululating cheer rippled among the African villagers. A whimper trembled among the Asians. The shopkeeper fell to his knees and clutched at the hem of the African's robe. The big man reached down and pulled him to his feet, thrusting him toward a guard and motioned that he be taken to the wall.

"You have no proof!" the Asian screamed.

The African spun around, his robe creating a cloud of dust on the ground. Until then he had not been confident of his own intent. "I have a lifetime of proof!"

The yard shuddered with the sound of gunfire. The weaver birds, startled from their nests, darted among the branches of the thorn tree. His eyes, blurred by tears, Kamau watched them, fluttering as though caught in a storm, and wondered what tomorrow would bring.

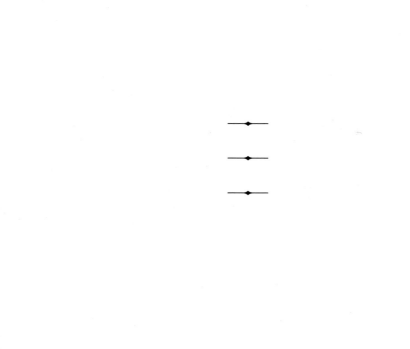

Only So Much
to
Reveal

When the police left, Matua locked up the main house and went to the servants' quarters behind the line of pepper trees to fix his lunch. There had been four of them, two Africans who had walked from the police station on the other side of the narrow stream, and two who had come from Nairobi by car. He thought about each of the men, as he added a few more pieces of charcoal to the cook fire. It had burned low during his absence. He fanned it into a new flame, and put the pot of meat and beans back to cook again. Then he sat down on the stone steps to think.

Overhead the sky was a clear blue, with puffs of high white clouds. If he raised his eyes he might see the tops of the flame trees that grew down by the stream, their scarlet blooms and broad green leaves obscuring the orange tile roof of the local police station just beyond.

Black or white, the police were the same, swollen by the authority of their uniforms into thinking they were bigger men than they really were. His friend Juma was no different. Since he had become a policeman there was no kindness in him, none of the old good-natured laughter. Only when his heavy boots were undone and set aside, and a freshly brewed bowlful of *pombe* began to gurgle in his stomach and flow in his veins, did Juma's face soften, his lips curl, and laughter fill his mouth. But not in the old way.

Today Juma had not come as a friend. Like the other three with him, he had come as the police, with his boots on. One lunge of a boot and a man would fall to his knees. Matua had seen it happen many times. And always it made the last meal he had eaten fight in his stomach.

The first time was in his village many years ago when he and Juma were boys. The police were all white men then and they came in their boots and uniforms, with their truncheons swinging at their sides. They were looking for someone.

Matua could no longer remember what crime the man had been accused of, but he remembered how he and Juma had watched from the shadows of one of the huts. When the man was found, he was kicked and beaten, and finally dragged away.

Matua shook off the recollection and leaned back against the stone step, sighing. Things had changed, but not in the way he had dreamed of. Independence had come and now Africans wore police uniforms side by side with Europeans. Juma was one of them. It bothered Matua more to see an African kick an African.

Yet today there had been a timidity about Juma that surprised him. It was the same with the other man who had come from the station house across the river, but Matua's quick mind found an explanation. The two black men were ill at ease in front of the big red-haired Englishman from Nairobi whose uniform was more elaborate than theirs and who had arrived by car with an Indian policeman as his driver. The Englishman's face was puffy and discolored, with streaks of purple in his cheeks. Rusty brows frowned over hard blue eyes and a bushy mustache twitched about his wet mouth like the tassels on a ripe ear of maize. The Indian wore a starched Sikh turban instead of the regulation hat, staring at Matua with coal dark eyes as the questioning began.

"When was the last time you saw the Bwana alive?" the Englishman asked.

Matua shook his head but did not speak. Long ago he had learned it did not serve an African of his station to acknowledge how well he understood the white man's language. Feigned ignorance allowed one to say less and learn more. His silence was rewarded. The question was repeated, as he had hoped, in Swahili.

"After dinner," Matua answered. "The Bwana said he did not want anything else, so I went to my room to sleep. It was nine o'clock."

"What noises did you hear during the night?"

Had he heard something? A cry? Or perhaps even a scream. How could he be sure? It might have been an owl or the wild screech of a civet cat thwarted in its search of prey. Perhaps what he had heard had been only the sound of his own snoring. But his answer to the red-haired European hid his uncertainty. "I heard nothing."

"Nothing!" The mustache twitched, the bloodshot cheeks reddened. "How could you not hear some sound? Look at this!"

They were in the sitting room where kapok lay in heaps on the floor and clung in clumps to the sisal rug that Matua had brushed and swept only yesterday. White dust clouded the border of polished wood. Every seat had been slashed, every piece of furniture overturned and ripped apart. In the bedroom it was the same, the mattress in pieces, the pillows in shreds, feathers everywhere. It looked like a henhouse after a cockfight.

"My room is in the servants' quarters behind the trees." Matua pointed out the window. "It was very cold last night." It was true. He had even wished for another blanket. "My door was shut. I heard nothing."

The Indian turned to the Englishman, his head and turban moving as one plastered unit, his sallow face sly. "They sleep and it is as good as dead. But I think this one lies."

Matua gave no sign that he understood the English-spoken aside, but an old anger leaped in his stomach. It was eased a little when he saw the look that Juma gave the Indian. In it was his own hidden hatred, and once again he felt united with his friend, because together they were seeing in that sallow face the countenance of all the Indians at whose shop counters they had been cheated and abused.

Long ago the British had brought Indian laborers to East Africa, hundreds of them, and their families, to work on the railway. A few returned to their homeland, but the others settled along the coast of East Africa and inland. They became shopkeepers and merchants and gained control of all the commerce and trade in East Africa. In small villages and towns the Indian *duka* was the only shop. In large communities *dukas* were side by side, connected like beads on a string by hidden passageways where prices were set and word was passed when an African buyer appeared. If the price in one shop seemed too high it did no good to go to the one next door. The price was fixed and inflated, down the line, for everything—rice, tea, sugar, cloth, thread, a single needle. It is easy to learn to hate a man who will give you only half the amount of rice your money should buy, when half is not enough to feed your family, and the coin in your hand is all the money you have.

The British policeman scowled at the Indian's comment. Matua knew there was no love between them either.

The Englishman turned to Matua and continued his questioning.

"When did you return to the house?"

"At six-thirty this morning."

"Is that your usual time?"

"Yes."

"But you did not ring up the police station until fifteen minutes after seven. Is that correct?"

"It is correct."

"Why did you not call immediately? What were you doing from six-thirty to seven-fifteen?"

"I was making scones."

The mustache twitched and the words that came from the moist lips were punctuated with spittle. "What are you talking about? Scones! Your master had been murdered!"

"I did not know the Bwana was dead. I did not go into the bedroom right away."

"Why not? Did not this mess tell you something was wrong?"

Matua shook his head.

The Indian took a step forward. "Do not shake your head! Speak!" The Swahili command was an explosion of garlic breath in Matua's face. "You are taking time to think up some lies!"

Matua swallowed but looked straight into the Indian's small black eyes. "I do not know what you mean by lies. It is I who called the police." Matua glanced at Juma to see if he would support his statement, but Juma was staring straight ahead. The Englishman spoke, angrily, "I want to know when you discovered the Bwana was dead!"

"It was six thirty when I came into the house, by the kitchen door. Always I go to the sitting room to open the curtains, but this morning with the scones to make I did not go. I would do it later, while the scones were in the oven, after I had brought the Bwana his first cup of tea.

"It was seven o'clock when I took the tea tray down the hall to the bedroom. The door was closed. I knocked and went in. It was dark and I set the tray down on the small table inside the door and went to open the blinds. I stumbled over something lying on the floor. 'Bwana,' I called, but there was no answer. I backed away and turned on the light. The Bwana was lying on the floor dead."

"How did you know he was dead? Did you touch him?"

Matua frowned. "He did not need touching for me to know. There were many wounds and much blood. He was dead."

"When did you call the police?"

"Then." The answer was almost the truth. There was no need for him to say that he had run from the house first, to his own room, that he had sat on the edge of the bed shivering with terror and wondering what he should do, that he had even thought of running away.

But why should he run? He had done nothing. Where would he go? His village was far away and he did not have enough money for the bus fare. And what of the tea tray he had left in the Bwana's bedroom? The scones still baking in the oven? He could not leave without cleaning the kitchen. When the police came, and he knew they would come sometime, they would know he had been in the house and had run away. They would think he was the one who had killed the Bwana. They would come after him to his village. They would track him down as though he were nothing more than a wild pig.

Matua had covered his face with his hands, had tried to shut out the pictures forming in his mind of his children clinging to one another in the shadow of their hut, of his wife standing with the other women, watching as he was beaten and dragged away. It had not been the sight of the dead Bwana that had filled him with terror, but of the *panga*, lying beside him, its broad blade caked with earth and newly clotted with blood.

"I telephoned the police station where my friend Juma works. He was not there, but the others came. They took the body away and told me not to clean the room. Now you are here." He did not have to tell anyone about how he had almost run away. There is only so much that a man has to reveal of himself to other men.

"And the *panga*? Where is that?"

"They took the *panga* when they took the Bwana." He thought of it again, lying beside the dead body. Every African owned a *panga*, sometimes two. They were protection in the forest, a hoe in the field, an ax for splitting bamboo or chopping fire wood, a knife to cut a pawpaw in half and scrape out the seeds. All alike, with their solid wooden handles and broad blades, they could be bought at an Indian *duka* for fifteen shillings. One was hardly recognizable from another. But a man knew his own *panga*, just as a man knew his own woman.

"The *panga* was mine," Matua said, and saw the Englishman lift his head and look at him. The Indian looked too, and so did Juma and the African policeman beside him. "I had worked in my *shamba* yesterday, hoeing beans. When I was done I left my *panga* standing outside the door to my room, with the earth still on it. It was there when I went to sleep last night, but it was gone this morning. I would like to have my *panga* back when the police are through with it."

"Of all the bloody nerve!" the Indian exclaimed. "He wants his *panga* back!"

The African policeman beside Juma stepped forward and spoke for the first time. Matua did not know his name, but he had seen him with Juma once in a while in town. "A *panga* costs fifteen shillings. It is Matua's right to have it back."

"It's a murder weapon, you idiot!" the Indian shouted.

"What will be done with it when the investigation is over?" Juma asked.

"How should I know," the Indian said.

"You know." Juma's voice was louder now. "You will take it! And then you or your brother will sell it to someone for *more* than fifteen shillings. The *panga* is Matua's. It will be returned to him."

The hate that gleamed in Juma's eyes warmed Matua. Once more they were boys together.

"Enough of that," the Englishman commanded and turned his attention to Matua. "You heard no one come to your house last night?"

"I heard nothing."

"What was the murderer looking for?"

Matua frowned, not certain that he understood. "I do not know what you mean."

"The murderer was looking for something. Why else would he have done all this?" The Englishman nodded at the ruined furniture.

"I do not know. Perhaps it was money."

"But didn't the Bwana keep his money in the bedroom safe?"

"Yes, but I do not think there was very much money there. It is the end of the month now and the Bwana always went to the bank on the first day."

"Whatever was there is gone," the Englishman said.

"The Bwana said it was not a very good safe. That is why he did not keep much money."

"What did he keep in the house?"

Again Matua frowned. "I do not understand."

"The murderer wanted more than what he found in the safe. He tore up this whole bloody place to find it. What was it? What was he looking for?"

Matua shook his head. "I do not know."

The questioning went on for a while longer and then suddenly it ended. Matua was glad, because there was no more to be said. The Englishman told him to clean up the house. The landlord had been informed of his tenant's death and already had someone interested in renting the house. They would be coming from Nairobi tomorrow.

———◆———

Matua rose from the step outside his room, and returned to look at his cook fire. He had begun to smell the sweet odor of the beans and meat cooking together and he realized he was hungry. He was thinking how good it would be to have someone to share his meal with when he heard a footstep along the path on the other side of the pepper trees. He was not certain whether it was real or his imagination. And then all at once his breath froze in his chest. Not until that instant did he realize that if the murderer had not found what he was looking for, he might come back.

"*Jambo*," came a greeting through the trees.

"*Jambo*," Matua replied, his heart beating like a trapped bird in his chest.

"*Habari gani,* how are things?"

He recognized the voice and his heart grew quiet.

"Ah, Juma. You have smelled my meat and beans even from across the river."

They sat on the steps and ate with their fingers, dipping balls of cooked cornmeal into the stew. They spoke of unimportant things at first and then

Matua asked, "What do the police think about the Bwana's murder? Do they know who did it?"

"A robber."

"A robber? But who?"

"How can they know who? He did not leave his name."

Matua frowned. He did not like Juma's joke. "But the police are clever. They have ways of finding things out."

"What things? What can be found? Have you discovered something?"

Matua shook his head. "I have discovered nothing. It is strange that the Bwana was killed with my *panga,* but another knife was used to do the rest."

"And how do you know that?"

"The blood would have been gone from my *panga,* so would the earth left from my bean patch, if it had been used to open up the mattress and to rip the cushions."

Juma looked at him strangely, his eyes narrowing. "And what do you think is the meaning of that?"

Matua shook his head. "I do not know. Perhaps the murderer is someone not comfortable using a *panga.* What was done to the furniture took a long time."

Juma frowned. "That is a good thought, Matua. I am sure the English policeman from Nairobi did not think of it. Tell me though, why did you tell him the *panga* was yours? You do not need the fifteen shillings that much."

Matua looked up. "Why should I let the Indian have it?"

Juma shrugged. "But there must be another reason why you spoke of it."

"It is better I tell the police it is my *panga* than if they find out later. There would be trouble."

"How could they find out? One *panga* is like any other."

"There are differences. And the police are clever." Matua paused, realizing he had been talking about the police as if Juma were not one of them. "Besides, it is easier to tell the truth than it is to lie. A lie can be forgotten, but the truth, never."

Juma laughed and sucked the juice of the meat off his fingers. "Why then did you not tell the truth about what the murderer was looking for?"

Matua raised his head, startled. "What do you mean?"

"You have said it is easier to speak the truth than it is to lie. So why lie to me, your old friend?"

"I do not know what you are talking about, Juma."

"A long time ago, when you first came to work for the Bwana, when the Memsab was still alive, you told me they showed you diamonds, diamonds the Bwana had brought with him from Congo. They kept them carefully hidden in the house. But where, Matua? Where did the Bwana hide the diamonds?"

Diamonds. Matua heard Juma say the word again and thought to himself what a fool I am to have forgotten. Too late he saw that Juma had caught the look of recollection in his face.

"Now you remember!"

"I have not thought of them for many years."

"Well, think of them now. Where are they?"

Matua frowned. Only a fool or an old man could forget something he once knew. Why is it that I cannot remember? The Memsab spoke of them to me, and so did the Bwana, but only once. They said that some day if the coffee crop failed there would be the diamonds. It is not the kind of thing for a European to tell a servant. Why was it they wanted me to know? There had to be a reason. Why was I such a fool to boast about it to Juma? But that was a long time ago, when I thought of him as a friend.

"Come, Matua. We are old friends. Tell me where the diamonds are."

"I do not know where they are." Matua spoke with impatience, looking straight into Juma's eyes. Then he reached for the empty bowl and took it to the outside faucet to rinse it clean. "I must go back to the house now. There is much to do, with new people coming tomorrow."

Juma rose. "I will help you. Perhaps while you clean you will begin to remember. Perhaps together we can find the diamonds. Lend me one of your shirts, Matua. I cannot return to the police station looking like a houseboy."

Matua looked at Juma's starched uniform, the polished black boots and at the new gold watch that gleamed on his wrist. He had not thought a policeman earned that much money.

Without a word he went into his room to get Juma the shirt he had asked for. He wanted Juma to go, to leave him to his cleaning, but he would not say this because Juma would think he wanted to be left alone so he could find the diamonds. And in a way that was true, but not for the reason Juma would think. It bothered him that he did not remember. In the house where he had worked for many years, everything had its place. Clothes were in the closet, pots were in the kitchen cupboard, tea and sugar were in the pantry. The Bwana's money was in his safe. The diamonds, too, were somewhere. But they were not Matua's to own or steal, or to hide. Where had the Bwana hidden them?

While Matua swept and dusted and carried the stuffings of furniture out to a rubbish pile in the garden, Juma examined the furniture, probing into corners with a shiny knife he had taken from his trouser pocket.

Matua called to him, "Help me with this rug. I cannot clean it in here.

I must put it outside on the line and beat it."

Juma turned, and with a flick of his wrist, threw the bright knife into the arm of a chair, where it landed upright and quivering. Matua pretended not to notice. Since he had become a policeman a *panga* was not good enough for Juma. But what good was a small knife like that? It could not hoe, nor could it chop down a stalk of bamboo. Matua bent over the rolled-up rug while Juma took his end.

"The safe in the bedroom ... " Juma started to say as they heaved the large rug over the wire line outside the kitchen door, "... why did the Bwana not keep the diamonds there?"

"I told you, the safe was not strong." Matua squinted against the sun slanting through the curtain of pepper tree leaves, and looked over the rug barrier between them. How could Juma be so sure the murderer had not found the diamonds?

They went back into the house. With the rug outside it was easier to clean the sitting room. Juma helped him carry some of the broken furniture out onto the veranda and stack it in a corner. They took the mattress to the rubbish pile. Then Matua put on his sheep skin footpads and began skating over the wooden floors, rubbing in the coconut oil that made the wide boards gleam.

"I am thirsty after all this work," Juma said as he came upon the cupboard where the Bwana kept his whiskey. "Let us have a drink."

Matua shook his head. He liked *pombe,* the African beer of his village, but he had no taste for the white man's whiskey.

"What is this?" Juma held up a small green bottle. "I have not seen this kind of whiskey before."

Matua looked across the room at the bottle Juma was examining. "It is not whiskey. It is something called ginger ale, to be mixed with whiskey. When the Memsab was alive that is what she and the Bwana would drink, with a little ice. But afterwards the Bwana did not want anything but whiskey."

"Fix me a drink, Matua. A drink like the Bwana used to have with his wife. Pretend I am the Bwana of the house now and you are my servant."

Matua looked at him. "I will fix you one drink. And then you will go. You are keeping me from my work. There is much to do. New people are coming tomorrow. Perhaps if I have the house to their liking they will ask me to stay and work for them." He took the bottle of ginger ale and the whiskey and started toward the kitchen.

Juma called after him. "I will have my drink and I will stay while you clean the rest of the house. I am not satisfied that you do not know where the diamonds are."

Matua turned around. "I have told you I do not know. The Memsab and the Bwana spoke of them once, a long time ago. They did not speak of it again. What good would they do you anyhow?"

"Diamonds are worth a lot of money, Matua."

"Who would give you money for them?"

"Merchants in the Bazaar."

"Indians."

Juma shrugged. "If I have diamonds and I want money for them, I must go to who has money and who wants diamonds. Yes, Indians."

Matua shook his head. "They will cheat you and then report you to the police."

Juma threw his head back and laughed. "You forget, Matua. I am the police."

Matua smiled sadly. "Yes, sometimes I do forget." He turned then and went into the kitchen and took two tall glasses from a side cupboard. It was automatic. Whiskey and ginger ale belonged in two tall glasses. One for the Memsab and one for the Bwana. But that was a long time ago. He put one glass back on the shelf and went to the refrigerator for some ice.

He reached for the small tray on the right. That, too, was automatic. Always the tray on the right. Why never the other? He stood for a moment staring into the open coldness. A small smile moved on his lips. He reached for the tray on the left and carried both trays to the counter next to the sink. The refrigerator would need cleaning too.

Juma was leaning in the doorway, fingering the blade of his small knife, watching Matua thoughtfully. "What you said about the Indian merchant is true. If you went to him with the diamonds he would inform the police, but he would not tell the truth about how many diamonds you brought. He would admit to only two or three. Even one diamond would be enough to put you in jail for a long time. And the Indian would have all the rest."

"Why do you say this to me?"

"Because I want you to know that without me to help you with the diamonds they will do you no good."

"And what makes you think that with your help they would do me good? What good did they do the Bwana? I do not need your advice."

"And what do you mean by that?"

"I mean that if I knew where the diamonds were I would not touch them. And if they came into my hands I would get rid of them."

"You are either a fool or a liar!"

"Perhaps a fool, Juma, but I do not lie. Now here is your drink." Two ice cubes tinkled against the glass as he held it out.

Juma took it from him with his left hand, but his right hand shot forward, pointing the knife. "If I learn some day that you have lied to me, that the diamonds are already yours, you will be sorry!"

Matua stared into the eyes of the man, who as a boy had been his friend, and then at the clean blade of the knife in his hand. He was not afraid. Juma would not hurt him. Another murder in the same house would cause the European policeman with the mustache like the tassels on a ripe ear of maize to become suspicious. Perhaps he was suspicious already. Matua had admitted that the *panga* used to kill the Bwana belonged to him, but what of the other knife, the knife used to slash up the furniture. To whom did it belong? The Englishman must have wondered about that. He could not be the fool that Juma thought him to be.

Their glances met over the point of the knife, and Matua found himself wondering if the uniform could be blamed for the man. He had not thought the Bwana would mind dying. He was not young any more. He had grown old quickly after the Memsab's death. But it was not right for him to die this way.

The man who had once been his friend raised the glass to his lips and took a long swallow. "It is good. Why do you not have one?"

Matua shook his head. "I have work to do," he said and turned to empty the two trays of ice cubes into the sink. He turned on the tap and let the water pour over them. As they became small he swept them down the drain with his hands. He rinsed the empty trays and set them aside to dry. He smiled to himself. It had been a good hiding place. Later, after he cleaned the refrigerator, he would fill the trays with fresh water and put them back in their place. For a while it would be automatic for him to reach for the tray on the right, never the one on the left. Either way, it would not matter. The diamonds were gone.

Intruder in the Maize

Claire waited until the churning of the Land Rover's heavy wheels on the long gravel drive had faded into the softer sound of tires against murum, and then rose to dress for the day. She was annoyed to have wasted the last hour pretending sleep, but it was preferable to a confrontation with Jack.

It was pitch dark when her husband left the bedroom. Sunrise was almost an hour off. Undercover of darkness he was heading for the rise overlooking the field of maize. Once there he crouched down and waited until dawn came, hoping to catch his culprit in the act. It had been his pattern every morning for the last two weeks.

She slipped a sweater over her suntanned shoulders and left the house by the veranda door. As she passed the kitchen, she stopped to tell Kariuki he shouldn't bother with breakfast this morning. She would fix coffee for herself later.

She walked across the dew-soaked lawn, past the bottle brush tree, where sunbirds twittered among its red blooms. Overhead the East African sky was an intense blue, and stretched to infinity. High white clouds rose like mountains, to be climbed. She breathed deeply of the cool air. It was dry, but it did not strike her as thin, not even on that first day, a year ago, when they had just arrived. The only time she had felt the altitude was when she walked uphill, and then her breath came in quick, short pulls and her chest felt hard and tight. But that had past.

She continued to where the shrubs thinned and she could look down into the valley and to the opposite ridge. There were thatched huts scattered on the sloping hillsides. The familiar smoke of cook fires rose in the early morning air.

She spotted a man walking up along one of the nearby paths. His dark head was bent, obscuring his face, but from his dress, the short-sleeved white shirt and the dark trousers, she was sure it was Molo. He was one of the few farmers in the area who had adopted European dress, when he came to pay a call. He had a small *shamba* on the other side of the valley. Before she and Jack had come to Kenya, Molo had raised potatoes and maize, but last season he had set out his first real money crop—a half acre of pyrethrum, a plant with silver-green leaves and daisy-like flowers, from which an insecticide could be extracted.

Claire stood waiting for Molo, wondering why he had left his *shamba* so early this morning. It was the coolest part of the day, and the best time to work on the land.

"*Habari,*" Claire said.

"*Mzuri,*" Molo replied, but the look on his face did not seem to agree that everything was good.

There were a few more prescribed words for them to exchange before they exhausted her Swahili. Then they would switch to English and slowly Molo would come to the point of his visit.

He looked up at the sky. "The rains come soon."

She saw nothing that resembled a rain cloud. But the skies were strange to her, both night and day. The stars were not the ones she knew, nor were the clouds. Whatever the time of day, the sky was beautiful. Sometimes she wondered if Jack saw any of this, if he realized how much beauty surrounded them.

"Is the Bwana at home?" Molo asked.

"He left early this morning on *safari.*" She smiled awkwardly, still not used to the East African meaning of the word. It didn't always involve sun helmets and bearers and trekking through the bush. Most often it referred to any trip out of town, whether for a day or longer.

"The Bwana Red go with him?"

"No, they were planning to meet in town, and from there go up-country."

Tim Redmond had been in East Africa for twenty years, more than half his life time. His knowledge about the country and the people proved a valuable asset to her husband, but sometimes the fact that Red knew his way around, irritated Jack. Her husband did not like to be bested.

She admired Red a lot, but tried hard to avoid making comparisons between him and her husband, and went out of her way not to make Jack jealous. Whether Red had anything but polite feelings for her, she had no idea, for he showed no sign. Red was no fool. He and Jack had to work together, managing the sprawling farming cooperative.

"Is something wrong, Molo? Do you need more seed?"

Jack had come to East Africa on a two-year contract as an agricultural adviser. Ironically, he was Red's boss. Jack had taken for himself the responsibility of parceling out seed to the local farmers. It was given on a loan basis, to be paid for when a crop was harvested. Seed of any kind was a precious commodity, doled out on the basis of past records of repayment. Someone had put the idea into Jack's head that thieves were everywhere, and so he kept the sacks of maize seed locked in a storehouse at one end of the maize field.

On their arrival Claire had discovered that a concern about theft was part of the culture. The house, into which she and Jack had moved, had barred windows, locks on every door—not just outside doors, but all inside doors, closets and pantries.

"It's different with the seed," she had said to Jack. "I can understand your concern about the seed." In part she did, but the intensity of his paranoia bothered her.

"But I'll be darned if I'm going to lock up the pantry every time I leave the house, just so the houseboy won't help himself to a spoonful of sugar!"

She had pointed to a peg board on the wall. "Look at that! There must be a dozen different keys there. I won't live that way."

"I told you, the house is yours to run as you want," he said and then nodded toward where Kariuki and his helper were outside hanging the wash. "Just don't come crying to me the day one of them walks off with something that can't be replaced."

After that she put the few pieces of silver that Jack's family had given them in the wall safe behind the mirror in the bedroom and left it there.

One day when Red was having a beer with them, Jack brought up the topic. Claire knew he was hoping Red would support his thoughts on the matter, and persuade her to his view, but it was no surprise to her that Red was of a different mind.

"If I bothered to check, I suppose at the end of each month I'd find I was out a cup of sugar and maybe some tea. On a day-to-day basis Jinja helps himself to a banana or toast that's left over from breakfast. The banana would rot before I'd get around to eating it." He shrugged.

"That's not the point," Jack had countered. "They ought to be taught that what's yours is not theirs."

"There's a difference between stealing money and things of value and taking scraps of food." Red went on patiently. "When Jinja washes my trousers, he checks the pockets. I'm always leaving things in them—cigarettes, screws, keys, a few shillings. He keeps a basket on the shelf above the tub for all that stuff. I find the shillings there too, along with everything else."

Jack had looked at him narrowly. "Have you ever left an odd bunch of change, and looked to see if it's all there?"

"You mean have I ever tried to trap him?"

"If you want to call it that."

Red shook his head. "If I did that it would mean I didn't trust him. And he would know, and then the whole thing would break down and I *couldn't* trust him."

Jack had continued the discussion, long after Red would have been happy to let it go. In a final effort to win a point Jack had lashed out angrily, "The Africans wanted freedom, now they have to accept the responsibility that goes with it!"

"I couldn't agree with you more on that," Red said, "but I don't go along with your methods. You have to start out with trust. Suspicion without cause is a sure way to create a thief."

———◆———

Molo shook his head and told her he had not come for seed. "I would like to look at the field of maize."

Now she understood. He was asking permission to come onto their land.

"Bwana Jack thinks a wild pig is coming and stealing seed. He has been watching."

So, Molo knew of Jack's early morning vigils.

"I bet it comes around dawn," he'd told Red. "From that rise over there it would be an easy shot. I'll get him one of these days."

"What kind of gun do you intend to use?" Red had asked, uneasily.

"I don't plan to use a gun."

"Suit yourself, but setting traps can be slow. That's a big field."

She remembered Jack's disdainful boast. "I intend to use a bow."

Red looked up quickly.

"I'm a fair marksman," Jack went on. "I had some practice in the States."

Claire bit her tongue, and thought of the country club's manicured lawn, and the steady bull's-eye target.

"A couple of weeks ago I bought a bow from one of Molo's brothers and a dozen arrows. It's a different kind of weapon from what I've been used to, but it sure has zing."

"That might be a little light to do in a wild pig," Red said.

A grin spread over Jack's face. "I've got something else to help it along."

She remembered the frown that had creased Red's brow. "I'd be careful with that stuff. It's not something to fool with."

"Thanks for the advice. I never did have a wet nurse, and I don't need one now."

The recollection of the scene embarrassed her again.

———◆———

Claire followed Molo toward the maize field, in the direction of the lookout point where Jack had gone early this morning, before he'd left to join up with Red.

At the rise Molo stopped. She noticed he had his *panga* with him. The machete-like knife had a broad blade, and was used to cut grass, chop roots, dig potatoes, prune trees, and sever the heads of chickens. It was as much a part of the African farm scene as was the hoe in the States before mechanization. Usually when Molo came to call, he left his *panga* behind. She couldn't help but wonder why he had it with him this morning.

He used it then to point in the direction he wanted her to look. She followed the dark line of his arm to the end of the blade

"Pig come out of forest and walk low on belly through maize."

For a moment the slight furrow in the sea of green stalks eluded her, but then, as her eyes focused, it became clearer.

"You stay here, Memsab Simon," Molo said. Something in the softness of his voice struck her with surprise. He was not being rude, but protective.

"Molo, you don't think the pig is there now?"

"No, pig is gone."

"Then why can't I come with you?"

"It is better you stay here. Let me see first."

Molo might be a guest on her land, but she was a stranger in his country. With a shiver of uneasiness she stood watching as he descended the small hill and entered the field of maize. Overhead the sky was the same clear blue it had been minutes ago, with the same white, climbing clouds. There was no sign of rain, but something else had thrown a shadow over the day.

The maize was shoulder high, so that when Molo stopped suddenly, and stood looking down at the ground, she couldn't see what it was he was looking at. He walked forward, stopping again after a few paces. Then he walked quickly on, as though he'd found what he was looking for.

He had entered the field from the side bounded by the forest and had followed the path that had been broken for him. As the larger picture came into focus, Claire saw that the parting in the maize seemed to lead to the padlocked storehouse.

Oh, God! Some animal found a way into Jack's burglarproof store! Had her husband come here every morning for the last two weeks and not discovered this?

She stood watching Molo. Something he had said earlier set her to wondering. "Pig come out of forest and walk low on belly through maize." It was an odd way to describe an animal's foraging.

Had an animal made that path? Or had it been a man, a man trying to find a way to break into the seed store?

Molo had reached the storehouse and turned in her direction, calling to her in Swahili. "Come now."

Hurriedly, she started down the slope, propelled by a fear that something was terribly wrong. When she entered the maize field, she moved more slowly, her arms raised to protect her face from the slashing leaves. Her eyes were focused on the ground, and she saw what Molo must have seen—a stone smeared with blood and more blood on the low leaves. Ahead there were drops of blood, hardly visible on the red brown earth, but unmistakable.

Had Jack hit his target this morning? Had he only wounded it? She looked around her, trying to see into the impenetrable growth. The wounded animal might be hiding, crouching, ready to charge. How could Molo be so sure it was gone?

Her breath was coming in quick shallow gasps, when she reached Molo, who stood in the shadow of the storehouse. With his *panga*, he pointed to the ground, to a pile of dirt and a hole dug under the foundation. A sack of seed and an abandoned *panga*, used to dig the hole, lay on the ground.

At Molo's feet lay an arrow, its arrowhead and shaft bloody.

She suppressed a moan. An animal couldn't use a *panga*, nor tear an arrow from its stricken body! The succeeding thought was terrifying. Jack had shot a man!

But perhaps it wasn't Jack's arrow at all. He had told her he had marked his arrows, scoring the shaft. She had to find out. She had to know. She hesitated, and then with horrified determination took a quick step forward, her hand reaching out. Molo's shadow was upon her and his arm caught her shoulder and she fell back into a hammock of maize stalks.

A scream choked in her throat as she stared up at the black man standing over, his *panga* raised. It sliced through the air and caught the blood-smeared arrow and tossed it aside. He stabbed his *panga* in the ground. "Memsab, the arrow is poison. A scratch brings death." He held out his hand and helped her to her feet.

Terror filled her throat and she did not trust herself to speak. She looked at him and pointed to where the arrow lay. The question formed slowly on her lips. "Is it the Bwana's arrow?"

"Yes," he said. "It killed my brother."

Her hand flew to her mouth, silencing a cry. She did not know what to say. She stared at him helplessly.

"I am sorry, too," Molo said. "I am sorry that my brother became a thief. And I am sorry that your husband must die."

Oh, God, she thought, what did that mean? Could she reason with

Molo? If not, somehow she would have to get word to Jack. It was possible that he and Red had not yet left town.

She struggled to find the right words to say, when Molo began to speak. The words came slowly, thoughtfully, half in English, half in Swahili.

"Before the Bwana came to live here, my brother was watchman for the Bwana Red. He slept at night outside the seed store, the old one which we do not use any more. No one stole or they would know my brother's *panga.*"

Molo's eyes fell to the ground where the big knife lay. Then he looked at her again. "But then the new Bwana came and everything changed and my brother became a thief." He stopped. It was as much as he could say.

"But, if your brother was stealing the seed, why did he sell my husband a bow? Why did he give him the poison?"

"The bow he sold because he needed money, and because he thought the Bwana could not shoot well. But he did not give him poison. The Bwana got poison somewhere far from here, from someone he pay a lot of money."

Molo cocked his head, in response to some distant sound. She heard it then, too. It was the Land Rover returning.

"It is the Bwana Red," Molo said.

She looked, but it was too far for her to see who was in the vehicle. It bore down on them, coming as close to the field as it could. Red was at the wheel. The seat beside him was empty.

Red got out of the Land Rover and started toward them.

"Where's Jack?" she called.

"I left him in town. What's going on? He sent me out here, said there was something for me to see." His glance went from Molo to Claire.

"There was no wild pig in the maize. It was Molo's brother," she said. "He'd dug a hole under the storehouse."

Red frowned. "I guess that's one for Jack's side. I'd have said it would take a lot to make Molo's brother turn thief." A flicker of hope crossed his clouded face. "I suppose Jack caught him in the act."

Tears seared her eyes. "Jack didn't catch him. He killed him."

Red's face went blank with disbelief. He turned to Molo. "How did he do it? He wasn't that good a shot with the bow."

"The arrow came here." Molo touched the fleshy part of his thigh. "It would not have killed him, but the arrow was poisoned."

"Poisoned! Where did Jack get poison?"

Claire answered. "I thought he'd gotten it from Molo's brother. But Molo says no, that he got it somewhere far from here."

"That arrogant son of a bitch! This means trouble for all of us."

Molo shook his head. "No, Bwana Red. There will be no trouble. My brother is dead. And the Bwana will die. It will end there."

Red reached out and put his hand on the African's shoulder. "Molo, old friend, the viper eventually spends itself. Do not put yourself in danger by seeking its death."

"Do not worry, Bwana Red. The viper has already felt its own sting."

She looked from one man to the other. She had caught the proverb, but did not understand its application. She turned to Red. "Why didn't Jack come back with you? Where is he?"

"I left him at the dispensary. He cut himself, apparently on one of those damn arrowheads, enough to need a couple of stitches. I wanted to wait with him, but he didn't want me around."

She listened to each word, each progressive syllable, and her realization grew until the horror of it was evident in her face.

Red caught her hand. "God, I'm sorry. I know what you're thinking. Jack's all right. It's just a simple cut. You see the poison is applied to the shaft of the arrow, not the tip—for reasons just like this—it's so easy to get a scratch and that's all you need."

She shook her head. Slowly, she turned to Molo. "How did you know? How did you know the Bwana would die?"

"Many people were in town, waiting at the dispensary. They brought the news to my *shamba*."

"What's this all about?" Red said, turning to her. "I just told you. He'll be all right."

"No," she said. "No, he won't. You see he didn't know about applying the poison to the shaft. He put it on the arrowheads."

Prisoner
of
Zemu Island

*H*igh over Zemu Island, a needle of light pierced the blue African sky. In the shade of a jacaranda tree at the edge of the airfield Ras Lazaar watched the gleaming splinter of light sprout wings. A fusion of excitement and sadness held him, as he followed the plane's gradual descent. Before the revolution, he had traveled to the mainland by boat many times, but he had never flown. It was not likely now. The new African government did not allow Indians to leave the island.

He pushed aside the thought and waited for the plane to land. Thirty passengers were on board, twenty-nine Germans on a group tour of Africa, and an American woman traveling independently. The Germans would leave the island before nightfall.

As Director of Tourism, all arrivals were Ras Lazaar's responsibility, but the American was of special interest. The decision to grant her entry had not been reached without argument and a pointed threat, directed at him. Except for tourists, all visa requests were automatically denied by the new government. It was more than a year since an American had sought to come to Zemu Island.

"If this woman is not what she says she is, if she brings trouble to the New Republic of Zemu Island—you, *Indian,* will pay for it!" Prime Minister Masaka's finger had pointed like a gun at Ras' head, firing the Swahili with the slur of ethnic superiority. Ras' hatred of Masaka exceeded his fear.

When the plane touched the ground and started down the runway, Ras stepped out from the shade of the jacaranda tree. He was taller than the average Indian, with the traditional olive skin and gleaming black hair. His stride showed a trace of stiffness from the year-old leg wound. His recovery helped by the fact that before the coup he had played tennis and was a good swimmer. At twenty-six his body showed little evidence of the year's absence from exercise. His mind, too, had survived the trauma of the two-day revolution, which had decimated the Indian population of Zemu Island.

He had stopped asking why he had lived when so many had died, what instinct had sent him to the ground at the unfamiliar sound of gunfire, by what lucky accident a bullet had struck his leg and not his heart. The Africans had not killed him when they found him wounded and unconscious. Instead they put him in the care of the Cuban doctors who were part of the revolutionary force. The Africans needed him. He could read and write both Swahili and English. They named him Director of Tourism.

That Masaka should see a threat in the visit of the young American schoolteacher was in keeping with the Prime Minister's general paranoia, accompanied by frequent rages and bursts of irrationality. The pressures of ruling a country were heavy, even with the support of the people, but suspicion had quickly eaten at the edges of black unity. Word spread that the revolution had been instigated by a foreign power, not the rebellion of Africans against a repressive Indian government. Soon sober Africans began to ask questions. Some had begun to demand answers. Yukano was one of them.

The differences between Masaka and Yukano were more than physical. Masaka was six feet tall, with a round head and enormous hands that were forever washing one another. He spoke in a loud voice. Yukano was slight of build, with a thin face and narrow shoulders. His manner was calm and without bombast.

As the plane taxied across the airfield, Ras recalled the meeting held to discuss the American woman's request to visit Zemu Island. Immediately, Masaka stood up and in a loud voice declared his opposition to her visit. When he had finished, Yukano rose and spoke of Zemu Island's need to reinstate tourism as a source of revenue and prestige. "The American, June Hastings, asks to come not just as a tourist but as a scientist interested in Zemu Island's marine life. Do you recall the prestige that came to Tanganyika when Dr. Louis Leakey made his excavations at Olduvai Gorge and found evidence of prehistoric man? How do we know what there is to be found in the waters of Zemu Island?"

Masaka had eventually acceded to the majority, but Ras knew it was a defeat the Prime Minister was not likely to forget. It was hard to know, what sort of action he might take to soothe his wounded pride.

The plane came to a stop and the airfield came to life. Africans in ragged shorts and bare feet left the shade of the palm trees to unload baggage. Airport officials of the same skin color, wearing starched uniforms and hats decorated with gold braid, stood at attention to some unseen authority. The sun streamed down and the concrete airfield glistened with the mirages of running rivers and shimmering pools.

The first person to disembark was the German tour leader. Ras greeted him courteously. "Lunch is waiting for your group at the Manga Hotel," he said. "Local guides will give you a tour of our island."

The balding pink-cheeked man mopped his forehead and managed a smile, then went off to tend his flock.

Ras was free to study the young woman who was the last of the passengers to come though the plane's doorway. A warm breeze fluttered at the hem of her light blue dress. Her bronze hair was pulled back away from her face. She scanned the horizon of palm trees, and then started down the steps.

"You must be June Hastings," he said.

She hesitated. "Yes, I am."

"I am Rashid Lazaar. We have corresponded. I am with the ministry of tourism."

"Of course. I'm glad to meet you, Mr. Lazaar." She offered her hand. "Thank you for arranging my entry permit."

"My pleasure," he said, a phrase he realized he hadn't used with any real meaning in a long time. "I think if we go directly to Immigration we will save time."

"What about my luggage?

"That will be delivered directly to Customs. We'll go there after Immigration."

Her eyes were a pale brown, almost golden. There was a question in them. Her bronze head tossed. "Does someone from your office always meet a new arrival?"

"It is the policy of the new government."

"But I must be someone special to be entitled to the Director of Tourism himself."

The mischief in her voice was clear. It surprised him and reminded him of his sisters, and their playful jibes.

"You *are* special, Miss Hastings. You have not only chosen to visit Zemu Island, you have come for an unusual purpose. Zemu women and children have gathered shells for years and made necklaces of them, but no one has ever thought them of scientific interest."

"Maybe it's time someone did."

"Some in the government are doubtful, yet others have suggested that you will give prominence to Zemu Island by discovering something as important as what Dr. Leakey found at Olduvai Gorge."

She stopped and stared at him. "They don't really think that?"

"It is what has been said."

"By whom?"

Ras shrugged. "A man named Yukano." The name would probably mean nothing to her. Yukano had surfaced in the island's politics only a short time ago. Yet Ras thought he detected a flicker of recognition in her face. "Have you heard of him?"

"African names still confuse me. They shouldn't, after all this time."

He assumed she was referring to the last two years she had been teaching school in Kenya, information she had provided on her visa application.

"From a distance people of one culture often imagine those of another are all alike. Little thought is given to the possibility of great differences among them."

Her voice felt silent as they approached the immigration building.

Ras would have liked to continue the conversation, but it wasn't the right time. She was well informed, typical of emancipated American women he had read about. He had to be careful not to be guilty of what she had just described. She was an individual, who had come to Zemu Island for a special purpose. He suspected there was much he did not know.

The immigration check was routine, even to the insolence of the African clerk who looked at Ras and yawned widely. In the past twelve months Ras had learned to ignore such petty insults, but with the young woman at his side it was more difficult. He was glad when they were outside again and he led her to the car he had left parked near the jacaranda tree. "Your luggage is being delivered to a building at the other end of the airfield. It is just a minute's drive."

As he helped her into the front seat he thought about warning her that this would be no ordinary customs check. Two of Prime Minister Masaka's own men would be doing the search, and their instructions were to go through her belongings with exactness. If they found something they did not like, she would be put on the next plane.

He decided a warning would serve no purpose but to alarm her. He hoped her luggage cleared. He wanted her to stay. There was very little he had wanted so much in a long time.

Perhaps he would take her to Pwani Pwani. He had not been back since the day the guns had fired and his whole world had changed. He had thought he could never return, to walk over those sands where his mother and his sisters and the girl he had loved had played ball and gathered shells. In memory he saw them strolling along the beach, their colored saris catching the breeze, like butterflies in flight. Sunday after Sunday they had gone to picnic at Pwani Pwani. One Sunday all of them had died there.

"Tell me about the Manga Hotel," he heard June Hastings say. "Is it as beautiful as it used to be?"

Torn from his reverie, he glanced at her with surprise. "You know it?"

"I heard of it from someone who had been there years ago, when the Norberts owned it. They aren't still here, are they?"

Ras smiled. Anyone who had stayed at the Manga would remember the Norberts. "They're still here. They run the hotel for the government now." He was certain she was aware that the new regime had confiscated all private lands and possessions. "They have kept things up. It is a handsome building, white stone and coral, built around a courtyard that is always in bloom."

Purposely he did not mention the door. For some reason he wanted her to see it for herself, unprompted. He was tempted to add that a building, no matter how beautiful, did not make a hotel. Only guests could give it life. There had been no guests for more than a year. The few boarders were foreign technicians who had come in the wake of the revolution, from Cuba and Russia and China. They had come to work, not to play. The lanterns that had always hung in the flame trees, lighting the terrace on Saturday nights, had not been lit in a year.

Ras drove to the edge of the runway where the tropical forest began, and turned onto the narrow dirt track that led to the Customs House. As he parked beside a car already there, his heartbeat quickened. It was Masaka's car.

The shade of the trees was deep, but it was a relief after the brightness of the sun. Inside the *banda* it was darker still. Two Africans in Army uniforms stood behind a table on which her luggage lay, a blue suitcase and one small metal trunk. Their black faces shone in the glow from a pressure lamp whose eerie light did not reach into the far corner to make distinguishable the figure standing there. But a familiar movement of hands washing one another told Ras who it was. Masaka. He took a deep breath. He needed to stay calm.

———◆———

June unlocked the blue suitcase, and Ras watched as the two men began to paw through the layers of her pastel-colored clothes, looking into pockets, peering into the toes of shoes. She stood silent. The glance with which she touched Ras was fleeting, but in the strange light her eyes looked to him like warm gold. Once before he had known someone with eyes of that color, a little girl in Dar es Salaam, but that was long ago.

When he was a boy, he had gone there several times by dhow with his father, sailing first to Zanzibar and on to Tanganyika. They always stayed two days. The first day's business was to sell the copra they had brought from their plantation. On the second day they went to visit a man named Benji, an old friend of his father. The packet of money from the sale of the copra bulged in his father's pocket, as the two men sat together in the shade of a mango tree, sipping tea. Their voices were hushed, their heads bent in serious talk. On the other side of the garden Ras played with Benji's youngest son, named after his father. They played with marbles, drank orange Fanta and stuffed themselves with sweet cakes and savories. Sometimes the small girl, who lived in the house on the other side of the garden wall, joined them. She was about the same age as they were, but her coloring was different. Her skin was fair and her hair was the color of dark honey.

Each time he and his father left Benji's house the packet of money his father had received from the sale of the copra was smaller than when they had come, but the expression on his father's face suggested that things had gone as he had wished. Ras was always tempted to ask what business his father had with Benji that took so much money, but he knew his father would tell him when he was ready. That time eventually came.

"Some day things will not be good on Zemu Island. You and your mother and your sisters will have to leave. Benji is sending money for me to a bank in Switzerland. It is in my name and in yours. Should something ever happen to me, you will know what to do." Ras remembered how frightened those words had made him, and how little he had understood their full meaning.

Now he understood, but what good did it do? Those careful plans his father had made in Dar es Salaam, under the mango tree, while the sound of marbles clinked in the warm still air, had died on the beach at Pwani Pwani.

June Hastings turned the key in the lock and lifted the lid of the metal trunk. The two Army men turned away from the blue suitcase and stared at the contents of the trunk. Their eyes grew round and then narrowed. They leaned closer and then straightened, muttering in Swahili to each other and to the man in the corner of the room.

Masaka left the shadowed security of the *banda* wall and moved to the table. The young woman looked up but made no sign that his presence was a surprise to her. Ras felt his breath catch. He wondered if she knew who Masaka was.

The lid of the trunk held a collection of tools: files, tweezers, knives, hooks, brushes, a small rake and shovel. In the bottom of the trunk was a roll of netting, a half dozen liter-sized bottles filled with liquids, and several dozen clear plastic boxes of assorted sizes, separated by layers of cotton wool.

She turned to Masaka and spoke in a quiet fluent Swahili that surprised them all. "I have come to Zemu Island to gather specimens of seashells. These are tools I need to find the shells and to clean them." Her hand passed lightly over the contents of the lid and then moved to the items in the lower section. "The large bottles contain cleaning solutions— bleach, alcohol, vinegar, formaldehyde. These plastic boxes are for the shells after they have been cleaned. Each will be wrapped in a piece of cotton, to protect it so it will not be crushed."

She had turned in the course of her explanation so that her glance touched each of them, the two Army men, Ras, and Masaka. Ras felt a rush of admiration for her intuition. She guessed that Masaka would not understand a lengthy stream of English, and would grow angry if his ignorance were revealed.

She withdrew a small blue-bound book from the trunk, with a colored photograph of shells on its cover. Ras read the title: *Shells of the East African Coast*. She opened to several pages. Each had some text accompanying the photograph of a shell.

"This book describes shells found along the coast of East Africa. I would like to do the same thing about shells in the waters of Zemu Island."

One of Masaka's large hands reached out for the book. He looked at its cover and turned to look inside. He snapped the book shut and thrust it at her. "You will make a book like this about Zemu Island?"

"I would like to."

"Where did you learn to speak Swahili?"

"In Kenya. I taught English in a school north of Nairobi."

Masaka's hands had begun moving one over the other, alerting Ras that when Masaka spoke again, it would not be with an even voice, but with the irrational anger. How would the American woman react?

"Kenya has declared Swahili its national language! Why do they still teach English?"

Something in Masaka's expression had evidently prepared her for the attack. She frowned thoughtfully. "English is just one of many subjects taught in Kenyan schools, like arithmetic and history and geography."

Masaka stared at her and then his face closed over. He motioned to the two men standing mute behind the table. They followed him out the door.

Ras looked after them, relieved, yet gripped by uncertainty. It was not like Masaka to give way so easily.

"Is it all right for us to leave now?"

Her voice took him from his thoughts. She had been calm through it all, but he saw the relief in her eyes. "Yes, of course. Let's go. It's time for lunch. The Norbets will be waiting."

"Let's hurry." She smiled mischievously. "I'm so hungry I could eat a horse!"

"You will insult the Norberts with that kind of talk!" They were both laughing. He felt strangely free. He had to remind himself that he was still a prisoner on Zemu Island. But the gloom of that reality did not weigh on him so heavily.

After he put her suitcase and trunk into the boot, and they were inside the car he turned to her. "Did you know who he was?"

"Masaka? Not right away. It was too dark at first. After the revolution there were lots of photographs of him in newspapers and magazines, standing on the veranda of the old Sultan's palace with the new flag draped over the railing. I was a bit worried when I realized who he was."

"You didn't show it."

"I felt it. It's the first time I've had a head of state come to the airport to check my luggage."

"I told you that you were someone special."

"You didn't say *that* special." She leaned back, resting her head against the seat. "Ras, are we going to be seeing a lot of Masaka?"

The road from the airport to the Manga Hotel was narrow. He was behind a donkey cart laden with bananas, moving slowly. It was easy to turn and look at her. She had called him Ras, not Rashid. There were some things about her that were indeed puzzling—the easy comfort he felt, the strange sense of the familiar.

"I cannot speak for Masaka. He is not a predictable man."

"Or the most stable. I heard that on the mainland, but I thought it might just be gossip, or wishful rumor. But it's not. That man is cracking up. It's nothing to rejoice about. Zemu Island could be in for a lot of trouble with someone like him in power."

"That is very dangerous talk," he said.

"And I should know better. You might turn the car around and head straight back to the airport. Please don't. I'd be so disappointed. I've wanted to come here for a long time. I never thought I'd get the chance. It's a long way from Boston."

"Is that where you come from?"

"It's my mother's home, where my parents met. We went there to live after my father died ten years ago. He was a doctor. We traveled a lot when I was small."

"You had been to Africa then, before teaching in Kenya?"

"Yes," was all she said.

The last turn brought them into the center of Zemu town with its narrow Arab alleys that twisted and cut back on each other. To a stranger they were a mysterious labyrinth, but to Ras they were home. As he drove, he could not help but see her intense interest. He drove slowly.

A sense of pride stirred in him when he pulled up in front of the hotel. The white walls appeared almost opalescent in the brilliance of the noonday sun, interrupted at intervals by bougainvillea tumbling in scarlet cascades. The stairway entrance led to a massive double door carved of ebony. Spikes of polished brass were embedded in the oiled wood and gleamed in the equatorial light.

She was silent beside him, her profile intent and still. When she turned, her eyes were shining. "It's magnificent. You were right, not even an elephant could batter that door down."

"An elephant?" He stared at her, chasing a distant memory.

There was a gleam of mischief in her eyes, as she held his gaze. "You don't remember? How absolutely horrid of you!"

He had heard those words before, a child's voice, on a day long ago, when the blue marble flew from his hand and hit the white one swirled with red, and split it in two. *How absolutely horrid of you!* She had stamped her foot and run off, disappearing behind the garden wall.

The great double door of the hotel swung open, and an eager young African in a starched white uniform and red fez came down the steps. "*Jambo, Memsab, Jambo, Bwana.* Welcome to Manga Hotel."

Winky Norbert was waiting for them at the desk inside. He shook Ras's hand and smiled at the young woman at his side. His wiry mustache twitched. "Good you didn't get here a while ago. Sheer bedlam with that tour. Couldn't please one of them, no less the lot. If they can't give Zemu more than four hours I'd rather they stayed away."

"That'll do with the complaining, Winky." Margaret Norbert appeared from the narrow doorway. "You know very well you loved every minute of it. You haven't been so chipper since the last tour. Twenty-nine lunches are twenty-nine lunches. Makes me feel we're still running a hotel."

She turned to June with a smile that deepened the wrinkles around her mouth and eyes. "Welcome to The Manga. I don't have to guess who you are—June Hastings, our first real guest in a long time!"

June smiled. "It's lovely to be here. I knew it would be. Is there any chance you've given me a room overlooking the courtyard?"

"Take your pick. You can have one next to the Cubans or across from the Russians. The Chinese prefer the hotel down the street."

Winky patted his wife's arm. "Stop twigging the girl, Maggie."

The woman smiled at her husband and June. "We've given you a room on the second floor. It looks right out onto a forest of bougainvillea. I think you'll like it."

Maggie Norbet was true to her word. The room had a small balcony, overlooking a courtyard filled with all the tropical flowers June had grown to love. If Ras had not been waiting she would have lingered, but they had many things to talk about.

They ate quickly, over the protests of Winky, who wanted them to linger. His wife came to the rescue. "These young folks are anxious to do some exploring before the sun sets. We'll see them back here at dinner time."

The road to Pwani Pwani wound along the edge of coconut plantations and through the ripening groves of clove trees. The humid air was heavy with the fragrance of an earlier crop, already harvested and drying in the sun. June had changed into a short blue dress that bared her suntanned arms. Under it was a bathing suit. She was leaning back against the seat, her hair blowing in the soft breeze.

"You've had time to remember," she said.

"I never forgot. But it was better to pretend. If I had allowed myself to think, I could not have let you come. This way it has happened without my really knowing."

"It's that bad here then?"

"Why have you come?"

"Benji sent me."

"Benji? Benji died three years ago."

"I'm talking about Benji, the son."

Ras thought of the small boy with the dark eyes with whom he had shot marbles and drank orange fanta. He was a man now and playing a different game. The last time Ras had been to Dar es Salaam young Benji had been at school in England.

"Where is he now?"

"I saw him in Nairobi, but he is leaving for New York soon."

Ras shook his head sadly. Nairobi. New York. And he could not even go to Zanzibar. "Benji sent you. Why?"

"To find out what is happening here. No one on the outside really knows. So little has leaked out. I wasn't honest with you when I said I hadn't heard of Yukano. When you asked, it wasn't the right time to talk about it. I have heard of him. Some people think he should be ruling Zemu Island, not Masaka. He would allow the British to return. He would seek American aid, not only from the Communists."

"What would Yukano do for the Indians? Give them back their lives?" He'd spoken so bitterly that he knew she could make no reply. He took a deep breath. "Benji has a plan?"

"It is not just Benji. There are others he is working with. But they need someone they can count on in Zemu. Benji wants to know if you will help."

"In what way? To make Yukano head of Zemu Island?"

"Your problem with Yukano is that, like Masaka, he is an African." She had spoken softly, with no edge to her voice, but even so, Ras was hit by the bite of her words, the accusation and the challenge.

She was no stranger to East African politics. She knew the deep animus that lay between African and Indian. Tumult and bloodshed had accompanied the fight for independence. The outcome had thrust the Africans into power. For those who had been born to the old way it would never be easy to accept black authority. But to fight it, or pretend that was not the way the tide ran, was to put your head in the sand.

Ras told all of this to her, and then shook his head. "I know the differences between men. Except for the color of their skin, there is no other likeness, common to Masaka and Yukano. Zemu will rot under the rule of a man like Masaka. With someone like Yukano there would at least be a chance to bring back life to this island, and hope." He fell silent, glad that she did not rush to speak, giving him some time to think.

"But how?" he asked after a while. "It would not be enough to get rid of Masaka. They would only put someone else like him in his place. And it would be dangerous, more dangerous than you can imagine. Masaka may be stupid, but those behind him are not. I do not think it was his own intelligence that made him suspicious of your visit. He was warned."

"But after today no one will be suspicious."

"What makes you say so?"

"Today we are going shell gathering. I am sure we will be watched. But after they see all the trouble we go to get a few shells, they will be convinced that shells are the sole reason for my visit."

"Then it is not a pretense?"

"It is, and it isn't. Marine biology is my field. I will write a book about the shells I find here. It will be published and copies will be sent to members of the government. If any doubt over the purpose of my visit still lingers, it will disappear when copies of the book arrive. In Yukano's argument with Masaka, urging that I be allowed to come to Zemu Island, he went a bit overboard when he talked of Olduvai Gorge. The whole world was impressed with what the Leakys found there. But Africans are also impressed by books, which offer praise, not criticism. My hope is that Masaka will be reassured, and so will the Cubans and the Russians. Eventually, tourists will be eager to visit Zemu Island, once again. Word will spread about this tropical paradise. Masaka and his henchmen will feel secure, and assume there is no one interested enough in the welfare of this small piece of land floating in the Indian Ocean to plan a counter revolution."

"Those are big thoughts," Ras said, "and dangerous. Such plans would take a long time, not just months, but years."

"Neither Benji, or the others working with him, have any illusions that it will be easy. Yes, there will be months of careful planning, but they cannot do it without help from someone here on the island. In your position as director of tourism you are permitted to receive and send letters, a privilege others on Zemu are denied."

"Every letter I write or receive is scrutinized."

She nodded. "I know. We would use a code."

He listened to her unfold a plan that could not work without him. It was a mad plan that had greater chance of failure than of success, but it offered hope. Until she had come he'd had no hope, no hope at all.

Driving slowly, he continued along the narrow road, looking for a sandy track that branched off to the left in the direction of the sea, leading to Pwani Pwani beach. It would be grown over now, perhaps not passable by car. "There it is," he exclaimed, pointing to a gnarled dead tree that had always been their sign post. He inched the car forward. Branches arched over the once open path, strung with thorny vines and moss.

"Close your window so you don't get scratched," he said and rolled up his own.

The perfume of ripening guavas drifted into the car and brought with it the memory of the last day he had been here with his family. His mother and his father, along with his sisters and the girl he had hoped to marry, had been walking along the beach. He had stayed behind, picking guavas, when the first shot came. Others followed, bullets skipping across the sand. Like dolls, his mother and his sisters had fallen, brilliant piles of crumpled saris on the sand. His father spun and fell, and died beside them.

Ras lay, flattened in the underbrush of vines, the guavas he had picked squashed and wet and oozing against his chest, warm like the blood in which his father lay. Then pain exploded in his leg. He fought the blackness threatening to engulf him, wanting to remember at least one face among the bearded strangers, who had fired the guns and killed every member of his family. Masaka.

When he stopped the car, his hands were clenched around the steering wheel. He took a deep breath and leaned forward to stare through the windscreen. Flashes of water glimmered through a denser tangle of green. The beach was not far off.

He opened the car door and reached under the seat for the *panga* he kept there. The broad blade sliced through the ropy lengths of vines as if they were bits of string. Sap oozed and trickled over his hands and arms.

When the path was clear, his arms fell to his sides, the point of the *panga* stuck in the sand beside his foot. His chest heaving, he turned and saw her standing by the car, watching him, her eyes full of questions.

"My family always came here to Pwani Pwani. It was our special place. They all died here that first day of the revolution. I was picking guavas. They were walking along the sand. I have not been back, not until today." His dark eyes looked deep into hers. "I'm glad you are with me. It is time. I am ready."

She smiled gently and held out her hand. "Let's go then. There's lots to do."

They each took a handle of the metal trunk and carried it onto the beach where they placed it in the shade of a palm tree. He left her to open it while he returned to the car for the two buckets she had borrowed from the Norberts.

Along the way he glanced on both sides into the dense tropical growth for a sign of someone hiding there. They would be watched, but they would never know by whom or by how many. Once before, the forest had camouflaged the presence of the enemy.

He started back toward the beach with the buckets. He looked for the tree where he had left her with the trunk. She wasn't there. His heart stopped. Then her voice floated toward him, and he spied her arm raised in the water, waving to him, splashing. He tore off his clothes and raced into the shallow waves. They swam for a while, and then returned to the beach. She looked for shells along the water line.

"Here's a beauty," she said. "Look at it." She held a brown and white spiraled shell in the palm of her hand.

"There must be hundreds of them just like that all over the beach," Ras said.

"Most of them are chipped or cracked. The shells I take back must be perfect. This is a Speckled Turret Shell, otherwise known as *Terebra oculata*. It seems unblemished."

"What about this one?" Ras extended his hand.

She reached for it without looking, and then glanced at her palm. "You don't take me seriously at all!" He could almost see her foot stamp.

"Oh, but I do." He tossed the small stone away and gave her a handful of shells he had collected.

"These look like good possibilities. I'll check them out later. Now I want to set some traps in the rocks close to shore. Some shells are nocturnal. It won't take long. Then we can swim until the sun goes down, and come back tomorrow."

She cut squares from the roll of netting that had been in the trunk, and with thin wire gathered them into makeshift baskets. A small piece of meat from the Norberts' kitchen served as bait. They laid the traps together, anchoring them with small stones. As they worked, their heads were close, almost touching. She spoke softly. "Someone is keeping an eye on us. We could be setting mines. Someday we will."

She looked up and her eyes held his for a moment, the expression in them intent and serious. Then in the next instant she was laughing and running into the water.

The sun was low in the sky, a fiery orange ball that lit the surface of the turquoise sea with ribbons of orange and gold. Between the breaking waves the water flowed like the soft folds of an iridescent sari. Ras raced after her and dove into the water, feeling the salt sting his eyes, blurring the memory of a girl he had loved, who on the last day of her life, had worn a sari of green, threaded with bronze and gold.

He swam alongside the American woman he had known as a child. "Can you swim to those rocks? At the last one there is a deep pool and a cavern. If the light is right it is a wonderful sight."

Drops of water clinging to her eyelashes sparkled and flew away when she nodded and began an easy stroke beside him.

It was a long time since he had made the dive and he wanted to be certain the passage was still clear, certain no rock had dislodged itself. He warned her to let him lead the way. Her hand was in his as they swam underwater to an archway of rock leading under a ledge in the rock ceiling.

It was the purple coral he had wanted her to see, the sea anemones and the swaying ferns whose undulations were said to have teased love-starved sailors into thinking they were mermaids. It was a perfect time, the sun and the tide were right. There was a space where they could rise to the surface and rest before they dove again.

"I've never seen purple coral before," she said.

"It is purple only in the water. It turns brown when it hits the air."

He was ready to dive again, anxious to show her more.

"Wait, Ras. The sun will set soon. This is a good place to talk. No one can hear us, no one can see. There are other things you must know, about Yukano and the money that is yours in Switzerland, and the code. It's important that you know the code now. Should anything happen to me, then you could still get in touch with Benji."

"Nothing will happen to you."

"I could drown."

He shook his head. "You swim too well." He smiled to himself, measuring the differences between them. He wanted to show her the mysteries of an underwater grotto, he had explored as a child, and she wanted to plan a revolution.

She looked at him, her eyes doubtful. He nodded. She needed him. Benji needed him. He would be their tool, as Masaka had been the tool of the foreigners. Was there a difference? Would the people of Zemu Island feel any more loyalty to the man who counter revolutionaries would put in the Sultan's palace than they did to Masaka? How many people would die?

Despite his questions he knew he would do what Benji asked. Not because he wanted revenge, or because the success of the counter revolution would make him free, but because it gave him hope. And without hope no man can live and stay whole.

She spoke quickly then, but clearly, and explained the code to him. It was fairly simple, but with enough complexity that it could not be broken easily.

He took her hand for a moment, wishing he could explain what her coming had meant to him. But even if he were able to say it, he was afraid she would think him sentimental and not ready for the task that lay ahead.

They swam toward the shore in the sun's last golden path. In minutes night would fall. The sun set quickly on the equator.

They left the water. The evening air had cooled. She began to run, her wet hair streaming behind her. Playfully, she called over her shoulder, "Catch me if you can!"

She was headed to the forest's edge, where they had left the trunk, where dark shadows moved among the guava trees. Ras saw the bearded men, camouflaged to look like trees, waiting, ready to fire.

He stood as still as stone, his feet sinking deeper and deeper into the wet sand. His voice was trapped in his throat, unable to shout a warning. He waited for the first shot to fire, and closed his eyes, so he would not see her body spin and crumple to the sand.

"Ras," he heard her calling him. "What's keeping you?" She beckoned him toward her with a wave.

He shook his head against the nightmare of his memory and ran toward her across the sand.

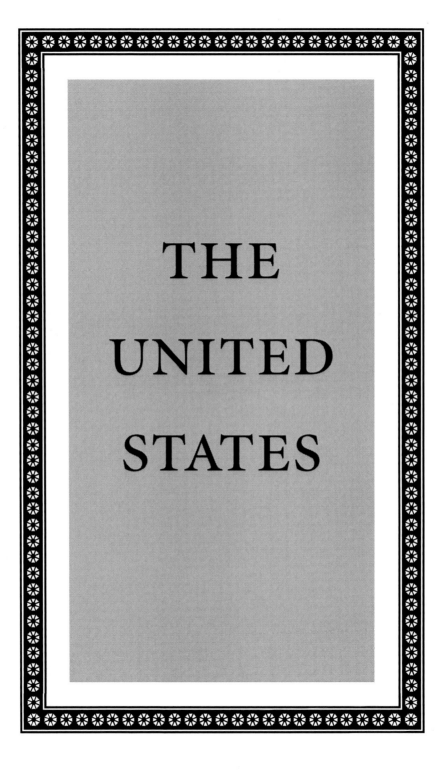

THE
UNITED
STATES

Recipe Secrets

*A*fter the real estate agent left, Larry stood in the front doorway of the house where he and Evelyn had lived for most of their marriage and contemplated the quiet tree-lined street. His glance drifted from house to house, each on an over-sized lot, beautifully landscaped, typical of suburban Philadelphia.

"I'm not sure I even want to sell," he told the woman when she first arrived. "It's only a possibility."

An accommodating smile had multiplied the wrinkles of her grandmotherly face, framed in wisps of gray hair. "I understand. Big decisions need to be taken in stages. It's hard to leave a house you've lived in for so long."

"Twenty-one years," he said with something of a sigh and hoped it didn't reach her like a pitch for sympathy.

She appeared not to notice. "This is a marvelous house and a lovely neighborhood. When you decide, you'll have no trouble selling. Could we start with the kitchen? For me that's the heart of a house."

He'd wondered if it had been that for Evelyn. No question, it had been important to her, but the heart? He wasn't all that sure. He led the way and stood aside, as Mrs. Brody slowly took in the last of his wife's redesigns. His reward was the woman's small gasp. Her gaze traveled over the black and white cabinets, marble counters, and the broad sweeping length of a center island. Her eyes widened when she entered the breakfast room where floor-to-ceiling windows gave view to a terraced garden, banked with specimen evergreens and flowers that changed with each season. It was the middle of June. Mounds of white peonies alternated with clumps of salmon-colored poppies.

"It's magnificent," she said.

Larry nodded, thinking, so were the earlier kitchens, and the other gardens. Evelyn had never been satisfied.

"The Wilsons told me your wife was a professional. I can see how important this space was to her."

It was Madge Wilson who had given him Mrs. Brody's name. "She's not pushy, and you can learn a lot from her," Madge had said, and so he had made the call.

"Phil Wilson and I play golf together. Evelyn and Madge were best friends."

"I understand your wife was a food and flower stylist. I'm not sure I know what that is."

"I'm not the best to explain it. Evelyn was a terrific cook and liked to fiddle with flowers. At some point she turned a hobby into a profession. She prepared food and flowers for magazine ads and TV commercials. She did things like paint a roast turkey with shellac to keep it looking shiny and crisp. Madge can tell you more."

They toured the rest of the two-story house at an efficient pace, and in less than an hour were seated in the living room going over a few details. "Have you thought where you might move?" Mrs. Brody asked.

"Something much smaller. Maybe one of the townhouses on the golf course. But I need more time. I don't know where to begin with all of this." He waved an arm, embracing the sprawling house and its contents.

"An inventory of each room will help. Decide what you can't part with, and then what you hate." She gave a sharp little laugh. "I won't bore you with how I know about that, except that my late husband collected bird cages. I got rid of every last one."

Larry felt himself grinning, not at what a house full of bird cages must have been like, but the prospective fate of the big painting in Evelyn's study, by that long-haired artist who called himself Aztek.

"When you're ready," Mrs. Brody went on, "I can recommend people who run estate sales. You give them a list of what stays and what goes. They find buyers for the bigger things. The rest they tag and sell. You don't even have to be around, in fact it's better if you're not."

At the front door, she smiled. "It helps to start by throwing things out. The kitchen is a good place to get the feel for that—stale cereals and cookies, all those baking ingredients your wife kept on hand."

After she had gone, Larry found himself staring at the enormous painting that hung on the wall in Evelyn's study. It was one of the pieces from Aztek's first show, his gift to Evelyn for doing the reception for the exhibition. Larry wondered if his prejudice against Aztek's long hair and phony name had gotten in the way of fair judgment. He shook his head. It was no more to his taste now than it had ever been. He remembered telling Evelyn she'd been short-changed, her cocktail tidbits and flower arrangements had stolen the show. Aztek's paintings were just a joke. It had been a nasty remark. He regretted it.

Fury had leapt in his wife's gray eyes. "You don't know a thing about art. Aztek is going to be big."

She turned out to be right. A gallery owner from Manhattan had come to the show and was smitten with what she saw. She took some paintings back to SoHo, where they sold at good prices. They were all from Aztek's egg period—large canvasses, dominated by large ovals, with smaller ovals inside.

Larry eyed the big purple and yellow oval on the wall and moved closer to examine the crowded illustrations framed in other eggs. The worlds of activity surprised him—a picnic in the woods, a volley ball game, an outdoor cafe, a ballet class. In each of the scenes Aztek had painted himself as the dominant figure—lean, tall, darker-skinned than he really was, his hair in a long plait down his bare back.

A ripple of discomfort crept over Larry as he looked from one scene to the other, and realized that the figures were caricatures of people he knew. It was a shock to find himself at the picnic, lying on his back, asleep. Well, not everything about him was asleep. Jesus! He was naked. So what? So was everyone else, just not so prominently.

It was a bigger jolt when he found Evelyn, alongside the ballet bar with her leg raised high. He stared in stunned disbelief at the tiny strawberry mark in the crease of her inner thigh. Aztek had painted it as a rose, which is exactly what it looked like in real life, up close.

Like warm oil, a memory slid over him, transporting him to a hotel room overlooking the Gulf of Mexico. The sun poured in through wide-slatted plantation blinds and the shadows of palm trees traced intricate patterns on the walls, but he hardly noticed. He was too absorbed in stroking the satiny skin of the woman who lay at his side. He leaned to kiss the softness of her inner thigh, and saw the rose for the first time.

He stood in the shadow of Aztek's canvas, trapped in the meaning of what was there. There was only one way Aztek could have known about that tiny mark.

When the phone on Evelyn's desk rang, it was only after the third ring that he managed a croaking hello.

"Larry?" He recognized Madge's hesitant voice. "Did I wake you? It's Madge."

He shook his head, fumbling for a sensible response. "Mrs. Brody just left. She's given me a lot to think about."

"Good things, I hope. I just called to remind you about tomorrow, Sunday night supper at our house. No need to wear a tie. It'll be just the three of us this time." She laughed goodnaturedly. She was referring to the cocktail party she and Phil had given two weeks ago. He had been less than attentive to the two single women invited for his benefit. They were attractive enough, but he'd felt no spark. That was how it had been since Evelyn died. It was as though he'd lost interest in the game.

He brought up the issue when he went to his doctor about a pain in his shoulder the next week. After dealing with the shoulder and writing out a prescription for tendinitis, Hubbard settled back in his chair.

"So, your libido is a bit low and you're a little depressed. It isn't at all surprising. It's not even a year, since your wife died."

"Five months," Larry said, and recalled the day.

He'd come back from a week-long business trip and spent the day at his office, catching up. Around lunch-time he left a message on Evelyn's machine, saying he'd be home between six and seven. He suggested dinner out. Maybe Phil and Madge were free.

He hadn't expected to hear from her. She would either act on his suggestion or choose an alternative. If she had something of her own to do, he'd find a note.

It was six-thirty when he turned into the driveway and hit the garage door opener, already savoring the idea of the Scotch he'd pour himself as he turned on the news. But the thought evaporated as his attention swerved to take in the length of green garden hose trailing alongside Evelyn's car. One end was taped securely into the exhaust pipe, the other threaded through the driver's window.

———•———

"You came to see me after the funeral," he heard the internist say. Larry saw him, eyeing him over the rims of his half glasses. "You asked me if your wife had been ill."

Larry nodded. "I remember. You said she was in good health. I guess I was looking for a reason. According to the police, most suicides leave a note. Evelyn didn't."

Hubbard came from around his desk and Larry knew his time was up; there were other patients waiting. He put his arm around Larry's shoulder. "You'll be okay. It just takes a while. Any death is hard. This is one of the hardest. Keep in touch. I'm here if you need me."

———•———

At some point in his wanderings though the house, Larry decided he was hungry. It was past one o'clock. A beer and a corned beef sandwich at the Red Dog would be just the thing, with a stop at the liquor store for some empty boxes. After lunch he'd start on the kitchen cupboards.

When he reached the mini mall, a flower sale was taking up the center space and he had to park off to the side. All the flats and pots of summer blooms reminded him of Evelyn's talent with flowers. It was amazing what she could do with a few twisted branches and a couple of blooms. Some arrangements were much more elaborate, like the ones she had made for Aztek's shows—driftwood and rocks, that weren't really rocks, but pottery shaped in that form, hollow and lighter in weight. Displayed on their own pedestals, her arrangements were stunning works of art. One time he asked her where she got her ideas.

"It has to do with balance and form," she said without warmth or elaboration, and he knew he had been dismissed.

He had thought a lot about their marriage since her death. He wondered how they had gotten into living such parallel lives, hardly intersecting at all. From the beginning his job with the pharmaceutical firm had meant long days, spilling over into weekends. Evelyn had accommodated, seeming to find ways to keep herself entertained and occupied. Even when his travel increased, she didn't seem to mind.

He got the hang of having a good time on the road. Taking his golf clubs along had opened up things. There was that game, and the other— women. Most of them had been married, bored, looking for some fun. There was hardly a city in his territory where he hadn't found someone to fool around with. Things changed after he met Hadley. He lost interest in the others, and began thinking of spending his whole life with her, but it had never come to that.

What a sport she had been, always on time, at the Providence airport waiting for him, in that sharp little red Mustang she drove with the top down when the weather was right, looking like she'd just jumped out of the shower and had tossed her hair dry. Off they'd go, headed for one of the fancy New England inns she had on her list. The syndicated travel column she wrote under a pseudonym, gave her a ready excuse to take off, so that her husband, who was with a brokerage firm and worked long hours, never questioned her being away.

It lasted almost two years, and then suddenly it was over. No explanation. One day he called and heard a recording saying the number had been disconnected, no forwarding number.

He had toyed with the idea of driving by her house and just ringing the bell, or hiring someone to do the same thing, and say they were making a survey. But then what? He dropped both ideas. He had no interest in messing up her life. But the way it ended still had him wondering. It didn't fit with Hadley's open style.

———◆———

The next Sunday morning he tackled the kitchen cupboards. He tossed out stale cookies, crackers, cereal and whatever else looked old and tired.

He filled the boxes he had gotten at the mini mall with things the food bank could use, and set aside bars of baking chocolate and cans of nuts to give to Madge. She was a good cook, but no match for Evelyn, especially when it came to pies. No one made a pie like Evelyn. Apple, peach, cherry, the fruit almost didn't matter. It was the warm, flaky, buttery crust that melted in your mouth and made you ask for more.

Thinking about it brought on a painful recollection of the day he and Phil had finished a golf game and were sitting over beers. It was probably three years ago.

"Say Larry, Madge's birthday is next week. I'd like to give her something special. It's something she really wants, and can't buy. What would it take for Evelyn to give me her pie recipe?"

Larry remembered his stunned surprise. "What do you mean, what would it take? Madge should just ask her."

Phil's face reddened. "She did. Evelyn refused. She says it's a family secret."

Larry guessed he must have laughed, a shaky cover for his embarrassment. "I don't understand those kinds of secrets," he said awkwardly.

He still wondered how Evelyn could have done that to Madge. They were best friends.

He finished sorting through the food cupboards and turned to the closet next to the refrigerator. It was lined with shelves, crowded with cookbooks. On the middle shelf, right out in front, was a bright yellow recipe box, the kind that fit 3x5 index cards. The pie recipe still on his mind, he wondered if this was Evelyn's secret file. He reached for it eagerly and took it to the breakfast room and sat down. In the brighter light he saw the white card taped to the lid. Evelyn's handwriting leapt up at him. *For Larry only —Destroy on my death. Evelyn*

After he got over the initial shock of what he'd just read, he focused on the date she had written below her name. It was the day she died. He felt as though he had been punched, and held on to the edge of the table to steady himself.

He closed his eyes, struggling to understand. She'd left him no note of farewell, no explanation for why she had taken her life, yet she left him instructions about the disposition of her recipes. Why the Hell hadn't she destroyed them herself!

Angrily, he opened the file. He would start with A. What would he find—Apple Pie, Apple Strudel, Apple Tart? And behind B—Brownies? And when he finally got to P? Would he find Pie Crust, a family secret ?

He looked at the first card and got a second jolt. A hot current of disbelief ran though him, jangling every nerve. His hands were trembling as he turned to the second card and then the third. His heart was doing strange flips as he moved through the alphabet, through the eastern seaboard cities where he had traveled over the years.

ALBANY—Cheryl

BOSTON—Judy

CHARLESTON—Darlene

His head was throbbing and his mouth was dry when came to P.

PROVIDENCE—Hadley.

He brought his hands up to his face and covered his eyes, but there was no blotting out what he had seen. The cities were in capital letters, the women's names in lower case, and their addresses, all written in Evelyn's careful, slanted script. She had known about them all.

For a long time he sat like a child hiding behind his hands. He felt publicly disrobed.

He wouldn't have cared about all the others, but Hadley had been different. Discreet was the word they had used. They had talked it over and agreed he would never call her from his office or from home. He always called from a pay phone and never with a credit card. All hotel and restaurant bills he paid for in cash.

Their phone arrangement was simple, but secure. When she answered, he would say, "Mrs. Noble?" If she laughed he would know the coast was clear. Otherwise, he would hang up and call at another time.

His hands dropped from his face and he stared out into the garden. Shifting clouds had obscured the sun, bringing on a premature darkness that turned the windows into mirrors. At every angle, he faced the reflected image of his sagging shoulders.

He had no idea how many women there had been before Hadley. A few were just one-night-stands, others went on for a while. He thought of the energy it had taken to court and persuade, to set things up, cover his tracks, and have everything go off without a hitch. All that, and Evelyn had known. How had she found out about Hadley?

A clock in the living room chimed. In an hour he was due at the Wilsons. If only he could call them and say something important had come up, or that he wasn't feeling well, but he couldn't do that to them, nor would they buy it. It would only bring on questions that would be impossible to answer.

He began to wonder just how much Madge knew. He was aware that women shared confidences in the way men did not. Had Evelyn talked about his out-of-town activities? What about Evelyn's affair with Aztek? He guessed Madge must have known.

How quickly he had accepted the affair as fact. Well, it was pretty plain. And it explained a lot—Evelyn's rage when he'd put down Aztek's art, the flower arrangements she designed for all his shows. Had she been in love with him, or had it just been a frolic? How long had it gone on?

———◆———

He found the Wilsons where he expected they would be on a warm summer evening, settled into chairs on the patio beside their rambling stone house. Phil served drinks and Madge brought out a plate of spiced shrimp. Whenever he got together with them, which was often, Madge made a point of mentioning Evelyn, cautiously and only in passing. Sometimes he wondered whose grief she was tending, his or her own.

He had to be careful tonight. There was a lot on his mind and he wasn't sure just how much he wanted to say, if anything at all.

As she passed him the shrimp, Madge asked him about Mrs. Brody.

"She was terrific," he answered honestly, seizing the neutral topic. "Helpful, like you said. She got me started on cleaning out. She suggested I hire an estate sales agent when I'm ready."

They discussed that for awhile and then drifted on to other things—the proposed widening of a road alongside the library, the golf tournament scheduled for the fall. Just as darkness began to fall they moved inside to the screened porch where Madge had dinner ready—poached salmon with a dill sauce, potato salad and fresh asparagus. They drank a lot of wine.

"I've a surprise for you two," she said when she rose to clear the table. "For dessert, I've made one of Evelyn's pies."

Larry had been playing with the stem of his wine glass, which Phil had just refilled, and almost tipped it over. "You have Evelyn's pie recipe?" Disbelief roughened his voice.

"I'd given up trying to pry it out of her," Marge answered with a half-hearted smile. Then just last year, she just gave it to me, but she made me swear I wouldn't tell."

Larry, too, forced a smile, but for a different reason. What he had found in the yellow file, which had held the promise of Evelyn's recipes, had been too bruising to leave him with any interest in Evelyn's recipe secrets. Yet, he was glad Madge had the pie recipe. She'd wanted it for so long. Surprisingly, it made him feel a little better about Evelyn. Even so, there was a knot in his stomach when Madge appeared with the pie.

It was lightly dusted with powdered sugar, attractively centered on a fluted glass plate. He could tell from the fragrance that drifted toward him, it was warm, the way Evelyn had always served it. Madge cut generous slices for each of them, and then waited expectantly. Larry took the first forkful and felt the mingling of fruit and flaky crust spread across his tongue and slide smoothly down his throat. "Wonderful," he exclaimed with a prolonged, exaggerated sigh.

Madge laughed, a happy, affectionate trill. "Evelyn was such an artist when it came to food, I was just flabbergasted when she told me the trick."

Slowly, Larry lowered his fork. "What do you mean?"

A look of surprise arched Madge's brow. "You weren't in on Evelyn's secret?"

He shrugged, faking an indifference he didn't feel. Trick. The word bothered him. A lot of things were bothering him. "I always enjoyed the food Evelyn prepared, but I can't say I was interested in her recipes."

"It's a store-bought pie, right off the supermarket shelf. Evelyn's trick was to spread a quarter of a pound of sweet butter on the top and bake it for twenty minutes. I'd always thought it was some complicated recipe. Everyone did. She said it was a family secret."

"Jesus," he said, too embarrassed to say anything else.

Madge quickly poured coffee, and Phil, gifted in bridging awkward moments, returned to the real estate agent's suggestion. "An estate sale is the right idea, Larry. You've got too much stuff in that house to handle alone."

"I'm sure that's what Mrs. Brody thought, though she was too polite to say. She told me her husband collected bird cages. She got rid of them after he was gone." He laughed. "You know what that made me think of? That big egg painting of Aztek's—the one he gave Evelyn. I've always hated it."

The words were out before he had time to think about where the subject might lead, but again Phil came to his rescue, or so it seemed.

"I'd be careful with how you dispose of that," he said. "I suggest you go to Sotheby's or Christie's. An Aztek brings a hefty price these days."

"Oh, come on, Phil. He may be a better artist than I ever gave him credit for, but you make it sound like he's up in the stratosphere."

"Phil's right," Madge said softly. "With so many of his paintings destroyed in that fire, the few left have just skyrocketed."

Larry frowned. "What fire?"

Beside him he heard Madge's quick breath. Across the table Phil cleared his throat. Larry looked from one to the other, waiting. It was Phil who spoke.

"Aztek was having a big show in New York, part retrospective, part new stuff. Some of his earlier paintings were on loan. He and the gallery owner were working late the night before the opening. There was an explosion and a fire."

Larry's frown deepened. How come he didn't know about this? "Was a lot destroyed?"

"Everything," Madge said softly.

Larry saw her press her lips together to keep them from trembling. He wasn't sure what to say. He was having trouble digesting it all. "Aztek must be pretty busted up, losing everything he'd worked on for so long." He paused, startled that he was actually feeling sorry for a guy who had slept with his wife and then bragged about it by painting her nude.

"It wasn't just the paintings that were lost," Phil said, haltingly. "It was a pretty brutal fire. Aztek and the gallery owner were killed."

"Jesus! When did this happen? How come I didn't know?"

"You had enough on your mind," Phil said. "It was the same day Evelyn died."

He drove home slowly, mindful that he'd had too much to drink. He normally didn't go for brandy, but after the second bombshell of the evening, he let Phil pour him a hefty snifter.

He had never liked Aztek, and since this morning, he had good reason to like him less. But his death bothered him. Larry kept seeing the image of the artist's lean naked form dominating each of the scenes in the painting in Evelyn's room, suddenly consumed by flames. He shuddered and gripped the steering wheel to steady himself, but realized there was something else that had him spooked. It was the awful coincidence of the fire happening on the same day Evelyn had taken her life.

As soon as he got home he went straight to the kitchen and poured himself a glass of ice water. He drank it slowly as though it was some potent medicine with the power to settle his nerves. Over the rim of the glass he saw the yellow recipe box on the table where he left it. It seemed to blink at him.

After Providence and Hadley's name he hadn't gone any further. What did it matter who Evelyn had known about? Still, he sat down and went to the end of the file. There were a few more white cards, filled out in exactly the same way. The women's names rang some distant bell, but their faces were a blur. There was a blue card at the very end.

Maria Fernandez—New York City
Spring Street
West 57th Street

———◆———

He stared at the name and the two addresses, and then said the name out loud. Maria Fernandez. It had a familiar ring, the way the name of an actress or a singer might have, but he was sure he had never slept with a woman by that name. Yet Evelyn had included it in the file with all the others, set it apart, out of alphabetical order, on a different colored card. That meant something. But what?

In the middle of the night he woke and lay wondering if Maria Fernandez could be the name of a detective Evelyn had hired. How else could she have found out about Hadley?

When morning came he stood under a hot shower and made his decision. He would take time off from work and get the house ready. The sooner he could sell it and move out the better.

He'd just finished a quick breakfast when Phil called to set up a golf game the next week end.

"It's tempting, but I've made up my mind about the house. I'm going to sell. I've got a lot to do."

"That's great. Call me if you need any help."

"I will. By the way, thanks for dinner last night, and thank Madge for me."

"You can do that yourself. She should be at your place in about an hour. She's on her way to buy some geraniums. You left your jacket here. She'll leave it by the front door, if you're out."

"I'll be here," he said, and then suddenly, took a chance. "Say, Phil, you know anyone named Maria Fernandez?"

Even over the phone, he sensed Phil's surprise. "Well, I can't say I knew her. I met her a couple of times ...."

"Who is she?"

"She had a gallery in SoHo, the one that gave Aztek his big break. Later she opened a place in midtown, on 57th Street." Larry heard Phil take a quick breath before he rushed to finish. "She was with Aztek the night of the fire. It was her gallery that burned. She died, too."

He was in the garage with the door open, waiting for Madge, and sorting through garden tools when she pulled into the driveway.

"Not only do I get a great dinner, now it's special delivery," he said and opened her car door, eager not to have her hurry off.

"It was on my way," she said, handing him the jacket.

"How can I thank you? Not just for dinner last night, but for everything else you and Phil have done." He paused, afraid he couldn't go on. He wasn't sure he could do it, not to Madge. He would be careful and not push too hard. Above all, he didn't want to hurt her. No, that wasn't true. There were things he needed to know.

Her expression showed concern, as she stood waiting for him to go on.

"You've both been so great through all of this. I had no idea all of what you had been dealing with. It couldn't have been easy."

She nodded. "I won't pretend. It wasn't."

"We'd been married twenty years, but there was so much about Evelyn I didn't know. I was in her study just a little while ago. There are albums with photographs of food she prepared for events I never knew about, photographs of flower arrangements, and the lists of prizes she won ..." His voice trailed off. There was a lot more that he had seen that had set him back on his heels, but he'd said enough.

A look of sadness moved across her face. "What can I say, Larry? It wasn't all your fault. She was my best friend, but Evelyn had a side to her I didn't understand. I never understood the two of you. You were never around, and when you were you didn't seem to register anything she was doing. And she didn't seem to care." She stopped abruptly and shook her head. "I'm talking too much."

"No, you're not. You knew us both. You were Evelyn's closest friend."

Madge lowered her eyes, not quickly, but in a way that said she wanted time. When she looked up, her expression was uncertain.

"Evelyn was into so many things. Years ago she and I talked about starting a business together—a book store, a gift shop. They were such simple ideas. They didn't work out, but we stayed friends. It took her a while, but eventually she found her niche."

"What was that?"

"Oh, Larry! There was a little laugh and a note of exasperation in Madge's voice. "She was a food and flower stylist. You knew that."

"Is that what she called herself?"

"That's what the advertising industry called her. It's a profession. She was good at it. She developed a lot tricks."

There was that word again.

"Sure, I knew the basics of what she did. Some of it didn't register, as you said. Maybe a lot of things didn't, like her affair with Aztek."

Madge's chin lifted and she sent him a level gaze. "So you knew. Evelyn thought you didn't."

Evelyn had been right, he hadn't known, not until yesterday.

"When did Maria Fernandez enter the picture?" He asked the question slowly, not liking himself one bit. It was the ambush question he had planned. It paid off. The guarded expression that came to Madge's face told him there was more to Maria Fernandez than he had figured out.

"Madge, this is hard for me, but I think it's worse for you. You were Evelyn's friend. I'm sure she told you things you'd rather not have known. She killed herself and left no explanation. I suppose I can learn to live with that, if I have to, but it isn't easy."

Her mouth puckered and tears flooded her eyes. She took a deep breath and reached for Larry's arm and motioned toward the gate at the side of the house. It led to the garden in back.

They settled into facing chairs. Although her composure had returned, her tears freshened as she looked around, at the graceful terracing of evergreens and early summer flowers. "It's so beautiful here. Evelyn had a talent for creating beauty, but that was only one side of her. Oh, Larry, that's the side I want to remember, but it's so hard."

He waited, saying nothing, deciding it was best to give her time.

"You asked me about Maria Fernandez."

He nodded. "I'm just guessing, but I assume she and Aztek became involved with one another. Was Evelyn upset over that?"

"If it had only been that simple," Madge said in a voice that was hardly more than a whisper. A turmoil of emotions flickered in her eyes. "Evelyn knew Maria long before Aztek came on the scene. Maria was part of the New York set Evelyn got into, artsy people. It drew her like a magnet. She was there all the time. She and Maria . . . well, they developed a relationship."

"A relationship?"

"Larry, I'm not good at this. I never understood what was between Evelyn and Maria. I think Evelyn was experimenting with things she didn't understand."

He tipped back his head and stared up at the sky. I don't believe it. I don't believe it. But he did. Some of the photographs he had found in Evelyn's study had prepared him.

"How did you put up with all of this?"

"I didn't know about Maria, not for a long time. It came later, after Evelyn told me that she and Aztek were having an affair. I thought he was weird, and I told her, but she wasn't interested in hearing any of that. At some point, Evelyn began to suspect that Maria and Aztek were spending time together, and not including her. They weren't a threesome anymore. When Evelyn found out they had moved in together, she went wild. I remember the day they told her they were in love. They were going to be married right after Aztek's show. Evelyn had been jilted by both of them."

Madge's eyes were dry, but there was a constant tremor in her voice. "Evelyn rallied and put up a crazy front, pretending everything was just fine, but I knew it wasn't. She set about making the most elaborate flower arrangements for Aztek's show, and for the wedding. It was to be in the gallery, right after the opening." Her voice broke, and her hand flew to her mouth, stifling a cry. "Oh, Larry, I should have known. I should have done something to stop her."

Larry's heart froze.

"I should have talked to her," Madge went on in a frenzied rush. "I tried, but you know how she could be. She wouldn't listen. I suggested that she see a therapist. I even gave her some names. But it was no use." Tears were running down her cheeks, her hands were clenched in her lap. She took a deep breath and wiped her eyes. "Maybe I should have told you."

Oh, yeah, he thought to himself, I would have been a big help. "Does Phil know all of this?"

She nodded, "Most of it. He says we should try to forget it. There's nothing we can do about it now. I think he's right. I'm glad you know. It will be easier when we get together now. There was always so much Phil and I had to avoid."

He couldn't remember what he did after Madge left, but later in the day he saw that there were more bags and boxes in the garage. The simple-minded task of cleaning out allowed him to keep thinking, going over all the things he had learned in the last twenty-four hours, but there was a missing piece. Whatever it was eluded him, fluttering in some corner of his brain, like a tease. It made him wonder if he already knew, but was afraid to confront it. When it finally came, he rejected it as the product of his mind gone haywire. It was crazy to think that Evelyn had done anything to orchestrate the deaths of Aztek and Maria, but the idea, once admitted to his consciousness, wouldn't leave. The coincidence of Evelyn's death on the same day was too much to accept as chance. His suspicion swelled and grew into an even darker horror—that Evelyn might also have done harm to Hadley.

He decided to start with Hadley. There were inquiries he would have to make, discreetly, so that if his suspicions had no basis, there would be no repercussions. He drew a line down the middle of a yellow pad. On one side he wrote New York and on the other Providence. He listed all he'd learned from the Wilsons about the gallery fire, but when he turned to Providence his knowledge was a blank. Something had happened there that was out of the ordinary. He was sure of that. It seemed the only explanation for Hadley's abrupt silence, her inexplicable departure from his life, without warning, and the suddenly disconnected phone.

If his most extreme fears were true, any inquiry, to any authority would send up an alarm, invigorating an investigation that had dried up or been put on hold, waiting for a break. An alert that would connect an incident in Providence to the fatal fire in New York would bring the FBI to his front door. His life would be torn apart.

He was losing courage.

Maybe he should heed what Phil had said to Madge. "Try to forget it. There's nothing we can do about it now."

He began to wonder why the Wilsons had kept the fire a secret from him all these months. By itself it would have been a piece of news. With-holding it, gave it bigger meaning. What was it Madge had said? "I should have done something to stop her."

What in God's name had Evelyn done?

He wandered through the house, as if in some forgotten corner an answer might be hidden. In the living room, he stood by the piano Evelyn had once played. He couldn't remember when she had stopped. A fringed, silk shawl was draped across it now, anchored by a grouping of three large rocks. They weren't rocks, of course, but the pottery replicas Evelyn used in her flower arrangements. They had other uses. For a Fourth of July celebration, Evelyn had mixed sparklers among pussy willows and set them alight, startling and delighting everyone. Garden shops sold them as clever hiding places for house keys. There was one in the small rock garden outside the door to Evelyn's workshop on the side of the house.

He'd forgotten all about that room. He hadn't even shown it to Mrs. Brody. She would have liked seeing where Evelyn had worked. Fluorescent lights were hung over a long work table where she had done all her flower arranging. It was her private space, one he had not entered often, nor was he interested in exploring now. He'd not been there since her death.

He found the key, hidden in the hollow rock, and unlocked the door. Inside the lights flickered on, revealing a pegboard hung with a variety of wire clippers, shears and assorted other tools. The contents of the shelves along one wall rivaled those of a hardware store—drills, saws, a blow torch, tubes of glue, clay, spools of wire, bags of stones, marbles and cans of paints and other things he had little knowledge of. Everything was as he remembered, orderly and without surprise, except for the flower arrangement that was centered on the work table. It was as elaborate as any of Evelyn's he had seen. Shards of gilded wood and her signature rocks provided the background for dried flowers of subtle and exquisite color. An envelope was tucked among the foliage. His name was written in Evelyn's familiar hand.

So here was his letter. He should have known. This was the room that was most her own. This had been the heart of her house, not the kitchen, as it was for Mrs. Brody.

He hesitated, not sure he wanted to read the message she had left, afraid it would be just another trick—as the recipe file had been, and the pie. We cheated each other, he thought and reached for the envelope, and saw that it was just a card. There was no message. His name was all she had written. But that was enough. The card was already in his hand, tripping the wire that had held it fast.

The flash of blinding light came before the sound, before he felt himself lifted off his feet, before the heat and flames roared around him and his mind had lost its sense, but time enough for the horror of the full truth to reach him and make him glad for death.

A LEGACY OF QUESTIONS

A steady stream of people had come to pay their respects, but there was no one I recognized and no one who remembered me. It was no surprise, really. I'd been gone a long time. I introduced myself when it was appropriate and politely accepted their condolences. The room was cool, filled with the scent of carnations. The caskets were closed. For some reason we spoke in whispers.

I was ten when I left, twenty-one years ago. I hadn't known it would be for good, but it turned out that way. Ten is old enough to have memories, and I have some, but they aren't the kind Joel has of his childhood —hanging out in the school yard, kids sleeping over, playing hide and seek, and family vacations.

I've been to his family's summer house on Lake Michigan, a ramshackle place with a wrap-around porch and a loft that can sleep twelve. I'm green with envy imagining all the fun he had as a kid. I've tried hard to explain how different my life was, but he doesn't get it. I can't blame him. It's too hard to imagine.

We were married in Chicago, four months ago. It's where I went to college and then stayed on, accepting an entry level position at an advertising agency. I'm now in charge of one of the creative teams. Joel is an attorney.

According to my boss I'm good at word images that enlighten and persuade. Three of my ad campaigns have won awards, but for some reason I haven't painted a convincing picture of my childhood for Joel. He thinks I'm exaggerating when I tell him I never played at anyone's house or had a friend come home with me after school.

It looked as though the last of the visitors might have come and gone, but it was another hour before the funeral parlor would close. We would stay until then.

"You didn't know anyone? Joel asked.

"It's been a long time."

"So who were all those people who came?"

I had wondered that, too, and guessed at the answer. "It's the polite thing in a small town. They lived here all their lives," I said looking at the caskets. "They shopped in town." My voice trailed off, and then revived with a fresh thought. "They owned the mill. Maybe some of the people who came work there."

It was only yesterday, at their lawyer's office, that I learned about the mill. They owned it. And they left it to me. "To our only daughter, our sole heir...."

"How could you not know about the Loring Lumber Mill?" Joel exclaimed after we had left the lawyer's office. "Loring is your maiden name."

"I know that," I said with a laugh, trying to ease the tension rising between us. "Their whole life has been a mystery. This is just another piece." I knew Joel would want a better answer that, so I hurried on.

"They never mentioned it. You heard what the lawyer said. It's ten miles outside of town. They didn't have a car. We never went anywhere...." I stopped, detecting a whine in my voice.

"Neither of them worked. Didn't you wonder where their money came from?

I guess I hadn't. "I was just ten when I left here. Is that what kids think about at that age? It was different for you. You had two older brothers and a sister, and lots of friends. You had comparisons to make. I didn't."

I tried not to think back on that conversation, as we sat waiting for the long day to end. I was feeling tired, and I wondered why. There had been so little for me to do. They had prearranged everything, their lawyer told us, orchestrated to the last detail, down to the blanket of white carnations that covered their twin caskets.

Beside me Joel uncrossed his legs and looked down into the space between his spread knees. I followed his movement and studied his profile, the curve of his dark lashes, the line of his jaw, his head of shining black hair. We were opposites in more ways than one. Uncle Daniel said my hair was the color of honey. My eyes were blue.

If only Uncle Daniel were alive. He had known them both, and we had known them together. It would be such a help to have him here. I would have let him know that Joel and I had plans to visit The Sisters, and soon after, I would have phoned to tell him that they had passed away. But there was more that I would have had to say. I was relieved not to be faced with that. There was no one else I needed to tell. I reached for Joel's hand. This isn't easy for him, either. He sensed my shift in mood and brought my fingers to his lips. "It will be over soon," he said softly.

I nodded. We'd left Chicago four days ago. It felt more like a year.

We both turned as an elderly man appeared in the doorway of the room in which we sat. He stood there for a moment before making his hesitant way down the aisle. He was using a cane, but that wasn't what caught my interest. There was something about the angle at which he held his head, the peculiar lifted hunch of one shoulder. My gaze was fixed, chasing the illusive thread of memory. He stopped before the drape of white carnations and bowed his head.

It came to me in a rush. As I rose to greet him, I kept looking over his shoulder, for the ghost of the heavy leather bag he had always carried. It was from its bulging depths that Uncle Daniel's postcards had come, mailed from Bombay, Capetown, Sydney, Tierra del Fuego, ports where his ship had called. They were colorful, brief messages often obscured by the ink of postage marks. Sometimes there was a letter in an envelope addressed just to me.

"Mr. Dell." I said softly. The name came to me from a tunnel of dark memory, where he was one of the brightest spots. I was quick to tell him who I was. It wasn't likely he would remember me.

He shook his head in wonder. "You know me after all these years? You were just a little tyke, not even going to school yet, when you started waiting on those front steps. You were there most every day. You were my best customer."

His voice had grown rusty, but at the heart of it was the warmth I remembered. He knew the steps were as far as I had been allowed to go.

Joel had come up beside us and I introduced them to each other, leaving out the most important thing, that the postman had been my link to Uncle Daniel.

We talked for a while and when there was no more to say, Mr. Dell turned to leave. "They were as good as one, those two, never apart. They went together. I'm sure it's what they wanted." He was right. They were one, not just of face and bearing, but of mind, voice and attitude. It was only birth that had thrust separateness upon them, but barely. The Loring Sisters came into the world two minutes apart. I was the daughter of one, the niece of the other.

What memories I have of those early years, in the house on Eagle Street, are through a veil of organdy. Sheer starched curtains, washed and ironed by hand, were at all of the windows of the two-story house. The sisters added bluing to the rinse water to make them pure white. It's through this filter that I still see them, their silhouetted profiles framed by the curved bay window at the front of the house. Their chestnut hair is piled high in like coronets. They sit in straight-backed chairs, watching for me to come home from school.

It's only after I've climbed up the front steps and have opened the front door into the vestibule, and passed through the second door, that the image sharpens. Across their lap of touching knees, a wooden hoop holds taut a table cloth they are embroidering, white linen, with a cross-stitch design. Their slender hands work in harmony, directing their blue-threaded needles to pierce the fabric and withdraw, pulling to the thread's length, returning to make another stitch.

I watched them one day, a queen of cards folded in half, brought face to face with herself, wishing one of them would finish her square of crosses first, wanting to know who was my aunt, who was my mother. Of course, I asked. I was not without curiosity, or rebellion, as Joel thinks, at least not at first. But their response is hard to explain to someone like my husband, or to anyone who has never experienced the punishment of silence. It could go on for days.

If there were anyone who knew the secret, I was sure it was Uncle Daniel. I always planned to ask him, but there were long and uncertain stretches between his visits, so that when he finally came I was so filled with delight, that I forgot—or maybe I was afraid to ask.

There were times when I wondered if Uncle Daniel was real, or if I had made him up. I was afraid he was like the friends who came to play with me at night, after the lights in the house were out. We'd hide under the covers, and play games and tell stories, until I fell asleep and they became part of my dreams.

Just when I was almost sure Uncle Daniel had to be part of a story I made up about a sailor whose ship had gotten lost at sea, Mr. Dell would come along and rest his mail bag on our front steps, and smile. Not the usual modest turn of his lips, but a big crooked grin that spread almost to his ears. It was the signal. There was something in his bag for me from Uncle Daniel.

It was a special day when Uncle Daniel came to visit. It was often at Christmas or Easter, not on the exact day, but around then, depending on when his ship was in port. He was a merchant seaman. The table in the dining room would be set with fine china and polished silver and a cloth that was so white it was almost blue. There were covered dishes that held steamed dumplings, lolling in warmed melted butter, roast beef with juices that ran rich and rare, or sometimes a goose with browned crackling skin and dark spiced apples. Uncle Daniel carved the roast and then later said he hadn't eaten so well or so much since his last visit. He would pay his compliment to them both, with one glance. He called them Dora, which is what I called them and what they called each other. Only on their birth certificates, and now their certificates of death, were their names different: Theodora and Dorothea.

After dinner Uncle Daniel always liked to go for a walk, and asked me to go with him. It was our special time together. When the weather was right, we followed alongside the railroad tracks that ran behind our house, or went into the fields toward the lake where the mallards came in spring. In the back of my mind there was the question I wanted to ask him about my mother, but I always put it off for another time.

He had a lot to tell me about the places he had been, but even more than his sea journeys he talked about Florida. It was where he said he wanted to live some day. I knew he meant it because whenever he began to talk about it, he'd stare off at some distant point, the way I imagined he did on board ship, when he was in search of the next sight of land, afraid it might not be there.

When his gaze was mine again, his blue eyes were bright and he'd be smiling. "It won't be a big place, but it will have a few orange and grapefruit trees. And it will be right smack on the water, with a dock where I can tie up a small boat. Then, you and I can catch some worthy fish." This last, he said with a grin. He'd taken me fishing in the creek behind the old cemetery one time. He'd cut a sapling for a pole and we went to Keeler's Emporium for hooks and line and some sinkers. We used worms for bait. Our biggest catch was an eight inch perch. Sometime afterwards, he sent me a photograph of a fish he'd caught in Florida. It weighed thirty pounds.

He never stayed more than two nights, and when it came time for him to leave, my eyes would sting, but I knew not to cry. He kissed me three times, on each cheek and once on my forehead. I wondered if when I got older, he wouldn't kiss me anymore, if our farewells would be like those he exchanged with The Sisters. He held out his hand to them, and they, shoulders touching, would offer him theirs, two hands entwined as one.

The year I was ten, it wasn't Christmas and it wasn't Easter when he came. It was late summer, on a day when The Sisters had picked the last of the purple grapes that grew over the arbor in the back yard. Sterilized empty jars were lined up on the kitchen counter, waiting to be filled with the jelly that bubbled in the big kettle on the stove. A tangy sweetness filled the house.

There was a sound at the screen door leading from the backyard and a deep voice, calling, "Dora?" We all three turned and there was Uncle Daniel on the other side of the screen—tall, handsome, clean-shaven and sun tanned.

The Sisters reached up to touch their hair, which the steamy kitchen had sent curling in disorderly wisps about their faces.

My own surprise was sharp and quick. I'm sure I cried out his name, but for them the shock was more complicated. I heard their twin gasps and turned in time to see their cheeks, already flushed from the heat of the stove, take on an even more shimmering glow. Their eyes lit up in a way I had never seen before. But it was all gone so soon, I wondered if I imagined it.

While they finished making the jelly, I went upstairs to help Uncle Daniel unpack. My bedroom was at the top of the stairs. His was at the end of the hall. It had a double bed and a chifforobe and a desk. No one else ever stayed there. The Sisters' bedroom was downstairs, off a long hall past the kitchen.

After supper, which wasn't as grand as when The Sisters knew ahead that he was coming, I was ready for our usual walk, but instead he patted my hand and asked me to go to my room for a while. There were things he needed to talk to The Sisters about.

Soon I heard his voice from the foot of the stairs, calling me to come down. His eyes were bright and he was smiling. He had big news. He was done with his long sea voyages. He had bought the house in Florida he had always talked about. It was made of pink stone and had palm trees in the front yard and orange and grapefruit trees in the back. Best of all, it was on the water with a dock where he could tie up his boat.

I'd never seen a palm tree, or grapefruits or oranges growing on trees, or the ocean. It wasn't really the ocean, it was the Gulf of Mexico, but it was beautiful and went on forever.

There was another surprise. I had never thought about Uncle Daniel being married. I wondered if The Sisters knew. Maybe that was something else they had talked about the day of the jelly-making.

Aunt Flo had a bright laugh and if something went wrong, like a pot of spaghetti boiling over, we'd hear it, followed by "Oh, damn!" She had short blond hair and wore rose polish on her finger nails.

For a while I thought I was just visiting, and I guess that was how it had been planned, a trial. But then Christmas was almost with us, and over lunch one day, Aunt Flo turned to Uncle Daniel and to me, "What should we send The Loring Sisters for Christmas?"

I had written to them, short letters and postcards with pictures of pelicans and palm trees and orange sunsets. I told them about Uncle Daniel's boat the *Sweet Life*. I was learning to swim, and I liked school. They wrote back, short notes which were mostly about the weather.

We sent them a basket of oranges each year after that. A thank you note followed, signed in their usual way. DORA.

Joel can't understand why I never went back to visit them. He might stop asking if I came up with a better answer, but I have none, except that I got caught up with living in Florida, with Uncle Daniel, Aunt Flo, a new school, and friends.

I was in my third year at college when Uncle Daniel died. He had gone out on his boat, just as he did every morning when the weather was right. When dinnertime came and he wasn't back, Aunt Flo called the Coast Guard. They found the *Sweet Life* drifting at anchor, close to shore. He had died of a heart attack. I wrote to The Sisters, and received a short note.

I never knew how much Aunt Flo knew, how much she imagined, if Uncle Daniel had told her anything at all, or what there was to tell. I had never gotten around to asking him my question.

After college, I stayed on in Chicago, content with my progress at the ad agency, happier after I met Joel. Aunt Flo died two years after Uncle Daniel. Joel never met either of them. When we decided to get married we sent an announcement to The Loring Sisters. Their reply came soon, in the same careful handwriting that had been the slender thread of our connection through the years, but I was surprised by what they wrote.

"It would be nice to see you after so long, and your young man. Please come."

They had never asked me to visit before.

I wanted time to sort out how I felt about such a visit. Joel liked the idea, and I couldn't summon up an argument strong enough to oppose him, so we settled on a time.

Joel had never been to New England, so we chose local roads for our two-hour drive from the airport to the town where I was born. We drove through village squares, heralded by steepled white churches, along brief stretches of countryside, where mountain laurel was in bloom.

I had no idea what I would remember of the small town where I'd been born, but it didn't accommodate the sprawling shopping center on its outskirts, or the spread of a housing development where farmland must have been. Yet as soon as Joel made the turn onto Main Street, it was as though I had opened the pages of an old photograph album. There was Dawson's Drug Store, with its oval ice cream sign. Uncle Daniel had taken me there for my first ice cream soda, a black and white, with extra whipped cream on top. We sat at a counter on high stools that had caned seats.

A few doors down was Keeler's Emporium where we'd gotten our fishing gear, and where The Sisters bought their embroidery cotton. My memory petered out after that.

The rest of the pages in the album were blank, until we turned onto Eagle Street and parked in front of a gray, two-story house with its stairway of brick steps leading to the front door. They were where my memory had left them, seated in the curve of the bay window, twin profiles silhouetted behind the curtained glass. They were waiting for us.

I hesitated as we started up the walk, and for reassurance reached for

Joel's hand, but then let it go at the front door. It swung open at my touch, into the vestibule with its second, curtained door. I knew its glass knob would be cold in my hand.

An afghan covered their lap of touching knees and trailed to the floor, almost hiding the wheels of the chairs in which they sat. Their once shining dark hair, though still wound in matching coronets, was faded and gray, their faces lined and pale. They reached out in the gesture that was etched in my memory, their twin hands entwined.

It was Joel who got us through the first few minutes, chatting in his easy way about our flight from Chicago, our drive from Boston, through small New England towns, past vestiges of farmland, marked by stone walls. Soon, my voice joined his and we fell to entertaining them.

When the afternoon had taken us to early evening, they said they had a few things to do in the kitchen. No, they didn't want our help. Our room was at the end of the hall upstairs. Perhaps we would like to rest.

———◆———

In Uncle Daniel's old room, Joel took me into his arms. "How lucky Daniel took you away from here."

I leaned into his embrace and closed my eyes for a moment, grateful to have him holding me, but I knew he had more to say. I tried to prepare myself.

I had told him almost nothing about my family when we first met, waiting until it seemed he would have a permanent place in my life. The strangeness of my situation made people curious, and although I couldn't fault them for that, I'd learned to spare myself the explanations, unless it mattered that they know.

"They are definitely spooky," he said.

I smiled with relief at the word he chose. "I tried to tell you."

He nodded. "I thought you were exaggerating—the way you sometimes do."

He was right I did embellish at times, for effect is how I explained it. A gale had more entertainment than a wind, but imprecision didn't sit well with Joel. His nature, reinforced by legal discipline, preferred facts.

My childhood had been filled with fantasy. A therapist once said it was the way I had gotten through. In the advertising world, it was a talent to be able to fanaticize and stretch the truth, to tell stories and create worlds. But when I told Joel about The Sisters, I had not done that. They needed no exaggeration.

"Seeing them is like looking at a trick mirror," he said. "The same hairdo, the same dress, even the same little gold bird pin, worn to the right of the collar. They could be one person." He shook his head in troubled wonder. "But it's not just their looks. Their thoughts and all their movements seem synchronized. It's the damndest thing I've ever seen."

I smiled with relief. Finally, I had made some headway.

Dinner was announced when they opened the dining room's double doors, in their wheel chairs, together, with the ringing of the crystal bell they had used on the occasions Uncle Daniel came to visit. The table was laid as it had been then. The silver shone, the table cloth was starched and white. The difference was that Joel carved the roast. Throughout the meal Uncle Daniel's voice echoed in my ears.

When dinner was over, they refused to let us help them clear, or clean up, insisting that we leave them to their task. Perhaps we would like to go for a walk.

We headed down the street in the direction of town. In the quiet dark, Joel took my hand. "How do you suppose they manage if they're so bound to those wheel chairs?"

"Maybe they have someone come in to help."

"You mean there was someone hiding in the kitchen this evening?"

"Oh, Joel," I said laughing, "I doubt that, but at other times."

"You know what I think?"

I shook my head and waited. I should have known he had a theory.

"Only one of them needs a wheel chair. The wheels on one are brand new. On the other they're well worn."

I stared at him. "That's crazy."

He pulled me toward him, grinning, and kissed me. "Spooky is the word I used."

———◆———

The next morning, sun streaming in from the bedroom window woke me. I raised myself on an elbow and saw that Joel was already gone. He had signed up for a marathon in the fall and got up early every morning to go for a long run. I knew he'd been looking forward to the challenge of a new terrain. I just hoped he wouldn't be gone as long as he sometimes was.

I washed my face and brushed my teeth and headed downstairs, anticipating the sounds of breakfast under way, the smell of coffee perking, but the house was still. The kitchen door is probably closed, I thought, and the dining room, too, if the pattern of last night were any gauge. But a glance over the stair rail revealed the dining room doors were open wide. The dark wood of the table was stripped of the table cloth and bare, except for the crystal bell and a square white doily.

There was no one in the kitchen, and I found myself at the sink, looking out the window into the yard. Once there had been a footstool for me to stand on so I could reach the faucet to wash my hands. Except for the railroad tracks in the distance, the view held no memories. Over-grown forsythia was in bloom along the fence line.

I explored the pantry and found the hallway that went past the door to the cellar and then further on to where their bedroom was. I walked softly, my footsteps cushioned by sneakers.

A collection of sepia-colored photographs was hung on the long wall, and I looked at each one. Most of them were of The Sisters, taken at the time of their high school graduation, in caps and gowns, diplomas in hand, then in long white prom dresses, looking like brides. I thought I had seen some of them before.

To my surprise, I found the door to their bedroom open and would have turned away, but it was as though I had come upon another photograph. The same sepia twilight that suffused the photographs filled the room. I wondered at its source and then realized it was the sun, sifting through the filter of ecru-colored shades that were drawn across each window, framed by organdy curtains tied back in a swag. The tawny light softened all edges and transmuted what was really there.

My child's memory had them seated on the wide bench in front of the vanity, with its wings of angled mirrors. That they might look beyond their own reflection and find me standing there sent an echoing shiver of fear along my spine. It would take a simple upward glance into the silvered glass for them to see me watching. The dare was hard to resist. Sometimes I stayed watching as they brushed their hair, until the fear of being caught and the dread of punishment made me shrink back out of sight.

I glanced across the room to the four-poster bed where I saw the outline of their twin shapes lying side by side. At the foot of the bed, a wheel chair stood in solitude.

The other was in the kitchen, folded and tucked against the side of the broom closet. I stared at it, wondering at their need for pretense. Had it been just for us? I doubted that. I suspected the reason was deeper, and more tragic. Perhaps their life-long wish to move as one had been dealt a blow. Had fate played a mean trick and visited infirmity on one, and not the other, making them different? They could not tolerate that.

It was another question to add to all the others I hadn't asked. I could walk away from this one, too. Joel, who had guessed about the wheel chairs, would want to probe.

I returned to the window over the kitchen sink and looked beyond the yard, and began to wonder why I had let Joel talk me into coming here. And now he was off on his damn run!

A piercing swell of anger rose within me, directed as much at myself as Joel. I should have told him to wake me. I could have gone with him on his run. I needed to get out. I turned and headed for the front door.

As I passed the dining room, the tug of old memories had me hesitate. I thought again of Uncle Daniel and how his buoyant spirit had defied the strange confines of this house. The tidied table looked abandoned and forlorn. The white doily needed straightening.

When I got up close, I saw it was an envelope. "For Dora," was written on it. It was meant for me. I was Dora, too.

The flap was sealed. I held it in my hand for a while, staring at the script that had been my link with them through the years. I had come here to visit them. What had they written, that they would not say?

Dear Dora,

Perhaps you know by now that you are Daniel's child. When we were young we used our identical likeness to tease. We tricked him into thinking there was only one of us. When he guessed the truth, we would not let him choose. Even he never knew who bore his child. We made our choice to live as one, and now that illness threatens, we have chosen to end it that way. We wish you happiness. DORA.

I read it for a second time, and put it into the pocket of my jeans. I'm not sure if I understood what they had done, but when I walked back down the hall and entered their room, I kept my eyes averted from where they lay. At one of the windows I lifted a shade. Outside the sun shone. Dew sparkled on the grass. Across the yard the grape arbor sagged under the weight of vines grown wild.

—◆—

When Joel returned, the camouflaging sepia light in their bedroom was fully gone. He saw their night table with its open drawer, small bottles emptied of prescriptions, saved over the years. The doctor, whose name I'd found on one of the labels answered my urgent call, and was with me when Joel returned. A letter addressed to their lawyer was in a long white envelope on their bedside table, propped up against a lamp.

It is by our own hand that we have chosen to leave this world.
Dorothea Loring and Theodora Loring.

I had never seen their full signatures before.

—◆—

It's a relief to be outside, away from the scent of carnations. The late afternoon sun is pleasantly warm, after the chill of the air conditioned funeral parlor. My hand is looped through Joel's arm as we start across the parking lot toward our rented car.

"I can't get over it," he says. "The mailman was the only person you knew." He shakes his head in disbelief. "I thought there'd be some friends from school, someone your age."

His words have the effect of a fist hard against my chest. It takes my breath away. My throat tightens. I whip around to face him. My voice is brittle with rage. "Haven't you heard anything I've told you? How many times do I have to say it? There were no friends!"

His mouth begins to open, but I've turned on him, again, pounding my fist hard against his chest. They are feeble blows, but he's startled by them.

My voice has begun to rise and I rein it in, to keep it from becoming a scream. "You've got to stop it, Joel. No more questions. There are no answers."

He waits a moment and then, with a look I know precedes a reasoned argument, he says, "There are always answers. You just have to look for them." He reaches to take my hand. I keep it from him.

"No." My voice is cold and hard. "You may want answers, but I don't. And I want no more questions." For a moment I think he is ready to let it go.

"Okay, you win, just one last thing. They planned things so carefully— their deaths, while you were here. I can't believe they wouldn't leave you an explanation."

I guard my surprise, impressed that he has imagined what they have actually done. I haven't shown him the letter, nor will I. It will only feed his inquiry.

Suddenly a thought comes to me. When he left the house to go for a run yesterday morning, did he see the envelope on the dining table, sealed and addressed to me?

He might not have noticed it. I take a deep breath and walk ahead of him to the car. It's another question I won't ask.

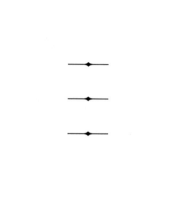

Last Harvest

He leaned back against the kitchen counter of the one-room apartment they shared off campus. His thumbs were hooked deep into the pockets of his Levis. "I've got to go. There's no way out of it."

She looked up from the book in her lap, open to the same page it had been when he'd walked into the apartment fifteen minutes ago. She closed the book and put it on the floor beside her and uncrossed her legs from their lotus position. Slowly she stretched out and rested back on her elbows. Her dark hair fell in a drape past her shoulders.

They were almost mirror images of each other—young, lean, wearing Levis. Their sweatshirts were different. His was gray. Hers was light blue. Whenever she wore it, Peter would say it matched the color of her eyes.

"Look, I don't *want* to go," he said.

She stared at him critically, the expression on her face a challenge. "Then don't."

He straightened and freed his thumbs, slamming the fist of one hand into the palm of the other. "You know it isn't that easy!"

"Who said anything about it being easy? But I don't think it's as hard as you're trying to make out. There are three of them. That should be enough. If they want to take the chance, let them. They don't need you."

"They need the car."

"Lend it to them."

"My car? Are you kidding?"

"All right then. Let them find someone else, who has a car. Let them rent one—if the car is what makes you think you have to go."

The chill was fading from her voice. She heard the fading and she knew he'd heard it. She wasn't going to lecture him any more; she wasn't going to ask him not to go. She had been on the verge of begging him and she'd never done anything like that before. In a way it had frightened them both.

He crossed the space between them and knelt beside her. He touched her hair and looked deeply into her eyes. His voice was soft. "I know what you're saying. I hear you. And I understand. But I can't pull out, not now. There isn't time for them to get anyone else. Tonight's the last of it. There'll be a frost tonight and rain tomorrow. That'll finish it until next year."

He looked away from her, out the window. "The sky's clouding up. I hope it holds out for a few more hours." Absent-mindedly his hand slid down the length of her hair and then began to trace the familiar curves of her body. With a sigh he sank down on the floor alongside her.

Next year, she was thinking to herself as she lay beside him. That's right, there's next year—one last year of college and another harvest. "You told them what I found out about old man Purdy?"

"I told them."

"What did they say? How are they going to handle that?" She sat up, and looked down at him. "What are they going to do about the farmer?"

"Look, Purdy isn't going to be any problem."

"What do you mean no problem? What have they decided to do about him?"

"Oh, come on, Sheila, stop giving me the third degree." He tried to roll away from her, but she straddled him, pinning him down with her hands on his shoulders.

"Tell me. I've got a right to know. If it hadn't been for me you wouldn't know anything about Purdy. You . . . ." She stopped, struck by her new word choice. All along she had been talking about *them,* as though Peter were not a part of it. But he was. "What are you going to do to him?"

He sprang up, knocking her away from him. "Nothing, damn it! What's the matter with you? What kind of guy do you think I am?" He stood above her, staring down at her angrily, ignoring the fact that she was holding her elbow which had hit the hard floor with a sharp crack.

She grimaced against the pain and fought the tears that sprang into her eyes. She swallowed and got her voice under control. This was her last chance to convince him. "Didn't you understand what I told you? Purdy will be waiting for you. Every night for the last two weeks he's been sitting on that back porch of his, waiting. If you know there'll be a frost tonight, so does he. He'll know tonight's your last chance. He'll be there with his spyglass just like that little kid said. He'll spot you and go right to the phone and call the police." She didn't go into what getting caught would mean. She'd been over it all before—prison for God knows how many years.

"He may try, but he won't get anywhere. We're going to cut the telephone wires, and just in case he decides to use his car we're letting the air out of his tires."

She stared at him, the words registering. She almost laughed. They weren't going to hurt the old man. She hadn't thought of anything so simple—only a prank, really. She was so relieved that even the pain in her arm was nothing, but then almost as quickly as her relief had come, it was leaving her. She had lost the argument.

There was nothing else she could say now that would keep him from going. All she had left was the hope that everything would go all right, that when dawn came tomorrow she would wake and Peter would be beside her and it would be all over and done with. And when the Christmas holidays came, two months from now she could look back and smile at all her fears. The money he would make on the deal would let them leave the bleak winter prairie for a couple of weeks and drive south into Mexico, and get some sun.

She let her imagination float with the fantasy, needing it to blot out the terrifying alternative. When they would recross the border back into the States, the border guards would check again and again, as they had last year; but they'd find nothing, because there would be nothing to find. They might question the stack of Mexican newspapers on the floor of the trunk compartment, but discovering that's all they were—newspapers—they wouldn't even be interested in Peter's explanation that he was doing a paper on Mexican journalism for a college course. Who would suspect that the destiny of the Zaragoza and San Pedro papers was to wrap prairie-grown marijuana, so it could pass for the higher-priced Mexican variety?

A cold wind tore at their jackets when they left the apartment a few hours later. The sun had almost set and the sky was streaked with dark clouds. They walked to the car together. Sheila reached up and kissed his cheek and then turned and rounded the corner where she could get a bus.

The envelope of census material was under her arm. She didn't know if she'd make any calls today, but she might try. It would give her something to do. The temporary census job didn't pay badly and she could fit the interviews in when it was convenient. Like now, if she wanted. She would go out of her mind if she stayed in the apartment alone, waiting.

Usually the questions and answers went easily. But sometimes not. Like when she had gone out to the Purdy farm, two weeks ago, where Brewster Purdy and his sister Elizabeth lived. It had been chance that she'd been given the group of five farms to do. If she hadn't Peter's car to use she would have had to turn it down. It was a long drive, almost an hour in a direction out of town they rarely went.

You really couldn't call the Purdy place a farm any more. The last hog had been slaughtered years ago. Purdy still planted a garden—tomatoes, squash, beans, potatoes, corn—but most of his land was untended now. What had once been wheat and cornfields was overrun with weeds.

It was Elizabeth Purdy who answered the doorbell the day Sheila pulled up to the farmhouse in Peter's old beat-up car.

"No one's rung that bell in years," the gray-haired woman said with a hesitant smile. "It's a wonder it works. Most people use the knocker."

Sheila had smiled. "I'm from the city. There aren't many knockers there. I guess I'm used to ringing doorbells. Are you Miss Purdy?"

The woman nodded.

"My name is Sheila Evans. I'm helping out with the census." She showed her identification card.

"Who's that?" a voice bellowed from somewhere inside the house.

The woman frowned and leaned toward Sheila. "That's my brother. He's in an ornery mood today. Worse than usual. He's been like that ever since the government took away his subsidy. It never made no sense to me for the government to pay him for not plantin'. It didn't seem right, but then Brewster said I never had a head for such things. It's hard, though, when you're used to havin' money come in and then suddenly it stops. It's worse on people like the Stocktons down the road with all those little kids to feed." Elizabeth Purdy turned and called over her shoulder. "It's a young lady. She's come about the census."

A small wiry man appeared in the doorway. He was an inch or so shorter than his sister. It was hard for Sheila to believe that such a small body could house such a loud voice. His hostile gray eyes studied her and she knew, for this farmer, it hadn't been worth her trouble to put on a blue blazer over a white shirt and jeans.

"You say you've come about the census?" he barked.

"Yes, there are just a few questions I have to ask."

"Well, I've got one to ask you. When's the government goin' to give me back my subsidy?"

Sheila shook her head and tried a small smile. "I'm sorry, I don't know anything about that."

"You don't? Why not? You work for the government, don't you?"

"Well, not really. I'm just ...."

He wouldn't let her finish. "If you don't' work for the government then you have no business comin' here askin' us questions. I've a mind to call the police."

Sheila suppressed a sigh and decided it would be best to ignore the old man. She turned to his sister. "Does anyone else live here beside you and your brother?"

She got her answer and left, with the old man yelling out the door, threatening that she wouldn't get far, that he would have the police after her.

The Stockton place was the next on her list and she drove the two miles slowly, thinking about the old pair she had just left, wondering if there had ever been any happy times in their lives, wondering if the harsh life of the prairie had squeezed all the joy out of them, or maybe there had never been any joy to begin with.

October can be a pretty time in some farming areas, particularly in the northeast, with pumpkins and squash stacked in piles, and farm stands selling baskets of apples and pears, but not in the prairie states. Sheila looked at the flat land, stubbled and browning, stretching for miles.

She turned into a rutted driveway marked by a mailbox. Its black letters were chipped and faded. The name Stockton was barely distinguishable.

A brown and white spotted dog leaped playfully at her heels when she got out of the car. As she leaned down to pat its head, she heard the wail of a siren and turned to see a black and white police car, its red dome light flashing, turn into the driveway and screech to a halt, showering dust. The occupants of the farmhouse spilled out into the yard, a half dozen children and a thin woman in a faded blue print dress. The gaunt wind-burned man beside her was dressed in a pair of ragged coveralls.

"What's the trouble, George?" he asked with a curious glance at Sheila.

"Don't know yet. Just answering a call from Purdy." The patrolman turned to Sheila. "You the gal who's just been to the Purdy place?"

She nodded. "He said he'd have the police after me, but I didn't think he meant it. I'm a census taker, but I don't think Mr. Purdy believed that." She unclipped the identification card from the folder under her arm.

The policeman looked at it and frowned. "Have to satisfy a man like Purdy. He makes a lot of noise. Sometimes what he has to say is worth listening to."

He left then and Mrs. Stockton took Sheila's arm. "I bet you could use a cup of coffee after that scare. Come on into the house. No need for George to have used his siren like that. You'd think he was chasing some criminal. Gave me a fright the way he pulled into the driveway, throwing up dust. Smart aleck, that's what he is."

"He's just doing his job, Amy, same as anyone," Mr. Stockton said wearily. "Only he's gotta jazz it up a bit."

He held a chair out for Sheila and she sat down at a wooden table, with a finish worn smooth by repeated scrubbings. There was a plate of cupcakes in the center, freshly iced. There were eight of them, one for each member of the family. Now they had a guest. Sheila looked around at the faces of he children, round-eyed, semicircled by shadows. They were thin and looked tired, just as their mother and father looked tired.

With a pang Sheila realized she was looking close into the face of poverty and there was nothing she could do about it. She accepted the coffee that was being poured for her and hoped they would believe her when she said she'd just had lunch and was too full to eat one of the cupcakes they invited her to have.

"Old man Purdy is getting on," Mrs. Stockton said. "He's starting to have some foolish notions. Seems worse since they took away them subsidies." She turned to the tallest of her sons who looked about twelve. "I want you kids to stay away from there. Don't pester that old man none."

"We don't pester him, Ma," the boy said. "We just watch him from the old barn."

"Watch him? Watch him doing what?"

"He sits out on his back porch all day, watchin' the road along by the old railroad tracks. Sometimes a car stops and some big kids get out. Ol' man Purdy has his spyglass on them. He sees them cut down the weed that's growin' there. They fill up the car and take off. Ol' man Purdy calls the police. The kids get picked up and Purdy gets a reward."

Stockton leaned forward and looked at his son. "Are you sure about this, Willie?"

"I'm sure. Most of my friends know about it. And there's something else. You know that cornfield behind his house, the one he didn't plant this year? It's full of weed growin' real thick. He's just waitin' for somebody to come and get it. He stays out on that porch even after dark, waitin'."

"How do you know that, Willie?" His father's voice was stern.

Willie's thin face whitened. "Sorry, Pa. We won't do it again, but Jim and I snuck up to the house the other night and saw him sittin' there."

The boy next to Willie nodded his head. "He had his pipe goin' and ever' once in a while we could see it glow up. Say, Pa, how much money do you get for bein' an informer?"

Mr. Stockton glared at his son, and seemed about to raise his hand, but then, perhaps because Sheila was there, let it fall to his side.

That had been two weeks ago, but the memory of her visit to the two farms was still with her. She had her collar turned up against the wind and was glad when she saw the bus come round the corner. It was colder than she had thought. She should have worn a scarf. She found a seat by the window and stared out at the darkening evening trying to get her thoughts under control. The bus was warm, but she was still cold. It was a chill of a different kind, not from the outside, but from within.

The Purdy place was the last on Peter's list. All the others, marked carefully on the map made from scoutings done early in the summer, had been successfully hit and harvested. The stalks were hanging in garages and apartments and dormitories, upside down, so the sap could flow into the leaves, drying, waiting to be processed. There were none in the apartment she shared with Peter. He'd given in to her on that. Only the Mexican papers they'd bought last year were under the bed they shared. They would be gone, if everything went as planned.

She got out at the bus stop she had headed for, but now that she was there she didn't feel like ringing doorbells. It was probably too late anyhow. People would be having supper. She went into a diner, found an empty booth, and ordered a hamburger and coffee. She could see the corner where the bus had stopped. She could have stayed on the bus, gone to the end of the line, and come back, but she hadn't thought of it. The coffee came and the hamburger. She ate it, thinking of the Stocktons and their thin faces and hungry stomachs. Her own churned as she thought of Peter and what he was doing.

She woke at two o'clock the next morning. The place in the bed beside her was empty. The apartment was lonely and still. She got up and went to the window. Against the street lamp she could see a light swirl of snow. Peter had been right about the frost. She looked down the street, hoping to see the lights of his jalopy come around the corner. She stayed there a long time, watching, waiting.

When dawn came and Peter hadn't come home, she knew for certain something had gone wrong. She didn't know what and she didn't know how to go about finding out. She couldn't call the police to ask if they'd picked someone up named Peter Finley. Maybe he had managed to get away.

At ten o'clock she took the bus to school and got off at the south end of the campus. The sun was out and the air was crisp. The yellow roses that had been blooming along the path to the library were brown and withered, their heads drooping, hit by last night's frost.

A group of students she didn't know came down the library steps. One of them had a transistor radio and she caught a snatch of a song Peter sometimes whistled while he shaved. The melody lingered in her head, even after the group was gone.

Hearing the radio gave her an idea. She turned around and began running back along the walk to where she had gotten off the bus. Another one would come soon that would take her back to the apartment. If she were lucky she'd be there by eleven, in time for the local news.

She burst into the apartment and snapped on the radio. It was a two minutes past eleven. A voice came on, a child's voice, frail, earnest, familiar.

"I'm gonna get a bicycle. That's what I'm gonna do with part of the reward. The rest I'm gonna give to my Pa."

Her breath caught as she listened. She saw the scrubbed kitchen table and the plate of eight cup cakes, the white face of the thin little boy, "Say, Pa, how much money do you get for bein' an informer?"

The Oak's Long Shadow

The tentative voice I heard, when I picked up the phone had the pull of a child's memory. It swept me from my Manhattan apartment to the house in North Carolina where I had been born, where tree toads still sing at night and dawn comes up when the first cock crows. It was where my eighty-three-year-old father still lived, and where Alma had been coming every day for as long as I could remember.

I began listening backwards for some clue to why Alma had called. We talked once a week when I phoned home, but she never called, unless something was wrong.

"Miz Katy ...." I heard the long pause, and then her quick determined breath. "Yes, it's me, child. I've got some sorrowful news. It's your Daddy ... he's gone."

So there it was, the words I knew would come some day. "Oh, Alma." My voice was a whisper, full of the child in me. I was thirty-two years old.

"Miz Katy, there's more I've got to tell you, but you'll at least be glad to know that he went fast."

The image of my father in lingering pain faded, but there was enough in her words to keep me on guard.

"Child, no easy way to say this ... but your Daddy didn't die no natural death."

———◆———

All through the night, in a sleep, twisted with dreams and periods of wakefulness that offered no answers, I kept hearing Alma's words, so it was a relief when morning came and my flight from La Guardia landed in Raleigh and I was behind the wheel of a rented car, headed for Elkton. I'd driven those forty-five miles dozens of times and watched the spread of urban development gradually devour the land. Each time another piece was gone, but so far, close to Elkton, there were still long stretches of fields where summer crops thrived under a hot sun. They swept by in a comforting green blur, lulling me into a reverie of earlier trips home, and I let myself be tricked into thinking that when I turned down the stony road that led to my father's house, he'd be on the porch, sitting in his high-back rocker, waiting for me.

I was in the thrall of that thought when the familiar fork appeared, marked by a cluster of mailboxes. My father's name, in black letters, was on one. Warren Cobbs. I got out to see if there was any mail and found a flyer announcing the annual Fourth of July Firemen's Fair, in two weeks. I stood there, squinting against the midday sun, feeling its heat after the car's air conditioning, listening to the familiar sounds around me—the hum of bees and the sawing sound of grasshoppers.

The sound of my car's tires crunching on the stony road, alerted Alma to my arrival and even before I'd gotten out of the car the porch door swung open. She was in a blue cotton dress, ordered from the catalogue store, in a style long enough to cover her tall, ample frame. There was more white in her gray hair than I remembered. But my glance slid past her to the giant tree that lay on the ground. It had fallen two weeks ago during a heavy summer storm. I'd heard about it over the phone, but nothing either Alma or my father had said quite prepared me for what I saw.

The oak was close to a hundred years old. It lay stretched from deep inside the Harrison yard next door to our front porch steps. Its wide spread of branches, dense with the leafy growth of early summer, established an instant forest between the two houses.

About ten years ago the tree had begun to list in the direction of my father's house and became the subject of a debate between my father and his neighbor, Cliff Harrison, a few years older than my father, and also a widower. Their argument took the form of letters. Harrison wrote his in a shaky hand, while Dad typed his on an old Underwood and made carbon copies. He kept their correspondence neatly filed in an antique chest which stood on a table next to his desk.

The chest, like everything in the house, had its own history. My father had found it in Zanzibar, where he had stopped on one of his voyages when he was in the Merchant Marine. That was long before he married my mother. She had been twenty years younger than he was, and died when I was in high school.

All of this and more sped across my mind as I stared at the tree and then turned and hurried across the hot drive and up the steps. Alma and I put our arms around each other and stood that way for a long time. Neither one of us cried. I knew how she felt about tears and somewhere along the way I had adopted her view. "Once you start, it's hard to stop. I just stay away from them as best as I can."

Alma had lunch ready, so we went inside and sat at the table in the kitchen by the window that looked out on to what had once been an herb garden. There were things we needed to talk about before I went into town to see the sheriff, but I wasn't ready for that just yet and I knew Alma wasn't either. She asked about my job at "that big city magazine," and I asked her about her family. Her husband had died a long time ago, but she had raised four children and got them all through high school. Two had gone on to college. None of them lived in Elkton now.

"They all doin' just fine, except for Roland," Alma had told me over lunch. "He's been livin' in Chicago, you know, but his marriage has gone off the track. A few weeks ago he sent young Rollie Junior down here to stay with me."

I remembered Rollie, a high-spirited six-year-old who'd spent a month with Alma two summers ago. I'd taken him to the Firemen's Fair that year. He was too small to ride the roller coaster alone, so I had gone with him. I called it quits after the second time. He hadn't liked that.

"I love that child," Alma sighed, "but I'm out of energy for takin' care of an eight-year-old. The first day he was here he got into a scrape with two fellas, not much bigger than him, but I know those boys and they don't fight fair. After that, I started bringin' him over here. He and your Daddy got on real well. They'd sit out on the porch, with Mr. Warren tellin' him stories about the days he was a sailor. That's what Rollie says he wants to be now."

After we'd finished lunch and the last dish was washed and put away, Alma took off her apron and led me outside onto the porch. We settled ourselves in the two rockers that had always been there and she nodded toward the fallen tree.

"It was truly somethin' when it fell. It was like the world was makin' some big announcement. Your Daddy and I were inside listenin' to the wind and watchin' the rain come slicin' down. Then all of a sudden there was this roar. It sounded like thunder, but it wasn't comin' from the sky. It was that old tree tearing up its roots."

She took a long, deep breath then and I could tell she was getting ready to talk about my father.

"Your Daddy came out here yesterday, like he did every morning, to read his paper and take another look at that tree. I was inside and had the sweeper runnin', so I couldn't hear anything but that. When it got to lunchtime, and he hadn't come in, sniffin' around the kitchen, like he usually did when his stomach was complainin', I came out here to get him. I supposed he'd just lost track of time, sittin' here lookin' at that tree, get-tin' ready to write another one of his letters to Mr. Harrison. I expected he was gonna give me one to put in the mailbox on my way home. I tried tellin' him it would be easier if the two of them talked to one another, instead of writin' all those letters, but I wasn't able to bring his mind to that."

She stopped then and pointed toward the floor at my feet. "Right there is where I found your Daddy, all in a heap. I thought he was just collapsed, but when I took his hand, I knew he was gone. I phoned the Rescue Squad right away, and came back out here with a blanket to put over him. Child, I got right down here on this porch floor alongside your Daddy, wishin' there was somethin' I could do for him, but I knew there was nothin'. I just thanked the Lord for makin' it so quick. I told him, 'Lord, Mr. Warren would have appreciated that.' About then was when I saw his eye. I didn't see it before, because of the way his head was turned. But I saw it then." She shook her head. "It's somethin' I'm not likely to forget."

———————

I dropped Alma off at her house on my way to see the sheriff. The man with a smile, almost as big as his mustache had retired a few years ago. He and my father used to play poker together. The office was pretty much as I remembered it, and so was the uniform—black pants and a gray summer shirt with a silver star pinned on the pocket, but the man wearing it now couldn't have been more different.

Sheriff Billie Jenkins was thick-shouldered and muscular, with bright red hair slicked back from his temples and forehead with jell. He was probably my age.

"Katherine Cobbs," he repeated in a way that made me think he didn't know who I was. His look was sullen.

"My father is Warren Cobbs . . . ." I started to explain, but he cut me off.

"I know who you are. That colored woman at the house told me you lived in New York City. I was just wonderin' how you got here so fast."

There was an unmistakable slur in his voice when he referred to Alma. It took some effort for me not to react. "I got an early flight to Raleigh this morning," was all I said.

"I suppose you're wondering about the body. We can release it anytime. Palmers is the only funeral parlor in town. I suppose that's where you want it to go."

I frowned, trying to decide if he was just an awkward man, or was he being intentionally rude. "I used to live here," I said slowly. "I know this town. Palmers handled things when my mother passed away. But before we get into that, I'd like to know more about how my father died."

He had been slouched in his chair, but he straightened then. "What do you mean, how? It was a bullet . . . went right through his eye. Whoever did it was a good shot."

"A good shot!" I recoiled. "What kind of a remark is that?"

"Remark? It's no remark. It's a fact." He gave me an odd, questioning look. "Why, you think it was an accident?"

"I don't know what to think. That's why I came to see you."

His eyes narrowed and he began twisting his mouth in a way that suggested he was chewing on a difficult thought. His voice was softer when he began, but it was too much of an effort for him to keep it up.

"You know this here isn't New York City. Your ole man wasn't wanderin' around Times Square and got popped off in some gang war. He was shot on his own front porch. You think that was an accident? That may make sense to you, but not to me."

"None of this makes sense to me," I said, trying not to let my anger show. "Look, my father was old and frail. He didn't even go into town anymore. The furthest he went was his front porch. He wasn't bothering anyone."

The grin came slowly and the relish behind it took me by surprise. "He must have been bothering somebody," he said and leaned back. "How about the ole guy next door? I hear him and your ole man have been feuding over that tree for years."

"Mr. Harrison? You can't be serious."

"It's the first thing that came to me, but then I found out he's got a withered arm and uses a wheelchair. No way he could have lifted a twenty-two rifle and got off a shot like that."

"Is that what killed my father?" I seized upon a tangible fact.

"Light-weight hunting rifle, aimed right, it can do the job. I don't suppose you see many of them in New York City. There it's somethin' small or sawed-off … easy to conceal. Around here everybody has a twenty-two, two or three, more than that, even."

I was on the verge of reminding him that having lived in Elkton half my life, I knew what a twenty-two was, but I never got to it. The door to his office burst open then and two boys, about nine and eleven, tumbled into the room. They had the sheriff's unmistakable red hair.

I started to smile, but never completed it. The sheriff leapt out of his chair, giving it a shove that sent it slamming into the wall behind him, adding another dent to the collection already there. He came around his desk with his fist raised. "I told you two to wait in the car."

"Pa, we only wanted …." The younger boy's words were cut off. His brother yanked his arm and dragged him back through the doorway. I sat still, listening to their footsteps running down the hall.

The sheriff closed the door after them and made his way back to his chair. "My wife and I are split. I get them June, July and August. It's the worst bargain I ever made. Be easier raising wild dogs than those two."

"Children are a big responsibility," I said feebly, feeling the need to say something, but confident that anything meaningful wouldn't be appreciated.

"You married?" he asked.

I shook my head. "Sheriff, I don't mean to be rude, but let's get back to my father. What are you doing about investigating his death?"

His jaw tightened. "Look here, like I told you, everybody around here has a twenty-two. There's no way we'll find out who did it. Tryin' would be a waste of time."

———◆———

I drove along Main Street toward the railroad station and back again, needing to give myself some time to settle down after my encounter with the sheriff. Trains didn't stop in Elkton anymore. The station house had been turned into a diner since I'd been home last. There were other changes too—a new pizza place on the corner of Elm alongside a video store. The yard goods shop was gone. At Magnolia, I turned left and drove halfway down the block and parked in front of Palmer's Funeral Home.

———◆———

The house felt empty when I returned, but the feeling had more to do with my thoughts than that I was alone in the house. The body I had looked at was my father's but it wasn't the man I knew, or the way I would remember him. Yet seeing his inert form confirmed in a real way that he was gone. Forever. I kept thinking of that as I wandered through the old house, through the upstairs rooms that hadn't been used much in recent years. When the stairs had become too difficult for my father to navigate, he had moved into a bedroom downstairs.

In the room that had been mine, the pink flowers in the chintz curtains at the windows and the spread on the bed weren't as bright as they had once been, but Alma continued to wash and starch-iron them every spring and fall, so they looked fresh and delicate rather than faded. The phone I'd gotten for my thirteenth birthday was on the desk in the corner of the room, white, yellowed now.

I was saving my father's study for last. It was the room I could always imagine him in—seated at his desk, going through old papers, some from his days in the Merchant Marine. Across the hall was Alma's room, where she had stayed so many nights during the last months of my mother's illness and other times when we needed her. A white chenille spread was on the bed, and a cross of folded palm leaves, saved from some long-ago Palm Sunday, was on the wall over the head board. Propped up against a lamp on the dresser was a colored snapshot I hadn't seen before—Alma's grandson Rollie and my father, on the front porch.

Rollie had sprouted since I'd last seen him. A yellow bandanna tied around his head made him look older and street-wise. The streets of Chicago, I thought, and imagined the handful he was for his aging grandmother. Part of the fallen tree was in the photograph, so I knew it had been taken recently. I picked it up and held it close, looking at my father's face. He was smiling.

I crossed the hall then and went to sit in his chair. I slid my hands along the satin wood of its arms, imitating a mannerism of his. "I never need to polish that wood. Your Daddy did such a good job." Alma's voice joined in with my thoughts as my gaze traveled around the room, over the books that filled the dark shelves, the family photographs and maps that were on the walls. Finally it settled on the Zanzibar chest, which was on a stand beside the desk. I reached to open it, but let my hand rest on its lid, recalling my father's younger voice, "Smell it. See if you can guess what used to be packed in there."

I had been three years old, maybe four, but already wanted him to know how smart I was. I was on his lap and after leaning forward to sniff the open chest, I pressed back against the curve of his arm and looked up into his face. "Cookies," I said, and waited for the spark of approval to appear in his gray eyes. Instead, he shook his head.

I wiggled out of his arms to stand in front of him. "Cookies," I said stubbornly. "The kind Alma makes … with those little hard black things for eyes and a nose and a mouth."

I heard his deep chuckle and relived the thrill his approval always brought. "Smart girl. Those little hard black things are what you smell—cloves, all the way from Zanzibar."

With the memory lingering, I opened the chest and took out the sheaf of correspondence between my father and Cliff Harrison. With it came the distinct scent of cloves. I smiled. I'd caught Alma one day, after she'd finished polishing its brass fittings, dropping a few kernels of the dark spice into the chest. "Let this be our secret," she said. "I don't want your Daddy disappointed and not smell all those memories from Zanzibar."

Memories. I turned to the papers in front of me. I'll always have those.

Most of the letters were one-liners, quick and sharp, all about the tree.

"I suppose you've noticed the oak is down," my father wrote just two weeks ago.

"My sight may be going, but it's not that far gone," was Mr. Harrison's reply.

"Standing, that tree was on your property. Now most of it's on mine."

"I'd say that's more your problem than mine."

When Dad read those terse lines to me over the phone, just a few days ago, I'd thought he was exasperated with the situation. "Let me call Baxter's," I'd said, referring to the hardware store in Elkton. "They're bound to know someone who'll come out with a rig and a chain saw. They'll get rid of that tree in a day."

My father laughed, a low easy chuckle. "And then what would I do for entertainment? No, I think I'll wait awhile."

I sat there, replaying his words, and on impulse decided to give his neighbor a call. The Harrisons had moved into the house after I'd left for college, so I never got to know them, except to wave on my trips home.

His housekeeper said Mr. Harrison was resting, but she was sure he would enjoy a visit. Tomorrow morning at about eleven would be a good time.

I called my father's lawyer after that. I had talked to Russell Worth from New York last night, but there were more things to discuss with him now, particularly my frustrating encounter with the sheriff.

Russell Worth came from an old Carolina family with a big reputation and strong political connections. I reached him at his office in Raleigh. "Sounds like Billie Jenkins needs a fire lit under him," he said after I described my meeting with the sheriff. "A visit from the State Police might do just that. I'll see what I can arrange. I'll also make a few calls and see what people have to say about the sheriff himself. I'll be in touch tomorrow, before noon."

◆

The sun had only begun to come up when I woke the next morning. I fixed myself some coffee and took it outside onto the porch and sat there watching the slender bands of silver light, that would be fierce later in the day, begin to filter through the foggy haze. The forest of the tree seemed more dense than yesterday, cloaked as it was in the vapor of early morning. I went down the steps to take a closer look and ended up walking along our property line toward the road and crossing over into Mr. Harrison's yard. It was the dark irregular shape of roots, upended in a great tangled mass that drew me. I stood for a few minutes gaping at the red clay cavern of a hole they'd left. I followed the giant length of log, to where the limbs began. Some were the size of small trees, crisscrossed and sprawled on the ground, fanning out and upward. The foliage was so thick and fresh, it looked like new growth. "Even lying down that oak's got a lot of juice left in it," my father would have said.

I came to a place where the ground was trampled, and small branches had been pulled aside and snapped back to make an entry way into the heart of the tree. I bent over and edged my way in, following a narrow path. Branches which clawed at my hair and tore at my clothes made me glad that I was wearing jeans and my shirt had long sleeves. I shielded my face with my hands. The path ended in a small clearing, where patches of sunlight filtered in through the overhang of the tree. Here the ground was littered with broken twigs and tattered leaves. What looked like pieces of colored paper caught my eye. Closer inspection revealed them to be crumpled candy wrappers and empty soda cans. I stared at them for a long moment and then looked up, and gasped. Through an opening in the leaves, I saw that I was directly in line with my father's front porch and the rocker where he had been sitting when he was shot. My heart beat wildly as I took in the meaning of that line of vision, and I spun around, wanting to get away. A branch whipped across my cheek and I realized the way out was no easier than the way in. I put up my hands to protect my eyes, and almost didn't see it, a yellow bandanna, snagged on a broken limb.

———◆———

It was years since I had been inside the house next door. A family named Miller had lived there all the time I was growing up. Gil had been two years ahead of me in school and I'd had a crush on him forever. The summer his leg was in a cast we played checkers at a round table by the bay window in his living room. The window was still there, but everything else was different.

"You'll forgive me if I don't get up," Mr. Harrison said with an impish smile, and patted the side of his wheelchair as though it was the flank of a horse. "It's nice of you to come to see me. I was expectin' Alma might, but I guess she's had her hands full. I saw the Rescue Squad the other day. I could tell from the way they carried your Daddy away, he was gone. If it's any comfort, he had a long and good life."

I nodded. "Thank you. I think he did."

"You know, we weren't what you'd call friends, but I'd say we had an understanding. You see we were in the same boat. Alone. Growing old. In houses too big for us, houses we didn't want to leave." He paused and his lips spread into a smile. "We had that tree."

I tried not to show how much his words affected me. My father had been lonely, but he had never let me know how much.

"We had a good run with that old oak. We started arguing about it right after my wife died, nine years now. You were gone by then. I don't know how much you knew about that."

"Dad told me some, but not all, I'm sure."

"I know what you must have thought . . . a couple of old fools, fightin' over a tree. We were that, all right, but it kept us on our toes and gave us something to think about. Maybe we took it too far." He frowned and leaned forward. "I'm afraid that tree had something to do with your father's death."

I stared at the old man, wondering what he could mean.

"Tell me what happened to him," he said. "Come on now, don't be afraid. I have a right to know."

"Alma found him on the porch. She thought he might have had a heart attack."

He nodded impatiently. "But it was something else, wasn't it?"

"He was shot."

"That's what I thought! That's what I heard—a rifle shot."

Right away I wanted to ask if he had seen anyone, but stopped when I saw that he had more to say.

"You know it isn't every day a tree like that one goes down. If we weren't on this back road, there would have been a lot of sightseers, coming to look at that tree. But what I'd been seeing out there was something different. It wasn't somebody standing in the open, gawking, like I saw you doing this morning. That's some hole, isn't it? No, what I saw was someone trying hard not to be seen. Somebody was hiding out in that tree."

———◆———

Alma was in the kitchen when I got back. I'd left a note for her on the hall table, saying I'd gone to visit Mr. Harrison.

"Oh, that poor man! I'd been meanin' to go over and talk to him. He must have seen all the commotion over here, but I just plain forgot. His regular lady Georgene is recuperatin' from an operation, or else she would have been over here by now. There's someone from an agency comin' in until she gets back on her feet."

Alma had a load of wash she wanted to do, so I left her and went upstairs to call Russell Worth's law office. I got his secretary. "I'm so glad you phoned. I called twice today," Mrs. Gaines said, "but there was no answer. I got concerned because Mr. Worth is in court today and he's not going to be able to make it to Elkton as he hoped. But he wanted to be sure you knew he arranged for the State Police to be at your place at one o'clock today. Sheriff Jenkins has been asked to be there too. He doesn't know anything about the detectives coming. He thinks Mr. Worth needs him to sign some papers."

I saw that it was almost twelve-thirty when we finished talking, and although I wanted to talk to Worth himself, I knew Mrs. Gaines would pass on what I'd learned from Mr. Harrison. That might not be necessary with the detectives on their way.

I started downstairs then. It was time I talked to Alma. She needed to know what was going on. I'd noticed she'd already made my bed and picked up my shirt and jeans, which I'd left in a heap on the floor. They were probably in the wash right now. I met her at the foot of the stairs.

"I was just coming up," she said. "Miz Katy, where'd you find this?"

The yellow bandanna was in her hand. "It was in the pocket of your jeans. I'm almost sure it's Rollie's. Those two boys I told you about, who ganged up on him a couple of weeks ago ... they took it from him. He didn't give me a minute's piece, wantin' another one just like it, but I couldn't find one anywhere around here. Them red ones are a dime a dozen, but this here yellow kind is hard to come by."

"Alma, where's Rollie now?"

She looked surprised. "He's back in Chicago with Roland. I thought I told you ... he left here the day before your Daddy died." Tears welled in her eyes. "That's somethin' else I thanked the Lord for. If Rollie had been here, he'd have been sittin' right alongside your Daddy. I might have lost him too." Her shoulders began to shake.

I put my arms around her and closed my eyes and said my own silent prayer. I hadn't gotten around to telling her that I'd seen the snapshot of Rollie in her room. She had no way of knowing what had gone through my mind when I found that yellow neckerchief, hanging in the tree.

The sound of a car horn honking outside gave us both a start.

"Oh, Lord, that's the sheriff! I forgot all about him. He came a few minutes ago, asking to see you. I was on my way up to tell you. You be careful of him, Miz Katy. If my son Roland was here he'd say that sheriff is a man with an attitude. I'd say he just plain mean. Those boys of his don't have a chance of bein' any different. It was them who roughed up Rollie."

I gave Alma's arm a squeeze. There wasn't time to tell her anything now, and I was just as glad. There'd be time later and maybe some things wouldn't need to be said. I headed toward the door, calling over my shoulder, "I think we'll need some iced tea."

A wide-brimmed hat shaded the sheriff's face and the kind of sun glasses you can't see into, covered his eyes. He was leaning against his car which was parked in the hot sun. I was surprised to see that his boys were in the back seat, which was separated from the front by a metal grill.

"You got some kind of trouble out here?"

I had been about to apologize for keeping him waiting, but I decided not to bother. "You seem to have a short memory, Sheriff. My father was shot, remember?"

"I thought it might be something else. I got a message his lawyer wanted me out here. One o'clock. It's almost one now. Is he comin', or isn't he? This is my afternoon off and me and my boys are about to go for some recreation."

I glanced at the boys. It had to be an oven in that car. As though reading my mind, and perhaps emboldened by my glance the younger one called out. "Hey Pa, it's hot in here. Why can't we get out?"

The sheriff spun sidewards and brought his fist down on the roof of the car. The boy slumped down.

The sound of a car turning into the road distracted me from the boys' plight and I watched a dark sedan move toward us, churning dust as it came. It pulled in behind the sheriff's car. Two men in plain clothes stepped out.

"Is one of these your father's lawyer?"

I didn't have to answer him. The taller of the two men spoke up. "We're with the State Police. I'm Detective Manning. This here is Detective Richards. You must be Katherine Cobbs," he said turning to me.

I nodded. "And this is Sheriff Jenkins."

"That's right," the sheriff said. "What are you fellas doing out here?"

"We'll get to that," Manning said, "but it's kind of hot out here. I wonder if we could all go inside."

I nodded toward the sheriff's car. "Those boys should come on in, too."

"Let's go, Sheriff, and bring those boys of yours along, or we'll be having to treat them for heat stroke."

———

A tray with a pitcher of ice tea and glasses was already on a table in the living room, when we trooped in. Alma directed the boys to sit on the wooden bench in front of the fire place, and brought them each a glass. Their thirsty gulps resounded in the quiet room.

"What's your name son?" Manning asked the older boy.

"Billie Jenkins."

"Same name as your father?"

The boy nodded, his expression wary.

"My name's Jamie," the smaller one piped up.

"And who are you named after?"

He shrugged and looked across the room. "Pa, who am I named after?"

"Your grampa."

"Which grampa?"

"You ask too many questions," the sheriff said and turned away to look from one detective to the other, "What brought you fellas out here?"

"You don't give up, do you? Let's say it's a special assignment," Manning answered, his words almost lost in the sound of a car skidding to a stop outside. Its doors opened and slammed shut.

"What the hell's goin' on here?" The sheriff was on his feet.

"Take it easy." Manning motioned him to sit down. "It's some of our folks. They've come to have a look around."

"Look around at what?"

"Around the house, and around that tree," the detective answered smoothly. "Whoever shot Mr. Cobbs might have left something behind."

The sheriff had left his hat on the hall table and his sun glasses were in his shirt pocket. His face seemed bare. "Like I told her ..." He gave me a quick side glance. "Her ole man was shot with a twenty-two rifle. It'd be like looking for a needle in the hay trying to find out whose it was."

Manning frowned. "That's one way of looking at it, but it sounds like a shortcut."

The sheriff stiffened and for a minute I thought he was going to rise to the challenge, but something made him change his mind.

I had been watching the boys. The older one kept looking down at the floor, but Jamie was sitting up straight, his eyes wide open, and riveted on the detective. "What are you lookin' for?"

"That's a good question," Manning said and leaned toward him. "We look for lots of things. Suppose someone had a flashlight and left it behind. The flashlight would have fingerprints on it, wouldn't it?"

Jamie frowned."Guess so. But it wasn't dark. We didn't need no flashlight. We ..."

His brother grabbed for him. "Shut up, Jamie. Just shut up," he pleaded. The bench toppled over and the boys rolled onto the floor.

The sheriff started across the room. Manning rose. "Leave them be, Sheriff. They're not hurt."

Confusion showed on the sheriff's face, as the boys got to their feet and righted the bench, and sat back down.

"Sheriff," my voice wasn't all that loud, but it startled him and his head snapped around. "You told me whoever it was had to be a good shot. You're a good shot, aren't you?"

"What's that supposed to mean? Of course I'm a good shot."

"Pa hits the bull's eye all the time." Jamie's proud voice, filled the room. "Billie's good, too. I'm not so good yet." He lowered his eyes but only for an instant. "I'd be a lot better if Pa gave me more chances. When just Billie and me go shootin' together, he gives me lots of chances. The other day he let me have the first shot. We were gonna shoot out the light on the ole man's porch. I missed it, but I scared the ole man ... he fell right off his chair. Billie woulda gotten the light for sure, but he didn't take no shot. He grabbed me and said we hadda go."

———◆———

It was nine o'clock and the night sounds of crickets and tree toads filtered in through the open windows. Alma and I were sitting across from one another at the kitchen table, tired, but not ready for sleep. I had found a bottle of bourbon on the pantry shelf and had fixed myself a drink. Alma was having a glass of milk.

She shook her head. "It's hard to believe so many folks knew so much bad stuff about that sheriff and just turned their heads the other way. Beatin' those boys up whenever he felt like it … and then givin' them treats by lettin' them play with guns … it makes no sense."

I didn't understand it either, but you only had to read newspapers to know that those kinds of things were happening all over.

Russell Worth had telephoned in the late afternoon, after the police had left. "I'm glad things worked out," he said. "It didn't take but a few calls to get a line on that sheriff. From the bank president on down everybody said he was a bad apple. I had no idea what would come of sending out those detectives, except one way to handle a bully is to set him up against a bigger bully. That's what they were supposed to do … bully him. We were just lucky those boys were along. Otherwise it would have been awhile before we got to the bottom of things."

Only in a town like Elkton could things have been wrapped up so fast, I was thinking. The day after tomorrow was my father's funeral.

Across from me I saw Alma nodding, but then her eyes flickered open. "I was just thinkin' about your Daddy. I don't know if he knew about me dropping a few cloves in that Zanzibar chest of his. I suspect he did. I'd like to take some with me when we go to the cemetery. I think he'd like it if I sprinkled a few over his grave."

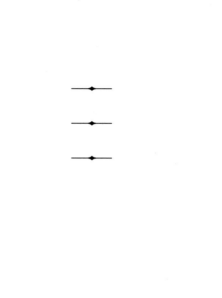

THE

WASTE

PILE AT

APPLE BOW

He'd seen the destruction of the land from the air, the hills and hollows of the earth's flesh, scarred and scabbed. But from the plane window it had been distant and unreal. It wasn't until the TV news correspondent had begun his climb up the steep mountain path, following the old miner that he began to understand what the big mining companies had done to Appalachia.

By the calendar it was spring, but the only evidence of the land's rebirth was an occasional stalk of fern pushing up a clot of rotting leaves. His eyes smarted from the smoggy haze that hung like gray angel's hair from the branches of the unleafed trees. Steve Jaros licked his lips and felt the grime of coal dust rough on his tongue.

On the path ahead of him he heard the miner cough and he listened to the lingering rattle in the old man's chest. It was the only sound in the stillness beside that of their footfalls on the trail. There were no bird songs, no rustle of squirrels and chipmunks in the underbrush. There was no sign of any animal life, at all.

The strip mines and the smoldering piles of coal waste that had been blackening the hills for years were now wrenching the last bit of life from the air and the soil.

He shifted the strap of his camera on his shoulder and undid the buttons of his suede jacket. Though the air was cold and raw, the exertion of the uphill climb had made him warm. Usually the camera wasn't his to carry, but when he'd learned that the mining company was refusing to talk to newsmen and that the miners were being equally silent, he'd decided to enter Apple Bow with a minimum of fanfare. He had come alone, leaving his cameraman and sound man back at the small hotel in Jackson, on the other side of the mountain.

The decision had one severe drawback. It meant he was limited to using the Filmo, a small camera without sound. Yet, had Charlie and Usher and all their equipment been with him when he'd walked into the school-house, converted into a make-shift rescue shelter, he would have met with an even colder wall of reserve. He wouldn't have got any answers at all. He wouldn't be headed now for what was left of the waste pile overlooking the hollow of Apple Bow.

At least that's where he hoped Newt Boyd was taking him. He wasn't really sure.

For more than half an hour they had been walking in silence, single file, following the steep rutted trail. Ahead of him, gun and game bag slung over his shoulder, the frail old man leaned into the steep incline. Now and again his shoulders shook with a fit of coughing.

When the trail showed signs of leveling off, Newt Boyd stopped and turned around. "Let's set here a minute." He moved off to the side and settled himself on a large boulder.

Across the way from him, Steve leaned against the trunk of a tree. As he slipped the camera from his shoulder he saw Newt peering at him, faded blue eyes staring intently from under drooping lids. The miner cleared his throat and Steve had the feeling that the pause in the trek up the hillside might have another purpose besides a rest.

"I suppose you heard the company's claiming that floodslide was 'An Act of God.'"

Steve nodded. He'd heard the no-liability position the company had taken and he'd read the terse statement that used just those words.

"They're blaming the rains. Well, rains come every spring. But the company held off until the clouds were hangin' right in there between them hills before they did what they should have done months ago. The thunder and lightning was crackling so hard you couldn't hear nothin' on the radio. The rain was coming down in sheets. That's when they tried to blast, hoping to shore things up. But it was too late. There were nothin' that could've changed the course of that slide then."

"Are you saying the company *knew* that waste pile at Apple Bow was in danger of collapsing?"

"Sure they knew! Everybody around here knew it was restless. For more than a year we'd been listening to the rumbling and the shifting deep inside that heap, watchin' the water build up behind it, seein' it start to seep through. A survey done last year by some government inspecting team put Apple Bow on the list of piles to be shored up. But the company knew nobody was gonna come around to check, so they did nothin'—until it was too late."

Steve cast a frustrated glance down at the camera on the ground. It would do no good to film Newt Boyd without sound and there was sure no point in wishing Charlie and Usher were standing beside him now.

His only chance of getting the story that would establish the mining company's negligence was if he could persuade the old miner to repeat the things he had just told him and say them once again in front of a camera with sound.

Newt turned sideways and pointed toward a distant spot through the trees. "See off there. There's another pile just like the one at Apple Bow."

Steve's eyes focused on a blackened mound, hooded by a layer of gray cloud. That's what Apple Bow had looked like, before the water had gathered behind it and turned it into a hurtling avalanche of rock and mud and coal waste. One hundred and twenty-four people had been killed and more than 3000 had been left homeless.

"There's hundreds of others of them piles, scattered all over these coal hills, all sitting and waiting until somethin' starts them shifting. Once they start there ain't nothin' that'll stop them."

There was no point in waiting any longer, Steve decided. Now was the time to broach the subject of filming the waste pile at Apple Bow. He could get what he needed with the Filmo. Later he'd try to persuade Newt to talk to him in front of the sound camera that Charlie and Usher had in Jackson.

"How about it, Newt? How close can we get to the pile at Apple Bow?"

The miner was gazing off in the distance, still looking at the other smoldering mound. His head turned slowly.

"You'd have to get mighty close to get any pictures of them bore holes where they put the powder when they tried to blast. The company's posted guards to make sure nobody comes snoopin' around. They got guns and orders to shoot anybody trespassing."

Steve knew about the guards, though he hadn't known they were armed. The way he saw it, the company's aggressive silence made it a sure bet they had something to hide. The miners weren't talking because they had something to fear. These suspicions, side by side, aroused not just his interest but his anger.

"There's gong to be an official investigation in a few days, Newt. Then the company won't be able to keep anyone away. I can't wait. I want that film now."

"Well, it ain't gonna be easy. Anybody going in there has a good chance of getting his head shot through. This ain't the first time a dam's broke in these parts and it's been the company's fault. It ain't the first time we had to go digging for our dead. There's always some hollerin' right afterwards and politicians make a lot of promises, giving us to believe something's gonna be done. Nothin' ever is. You don't know how powerful these big companies are."

Newt looked away, and against the gray day his profile was sad and lonely. A scraggly beard camouflaged his sunken cheeks, but the loose brown coat did little to hide the dejection and fatigue in the thin rounded shoulders.

Up until then Steve hadn't been able to put his finger on what was driving him after this story, except that he knew he wasn't going to be satisfied with recounting the details of the disaster and letting it go at that. It made no sense to wait for an investigation to turn up new information. By then the story would have gone cold, losing the interest of viewers, and TV producers. He didn't want that to happen with Apple Bow. Too much was at risk. Too many lives had already been lost.

He was beyond pissed off by the company's arrogance, its pontifical stand that "An Act of God" had caused the collapse of the waste pile. He bristled at their self-exoneration, when all around him he saw signs of their negligence and their culpability. His eyes swept over the gray-brown woodland, as barren as any he had seen in war zones, and he tried to imagine what it had been like before the mining companies had come, when springtime had meant trees in leaf, a ground cover of wildflowers, and small animals and birds stirring in the brush.

Something else kept him after the story. It was what he saw in Newt Boyd's face, in the droop of his shoulders and the set of defeat in his bones. The same look of defeat had been in all the faces at the rescue shelter, except for the girl. He remembered the toss of her blonde head, the resolute set of her chin, and the fiery flash of determination in her deep blue eyes. She stood apart from the others because of her spirit. He hadn't had time to find out why. He had the feeling that she was responsible for Newt Boyd coming forward, which is why the miner was talking to him now.

Newt shifted his position on the boulder and cleared his throat. "There's somethin' you might not know. The company's got a way of drying up a man's living if he's heard complaining. That's one of the reasons them folks at the shelter wasn't saying anything."

"Why are you taking the chance, Newt?"

The old man shrugged. "Fed up. Tired of letting them get away with things. I'm not young any more. My family's grown. I got nothin' to lose."

Steve stepped over to where the miner was sitting and put his hand on his shoulder, and then stepped back. "Newt, the public has been stirred up by what happened here. But people have a way of forgetting things that don't involve them directly. They have to be kept stirred up until the investigation gets started. If there are enough angry people around, demanding answers, the company's negligence and the government's ineffective inspection system won't get swept under the rug this time."

"How're you gonna go about doing that?"

"By keeping the story alive, by showing people what these hills look like, close up, by letting them hear what the miners and their families have to say. To begin with, I want film of Apple Bow."

A light flickered in Newt Boyd's eyes, but in an instant it was gone. "You sure you understand what I've been telling you? Them guards have been hired to watch out for fellas like you. If they catch you spying or trespassing, or whatever you want to call it, they'll shoot, just as if you was a crow sittin' on a fence. And if needs be, afterwards, they'll say that's what they thought you was, a crow."

"Damn it, Newt, what else are you going to come up with? Are you going to take me there, or do I go alone?" Steve picked up his camera and slung it over his shoulder.

A grin creased through the scraggly beard. There was no mistaking the brightness in the faded blue eyes now. "Lorny said you can't tell a bird while he's all sleeked and strutting. You gotta get him a little ruffled to find out what's under all them feathers. That silk neck thing and that fancy suede jacket you're wearing had me thinkin' you might be all show and no innards. Guess I was wrong. Lorny will be mighty pleased with herself when she finds out."

He got to his feet with a sprightliness Steve hadn't seen before. "Let's go."

But Steve put a hand on his arm, "Who's Lorny?"

"My daughter. Seen you eyeing her at the shelter. Pretty thing she is, but sometimes she's got a mind harder than a hickory nut. She's waiting lunch for us and I expect she's gonna be a bit fussed. We're late."

Steve wasn't about to be sidetracked. "What about filming Apple Bow, Newt?"

"Let's eat first and talk later. Lorny's got a plan."

Steve shook his head, exasperated, but at least he'd been right about the girl. His curiosity mounted as he followed Newt back on the trail.

In a few minutes they rounded a bend and he saw a small gray house set back among the trees.

"Needs painting," Newt said. "Lorny was all for starting it this week. Said it would be good therapy, but I've not been of a mind. Since she's come, she's set herself to ironing curtains and washing windows, between helping down at the shelter. Long time ago her brothers and me promised her Ma we'd see she went away to school. Martha didn't want Lorny ending up like all the other women in the hollows, waitin' for their men to come up out of the mines. Lorny's been gone six years, graduated college most two years ago."

"Where does she live?"

"Up north, works in the big city, in that place they call the big apple. She went to school there, and found a job mighty quick. Came right down when she got the bad news. She's talking about stayin' on. It's sure nice to have her here, but I keep tellin' her this ain't no place for her to spend her life."

Their voices must have carried into the house because the front door swung open and Lorny Boyd appeared in the doorway, blonde head tossing, and an impatient hand on a slim jeaned hip.

"I should have known noon would mean closer to two!" A smile softened the reprimand in her eyes.

"Now let's not start in scolding, girl. I had a few things on my mind that needed straight'nin' out." He turned to Steve. "This here's my daughter, Lorna. Guess she knows you. Says she's seen you on TV. Can't say I have. Don't have a TV and when I get a chance to see one, don't watch the news. Don't watch them hillbilly programs either, makes us mountain folk out to be a bunch of dumb jokers."

Lorna Boyd smiled at Steve, holding out a slim smooth hand. "I thought you were still in Vietnam."

So, she had seen him on TV. "I got back a month ago. This is my first stateside assignment in a long while."

"How does it compare?"

An honest answer would have plunged them into a lengthy and morbid discussion, so he avoided it. "Any place you haven't been before is strange. It helps though when everybody speaks the same language."

"Do we?" There was the unmistakable glint of mischief in her eyes.

He responded with a slow grin as he followed her into the house. "There have been moments when I've not been so sure."

In a bathroom down the hall, where fresh white curtains framed a window that faced a hillside of scraggy oaks and pines, Steve splashed some water on his face and pulled a comb through his dark curly hair. For a moment he stared at his reflection, smiling, wondering if "sleeked and strutting" had really been her words. Was that the impression he'd made on Lorna Boyd?

She presented an interesting mix of city and country. Her time away from the hills must have changed her a great deal from the girl she had been.

When he returned to the kitchen she was at the stove taking a platter of fried chicken from the oven. She glanced up, I hope you're hungry."

"I didn't realize how much until I stepped in here." He sniffed the air appreciatively.

"Everything's ready and Dad's waiting for you." She nodded toward a round table by the window where Newt was already seated and three places were set.

"How about a mite o' whiskey?" Newt reached for a jug on the floor at his side.

"Sounds great."

Newt filled two small glasses. He handed one to Steve and waited. Steve tipped the glass to his mouth, bracing himself. He'd had mountain brew before. He was pleasantly surprised and nodded his approval. "Goes down nice and easy."

"Don't drink nothin' else," Newt said, with a grin. "Two's my limit though. Doctor says I shouldn't drink at all account of the cough. But the few extra days it might give me ain't worth it."

Lorna joined them at the table, adding a basket of warm buttered biscuits and a bowl of salad to the platter of chicken already on the table.

"How did you manage all this?" Steve asked as she held the platter out to him. "You were still at the shelter when your father and I left."

She glanced quickly at her father, and then back at Steve. "There's a short-cut. It takes only about fifteen minutes to get up here."

Steve raised an eyebrow and looked at Newt.

The miner shrugged. "There was some thinking I had to do. Some questions that needed answering. Takes a while to figure out a man. Ain't sure I got you figured all the way, but I got a pretty good idea. Wanted to give you enough chances to change your mind."

"One more and I might have."

"Don't think so. You're the kind, the harder it gets, the more you want it."

Steve wondered about that. "Could be."

"I think it's time we stopped being cagey and got down to business. First off there's somethin' you need to know." Newt paused, his gaze lowered, hovering over his plate. Then his head came up with a snap. "Four of our kin were killed in that slide at Apple Bow—my two sons and my daughter-in-law and my four-year-old granddaughter. They was having the little girl's birthday party. I should have been there, only I'd been to Jackson to do some buying. Got held up because of the rain."

Steve drew in a long breath.

"Don't bother trying to say anything. There ain't nothin' anybody can say. But that tells you straight, I got no love for the company. And neither does Lorny. But up until you came along we weren't in agreement as to what to do about it. Right after it happened, before Lorny come down, I near went crazy. I took my gun and I went out looking for somebody to blame. I guess I would have shot the first company man I seen, except I got a bad coughing spell and could no more walk than I could shoot, so I come on home."

Newt looked toward a corner of the kitchen where the rifle and game bag stood. Steve followed his glance and felt his own frustration boil. A great story was unfolding before him. A print reporter listened and then wrote the story. But without film and voice, Newt's compelling tale was worthless for television.

"Lorny's got different ideas from the rest of us who've never been out of these hills. Mountain folk have always stayed to themselves, not mixing even with each other much. Lorny says we have to change our ways. Doing things alone ain't gonna get us nowhere now. We got to organize, she says."

Lorna flushed, anger deepening the color of her eyes. She looked as she had at the shelter, determined and ready to fight.

She leaned toward Steve and spoke with quiet control. "You saw those people at the shelter today, patiently waiting to find out what was going to happen to them—women who had lost their husbands, miners who had to use their own picks and shovels to dig out their dead children. All of them homeless, victims of big-company negligence and power, grateful when a Red Cross worker gave them a bologna sandwich!"

She gripped his arm. "They don't know their rights or how to go about finding out what they are. Somebody has to help them! Someone has to show them how!"

Newt's head jerked in his daughter's direction. "Let's not start that again. I didn't send you up north so you could turn right around and come back here. This ain't no place for you, Lorny. Your mother will be crying in her grave."

She eased herself back in her chair and took her hand from Steve's arm. She looked at her father. "All right," she said softly. "We won't talk about that now."

"We're not gonna talk about it ever. Now that's settled." Newt banged his empty glass on the table. "Now suppose we get on with explaining your plan."

Lorna sat back, took a deep breath, and turned to Steve. "I'll take you to Apple Bow. We'll leave before dusk this afternoon and get there by dark. We'll stay overnight so we can be there at dawn before the guards get up. You should be able to get all the film you want, without their even knowing you've been there. If Dad took you, he'd be sure to get one of his coughing spells."

Steve looked at Newt. The pieces were beginning to fit. Up until now he hadn't been able to figure out the miner's reticence to take him to Apple Bow. Now he at least had some idea what was behind it.

"She's somethin', ain't she? Worked this all out herself, even before you showed up at the shelter. Claims she knew you were the kind who wouldn't be satisfied without digging into things."

"What do you mean before I showed up at the shelter? How did you know I was coming?"

Lorna smiled at him. "The man who tends bar at the hotel in Jackson is my uncle. He overheard you talking with your crew."

Steve shook his head, grinning. "You've got as good a spy system as I've seen."

Newt chuckled. "I didn't like the sound of this idea at first, but I guess it will work out all right. How's it strike you?"

"So far so good, but Apple Bow isn't enough." He pointed a finger at Newt. "I need you on film, saying the kinds of things you told me on the way here, about the company knowing the pile was unstable and doing nothing about it until it was too late."

"Lorny said you'd want that. That's why I'm going to Jackson this afternoon and get your two fellas and their equipment. I'll get them to the right place at Apple Bow."

Steve looked from father to daughter. "Is there anything you two haven't thought of?"

Newt shrugged. "Maybe. I'll get them and their stuff to the other side of Apple Bow, just across from where you and Lorny are gonna be. Between the lot of you, you should get all the pictures you want. After that's done we can talk."

Steve looked at Lorna. "Are you the TV production expert in this family?"

"I took an elective course in radio and TV techniques at college. I knew the camera you have with you now has no sound."

Steve eyed her appreciatively as she rose to clear the dishes from the table and returned with a pot of coffee. He forced his mind to return to the problem of the interviews he wanted. Now more than before it wouldn't be enough to talk only to Newt. Four members of his family had lost their lives in the slide. It would be natural for Newt's objectivity to be questioned. As gently as he could he explained the situation. "I want your story, Newt, but I need others, too. What will it take to get some of the other miners to talk to me?"

Newt's eyes narrowed and his thin lips pursed. A thoughtful expression came to his face. "After tomorra morning you won't have no trouble. I promise you."

Apprehension darkened Lorna's eyes. "What are you planning to do?"

"Ain't telling nobody. So there's no use your pesting." Newt pushed his chair back from the table and rose stiffly. Since it's a long ways to Jackson, I'm gonna take a bit of a rest. Lorney, make sure you wake me in an hour, if I ain't up yet."

Steve called after the miner, as he headed down the hall. "You can use the car I left a couple of streets from the shelter. It'll get you to Jackson a lot quicker."

Newt turned around and grinned. "I wondered if you'd get around to offerin', or if I'd have to ask. It's that blue Chevy, ain't it, parked just a few yards from the post office."

Steve shook his head as the miner walked down the hall, and then turned his gaze to Lorna. "I have to hand it to you two. You sure have led me up a mountain path."

This time her smile was only fleeting, overpowered by the concern in her eyes. "What do you suppose he's up to?"

"You're asking me?"

While Newt slept, Lorna drew a sketch of the area around the Apple Bow waste pile, showing Steve where she planned to take him. She also mapped out the approach his camera and sound crew would follow on the other side.

"I'm still not sure why I can't just take my crew and head up to that pile and start filming. Those guards can't shoot all three of us—and say we were crows sitting on a fence."

"I do believe we are beginning to speak the same language, she said with a quick laugh. "No, I don't think they'd shoot the three of you. But they wouldn't let you film either. So what would that accomplish? The only way to get what you want is to do it, without their knowing."

She leaned toward him. "Steve, do you understand what this will mean to the miners? It will show them that the company can be challenged. Maybe their knowing that will be enough to convince them they should talk to you."

Her face brightened. "I bet that's what my father plans to do—take a few men along with him and let them see for themselves what you want to do. People here don't know there's a difference between a TV news correspondent and whoever puts on those awful hillbilly programs. My father didn't. It took a lot of talking to convince him. He didn't trust you. Why should *they?*"

Steve shook his head. "You're right. Why should they? Why do you?"

"I've been out in the big wide world," she said with a smile. "I knew who you were when you arrived at the shelter. I know the kind of reporting you do, so I thought you might be able to help us get the goods on the mining company."

"You've been two steps ahead of me all the time," he said. "I promise you, I'll sure give it a try."

"My father doesn't like the idea of my coming back here to live. I'm not really sure I want to. But sometimes I think it's the only right thing. To leave here and get an education and not come back and help out … it doesn't seem right. "

"And here I've been hoping to see you in New York."

"That would be nice." She smiled wistfully. "It isn't easy to decide."

"None of the big ones are."

While she did the dishes, he wrote a note to Charlie and Usher, explaining what the plan was, enclosing the map she had made of the area surrounding Apple Bow.

Newt had been asleep almost an hour when the sound of coughing came from his room, deep and strangled. Lorna started down the hall, but stopped outside his door. In a while she came back to the kitchen.

"He's lived with it for so long now. But someday…" She left the sentence unfinished. She'd heard her father's door open.

It was a few minutes before Newt joined them. "You got all your things ready for tonight, Lorny?"

She opened the door of a cupboard and took out three bulging pillowcases. "Blankets, food, and something to drink." She felt inside the cupboard and handed Steve a heavy woolen sweater, a worn leather jacket, and a ragged scarf.

"It will be cold tonight. What you're wearing won't be warm enough and besides you don't exactly melt into the landscape."

He grinned. "I'll have you know I bought this jacket in Spain and the scarf came all the way from Bangkok."

"You don't say? Well, peacocks never were a part of these woods, and if they were, they'd be mighty scarce by now. So you'd better change your feathers or those guards will shoot you for the wrong reasons."

Steve burst out laughing. Then, with a glance that took in her yellow knit shirt and the trim Levis, he asked, "And what are you going to wear?"

"You won't recognize me when I've changed."

"You want to bet?"

Newt cleared his throat. "Listen, you two, this ain't no picnic you're going on. Don't go getting carried away with that kind of nonsense."

"What nonsense?"

"Listen here, girl, I'm not dead yet and besides my memory is pretty good. I can see it's a waste of time saying anything else, so I'd best just be on my way." He thrust out a bony, callused hand at Steve. "Maybe when this is all over you can do somethin' about them hillbilly programs. Meantime, keep an eye on her. She thinks she knows it all, but she don't."

Lorna kissed her father's cheek. "I'd forgotten how ornery you can be."

Newt started toward the door, then stopped, walked back across the room and hoisted his rifle and game bag over his shoulder.

Her hand reached out. "Pa." In the one whispered word her voice revealed the frightened echo of the child she once was.

Newt patted her hand. "Don't go frettin' none. I've lived a long time and I know what I'm doing."

After Newt was gone, and everything they were going to take with them was in order, Lorna took him around to the back of the house, where the spikes of crocus leaves had struggled up through the sour earth. "My mother planted a garden here years ago. This is all that's left of it." She shook her head and pointed to a winding downhill path that led to the shelter, the short-cut she had taken earlier.

"When I was a little girl there used to be violets to pick in the spring, and wild strawberries in summer. My brothers used to hunt squirrel and possum. One summer a flock of bluebirds flew into that tree over there, and stayed until the first frost. But nothing lives or grows here now, only human beings.

She fell silent then, looking off into the distance. He stood quietly beside her, giving her time to get past a collection of sad and complicated memories. When she turned to face him he was struck by how lovely she was, even in the baggy dark gray coat that belonged to her father. He reached for a stick and broke it in two, tempering the urge to take her in his arms.

———◆———

He woke to a dark night, a dim shadow of the moon, hidden by a heavy layer of clouds, but no stars. Beside him Lorna stirred. They'd made a bed of leaves covered by an oilskin and climbed into makeshift sleeping bags. He felt her breath sweep past his cheek, the soft silk of her hair brush his ear.

He lay still, not wanting to wake her. The night was long. He waited for the glow of a coming dawn before he woke her.

They untangled themselves from their coverings and rose, stretching cramped limbs. She poured hot coffee from a Thermos into paper cups, and they ate peanut butter and jelly sandwiches. When they spoke is was in low whispers. Voices carry in the sort of stillness that surrounded them. They were on the downward slope of the hillside, overlooking the high and the hollow of Apple Bow. As dawn lifted and the spread of light fanned upward into the sky, an ugly black sprawling shadow took shape in the shallow valley not far below, the dregs of the waste pile.

Steve began to film in regular intervals following the progression of dawn into day. Sunlight suddenly pierced the layers of cloud cover and with the accuracy of a spot light, illuminated a string of bore holes at the base of the collapsed waste pile. Lorna pressed his arm and pointed. He nodded and swept the area with the camera.

He lowered it and turned to her. "Look over there," he said softly, pointing to the opposite hillside. There was a brief glint of light, there one instant, then gone, and then repeated, with no set pattern.

"What is it?" she asked.

"Sun glancing off a camera lens. Your father got to Jackson. Charlie and Usher are where he said they would be." He wondered if Newt was with them. "Where are the guards?"

She held onto his arm and leaned forward, pointing to a spot just below them, in partial shadow, not yet discovered by the sun. He could make out the shape of a lean-to.

He changed the film in the camera and put the shot reel into a weather-proof bag.

"You stay here. I want to get a closer look."

Her blue eyes defied him and he knew there was neither time nor point to argue. Newt had warned him she was strong-willed.

The ground was soft from the recent rains and any leaves left from previous years were damp and made no sound underfoot. The greatest hazard was the possibility of slipping. There was enough low growth for them to catch onto, as they made a careful, slow descent.

The murmur of voices reached them and they stopped. Three figures emerged from the lean-to, burly men in heavy woolen coats. One had a shotgun, held lightly in his hand, the other two carried rifles. Steve raised the Filmo to his eye and followed the men as they fanned out into a semi-circle and walked to a midpoint in the hollow.

As the three men spread out, Steve could see that their heads were raised, their eyes scanning the encircling hillside. For a moment he felt a pair of eyes looking directly at him, but they slid away without acknowledgement.

Across the way the glint of light came and went again. The man with the shotgun called out and one of his partners lifted a pair of binoculars hanging from a strap around his neck and trained them on the hillside across the way.

Beside Steve, Lorna took a breath. Steve had the camera up to his face, and was getting it all. The guy with the binoculars let them fall to his chest and was bringing his rifle up to his shoulder.

"Steve!" Her voice beside him was an imperative whisper. He turned. Her face was chalk white against the dark gray of her father's wool coat. She was not looking at the man with the rifle. Her eyes were wide with terror, focused on the small bent figure coming up from the mouth of the hollow.

Newt Boyd picked his way amid the rubble of the wash, heading in a straight line for the three armed guards.

Across the way flashes of light glinted on the brown hillside. The guard's rifle was raised and aimed.

"Hey, what you fellas targetin'?" Newt's voice rang out loud and clear across the valley. "There ain't been no game in these parts in years."

Three guns swung and fired. Newt Boyd staggered and fell still to the ground. Over Lorna's agonized moan Steve heard the sound of gunfire coming from the woods below. A shower of black earth sprang up and spattered around the feet of the guards. Guns fell from their hands and their arms reached into the air.

A small band of miners started out of the woods, moving slowly across the blackened earth of he hollow.

Lorna buried her face against Steve's chest and quietly sobbed. He wrapped his arms around her and rested his cheek against her hair. On the opposite hillside, he caught the familiar glint of sun off the camera's lens. Charlie and Usher were there, with sound and film. Steve was sure they had got it all.

Slowly, Lorna raised her head. He looked down at her upturned face, into blue eyes blurred by tears, shadowed by sorrow and uncertainty. Her voice trembled when she spoke. "I was afraid of this. I knew he had a plan. I knew he was determined to do anything to get the goods on the mining company."

His eyes stung and his voice was husky when he spoke, "Your father didn't plan it this way, but he knew it could happen and he took the chance. We've got to make sure his effort isn't wasted."

She nodded, biting her lower lip, and then reached for his hand. They started down into the hollow together.

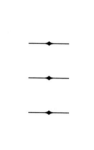

A Matter of Trust

Pete stood in the dark shadow of the east hangar watching the starry Mexican sky, his gaze steady on the northern quadrant, waiting for the plane's lights to appear. He was listening, too. Depending on the wind, the sound of the engine might come first.

Harry was fifteen minutes overdue—too soon to worry, except there'd been no radio contact with him for the last two hours. And no word from the drop spot either.

Pete sucked in his breath and let out a deep sigh. He and Harry had managed to survive two and a half years in Vietnam, scarred, but alive. To have it end for Harry in a nose dive on some piece of Arizona desert wasn't the way it ought to be.

Pete shook his head and tried to get rid of the grisly thought. Maybe Harry was just messed up a little and any minute would come limping in.

Then why not radio? And what about the ground? Why had they lost contact with them, too? Only a fool could think the two were not connected.

Come on, Harry, a familiar voice inside him screamed. Don't let your old buddy down. Don't make a fool and a dead man of me!

A few minutes ago Brewster had reminded him of something he had almost forgotten in his concern over Harry's return. "I'm sure glad we weren't dumb enough to trust him on this first run. You can never tell with a guy, not till you test him out."

"Hold on, Brewster," Pete had said. "Harry's only a few minutes late. Already you're blackballing him. Hell, what's fifteen minutes?"

"It's more than the fifteen minutes. Why haven't we heard from the guys on the ground? I've been trying for the last two hours."

Pete shrugged. "Maybe they had to scatter. Maybe they weren't there when Harry landed. Maybe Harry went off looking for them."

"Then why hasn't he called in?" Brewster leaned back in his chair and bit the end off a cigar. He struck a match on his knee and went through an elaborate procedure of lighting up. Letting out a bellyful of smoke, he looked at Pete. "I'd be a helluva lot more worried if those bricks had been the real stuff. This way all we lose is a plane."

"And a man," Pete said quietly.

"No loss if the guy is chicken or a thief."

"Boy, you sure have a lot of faith in your fellow rats."

Brewster stared at him through the cloud of smoke.

"I'm glad we understand each other."

That was when Pete had walked out the door into the soothing darkness of the night. Had he stayed inside he might have put a fist into Brewster's face. Maybe more than that. He had walked slowly across the airfield until he reached the hangar and then stood leaning against it, watching the sky, waiting.

Come *on*, Harry, the voice inside him screamed again. You can make it. Get the hell back here. I'll be a dead duck when Brewster finds out I let you fly the real stuff.

A faint hum touched Pete's eardrum and he turned his head to catch the sound, but it was too elusive to pinpoint. He scanned the sky, then turned and looked to the south. Harry might come in that way, depending on the wind. But none of the lights twinkling in the sky was moving.

The humming sound seemed to fade away. It might have been the motor of a small car somewhere in the distance. But there were no lights on the road, no distinguishable shadows moving on the dark flat horizon.

He couldn't stand still and wait any longer. He had to do something, if only walk. He started across the airfield, keeping in the shadows so that if Brewster were looking outside he wouldn't see him roaming around. He didn't want Brewster to get the idea he was nervous. That was hardly the word for the way he was feeling. He could do with a drink or a few pulls on some fresh grass. But there was a rule anyone who worked for Brewster had to live by. "Off duty, I don't care what you do, but when you're on my time you're clean. I don't want any dope heads around my planes."

A gust of dry cold wind scudded across the flat plain and blew dust in Pete's eyes. Tears flowed and washed the dirt away. The wetness that touched his cheeks made him realize he wanted to cry. The frustration of not knowing where the hell Harry was or what had happened to him or what Brewster would do when the whole thing came out was getting to him.

Why had he got into this rotten racket anyway? Maybe if he had tried a little harder and waited around a little longer, a job would have turned up. But he'd got tired of waiting, tired of being turned away with "Sorry, soldier, we're not hiring." Hell they weren't hiring. Who were all those guys working inside? Maybe it was the scars on his face they didn't like. Maybe it was his limp.

Brewster hadn't cared a rap about his scars or his messed-up leg. He just liked the fact that Pete could patch up a plane and make it fly even if all he had to work with was a coat hanger and a pair of pliers. And when Pete had told him about Harry, Brewster had said for him to come on down. "If the guy can fly as well as you say he can I don't give a damn what he looks like." And then Brewster had asked Pete the only personal question he ever had, and never brought it up again. "What the hell happened to the two of you—a fire bomb go off in your faces?"

"That's about it," Pete answered, but said no more. He didn't like to talk about it, and he tried hard not to think about it. He'd never forget the searing flames licking at his face, heating up the rims of his goggles so that they branded scars around his eyes that no plastic surgeon could fix. Hideous scars. But if it hadn't been for the goggles he and Harry would be blind.

He would never forget the screams either. Even in memory he couldn't tell whose screams they were, his or Harry's. In a way it was the screams that held them together, that bound them in some crazy way. He didn't know what was up with Harry now, why he was late. But he heard his screams, screams that maybe he wasn't even yelling. Pete was answering them, with his own. Harry, where are you? Come on, old buddy, you can make it! God dammit, get down here!

The night went suddenly silent. The hum he'd heard had not been repeated. He realized now what it had sounded like—a small plane coming in on a glide, the movement of the wind sliding off the wings.

Pete bent his head against a fresh swirl of dust and started back toward the office. Harry was half an hour late. It wouldn't do any good to stay away from Brewster now. Soon it would be time for Pete to tell him everything—that he hadn't followed orders but had let Harry take off with the real stuff.

He hadn't wanted Brewster to pull a stunt like that on Harry. Harry didn't need to prove himself, not to Pete. At least that was the way he felt five hours ago when he'd passed up the last chance to make the switch, when he'd stood at the end of the airfield watching Harry take off into the deepening dusk, headed north for the border. He was flying low so no radar could track him, following the course Brewster had plotted with him, headed for an obscure piece of Arizona desert where he could make a quick landing, unload, and take off again, in a matter of minutes.

What had happened? What had gone wrong?

Brewster was into a new cigar. The other lay half smoked in the big flat bowl of an ashtray on his desk. The room stank. Pete left the door ajar to let in some air.

"Any word?"

Brewster looked at him in an ugly kind of way. "Who from? Half an hour late on a two-hour run?"

"Did you try contacting the drop spot again?"

"What good would that do?"

Pete felt anger flush the scarred tissue of his face. "What good? Hell, we might find out what happened to Harry."

"We know what happened to Harry. He chickened out. He just didn't have it. I took a chance on him. I could tell he still had the shakes. It was my decision. I don't hold you responsible."

"You're saying he cracked up?"

"Cracked up, blew off somewhere, took a nose dive—I don't care what you call it. He isn't here now. What's the difference?"

"There's a big difference. Maybe he's out there somewhere and needs help. Maybe he landed at the drop and something went wrong."

"Like what?" A long puff of smoke billowed out of Brewster's mouth.

"Like the guys waiting didn't like the idea they'd made the trip for nothing," Pete said. Hell, I'm getting all mixed up. Harry *had* the real stuff. So nothing should've gone wrong at the drop.

Pete moved closer to the desk. He didn't like the sly smile that was beginning to play around the corners of Brewster's wet lips.

The smile spread. "You're saying that when they found out your buddy wasn't carrying what they wanted they mussed him up?"

"Didn't you tell them? Didn't they *know* this was a phony run?"

"Who said anything about it being phony?"

"You did."

"Yeah, that's right I did. But you're the one who put the stuff on the plane. You should know."

"Okay, Brewster. I let Harry fly with the real stuff. Pulling a deal like that on him would have been like knifing him in the back. Harry's the one guy in this whole rotten world I couldn't do that to. You should've known that."

Pete saw the smile on Brewster's face widen into a grin. "Sure, I knew. And so I took care of it myself. Only my timing was a little off. I waited too long to contact the guys in Arizona. When I tried to get them they weren't at the drop yet and there was no answer at the other place. They're a smart crew. They keep moving up until the last minute. So you see, they didn't know this was a phony run. But then I figured if everything you told me about Harry was true, he was the kind of guy who could take care of himself."

Brewster suddenly stopped talking and the grin died on his lips. Fear crept into his eyes. Pete felt a cold draft along the back of his neck and move down along his spine. Then he heard the footstep behind him and spun around.

He almost didn't recognize the man in the doorway. His khaki shirt and pants were in shreds, stained with blood from the cuts and bruises on his face and arms. Pete stared dumbly at the gun pointing at him.

"Yeah, Pete, it's me back from the dead again," Harry said, only it didn't sound like Harry's voice—the life had gone out of it. "I wonder how many times a guy has to die in this damn world. I thought I'd done all the dying I was ever going to do. Dying is easy. It's the coming back that hurts. But I had to come back this time, no matter how hard it was." He coughed and blood spattered on the floor.

"What happened to you, Harry?" Pete took a step toward his friend.

"Easy, Pete. Just stay put."

"What's the matter with you? What happened?"

"You know what happened. You were in on it, old buddy. When I landed that heap of a plane and hauled all that stuff out and those three tough guys checked it, they didn't like what they found and they let me know it, a little bit at a time. They thought they'd finished me and I guess I thought they had, too, but then something went off in my head and I started coming back. I picked them off one at a time. Three pops of this gun and there were three guys on the ground licking dust."

Pete stared into the dark hole of the gun barrel. Harry. The familiar name formed on his lips, but no sound came. He looked into his buddy's battered face and knew it was too late for explanations. The screams had started again, his and Harry's.

He heard the first shot and somewhere behind him a gurgling sound came from Brewster's throat.

Then the second shot sounded and Pete felt the leap of fire in his chest. With it the screams stopped and slowly the pain began to slip away.

Then he heard Harry's voice, close beside him, tranquil, soft, resigned. "This is it, old buddy. There won't be any coming back this time. Not for either of us."

The

Last

Rendezvous

*D*etective Kenneth Reid looked around, taking in the spring growth of the Connecticut woods, the ferns and mountain laurel, the wild honeysuckle and the layers of white dogwood blossoms overhead. His friends called him Kentucky. He still had relatives there, but he didn't visit often.

He remembered a woods like this when he was a kid. The thought held him for awhile, but then he glanced back down at the wet ground, to where the body lay.

"Well, I suppose you couldn't ask for a more peaceful place to die," he said, wanting to break the silence.

Beside him Charlie Player turned. His face was pale. Kentucky had never noticed the young man's freckles before, but he saw them now, like spatters of chocolate across his nose and cheeks. Kentucky waited, giving him time to pull it together. He was betting Player hadn't seen many bodies.

"There was no peace in the way this guy went." Player finally said.

"It doesn't look that way."

"I didn't know a body had that much blood."

Kentucky had thought that himself at first, but then he remembered last night's rain. With the layer of leaves on the ground acting like an oiled cloth, holding the rain, it looked like the man was lying in a deep pool of blood.

Kentucky didn't want to make anything big of it, but it wouldn't be fair not to point it out. "Head wounds bleed a lot, but some of what's here is rain water."

Player nodded.

They looked around, careful not to disturb the scene. The medical examiner and his crew were on the way.

Then for the experience, and to help him collect his thoughts, Kentucky had Player make some notes.

Detectives Kenneth Reid and Charlie Player respond to call from patrol car two. Possible murder victim, male, found in woods behind West Hills Golf Club.

Kentucky figured the man had been dead about twenty-four hours, which meant the murder took place sometime Sunday afternoon, maybe early evening. If it was murder, there was no mystery about the weapon. It was there right alongside the body, a golf club. It looked like a number two iron.

This was Cranford's second murder in a year. If things kept up, they'd have to add more than a detective unit. They might even get around to getting us an unmarked car, Kentucky thought. He and Player had been on the job three months. Cranford hadn't had an investigative unit before.

Two men from the medical examiner's office arrived, but not the ME himself. He was away for a long weekend. Kentucky and Player hung around awhile, to hear the initial reactions, and wait for the body to be identified.

The dead man's car was parked in a pull-off a hundred yards back, on the dirt road. An insurance card in the glove compartment and a driver's license in his wallet identified him as James Fullerton, 122 Oak Lane, Cranford.

Kentucky looked at Player. "He's been here all night. It's a wonder someone didn't report him missing. Let's go over to the Fullerton house and see what we find there."

Player drove. Kentucky was still learning his way around Cranford, having just moved over from Hartford. Player had gone to Cranford High and knew a shortcut behind the football field that would get them to Oak Street. "I used to have a girl that lived on Oak. I looked her up as soon as I got back here, but she's moved away."

———◆———

Sarah Fullerton locked up her shop at five-thirty, and headed for home, making a quick stop at the supermarket for some lemons. She'd decided to make the sponge cake tonight for her book club meeting tomorrow evening. If Valerie was still sick tomorrow, she wouldn't get home in time.

It was a while since Valerie had one of those headaches. Sarah wondered what had brought it on, but she hadn't asked. With as much time as they spent together in the shop, it would have been easy to get too intimate and too involved in each other lives. Neither one of them wanted that.

Sarah wondered how come Val had never married. Not only was she attractive, but she had a sweet temperament, and she was smart. Tall and blond, she had a terrific figure and played tennis like a pro. She coached at the indoor court near Essex, where she'd worked before they opened the shop together. She was thirty-six.

Sarah was forty-three. Maybe her question about Val not marrying could be answered by her own seventeen-year marriage. It hadn't been what she'd hoped for. Having the shop had finally given her the courage to end it. That was only two months ago, so she was still getting used to the idea, but at the same time she wished she hadn't waited so long.

There were other things she had been slow at discovering, like herself. She knew that her hair was her best feature. "The color of polished chestnuts," her father used to say. It had a wave to it, so with a good cut and a quick blow dry, she could look like she'd just left the beauty salon. Between that and the mascara and other eye make-up Valerie had persuaded her to buy on their trip to New York City last month, Sarah knew she looked better than she had in years.

She was thinking about that, and smiling to herself, as she looked out the window over the kitchen sink. She had just finished rinsing out the mixing bowl, when she saw a police car slow down and pull up in front of her house. She wondered what that was all about. Maybe the alarm at the shop had gone off.

———◆———

They introduced themselves as Detectives Kenneth Reid and Charlie Player, Cranford Police. They were wearing business suits. They showed her their badges.

"Are you Mrs. James Fullerton?" the older of the two asked.

"My husband and I are separated," she said. "Sarah Fullerton is what I use now." The older one had an interesting rugged face and soft gray eyes. The younger one was tall and lanky, and looked like he'd be a natural on a basketball court. He called the senior man Kentucky.

When she thought about it later, she was sure it must have happened differently, but the way she recalled it, Kentucky said they had come with some sad news. The next thing she heard was that Jim was dead.

Something else must have transpired, she was certain, but all she could remember was hearing herself say, "Come into the kitchen. I have a cake in the oven."

———◆———

The three of them were sitting at the kitchen table. She looked from one man to the other. Something in their expressions made her think they'd been sitting there for some time. The windows were open, and she could hear the kids next door, playing in the driveway. She'd started telling them about Cindy Clarke.

"She's a flight attendant, and lives near the airport in Providence. Jim told me that's where I could reach him. I've talked to him once, but I haven't seen him since he left two months ago."

She told them Jim had given her Cindy Clarke's address and phone number, "in case of an emergency," is what he'd said.

"What kind of emergency did your husband have in mind?"

"Something like the furnace giving out, I suppose, but I wouldn't have called him for that, not anymore." It was Kentucky who had asked her that. She heard the soft accent in his voice now, and realized that he was from the South. The nickname suited him. "I'm sure Jim hadn't thought about *this* kind of emergency."

She knew she had begun to ramble, and that her voice sounded uneven, as though she was in a car going over a corrugated road. She pressed her lips together.

Kentucky shifted in his chair. "Mrs. Fullerton, how did you feel about your husband leaving you for another woman?"

She stared at him, trying to think of how she wanted to answer that. If she told him the truth, she would sound pathetic. Well, that's what she had been, pathetic. But she wasn't now. "It wasn't all that new."

"What do you mean by that?"

"Jim had a history of going with other women. He had some sort of magic touch. He would listen to a woman and ask her questions and make her feel that what she said and thought were important. Most men don't know how to do that, and a lot don't care to. Combined with those blue eyes of his . . . well, it was hard for a woman not to fall for him."

The younger detective made a kind of clicking sound with his tongue, and Sarah turned to look at him.

"Sorry, Ma'am. That's a bad habit I have." He pushed his hair back off his forehead. "I was hearing what you said. That's a lot to tolerate in a man. How did you manage it?"

She guessed it was a question a lot of people might ask.

"It wasn't easy. But it was different after I opened my business. I don't mean that Jim was different. I was. I had something else to occupy my mind." She paused, looking for the right words. "His infidelity didn't bother me the way it had before."

She looked away then and thought about the shop, and how important it had become to her. How exciting it was to unlock the door each morning and step inside, knowing that it was hers, something she had built from nothing. Of course, without Valerie it wouldn't have happened. With Valerie's encouragement she'd taken a wild idea and turned it into a successful business.

"What kind of business do you have, Ma'am ?" Charlie Player asked.

"It's a shop on Bellevue. It's called SECOND CHANCE . You've probably seen it, a consignment shop, across the street from Pierson's Drug Store."

She glanced down at the table and saw with surprise that her hand was cupped around a coffee mug. There was a matching mug in front of each of the detectives. She looked toward the counter and saw the sponge cake cooling on a wire rack. The timer must have gone off. She must have taken the cake out of the oven, and made a pot of coffee. She had no recollection of that.

Her voice was thready when she spoke again." I used to think that if I knew who Jim was involved with, I could have some control over it." She stopped, not anxious to think about that period of her marriage, when she had taken to following him. That had been her lowest point. It made her skin creep to remember it.

Kentucky was looking at her, his gray eyes thoughtful.

"When I was first married I had a job with a printing company in Middletown, but the company moved to Baltimore. It couldn't have come at a worst time. Jim had just taken up with someone and I was too dispirited to look for another job. I helped out at the church and I did some volunteer work at the hospital. I did that for years, but it wasn't enough. Then I began to think about opening my own business."

"What kind of a business did you say you have?" Kentucky asked.

"Well, it's selling women's clothes, second hand clothes. With consignments you don't need much capital to start a business. With clothes all you need is hangers and a place to hang them. We started out in a small store on Spring Street, near the railroad station, but we have a larger shop now, in the center of town. It's turned into a good business. There are a lot of shops like ours opening up, all over the country. There was an article in the Sunday *Times* last month, about one in New York on Madison Avenue. It's been there for more than thirty years. Women don't hang on to their clothes the way men do. But they can't afford to just toss them out and buy new things. In shops like mine, one woman's discard becomes another woman's treasure." She stopped and smiled apologetically.

"That was a long answer about my business," she said and turned away, toward the window. It was getting dark. A breeze ruffled the curtains. Why was she talking so much? Her cheeks felt strangely cold. She touched them and discovered they were wet.

"I gave you her phone number, didn't I—Cindy Clarke's? This is going to be hard on her." She swallowed to get her voice under control. "She needs to know. You'll tell her, won't you? I can't do it. I've never met her. Jim told me she was twenty-eight. He was fifty last year."

Kentucky cleared his throat. "We'll be in touch with her, but we wanted to talk to you first. Do you know the airline she works for?"

"I think Jim said it was Trans Continental."

Sarah watched as he wrote that down, then looked up slowly and leaned toward her. "Mrs. Fullerton, you haven't asked us how your husband died."

She frowned. They had told her, hadn't they? Had she just assumed it was a heart attack? "He was always worried about his heart. That's the way his father died, and his older brother. I just thought ..."

Kentucky continued to study her, and for a moment it made her feel uncomfortable, but the feeling didn't last long. His gaze was so steady, she found herself wanting to hold on to it.

When he spoke, it was in a slow, even voice. "Your husband's car was found early this afternoon on one of the roads in the woods near the West Hills Golf Club."

She nodded. "He was a member of West Hills. He liked to play golf, and he liked the woods, especially when spring came. He used to park his car in one of the pull-offs and go to a place where there were a lot of dogwoods in bloom ... he took me there before we were married."

She was about to go on, but Kentucky interrupted her, his voice more firm than before. "Mrs. Fullerton, this is going to be hard for you, but you have to hear it. Your husband died in those woods, the woods you just described. The dogwoods are in full bloom. But it doesn't look as though he died of a heart attack. It looks as though he was murdered."

She looked away from him and stared straight ahead. She closed her eyes. She wanted to shut out the scene—that secluded, special place with the clouds of white dogwood. But there was nothing she could do to stop the images that moved across her mind. They were not new. She had lived with them for years. She had tried to push them down and layer them with other thoughts, but now they were fresh again. She brought her hand to her mouth and held back a moan.

"Ma'am." Player's voice startled her, her eyes flew open and her head jerked in his direction.

"Ma'am, what kind of work did your husband do?"

"He was an electrical engineer. He worked on contract."

"Ma'am. Did your husband have any men friends?"

"He got along with them in business. He golfed with some, but nobody close."

"What about hobbies, Ma'am? Was there anything special he liked to do?"

"He liked to repair things. He was a good carpenter. And, he liked to read. Whenever he met somebody new, he would find out what they were interested in, or what kind of work they did. Then he'd go to the library and come back with books about it."

"When you say somebody new, do you mean a new woman?" Player asked.

"Yes," she said quietly, and looked toward the door, and realized she was seeing Jim right now, walking in with a load of books in his arms. There had been a wide range of subjects over the years—speech therapy, rocks and jewelry making, singing, genetics, pottery, nursing, and most recently the airline industry and passenger safety.

"Ma'am." Player recalled her from her daydream. "Ma'am, your husband was killed sometime yesterday afternoon, maybe early evening."

Sarah looked at the clock on the stove. It was six-thirty. It would be dark soon. Jim had been dead a whole day.

"We've already checked with the golf club. He hadn't signed up to play yesterday, and no one remembers seeing him. Did your husband usually play golf on Sundays?"

"Usual isn't a good word to describe Jim. Sometimes he played on Sundays."

It was Kentucky who leaned toward her then, as soft-spoken as he had been before. "Ma'am, can you tell us where you were yesterday afternoon?"

Yesterday was Sunday, she had to remind herself. She'd gone to church in the morning. The service was at eleven. After that she and Pastor Bicks and his wife drove to Essex to a flower show. "We had planned to go to an afternoon movie, but Mrs. Bicks turned her ankle and we came back early. They dropped me off. I got home about four."

"And what did you do then?"

"I stayed here, made some supper, watched *Sixty Minutes,* read the Sunday paper, and worked on the crossword puzzle."

She was suddenly overwhelmingly tired. She leaned forward and rested her arms and the table, hugging her elbows. "I don't mean to be rude, but I'd like to be alone now."

Kentucky looked at Player and nodded. The two men rose. "Just one more thing, do you know of anyone who would have a reason to kill your husband?"

She stared at him for a long moment, and then shook her head. "I know what you're asking me, but I didn't know them all."

It was almost dark when they pulled away from the Fullerton house. At the top of the incline of Oak Street Kentucky had to swerve to avoid a kid sailing out of a driveway on a skate board. He thought of turning on the siren to give the boy a scare, but the kid was halfway down the hill already. There was no point in disturbing the quiet street.

"I'll drop you off at the station, and then I'll go on over to see the minister," Kentucky said. "You give the girlfriend a call."

"Sure. You don't think the wife did it, do you?"

Kentucky shrugged. "You know the way it's supposed to go. You start with the wife and then the girlfriend."

"Yeah, I know that, but that isn't what I asked you."

"Well the answer is I don't know. The wife is always my first guess, and I suppose I'll stay with that for now. It sounds like Sarah Fullerton had a whole harem full of reasons. But it's too soon to tell. Let's see what the minister and the girlfriend have to say. And there's the lab we have to hear from."

Player got out of the car, but didn't close the door. He leaned back in, folding himself over the door. Kentucky stared, marveling at his contortion.

"What makes a nice woman like that stay with such a bum?" Player asked.

Kentucky shrugged. He used to ask those kinds of questions. He didn't anymore. He'd gotten tired of not knowing the answers. "A lot of things. Security. Habit. Who knows?" He smiled. "Just because I'm at the half century mark, doesn't mean I have all the answers."

"Somehow I thought you did." Player grinned, straightened and was about to close the door.

"Hold it a minute," Kentucky called out. "That was nice work you did back there, coming in with those questions about what her husband did for a living. I thought she'd frozen up on us for good. Changing the subject right quick like that got her unstuck and going again. Where'd you learn to do that?"

Player kept grinning. "I'll tell you, over a beer sometime."

"I'll remind you." Kentucky said with a chuckle. "Get onto that stewardess now, and don't forget to check her story with the airline."

"Flight attendant," Player said and shut the door.

———◆———

The Presbyterian Church was a red brick building with a white steeple, on Sycamore Avenue. Reverend Bicks and his wife lived in a small wood frame house across from it. Kentucky hadn't met them before. The minister came to the door.

"I heard Cranford had gotten itself a detective squad," the minister said after Kentucky had introduced himself, and led the way into a small living room with lace curtains at the windows.

"Not a squad, exactly," Kentucky said, hiding a smile. "There are just two of us. It's something new for Cranford. We came on board three months ago."

"So I heard. And it's a good idea. Too bad, though. A few years ago there wouldn't have been anything for you to do here. But with the city elements creeping in, things are different. Everyone locks their doors and windows now, and if you're going to be away, you make sure somebody cuts your lawn.

Kentucky agreed and then went directly to explaining the reason for his visit.

The minister shook his head. "I can't say I was ever very fond of Jim Fullerton. My wife and I often wondered how Sarah put up with him. But murder, that's something else again. Sarah's a fine woman. She sure doesn't deserve this kind of trouble."

"Mrs. Fullerton said she spent yesterday afternoon with you and your wife."

"Yes, that's right. We went over to Essex. There was a flower show the ladies wanted to see. They were hoping to get some ideas for some new plantings for the front of the church. My wife tripped and sprained her ankle, and we came home early. She's still resting it. The doctor strapped it up and told her to keep it elevated for a few days.

"What time was it when you took Mrs. Fullerton home?"

"It was about three o'clock when we got back, but we didn't take her home. She had her car in the parking lot behind the church, so she left from there."

—◆—

Sarah had watched the detectives drive up the hill, and then she closed the windows and drew the blinds. When she'd rinsed out the coffee mugs, she went into the living room and flipped the switch that turned on the lamps at each end of the sofa.

She wanted to go back over everything they had said, but she knew she would have trouble remembering it all. She'd meant to ask them about just how Jim had died, but after she heard where his body had been found, her mind started to shut down. It was Kentucky who told her. "Our guess is that it was a blow to the head," he said.

It seemed he was going to leave it at that, but she got up the energy to press him for details.

"We'll know more after the autopsy, but it looks as though it was a golf club."

It had taken all the strength she had to control herself then, but now she sank back against the sofa pillows and closed her eyes and allowed herself to see it all. It was like opening an album of photographs that had been taken, carefully framed, snapped and then neatly pasted in proper sequence. No, it was more than that. Her memory had none of the limits of a camera lens.

It began with Jim driving her along the dirt road behind the golf course. It wasn't much more than a fire lane, with woods on both sides.

When he came to the pull-off, he braked slowly and then eased into it, careful not too get to close, not wanting to scratch the car. Then with the engine stopped, the hush of the woods engulfed them, magnifying the sound of the car doors opening and closing. Louder still was the slam of the car trunk. Jim had taken the number two iron from his golf bag, in case of snakes. They walked along the dirt road then, looking for an opening into the woods. All sound was muted by the soft moist earth, except for the occasional high note of a bird or the rustle of a squirrel. The heady scent of honey suckle filled the air.

Jim chose a different way into the woods each time, not wanting to beat a path and mark it for someone else to find. When he found a place that suited him, he'd take the lead and part the way, careful not to break any branches that would leave telltale scars. In the spring the sap was running and the new growth was supple, but even so their movements were deliberate and slow, adding a high charge to the counterpoint of their racing pulses, eager to reach their destination.

Finally, they arrived at the secret place, that small protected glade encircled by dogwood in white bloom. Then, like an actor on a stage, Jim would toss the golf club to the ground, and dramatically reach out and invite her into his arms.

The memory rose and swept over her with the force of a hurricane. She felt the tremble begin and tried to stop it, but it swelled and went on, rolling over her, out of control. She clutched herself and waited for the awful turbulence of longing and regret to pass, helplessly reliving the moment when their bodies touched. She cried out, and then at last began to sob.

———◆———

At police headquarters Player dialed Cindy Clarke's number for the third time. "Damn! She's probably off on a trip." He'd wanted to talk to her, before he called the airline. Then on the fourth ring she answered, a throaty voice, breathing hard.

He almost said he liked her voice, but decided he'd better not. Instead he told who he was, and asked how come she didn't have an answering machine.

"I hate coming back to a string of messages. I shut it off when I'm gone. If anyone really wants me, they'll call again."

"What makes you so sure?"

"Say, who did you say you are? This is the kind of call I don't need."

"Sorry," he said and told her again. Detective Charlie Player. He was glad Kentucky wasn't hearing any of this. "I'm with the Cranford Police."

"Are you collecting for the policemen's ball or something?"

He laughed, but not too hard. He had to get on track and fast. "Say, I've started us off in a wrong direction. I'm afraid I'm calling with some bad news. It's about James Fullerton...."

She went off like a rocket. A redhead, he'd bet. "What about Jim Fullerton? I kicked him out two weeks ago. So whatever you have to say about him, I'm not interested."

He took a breath and hoped she was ready for it. "I'm afraid the bad news is that he's dead."

For a moment all he heard was silence and then the throaty voice in a higher pitch. "You're kidding. What happened to him?"

She sounded all right, but you could never tell. He'd take it slow. "We found him in the woods near the West Hills Golf Club. It looks as though he died sometime yesterday afternoon."

There was a slight gasp that turned into a sour laugh. "Tell me if I have it right—all moss and ferns and honey suckle and dogwood trees?"

"You've been there?"

"I've been there, and so has half the female population in the northeast, probably. That's where Jim tried to take my best friend while I was away. She told me when I came home. I kicked him out."

Smart girl, he said to himself, and decided to go straight to the point. "Miss Clarke, where were you yesterday afternoon?"

"In San Francisco," she said without a flinch. "My flight got into Providence an hour ago. Why are you asking me that?"

"Well you see, it looks as though Jim Fullerton was murdered."

"Murdered! And you think I ..." He heard the beginning of another laugh, but it stopped midstream. For awhile all he got was silence, and then he realized she was crying. He waited, giving her time. Even a louse deserves a tear, he supposed.

When she came back on the line, her voice was steady. "I've been acting like this is some kind of joke."

"That was my fault," he said.

"Well, maybe, but I gave you some room." She paused. "Jim's dead. I mean dead, maybe murdered. Don't ask me why, but I thought about his wife and I just began to cry. I didn't know he was married, not at first. I met him three months ago, on one of my flights from Chicago. He'd been at a convention. He really didn't mean that much to me."

Player listened to her take a deep breath and wondered if she was going to cry again, but instead she said, "I don't know if his wife is going to want to hear this from me. But would you tell her how sorry I am?"

"I'll do that," he said. "Tell me, what was it about this guy that had you fall for him?"

"He was smart. He seemed to know about a lot of things. He was good at asking questions, and then listening. I think maybe it was the listening that got to me. Not many people know how to listen. Men, particularly, aren't good at that."

—◆—

Player had just finished checking out Cindy Clarke's story with the airline when Kentucky walked into the room. He could tell from the brightness in his eyes that he had some news.

"I just talked to the lab. There were no identifiable prints on the golf club, except for Fullerton's. Too bad, but no surprise." He settled himself into the chair alongside Player's desk. "His car made up for it, though. Enough prints and hair and make-up for a beauty parlor. That Fullerton was one busy boy."

Player shook his head. "I don't get a guy like this. All he was interested in was scoring?"

Kentucky shrugged. "Don't look to me for answers on that. How did you make out with the girlfriend?"

"She wasn't exactly bowled over when I told her he was dead. But she's in the clear. She was in San Francisco. And that checks out with the airline."

Kentucky nodded. "So that eliminates her. Did she have anything else to say?"

"It seems she and Fullerton parted company. She threw him out last week when she found out he'd been making moves on a friend of hers." Player frowned. "I asked her what was so special about him. She said he was a good listener, and that most men aren't. That gave me something to think about."

"And what did you come up with?"

"Hell, I don't know," Player said and leaned back in his chair. "What did the minister have to say?"

"The three of them went to Essex together, just like Sarah said. But they didn't bring her home. The Pastor said her car was at the church, and they left her there at three o'clock."

Player took a deep breath and blew out his cheeks. "So you think she lied to us?"

"We'll have to look into that." Kentucky said, in a tone that made Player wonder if he was disappointed. Player had the feeling the old blue grass bachelor was ready to strum his guitar for the lady.

Kentucky looked at his watch. "Let's get on over there. If she still has her lights on, we'll ring her doorbell. If not, we'll wait until tomorrow. I'd sure like to hear what she has to say about this."

Sarah had made herself some scrambled eggs for supper and was watching the news when Pastor Bicks called a second time. He asked her if she was sure she didn't wanted him to come over. She thanked him, but said she'd rather be alone.

"If you change your mind let me know," he said and then told her about his visit from the police. "It's the first time I met anyone from that new investigative unit. Detective Reid said it was just the two of them. He seemed like a likeable fellow."

"They were both here," Sarah said. "The other one is very young. He looks like he could still be in high school."

They said goodbye soon after that and she sat by the phone, trying to decide whether to call Valerie. If it was one of those bad migraines, Val wouldn't be out of it yet. Sarah decided to wait until the morning.

She thought about tomorrow. Kentucky had said they should have the autopsy report in the morning. After that the body would be released to the funeral home. She should stop thinking of him as Kentucky. It was too familiar. She'd have to close the shop for a few days.

In the living room she turned on WTFM, knowing she could get something soothing and soft there. Then took the pad and pencil out of the desk drawer and looked at the list of names she had begun earlier.

She had stopped caring about Jim and his women, or at least that's what she convinced herself she had to do. But it was always there—the knowing, hovering like a dark cloud, accompanied by wondering who it was. Who would be next?

Who had it been this time? Who had he taken to the woods yesterday? Had someone met him there? Or followed him?

She looked at the names she had written down. There were probably others that she didn't remember, and some she had never even known about. She leaned back against the sofa, and tried to think.

When the doorbell rang, she sat up with a start, realizing she must have dozed off. It was almost ten o'clock. The pad and pencil had slid off her lap onto the floor. She retrieved them and put them into the drawer. On her way to the door, she turned off the radio and stopped at the hallway mirror to smooth her hair. She turned on the porch light so she could see who was there.

"Sorry to bother you so late, Mrs. Fullerton," Kentucky said. "We wouldn't have, but your lights were on, so we decided not to wait until morning."

She led them into the living room, and motioned them into the two chairs across from the sofa.

After she had settled herself, Kentucky cleared his throat. "I'll get right to the point. We talked to Cindy Clarke."

She nodded. "I hoped that you would."

"Actually it was Player who talked to her. He'll tell you about it, but first I want to talk to you about our conversation with Reverend Bicks. You told us he and his wife dropped you off at your house at four."

Sarah shook her head. "Did I? I'm sorry I don't exactly know what I said. I said a lot of things." She felt herself flush.

"He told me you got back from Essex at three, and that you had left your car parked in back of the church."

"That's right. I drove there for the eleven o'clock service. We went to Essex in Pastor Bicks' car. It was a good thing. We'd never have made it had I been driving."

"How's that, Ma'am?" Player asked.

"I had no trouble getting it started, but I hadn't gone a block after I left the church parking lot, when it began to lose power. I managed to get it to Jerry's, on the corner of Bellevue and Maple. They're open on Sundays, but only for gas, and only until four. The attendant said I could leave it there overnight, and one of the mechanics would look at it in the morning. They had it fixed by nine-thirty today."

"You were without a car the rest of Sunday?"

"Yes. Why do you ask?"

She saw the two of them exchange glances, as though they were surprised by her question.

"I guess we need to be more direct about this," Kentucky said. He leaned forward, his gray eyes holding hers. "Did you kill your husband?"

She stared at him. "Kill Jim?" She sank back against the cushions. "I won't say I hadn't thought about it—lots of times. But contemplating something is a long way from doing it. No, I didn't kill him."

She watched the expression on Kentucky's face change, and wondered if she was reading something into it that wasn't there. He looked relieved. He nodded to Player, inviting him to take over.

"I talked to your husband's girlfriend," Player said. Ex-girlfriend, he thought, but he wouldn't get into that. "She was in San Francisco yesterday, so we know she's out of the picture."

Sarah started to say something, but stopped when she saw Player move to the edge of the chair, and awkwardly bend forward into the open spread of his bony knees, leaning toward her.

"Ma'am, you said the two of you never met—you and Cindy Clarke."

"That's right. She didn't say we had?"

He shook his head. "Ma'am there's something I don't understand.

Your husband left you for Cindy Clarke. And yet you were concerned about her. You asked us to make sure we let her know what happened. Can you explain that to me?"

Sarah frowned. "I'm not sure what you want me to explain. I assume she loved him, or thought she did. He'd probably given her enough reason to think he felt the same way about her. He was good at that, making a woman feel like she was important to him. The only thing is, it never lasted. I knew that, but Cindy Clarke didn't."

She caught Kentucky studying her again. She didn't quite understand the look on his face. It wasn't Player's puzzlement she saw there. He just seemed thoughtful.

"I just felt sorry for her," she said, looking back at Player. "You see, she had nothing to do with Jim's leaving me. That was Jim."

She glanced at Kentucky. The lines around his gray eyes were more pronounced than earlier. It was late. She was tired. He must be too. The younger man was still wound up. He had listened hard to what she had said, as though it was some complicated equation she was explaining.

"Ma'am, I hear what you're saying. But I can't imagine any women I know not wanting to claw each other eyes out in a situation like this."

Sarah smiled. "Maybe you just watch more TV than I do."

"Could be," he said and smiled. "By the way, Cindy Clarke, asked me to tell you she was sorry."

Sarah took a deep breath and swallowed hard, holding back the threat of tears. "Thank you for telling me that," she said. "The only thing I can say is Jim always seemed to pick nice women."

———◆———

They left soon after that, saying they would be in touch with her in the morning. She locked the door, returned to the living room, and stood there for a moment, looking around. The room felt empty. She turned on the radio again.

She was exhausted, but there were things she had to think about. She couldn't go to bed yet. Where would the detectives go with their investigation? She imagined how long it might go on, and of all the people they would want to question. One person would lead to another. She shrank at the thought of it. Cranford was a small town. How would she be able to stand the scrutiny, all the innuendo? And what about Valerie?

She went to the desk and took the pad from the drawer and tore off the top sheet. She stood there looking at the names she had written. There was one she hadn't put down, even though it belonged there. So many of Jim's love affairs had involved women she had known, and liked. Some had been her friends, whom he'd set about seducing.

With Valerie it had been different. Sarah had hardly known her. Val had lived in Saybrook then. They'd met briefly in the half-day orientation class for volunteers at Middle County Hospital, but afterwards they were assigned to different days. Sarah might never have known about Jim's involvement with her, if it hadn't been for the books on pottery he had brought home. The one thing Sarah knew about Valerie was that she was an accomplished potter.

A few months after that, Sarah found herself sitting next to Valerie in the hospital van. They'd been asked to accompany Elvira Morris, a sweet, elderly woman in her transfer to a nursing home.

If it hadn't been for the pink volunteer jacket Valerie was wearing, Sarah wouldn't have recognized her, and probably mistaken her for a patient. She was drawn and hollowed-eyed. Sarah didn't even have to guess at the cause. She knew. Jim had moved on.

Fortunately she and Valerie had Mrs. Morris to deal with that day. The poor woman had been in the hospital two months, and was confused by having to move. Her closest family was a son living in California. The nursing home had suggested the move would be less traumatic for Mrs. Morris, if someone she knew accompanied her to the home. As it turned out, Sarah and Valerie were her two favorite volunteers.

It was six months before Sarah saw Valerie again. But during that time she learned that the director of volunteers had noticed how bad Valerie looked, and had taken her under her wing, and seen to it that Valerie got some counseling. Word was that Valerie was on the mend.

Then Sarah received a note from Mrs. Morris's son. He was coming East for his mother's eighty-fifth birthday, and was having a small party and hoped that Sarah could come.

Sarah went. Valerie was there. After that, they began visiting Mrs. Morris together. It was on their drives to the nursing home that Sarah began talking about wanting to start a small business.

They'd opened the shop three years ago. Sarah had never let on that she knew of Valerie's affair with Jim, and as a result she talked about him as little as possible. They saw one another every week day, but went in different directions on weekends. Valerie played tennis and Sarah had her own things to do. A few times a year they went into New York and stayed the weekend. They went to the theater and they window-shopped along Madison and Fifth Avenues, staying in touch with the latest fashions. This August they were planning to take a trip together to Bermuda.

The shop was doing well and they enjoyed working together. Everything seemed to be going along fine, and then Jim had come after Valerie again.

Sarah saw it first in Valerie's eyes, a drawn haunted look of torment and despair. It was in Valerie's face on Saturday, after they had closed the shop and stood in the parking lot behind the bank. There were no customers to distract them, only the intermittent glare of the sun in their faces, as it shifted through the branches of a tall oak.

———◆———

Sarah leaned her head back against the sofa cushions and wondered when Valerie had decided to do what she had done. Had it just happened, or had she made a careful plan? Had she gone with Jim or had she followed him there?

None of that mattered. What mattered was what happened now. Would the detectives turn up evidence that would lead to Valerie? Sarah shuddered at the thought.

The questions kept piling up and Sarah felt as though her head was about to burst. There were all the other things connected with Jim's death to deal with. She had already told Pastor Bicks she wanted a simple burial, no service in a church that Jim had never attended. The minister hadn't tried to persuade her otherwise.

What she needed now was sleep. She rose and went into the kitchen and stood by the sink. She tore the sheet of paper with all the names, into tiny pieces, and pushed them down the drain. She switched on the garbage disposal and turned the water on, and shredded them.

———◆———

In Tony's Pizza Palace, across from the police station, the two large pies Player had ordered arrived and took over the entire table. Kentucky surveyed them. "Any chance I get to take a slice home?"

"Only if I hold back," Player said with a grin, popping a can of beer. "What do you think? Will we find out who did it?"

"It's hard to tell," Kentucky answered.

"Well, what would you guess?"

"I'm not much good at guessing. I talked to the lab. They said they'll have something interesting to tell us tomorrow morning."

"That's cute. Why, not tonight?"

"They've got their own way of handling things, and besides the big boss is away. They may feel a little insecure."

Player reached for a slice of pizza and Kentucky saw the steam rise. "Count to twenty," he said. "My sister always did. She never burned her mouth, not once."

"Thanks. I wish I'd had a sister. Three brothers is what I had, all bigger than me. They played football." He let the slice dangle in his hand. "Any guesses on what the lab has?"

"I told you, I'm no good at guessing, but that doesn't stop me from thinking. I don't know how they could find much in those woods, not with all the rain that night. I suppose that love nest will be just like Fullerton's car—another beauty parlor. Only God knows how many women he took there."

Player tipped back his head and opened his mouth. Half the slice disappeared. When he'd finished the rest of it, he looked at Kentucky. "Let me ask you something. Have you ever done it in the woods?"

"What kind of question is that?"

Player shrugged. "It's just a question. It's hard not to think about it, considering what we've been dealing with all day."

Kentucky reached for his beer. "Well, suppose I answer you this way. You've got kind of a short season up here in the north. Where I come from the dogwoods bloom earlier and the season stays warmer a lot longer."

Player let out a guffaw.

———◆———

Sarah woke at six. She had her breakfast, took a shower and blew her hair dry. She listened to the weather report and decided on a dark green suit and a silk blouse, and was putting on a pair of gold earrings when the phone rang. She picked it up on the second ring, trying to anticipate who it would be—Valerie, the police or Pastor Bicks.

His voice had a deeper twang on the phone than in person. He started out by apologizing for calling so early.

"It isn't so early," she said. "I've been up for some time."

He said he had something to tell her, and that she might want to sit down.

Sarah took his advice and sat on the edge of the bed. For the next two minutes she listened and didn't say a word. When Kentucky was finished, her heart was racing so fast she thought it would fly right out of her chest.

She didn't know where she managed to find her voice, but it came from somewhere. He'd said he couldn't come over right then, which is why he called, but he wanted to stop by to see her in the afternoon. She told him three o'clock would be fine.

When the phone was back in its cradle, she kept looking at it, taking deep breaths and trying to get herself under control. She had to get to Valerie, and fast.

She took a minute to think through what she had to say, and then dialed her number. When Val answered, she plunged right in.

"Val, I'm not even going to ask how your migraine is. You'll understand, as soon as I tell you."

"Sarah, you sound so upset or excited, or something. Are you okay?"

"Yes, I'm okay. Jim's passed away. He died of a heart attack." She almost bit her tongue at those words. Somehow they didn't quite describe what had happened. But she'd gotten the basics out of the way.

"When did it happen? Where was he?"

The police found him yesterday, in the woods behind the golf course. At first they suspected foul play. There were some bruises on his head, but the autopsy showed they weren't the cause of his death. It was his heart." She wanted to take a breath, but she didn't dare.

"I'm going to need some help, Val. My head's in a muddle. I need you to come over here. We need to close the shop for a few days. Then I want to go away. I thought, instead of waiting until August to go to Bermuda, we could go now." She stopped then, having said all she could think of saying. She hoped she'd covered it all. If Val started crying and talking about what had happened, she didn't know what she would do.

"Val?" Sarah waited.

Then Val's voice came on. "I'm on my way, Sarah."

———◆———

The sun was shining, and as Player pulled into the parking lot behind police headquarters, he was humming to himself. When he walked into the station house, the hum turned into a whistle. The desk clerk looked up, and pointed toward the back room. "Your buddy's been looking for you."

He found Kentucky bent over his desk, studying a report.

"What's up? It's only quarter to. We agreed to meet at nine."

"I couldn't sleep. Must have been all that pepperoni." Kentucky motioned to the chair alongside his desk. "Have a seat. I've got a message for you."

"What's that?"

"That stewardess called this morning, early. Said she had to fly to San Francisco, so she can't meet you at the *Moonlight Mile* tonight."

Player slid down in the chair and clasped his hands behind his head, and stretched his legs out as far as they would go. "Say, why are you doing this to me? I thought we did okay yesterday."

Kentucky nodded. "We did."

Player sat up straight. "Well then I've had enough of your southern wit. What's the word on Jim Fullerton."

"You're not gonna believe me when I tell you."

"Try me."

"They decided that the golf club didn't do the damage. It was a rock, a sharp piece of Connecticut granite."

"You mean someone hit him on the head with a rock?"

Kentucky shook his head. "The rock was in the ground. He fell on it."

"Jesus, Kentucky. Give me a break."

"According to the medical examiner the cause of death was a heart attack."

"Say, cut it out. This isn't funny anymore."

"I'm serious, I said you wouldn't believe me. Look for yourself. It's right here in the autopsy report. Have a look."

Player took the folder Kentucky handed him and read the top page. "I don't believe this."

"Well, I didn't either at first. But I do now. They figure Fullerton had the attack standing up and then fell forward. Under all those soft leaves was this sharp rock poking up. The head bruise didn't kill him, even though that's the way it looked at first. The lab almost told us last night, but since everybody had been thinking murder, they wanted to be sure."

"So that's the end of it?"

"Yup. That's it. Case is closed. Guess you might have some loose ends to tie up."

"Me?"

"I was just kidding about the *The Moonlight Mile,* but Cindy Clarke did call you. Here's the number she left. She said she'd be at home tonight. She's got a nice voice. Ask her if she ever sings blues?" Kentucky got up and stretched.

Player stared at him. "Did you tell her what the autopsy showed?"

"No, I thought I'd let you do that, just in case you run out of conversation."

"Boy, you are on some kind of roll this morning. What about Mrs. Fullerton? Shouldn't we go over and tell her?"

"I've already talked to her. Told her we couldn't come over this morning. But I'd I stop by this afternoon."

"Just you?"

"Well, I thought so. Doesn't take two of us, does it? Besides, I need some practice listening."

PUBLICATION SOURCES AND DATES

———◆———

The stories in this volume were previously published, as indicated below.

The Gambling Master of Shanghai
MURDER IN VEGAS
International Association of Crime Writers
Forge, Tom Doherty Associates, 2005
Edited by Michael Connelly

The Dance of the Apsara
DEATH DANCE
International Association of Crime Writers
Cumberland House, 2002
Edited by Trevanian

ELLERY QUEEN MYSTERY MAGAZINE

Love and Death in Africa, 2005
Assignment in Prague, 2001
The River's Child, 1999
Recipe Secrets, 1998
A Legacy of Questions, 1998
The Oak's Long Shadow, 1995
The Last Rendezvous, 1995
The Waste Pile at Apple Bow, 1973
Bitter Justice (Originally *A Matter of Justice*), 1973
A Matter of Trust, 1972
Last Harvest, 1972
Prisoner of Zemu Island, 1971
Only So Much to Reveal, 1970
The Ones Left Behind, 1969
Intruder in the Maize, 1967

Stories Reprinted in Anthologies

The Ones Left Behind

LIVING ON THE EDGE, Fiction by Peace Corps Writers
Edited by John Coyne, Curbstone Press 1999

Intruder in the Maize

BEASTLY TALES, Mystery Writers of America
Edited by Sara Paretsky, Wynwood Press, 1989

The Waste Pile at Apple Bow

MURDER ON THE AISLE, Mystery Writers of America
Edited by Mary Higgins Clark, Simon and Schuster, 1987

The Prisoner of Zemu Island

WOMEN'S WILES, Mystery Writers of America
Edited by Michele Slung, Harcourt Brace Jovanovich, 1979

BEST DETECTIVE STORIES OF THE YEAR
Edited by Allen J. Hubin, E. P. Dutton, 1972

Only So Much to Reveal

ALFRED HITCHCOCK PRESENTS:
STORIES TO BE READ WITH THE LIGHTS ON, Random House, 1973

ELLERY QUEEN'S HEADLINERS, World Publishing, 1971